Praise for Erica James

'An extraordinary deftness of touch, coupled with some searing insights into both how relationships fail, and can work' *Daily Mirror*

'A captivating novel of love, deception and misunderstanding' *Woman & Home*

'She writes with a wry sense of humour and this story quickly reels you in' *Evening Telegraph*

'With the turn of every absorbing page, you'll find yourself caught in the rapture and despair of each character as they find their way through this beguiling drama' *Candis*

'A big hug of a novel that leaves you feeling warm and fuzzy' *Woman*

'Delightful … a blend of emotion and wry social observation' *Daily Mail*

'Beautiful and heart-warming' *Sun on Sunday Magazine*

'An entertaining read with some wickedly well-painted cameo characters. It's a perfect read if you're in the mood for romance' *Prima*

'A captivating read: beautifully written and heart-rendingly sad' *Daily Telegraph*

'A wonderfully humorous novel' *Woman's Own*

'A poignant read with plenty of laugh-out-loud moments'
Heat

'A heart-warming, romantic story full of engaging characters, an emotional roller coaster' *Daily Express*

With an insatiable appetite for other people's business, Erica James will readily strike up conversation with strangers in the hope of unearthing a useful gem for her writing. She finds it the best way to write authentic characters for her novels, although her two grown-up sons claim they will never recover from a childhood spent in a perpetual state of embarrassment at their mother's compulsion.

The author of many bestselling novels, including *Gardens of Delight*, which won the Romantic Novel of the Year Award, and her recent *Sunday Times* Top Ten bestsellers, *Summer at the Lake*, and *The Dandelion Years*, Erica now divides her time between Suffolk and Lake Como in Italy, where she strikes up conversation with unsuspecting Italians. Visit her website at www.ericajames.co.uk or follow her on Twitter @TheEricaJames

Song of
the Skylark

ERICA JAMES

An Orion paperback

First published in Great Britain in 2016
by Orion Books
This paperback edition published in 2016
by Orion Books,
an imprint of The Orion Publishing Group Ltd,
Carmelite House, 50 Victoria Embankment,
London EC4Y 0DZ

An Hachette UK company

1 3 5 7 9 10 8 6 4 2

A CIP catalogue record for this book
is available from the British Library.

ISBN 978 1 4091 5957 5

Typeset by Deltatype Ltd, Birkenhead, Merseyside

Printed and bound in Great Britain by Clays Ltd, St Ives plc

www.orionbooks.co.uk

*For Edward and Samuel, Rebecca and Ally,
and a certain little boy of infinite adorableness.*

*I would also like to dedicate this book to the
publishing tour de force that is Susan Lamb.*

THANKS AND ACKNOWLEDGEMENTS

Thanks to J.P. Devlin for allowing me to poke and pry into his extensive radio station knowledge. And for the best Christmas tree ever!

Thanks to Neil Bright for his wealth of USAAF knowledge and for giving me an invaluable helping hand.

Thanks to David Deacon for being my local East Anglian expert. Is there anything this man doesn't know?

Special thanks to Trevor Newell for being an all-round top man, and also because he wanted his name in a book!

A cheeky thank you to one of my readers for letting me pinch her name – thank you Betty!

Lastly, thanks to Mary and Dave and Jack for all the laughs, and to John for coming up with Skylark Radio.

There were others, too, who helped me in so many ways in pulling this book together, and they have my grateful thanks.

I would like to add that this is a work of fiction and therefore allowances must be made for an author's right to make things up, or twist things round to suit the purposes of the story. I would also like to point out that the SS *Belle Etoile* never existed, other than in my imagination. I took my inspiration from the SS *Normandie*, one of the most beautiful ocean liners ever built.

*'Our dead are never dead to us,
until we have forgotten them'*

George Eliot

*'Someone has to die in order that the
rest of us should value life more'*

Virginia Woolf

Chapter One

Lizzie knew that there would be plenty of people who would
take the view that she was the author of her misfortune. But
the blame wasn't all hers. She had been made a scapegoat
and unfairly so in her eyes.

She still couldn't believe what had happened to her: one
minute she was riding high on the crest of a wave of ecstatic
happiness and the next she was unreasonably sacked from a
job she loved and, as a consequence, separated from the man
she loved. If that wasn't bad enough, and with no money
coming in, she couldn't pay the rent on her flat and in the
absence of any so-called friends rushing to offer her a spare
room to use temporarily, she had no choice but to leave
London and slink home to her parents in Suffolk until she
got herself back on her feet.

Not that she could tell her parents the real reason she'd

been sacked from Starlight Radio. She shuddered even now to recall the appalling moment when her affair with Curt had been so thoroughly exposed. To spare Mum and Dad the sordid details she had told them some story about the owners of the radio station having a draconian attitude towards relationships in the workplace and, with sweeping cutbacks to be made, she had been conveniently got rid of. The only element of truth in what she'd told Mum and Dad was the bit about a draconian attitude.

Now, at the age of thirty-two, here she was in her old bedroom surrounded by piles of bursting bin bags and boxes and effectively trying to squeeze toothpaste back into a flattened tube. No matter how hard she tried, there simply wasn't enough space in the wardrobes, drawers or shelves to accommodate what she'd accumulated in the ten years since she'd left home.

As was only right, the bedroom bore little resemblance to the room she had left behind. Just as soon as Mum had thought a decent time had elapsed, it had been redecorated and turned into the best guest bedroom, decked out with flowery curtains and matching bed linen, bars of fragrant Provençal soap strategically placed, along with neatly folded towels that no member of the family would ever be allowed to use.

She had been home for a week now and she really should have got the mess sorted, but the days had been mostly spent feeling manically sorry for herself and firing off job applications, all of them resulting in rejection emails that were irritatingly similar, with their matey flippancy wishing her luck. Luck? She should like some, thank you very much!

Poor Mum and Dad, it couldn't be easy having her back with them again. Not only that, they were still a long way from understanding why she'd ended her four-year relationship with Simon in favour of a man they'd yet to meet – a married man to boot. To all intents and purposes they had treated Simon as a bona fide son-in-law and Lizzie knew they were struggling to make the adjustment to not seeing him any more.

As happy as she and Simon had been together, marriage had never been discussed – the nearest they got to it was when Simon started talking about his Five-Year Plan and how he saw their lives rolling out in the future. As Lizzie was puzzling over her less-than-enthusiastic reaction to these projected hopes and dreams, Curt Flynn pitched up as the new Head of Programmes at Starlight Radio and in one fell swoop everything she had thought she'd loved about Simon paled into insignificance.

Forty-two years old, Curt was dynamic and fun – dangerously fun. He always seemed to know what she was thinking, and all it took was one glance from him with those flashing, intuitive eyes of his and she'd fall about laughing, often at the most inopportune moment. His sense of humour was scathingly cutting and delivered in a flat Mancunian accent she had originally thought was put on, a throwback parody of the Gallagher brothers. 'I'm from somewhere I bet you've never heard of, much less visited,' he'd said, when she had asked where he'd grown up.

'Try me,' she said.

'Levenshulme?' he'd told her. 'No, I thought not; even I would have to admit that it's not exactly a belting tourist destination.'

She'd immediately made it her business to Google Levenshulme – she was a researcher, after all. 'Most notable people from Levenshulme,' she'd said casually when she'd found herself arriving for work at the same time as him the next morning, 'the architect Norman Foster, the actor Arthur Lowe, the comedienne Beryl Reid and the original drummer from Oasis.'

Pressing the button for the lift to take them up to the studio on the fifth floor, he'd said, 'Never heard of them.'

'Not even the Oasis drummer?'

'Especially not him.' His expression was deadpan.

3

Alone in the lift, he'd turned full square to face her. 'I'm impressed that you went to the trouble of doing a background check on me. Do you do that for everyone you work with?'

Technically she worked *for* him, and liking the fact he hadn't played the boss card, she'd smiled. 'I live by the maxim that forewarned is forearmed.'

He'd laughed; a sexily louche laugh that had bounced off the mirror-lined walls of the lift. She had enjoyed the sound, had enjoyed knowing that she had amused him.

'I can see that I'm going to have to watch myself around you,' he'd said, putting a hand to the small of her back and nudging her forward when the doors opened. The touch of his hand had been like a bolt of electricity passing through her, a sensation she had never before experienced. *Bad Lizzie!* she'd reprimanded herself that evening when she was on her way home and guiltily replaying the moment.

A month later, and despite knowing he was married, she had agreed to have a drink with him after work one evening. She had known exactly what she was doing. So had he. 'There's no point in pretending we don't feel the way we do for each other,' he'd said bluntly. Knowing that he felt the same way about her as she did for him made her believe that it was meant to be, that his marriage had been a classic case of marrying the wrong person and for the wrong reasons. It happened all the time, didn't it? One in three marriages ended in divorce.

Telling Simon that she didn't love him any more was one of the hardest things she'd ever had to do. He was devastated, just hadn't seen it coming. But then neither had she. She did what she thought was the decent thing and moved out of the flat they had been renting together for the last two years. She found herself a small flat in Hackney, and that was where Curt would come and spend whatever time he could with her.

Initially the secrecy surrounding their affair had given Lizzie a frisson of excitement, but it wasn't long before it

4

became a burden. More than anything she wanted to share her happiness of being in love. In the end, the one person in whom she could confide, knowing she could trust him not to tell anyone else, was her twin brother, Luke. He was shocked and cautioned her to take care. It was advice that was typical of her brother – not for nothing had she nicknamed him Mr Careful when they were children. With hindsight she could see she should have heeded his advice.

When the affair was revealed and she was summarily fired, Curt had been in danger of losing his job too, but because he was married and had a young child, along with a hefty mortgage, the owners of the radio station had let him off. It was a bitter pill for Lizzie to swallow, that she should be so unfairly treated. Curt had promised her that it was only a minor setback, that when the dust had settled at work he would sort things with his wife and they would be together. In return he'd made her promise not to contact him, especially not at work. 'I need this job,' he'd explained, 'you can understand that, can't you? I can't afford to rock the boat again.'

It was Curt's promise that kept her going, gave her the hope to believe the awful situation in which she found herself was only temporary. He was adamant that, just as soon as he had the situation under control, at work and at home, it would all come right in a matter of months. 'We just have to play the game,' he'd said. 'Can you do that for me, Lizzie? Can you?'

She had said she could when she had his arms around her, but now – a fortnight since she'd last seen him – her resolve was crumbling. She didn't feel at all like playing the game. She wanted her job back, she wanted her flat back – but most of all she wanted to be back with Curt.

Just as tears of angry frustration rose to the surface of her self-pity, the ugly chacker-chacker call of a magpie in next door's silver birch tree came through the open window. It sounded for all the world as if the bird was laughing at her

5

and it had the effect of giving her the strength to fight off the tears. Going over to the window, she rested her elbows on the sill. Leaning out into the warm, still June air, she breathed in the lemony scent of the creamy-yellow rose that Dad had trained to climb up the back of the house. In the distance, in the delicately pale blue sky, a pair of swallows tumbled acrobatically above the field of rapeseed at the end of the garden. The dazzling blaze of yellow flowers had gone over now; come early August the harvest would begin.

And where would she be then? she wondered. Back in London, she hoped, starting a new life with Curt.

Chapter Two

Tess Moran was a great believer in doing her bit.

It was a trait that had been drummed into her when she was a child. Her mother had been responsible for that; she had brought Tess up to believe it was everybody's duty – hers in particular – to make the world a better place. Now in her early sixties, Tess knew no other way to be. Idleness was anathema to her and there was no such thing as a spare minute, every minute of the day was to be put to good use. Which was why, when she retired from working as a health visitor, she volunteered to become a befriender at Woodside, a care home for the elderly. Her role didn't actually cover caring as such, but she did whatever else was needed, whether it was playing the piano for the residents, reading to them, serving cups of tea, or just having a chat.

She had spent most of today at Woodside on her feet and now, as she drove down the long driveway and out through the gates, she was glad of the chance to sit down. The car was stifling hot from being in the sun and, opening the windows to let some air in, she wondered what awaited her at home and how Lizzie would greet her news that Tess had found her something to do while she job-hunted.

It went without saying that she and Tom loved both their children dearly and would do anything to help them, but they were guilty of having grown used to having the house to themselves, each of them carving out space in which they could enjoy their hobbies – sewing for Tess in Luke's old room, and local history for Tom in what had been the children's den when they were home from university. Having

Lizzie back with them was, to put it mildly, proving to be more of a challenge than they'd anticipated. But then really they should have known better; after all, one way or another Lizzie had always had a knack for upsetting the apple cart.

Whereas Luke had been an easy-going child who had moved effortlessly from childhood to manhood, Lizzie had tripped and fallen almost every step of the way. It never failed to astonish Tess that two beings could grow together in the womb and emerge so completely different.

As a small child Lizzie had once told Tess that she found it so very difficult to be as well behaved as her brother. 'I'm not good like Luke, am I, Mummy? I'm Bad Lizzie, aren't I?' Her young daughter's words had struck at Tess's heart, especially when Lizzie had asked if she was loved as much as Luke. 'Of course you are!' Tess had rushed to assure. 'Your father and I love you both equally.'

Insecurity in a child so young had meant that the strict impartiality of parenthood, which Tess had assumed would be her rock and stay, was not always the case when it came to Lizzie, and she invariably found herself defending her daughter, no matter what.

'The trouble with Lizzie,' Tom's mother used to say, 'is that she's hopelessly fickle; the girl simply doesn't know what it is she wants. She flits from one thing to another.'

There was much that was true in the statement, but whether fickleness could be blamed for the years of drama they'd endured, Tess couldn't say. As a toddler Lizzie had regularly thrown herself onto the floor, arms and legs flailing like a demented octopus, all the while screaming at the top of her voice. At the same age she had also perfected the skill of holding her breath for so long she would literally turn blue. Her teenage years weren't much easier, but by then Tom and Tess had learned to roll with the punches of whatever crisis revolved around their daughter, such as nearly drowning on holiday after drinking too much and going for a swim, or crashing the car the first time she drove it after passing her driving test, or losing her handbag and house keys, or setting fire to the toaster. Things just happened to her in the way they didn't to Luke. She was like a magnet for bad luck.

In common with most parents, Tess would have given anything for her children to have a trouble-free life – let somebody else's child experience the highs and lows, the dramas and heartaches, just let her own be spared any suffering. Yet as protective as she was of both Luke and Lizzie, she wasn't blind to their faults. Luke was like Tom and too easy-going for his own good, and Lizzie was invariably at the mercy of her pride and would refuse to admit that she had ever made a wrong decision.

That pride would very likely prove to be the problem now; it would dictate that she wouldn't be able to accept that her current predicament had been brought on by a terrible error of judgement. Lizzie should never have broken up with Simon in favour of a married man – a married man with a young child. It had been an act of madness. Every time Tess thought of the man's poor wife sitting at home while her husband was with Lizzie, her stomach churned.

They didn't know exactly why Lizzie had lost her job – there was something about her story of being made redundant that didn't quite ring true – but when Tom had started talking about her seeking legal advice for unfair dismissal, Luke had hinted it might stir up a hornet's nest that was better left well alone. Luke obviously knew more about what had gone on, but in loyalty to his sister he was keeping quiet. Which only served to worry Tess more.

The first she and Tom had known about this Curt character had been when Lorna had rung Tess – Lorna Duncan was not only Tess's closest friend in the village, she was also Simon's mother. 'How long have you known?' Lorna had asked, her voice tight with hurt and recrimination.

'Known what?' Tess had replied innocently.

'Oh, come on, Tess, you're her mother! Of course you know Lizzie's dumped Simon and taken up with some man

9

she works with. At least have the decency to be straight with me.'

So shocked had Tess been, both at the news and the tone of Lorna's voice, it was some moments before she could respond. 'But – but that can't be right,' she managed to say. 'Lizzie loves Simon. You know she does.'

In the uncomfortable silence that followed, Tess had thought of all the times when she had secretly allowed herself to plan Simon and Lizzie's wedding – a small marquee on the lawn at Keeper's Nook, the catering firm that had provided the buffet for her and Tom's thirtieth wedding anniversary, and a disco. Once or twice she had even joked with Lorna that they were practically family these days. It seemed impossible that none of that was going to happen now.

There was a lengthy pause before Lorna spoke. 'You mean you really didn't know?'

'I promise you, Lorna, this is the first I've heard of it. But surely there's been a mistake. Surely it's nothing more than a lovers' tiff. It'll blow over. Of course it will. I'll speak to Lizzie.'

Another of Tess's traits was to believe that there was no problem she couldn't fix. But in this instance, no amount of talking or reasoning with Lizzie was of use. Lizzie's mind was made up. She was sorry for upsetting everyone, but there was nothing to be done: she loved Curt now, not Simon.

Poor Simon, he was distraught. Tess and Tom had seen for themselves the state he was in when he'd turned up unexpectedly one evening. He was home for the weekend to see his parents and had called in on them at Keeper's Nook in the hope that they might be able to persuade Lizzie to change her mind. It had saddened Tess profoundly to see how upset he was, but knowing how stubborn their daughter could be once she'd made her mind up, all they could do was repeat how sorry they were and hug the lad they'd thought would one day be their son-in-law.

Since then relations between the two families had

deteriorated. Tess suspected that Lorna found her account-able in some way for hurting her precious only child. There had been no meals out together like they used to, or lazy Sunday lunches spent at each other's houses.

Tess had never believed that anger or the laying of blame served any good purpose but now, as she entered the village of Great Magnus and passed Orchard House with its im-maculate front garden of box hedging and roses, and where she hadn't set foot in some weeks, she felt a strong urge to be very angry indeed with her daughter. Not just for what she'd done to Simon, but to them as a family and their closest friends. Had Lizzie given any thought to the consequences of her actions? Tess wasn't proud of having these thoughts, but there was no denying the strength of what she felt.

Orchard House now behind her, she drove on slowly to the heart of the village with its elongated triangle of vil-lage green lined on all sides by a variety of prettily painted timber-framed cottages, their roofs a mixture of thatch, slate and clay tile. Not so long ago Great Magnus had boasted five pubs and a wide selection of shops, but now, and despite its growing population, it possessed just the two pubs, an antique shop cum tearoom and a community shop run by a rota of helpers, including Tess.

She passed the duck pond on her right and took the turn-ing afterwards, then, passing the church and going further down the narrow lane, she indicated right for Keeper's Nook.

A double-fronted Victorian red-brick villa that over the years had been treated to a mishmash of extensions, it was not what you'd call a looker. But it was the location that Tess and Tom had fallen in love with, in particular the swathe of open farmland behind the house. They had moved here from Essex the summer Lizzie and Luke sat their A-level exams. Tess always remembered that summer as being a good one.

She was out of the car when, from the depths of her hand-bag, she heard her mobile ring.

It was Luke's wife, Ingrid, a young woman who, if Tess

were completely honest, thoroughly intimidated her. She was a clinical and medical negligence lawyer and, having returned to work when Freddie was eight months, she radiated the kind of competency that Tess had never in her life achieved. There was a measured coolness about Ingrid, which meant she rarely said anything off the cuff, her every word seeming to be carefully weighed before uttered. Tess and Tom had always put this down to a Scandinavian influence; her mother was Swedish. She had been their daughter-in-law for three years now, but despite clearly making Luke happy, and being the mother of their delightful grandson, Tess didn't feel she knew Ingrid any better than when Luke had first brought her home to meet them.

'Hello, Ingrid,' she said now, packing into those two small words an excessive amount of cheerfulness. It was another effect Ingrid had on her; she made Tess behave out of character, as though she were trying too hard to please. The result was she always sounded horribly insincere.

Chapter Three

Over in Cambridge, throughout her conversation with her mother-in-law, Ingrid had been scrolling through her emails, dismissing anything that could wait until the morning and prioritising the rest.

The call now ended, she reached across for the form that Liam, the latest in a long line of office juniors, had left on her desk. Attached to the form was a handwritten note. She didn't know what was worse, Liam's appalling handwriting or the ridiculous text-speak he used to communicate with her – No *hury nd of nxt wk ok*. Just how much time did the boy think he was saving by writing in this idiotic manner?

Despite Liam's instruction that there was no hurry, she removed the cap from her pen and began filling in the details the form required of her. She hated needlessly putting things off; she preferred to get things dealt with as soon as possible, just as she liked to be honest and direct with those around her. Admittedly not everyone appreciated the candid approach she favoured. Twice now she had corrected Liam on his grammar and his spelling and both times he had looked at her as though he had no idea what she was talking about.

Luke's family were prime examples of people who didn't go in for the direct approach, preferring instead to tiptoe around the edge of what needed to be said. For Luke's sake Ingrid had learned to hold her tongue when around them, especially when it came to his twin sister who, in her opinion, was in dire need of a reality check – she was a thirty-two-year-old woman, not a child of thirteen, who believed the world revolved around her. It was high time that girl grew up and took responsibility for her actions – and herself. Running home to mummy and daddy when the going got tough was nothing short of pathetic at her age.

From all the stories Ingrid had heard about Lizzie as a child – usually told in a jocular how-did-we-ever-survive-it? tone – it never failed to surprise her just how indulged Lizzie must have been. Luke said that his parents behaved in the way any loving parents would: with patience, tolerance and love. 'Isn't that how we'd be with Freddie?' he'd asked her.

Holding her tongue, she'd kept to herself that she would never allow Freddie to behave the way Lizzie had. Her love for her son was absolute; she could never love him more, or less, but she would haul him quickly into line if he started to show the slightest similarity to his feckless aunt.

Ingrid had never let on to anyone, not even Luke, just what a wrench it had been for her to leave Freddie in the care of others so that she could return to work. The only way she could cope with the sense of loss she'd experienced was to absorb herself thoroughly in the legal cases she dealt with. It also served the purpose of leaving her no time to dwell on whether the nursery was looking after Freddie properly – did the nursery staff wash their hands enough, did they know what to do if he was choking, or had a fever, did they watch him at all times, was he drinking enough water during the day, was he learning anything, was he making friends? Her list of concerns was endless.

Having a child had been the biggest joint decision she and Luke had made so far in their relationship. They had both been perfectly content with the previous status quo, deriving all the happiness they needed from each other and their demanding careers, but then a friend's husband had died and from nowhere Ingrid experienced the stark fear that, if anything happened to Luke, she would be left with nothing of him; he would be gone, completely gone. Whereas a child, she realised, would provide her with a uniquely precious part of Luke, as well as the strength to face life without him.

Surprised by her turnaround, and her sudden anxiety about his mortality, Luke took some convincing, but before long he was as jubilant as she was at the positive result a pregnancy test kit gave them.

Now, the form duly filled out, Ingrid added it to the files awaiting Liam's administrations. Naturally precise and unhurried of movement, she straightened the files, squaring the corners to her satisfaction and wishing the rest of her life were as easy to order.

Hearing loud voices from outside, she rose from her chair and went over to the window that looked down onto the courtyard garden at the back of the elegant Regency building that was home to Cavendish Court Lawyers. On her return from maternity leave, she had been given this office following a reshuffle after the retirement of one of the partners. It had been made clear to her that she should consider herself lucky to be given such a prized space in which to work.

Luck be damned! She deserved this office as much as anybody else here. More so, in some cases. Actually, more so in *plenty* of cases.

Down in the garden a man wearing ear defenders wielded a chainsaw, the noise ricocheting off the surrounding walls. The conifer that was being chopped down had been exhaustively discussed. There were those who wanted to keep the tree, citing its importance at Christmas time when it was decorated with lights. Others said it should be removed as a matter of some urgency before it caused any structural damage to the building – the surrounding flagstones were already lifting in places.

Ingrid had readily agreed that the tree should go. Not only because it partially blocked the view from her window, but because it was obvious the tree had outgrown the space. Logic dictated her thoughts, not misplaced sentiment. Those in the firm who wanted a tree to decorate at Christmas could club together and buy one to play with if they cared so much!

Mercifully, the madness of Christmas was a long way off.

Right now she had a far more pressing problem. Over the weekend there had been a colossal flood at Freddie's nursery and it was only first thing this morning that the flood, and the extent of the damage caused, was discovered. With sewage seeping up from the drains, the job of putting things right was going to take weeks, if not months. Which left them well and truly in the lurch and was the reason Ingrid had rung Tess to ask if she and Tom could have Freddie on a Monday to Friday basis. Fortunately Luke had managed to take today off to look after Freddie and had said he would ring his parents to ask for their help, but Ingrid had insisted he let her make the call, saying she felt it showed more respect to Tess if she was the one to ask the favour.

However, the real reason she wanted to speak to Tess was to be very sure that her mother-in-law understood the ground rules, namely that Lizzie was not to be left in sole charge of Freddie at any time. The girl could not be trusted to look after herself, never mind a cherished two-year-old.

Down in the courtyard, the man with the chainsaw had revved it up a gear and was moving in for the kill. The tree, thought Ingrid, as the branches the other side of the window began to shake as if in protest, was a symbol of stubborn and futile resistance to change. There it had stood all these years insinuating its way, little by little, into a space where it wasn't wanted; now it had met its match and its demise was imminent.

In a window adjacent to hers, Ingrid spotted Julian Redman holding up a handwritten sign – SAVE THE TREE … for firewood! Seeing her, he grinned. She smiled back at her fellow voice of reason and held up a thumb of triumph and solidarity just as the tree gave a violent shudder and fell away from the window with a loud creak of defeat, followed by a thud to the ground.

Mentally cheering that today was a small victory for common sense, Ingrid turned away from the window and went back to her desk.

Chapter Four

'You might just as well give in graciously to Mum,' Luke said, watching his sister crawl around on all fours in the garden with Freddie on her back. She was pretending to be a camel for some reason – anybody else would have settled for a horse or a donkey and made the appropriate noises, but not Lizzie; she always had to do things differently.

'Since when have I done anything graciously?' she said, pausing to look at him.

'You could break the habit of a lifetime and give it a go, just to see how it feels.'

Lizzie let out a yelp. 'Hey, you back there, that hurts!'

Ignoring her words, Freddie giggled and tugged all the more on her hair, which she'd plaited specially to act as reins. 'Lizzie go faster!' he squealed.

'You want faster, do you, young man? Well, you'd better hold on tight, because this camel's about to turn into a racing camel, and you know what racing camels do, don't you, they go racing in the desert!' To shrieks of delight from her charge, she took off towards the end of the garden, then getting to her feet and with Freddie hanging on gamely, she turned round and thundered back towards Luke where he was sitting on the grass. Out of breath, she swung Freddie down and plonked him in Luke's lap. 'Your turn to entertain your son,' she panted. 'I'm all done in.'

'But you do it so splendidly. Isn't that true, Freddie? Auntie Lizzie really is the best auntie in the world, isn't she?'

'Thanks for bigging me up, but I'm the only aunt he has, so his experience is severely limited.'

In answer to Luke's question, Freddie wriggled out of his hands and threw himself on top of Lizzie, where she now lay on her back. 'I thought we'd sneaked out here to have a quiet chat,' she said with a grimace as Freddie sat astride her and began bouncing up and down, making clip-clop noises with his tongue.

'Come on, you,' Luke said, leaning over to grab his son, 'you've worn poor Lizzie out.'

Freddie pushed Luke's hands away. 'No, no, no, no, no!' he said, shaking his head violently from side to side.

'Look, sweetheart, just sit quietly for a while so your daddy and I can talk, and then if you've been extra, *extra* good we'll have another camel ride. Can you be quiet for me?'

He gave Lizzie's request a moment's consideration, then nodded slowly, pressing one of his fingers very firmly into the exposed skin of midriff where her top had ridden up.

'So come on, Luke, tell me why you think it's a good idea I give in to Mum and work at Woodside?' Lizzie said, while letting Freddie prod some more in the manner of a clumsy doctor examining her. 'Because I can't think of anything more likely to make me feel a million times worse.'

Five weeks had passed since Lizzie had moved back home to Keeper's Nook and at Mum's instigation, and considerable cajoling, she was about to start at Woodside as a volunteer helper. With all the appropriate background checks now carried out, it seemed a bit late in the day to be having a change of heart, especially as Mum had gone to so much trouble to set things up.

'Well,' Luke said, knowing he was on slippery ground, 'my question to you is do you have anything else in mind to do with your time? Apart from watching endless daytime telly.'

'Chance would be a fine thing! The minute I sit down, or even look like I'm about to sit down, Mum pounces on me. Honestly, it's like being a kid again. She keeps shooing me about the place. I swear she's worried I'll grow roots if I stay still for too long.'

Luke laughed. 'That's probably exactly what she's worried about. The last thing any parent wants is their grown-up child living with them on a permanent basis.'

Lizzie frowned. 'The last thing *I* want is to be here on a permanent basis.'

'So meantime you need to do something positive while you wait for the right job opportunity to come along.'

'If it ever does,' she said with uncharacteristic gloominess.

'It will,' he said firmly.

Still frowning, she said, 'Are you sure I can't come and stay with you for a bit? I could look after this little monkey instead of him coming to Mum and Dad.' She gave Freddie a taste of his own medicine and prodded his tummy, eliciting a happy giggle from him. 'I wouldn't be any bother. And you'd save me from the horror of Woodside.'

This wasn't the first time Lizzie had made this suggestion since a burst pipe had caused untold flood damage to Freddie's nursery, putting it out of action for an unspecified length of time. If it were left to Luke, he'd be tempted to say yes, it would make things easier all round. In fact, asking Lizzie to come to their rescue had been his first thought, but Ingrid had been quick to veto the idea. 'It would be like having a second child in the house,' she'd said, 'and frankly I'd lay odds on Freddie being the more sensible of the two.'

They had then briefly considered the possibility of travelling backwards and forwards on a daily basis, delivering and collecting Freddie to Mum and Dad, but living where they did, on the outskirts of Cambridge, it just wasn't feasible. It also hadn't seemed fair to expect his parents to do the toing and froing. But so far, the current arrangement was working well: Freddie loved being with his grandparents and being thoroughly spoilt into the bargain. They were here today, Sunday afternoon, to leave him for another week.

'You wouldn't last forty-eight hours, Lizzie,' Luke said

lightly to his sister in answer to her question. 'Freddie would wear you down to a husk and leave you no time to job-hunt.'

She gave him a bittersweet look, a look that told him she knew he wasn't being entirely straight with her.

In the silence that settled on them, punctuated by the sound of birdsong and Freddie humming to himself, Luke thought about the man responsible for his sister's predicament. He hadn't met this supposed love of Lizzie's life, but he'd heard a lot about him. Rather too much, if he was honest. His immediate response to Lizzie's confession that she was having an affair with a married man was one of shock. Even by his sister's usual maddeningly impetuous and headstrong standards, this was going some. He had wanted to tell her to drop the man like a stone, and fast; that no good would come of continuing the relationship. But seeing the change in her, how obviously in love she was, he'd known that she was beyond listening to anything that might pour cold water on the heat of her happiness, so instead he'd merely cautioned her to take care.

From a personal perspective he'd found her break-up with Simon particularly difficult because he and Simon had got on so well. They still did. Luke didn't like deceiving Lizzie, but he hadn't let on to her that he'd met up with Simon a couple of times for a drink when he was in London. The evenings they'd spent together had not been easy. The sad thing was, when Simon had become a permanent fixture in Lizzie's life, Luke had agreed with their parents that here at last was a boyfriend who would anchor her. Here was a boyfriend who with his gentle, even-tempered manner was the perfect foil for Lizzie's highly impulsive temperament. They were proved wrong. Maybe Lizzie wasn't ever meant to be anchored; perhaps she was destined always to be slightly adrift from the rest of them.

Of all the exasperatingly reckless things Lizzie had done, this business with Curt topped the lot, though. It even surpassed the memorable occasion when she'd tried to dye

Luke's hair for him and had used neat bleach, with disastrous results. Or the time she had surprised him by saying she'd got tickets for them to go to Glastonbury to celebrate their combined twenty-first birthday. It had been a fantastic surprise present and he'd so looked forward to seeing The Killers perform, as well as The White Stripes and Interpol. The day came when they set off for Somerset with backpacks bulging with a tent and waterproofs – only to find that Lizzie had forgotten the tickets. She'd sworn that he'd said he would bring them, and even when he showed her the text she'd sent him saying she had the tickets, she refused to climb down. She apologised eventually, admitting that she'd found the tickets Sellotaped for safe-keeping to her dressing-table mirror. And because her heart was genuinely in the right place, and he could never stay cross with her for long, he had forgiven her.

Lizzie had also confided in him the actual circumstances of her losing her job and if it had been anyone else, he might have laughed. But the thought of his sister being caught in flagrante at work left him feeling decidedly uncomfortable. For some reason he'd made the mistake of telling Ingrid – usually he was more circumspect in what he shared with his wife about Lizzie – and her horrified reaction, far from reassuring him that he was right to be shocked, had the opposite effect and made him play down his sister's crime as if it was the kind of thing that could happen to anyone. But deep down, some primordial instinct made him want to defend his sister's honour and beat the hell out of Curt Flynn for compromising her the way he had.

Being twins, the closeness that existed between them was about as powerful as it got. Ingrid claimed that the distance that existed between herself and Lizzie was because Lizzie was jealous of her for daring to steal her sacred brother. Luke had no idea if this was true, but it was a sad disappointment to him that Ingrid and his sister didn't get on better; all he could do was hope that with time that would change.

He was older than Lizzie by five minutes, and they were recognisably brother and sister, two very distinct peas from the same pod – both dark-haired with dark brown eyes, well-defined eyebrows and wide foreheads. But whereas he was six feet tall and, to his frustration, already beginning to show signs of filling out like their father, she was five feet five inches and as slim as she'd always been.

Observing her now, and seeing how unhappy she looked as she hugged Freddie close, Luke wished wholeheartedly that Curt Flynn had never made the journey down from Manchester to London. From day one Lizzie had loved her job at Starlight Radio and when the music station, based in Shoreditch, had branched out to cover the hot issues of the day, as well as a variety of amusingly quirky material, Lizzie had come into her own and relished doing the necessary research. But then along came Curt bloody Flynn, brought in as the exciting new programme producer, and bang went her job. And wasn't it just typical that the bugger had got off free, and it was Lizzie who had paid the cost and lost everything?

He was about to ask if she had heard anything from Curt when Ingrid appeared at the open kitchen French doors. Regarding his wife in the bright sunshine as she moved with the languid grace which had caught his eye when they'd first met, Luke thought, as he so often did, how effortlessly beautiful she was. She was wearing faded blue jeans that emphasised her long, slim legs and a simple white cotton blouse. Her Scandinavian blonde hair – that she complained was darkening as she grew older – was scooped up from her shoulders by a large clip, exposing her long neck.

Their paths had crossed at a corporate gathering of lawyers at Newmarket races. He'd just been to collect his winnings – a lucky guess on a horse that had come in first – and was returning to his table of fellow litigation lawyers when he spotted her backed into a corner of the room. He'd noticed her earlier during lunch and had thought how stunning she was; he thought the same then as he watched her, forced to listen to the large, florid-faced man in a pinstripe suit with a flamboyantly pink silk handkerchief stuffed into his breast pocket. Luke had recognised the deadly boredom in her blue eyes and knew the feeling all too well – there was nothing like a day of stifling VIP haw-hawing to make you wish you were somewhere else. She caught him looking at her and for a split second their gaze locked, the connection made. Then suddenly her expression changed and with the brightest of smiles, she put a hand lightly on the man's forearm and said something Luke was too far away to catch. Next thing she was coming towards him, weaving a graceful path through the crowded room. 'For the love of God, play along,' she said, her hand outstretched. 'Pretend we know each other and save me from having to speak a moment longer with that arrogant pig of a man. I told him there was something I needed to discuss with you.'

He played along, shaking her hand warmly and asking her how she was and why he hadn't heard from her in absolutely ages. She'd smiled and entered into the charade, then when the coast was clear and the florid-faced man had safely moved on to claim another victim, Luke had asked her what her name was and which law firm she worked for. From there it was but a very short step from wanting to know all about her.

Her name was Ingrid Vaughan, the only daughter of a British man who'd married a Swedish woman from Stockholm. She had spent part of her childhood in Sweden before moving to London. Her parents' marriage had not been a happy one: they had argued furiously and frequently, and when, in her mother's eyes, Ingrid's father conveniently died, he was quickly replaced by a series of men, culminating in a wealthy diamond trader from Antwerp who had no desire to have a tiresome young child getting in the way. So Ingrid was despatched to a boarding school on the south coast of England while her mother married her diamond trader and took up travelling the world in a level of comfort and style she had always known was her due.

All this meant that Ingrid grew up to be strong, independent and clever. Like Luke, once she had qualified, she'd discounted the lure of working for a big London law firm, preferring instead the opportunity to do well in a less pressurised environment. Had they not both applied to take up positions in Cambridge to pursue their careers, they would never have met.

Spotting his mother, Freddie clambered off Lizzie and ran to her. She lifted him up and kissed him tenderly on the cheek. Then glancing over to Luke, and giving him a quick smile, she said, 'It's time we were going.'

Chapter Five

She couldn't remember who it was who had shared this theory with her, but at the age of ninety-five, Clarissa Dallimore had seen enough of life – and death – to know there was a good deal of truth in it. The theory was this: people often choose when to die, wanting to hang on for the right person to be with them at the exact moment of death, or to take their leave once the final goodbyes had all been made and there was nothing else left to say.

Clarissa knew without a shadow of doubt that her time to depart was drawing very near and, as Ellis kept reminding her, why was she hanging about when there was nobody left to say goodbye to? What was keeping her?

The first time Ellis had appeared she'd been sitting in the communal garden, a few days after moving here to Woodside. He had waved to her from the other side of the lawn, over by the archway that led to the pond. Without a second thought she had waved back at him, her joy at seeing him again outweighing her surprise. The next time he'd appeared was at the end of her bed one night. Another occasion he showed up in the dining room during lunch. He hadn't been alone that day; Artie had been with him, along with Effie. Oh what fun it had been to see all three of them together! And how they had relieved the boredom of listening to that dreadfully tiresome man complaining that the meal they'd just been served wasn't seasoned enough. Effie had given Clarissa a complicit wink, sharing with her that she knew how unendurably tedious Clarissa found this particular dining companion. That wink from Effie had made her yearn for a time when she had been a slip of a girl, with a head and heart full of love, hope and adventure, when anything seemed possible.

But now the biggest adventure of the day for her was tackling the business of washing and dressing herself unaided – something she was determined to do for as long as she possibly could. Some days it frustrated her enormously how little she was capable of doing, but mostly she was resigned to it and was happy to reside inside her head and live life to the full that way.

Some days she felt compelled to explain to somebody – *anybody* – that this wasn't the real her; that she was so much more than this frail old lady living out the remaining days of her life in a care home. But who would believe her? More to the point, who would be genuinely interested?

As for sharing anything with her fellow residents, without being ungenerous, they mostly only wanted to speak about themselves and their own lives. Maybe that was because, in some cases, it was all that was left when you reached a certain age. In the days and weeks that had passed since her arrival, she had listened politely to those around her. Now and again she was guilty of nodding off, but from what she could see it didn't matter, for within no time she would be listening to the same story all over again.

With lunch now over, Clarissa waited for somebody to come and help her leave the dining room in the wheelchair that was supposed to make her life easier. How she wished she had the strength to wheel herself away!

Up until last year she had been able to look after herself perfectly well, but then shortly before Christmas she had slipped in the snow and ice. She had gone outside to the garden to feed the birds and to melt the frozen water in the birdbath with water she had boiled in the kettle. She had lain for nearly an hour in excruciating pain in the snow, hugging that kettle for warmth.

It had been the dustbin men who had found her. Luckily they collected her wheelie bin from the back garden, instead of expecting her to struggle to put it out by the front gate – had they not kindly carried out that task, who knew what might have happened to her as her neighbours were out at work all day, and her cleaner was not due until the end of the week. Even in the state she was in, she had managed to joke with the dustmen that if it was no trouble they could just throw her into the dustcart and spare people the bother of a funeral.

To her great regret that fall had been the end of her independence, for when she was eventually allowed home from hospital to recuperate from a broken pelvis, she was faced with the reality of having to employ the services of somebody to help her. Her doctor had been suggesting this for some time, but she had balked at the idea, hating the thought of strangers invading and taking over her life. All previous help she'd had by way of gardeners, cooks and handymen, and women to clean for her, had been on her terms, but a person to wash and undress her in her own home was another matter; it was so undignified. Nevertheless, she subjected herself to it, until one day, after a series of unsatisfactory carers, she accepted that she was wedged firmly between a rock and a very hard place and decided it was time to be sensible and make the move to a care home.

Woodside came highly recommended, small and friendly with the emphasis on personal and first-class quality care in a country house hotel environment. The brochure had promised her a carefree existence with all day-to-day worries lifted from her shoulders – and from those of her family. Since she had no family, all the weight was on her own shoulders, and had been so for a long time. Woodside, as the brochure further informed her, was located on the outskirts of Great Magnus in the heart of Suffolk, a true home from home for elderly gentlefolk. All of which added up to an expensive price tag, and while her financial situation was not what it had once been, she fortunately had the means to pay the exorbitant fees, and that was before selling her house.

She looked around her, realising she was entirely alone. Was anyone ever going to come and help her? It was then she saw a young girl hovering in the doorway of the dining room. Clarissa had noticed her earlier during lunch and thought how distinctly awkward she looked in her befriender's cerise-pink tabard. She didn't fit the profile of the usual women who worked here, or helped out on a voluntary basis; mostly they were older with a polished, cheerful manner about them. Mr and Mrs Parks, the owners of Woodside, were very strict on the type of person they took on – anyone who didn't make the grade was given their marching orders sooner rather than later.

With her unsmiling face, this girl in the doorway didn't look like she would last long. She bore all the hallmarks of somebody who wished they were anywhere but here. Yet hidden behind the awkward expression, Clarissa detected a pretty enough girl, a girl who was older than at first she thought, in her late twenties, perhaps. Her skin was clear and refreshingly devoid of make-up and her hair, thick and dark, was pulled back from her face in a ponytail. She was an unhappy girl, Clarissa found herself thinking, but then she herself might have been unhappy at that age if she had been forced to wear such an unflattering garment as that pink tabard.

The girl approached her. 'Mrs Danemore?' she asked.

Clarissa couldn't help herself. She looked around the empty dining room and shook her head. 'I'm not acquainted with anyone of that name here,' she said.

'Oh,' the girl said, her brows drawn in a delightfully studied expression of confusion.

'I am, however, on very good terms with a Mrs Dallimore. Perhaps,' Clarissa added mischievously, 'that's who you're looking for?'

The girl hesitated. 'Dallimore ...' she repeated, her brows

still drawn. 'Yes, that's right. Do you know where I can find her?'

Clarissa took pity on her. 'I'm afraid I was being a little disingenuous with you; *I'm* Mrs Dallimore. You must be new.'

'I am. This is my first day. Sorry I got your name wrong. I'm usually fairly good with names.'

'That's quite all right. First days are always difficult. How's it going?'

'So-so. Do you want me to take you back to your room for a nap?'

'No thank you. I'd like to go outside to the garden, if it's not too much trouble.' She was hoping Ellis might put in an appearance out there.

'No trouble at all,' the girl said breezily.

Her words were spoken rashly as it quickly became apparent the girl didn't have a clue how to manoeuvre a wheelchair. They eventually reached the garden having bumped into countless chairs and doorways before culminating in nearly tipping Clarissa out of the wretched thing when the girl tried to negotiate a route around a large terracotta pot on the terrace. 'I'm sorry, I'm so useless at this,' she said with a heartfelt sigh when they'd reached their destination. 'I've only ever pushed a pram before; it's those little wheels at the front, they have a mind of their own.'

'You have a child?' Clarissa asked, surprised. Based on what she'd seen so far, she'd no more trust the girl with a child than she'd ask her to perform brain surgery.

'No, a nephew; he's my brother's little boy. Do you want me to fetch you anything? A cup of tea, or maybe something to read?'

'Actually, I think I'd like you to take me back inside and find a carer to help me to the bathroom, please.'

The look of horror on the girl's face was a picture and once again Clarissa took pity on her. 'You must forgive an old lady a somewhat wicked sense of humour,' she said. 'I shall be perfectly content to sit here on my own and admire the view. Apart from that, it would be selfish of me to keep you from entertaining the others with your ability to wreak havoc at every turn.'

The girl looked at her hard and just as Clarissa was wondering if she'd gone too far, a smile brightened her face. 'With any luck, especially if you make a formal complaint, I'll be asked to leave by the end of the day.'

Clarissa chuckled. 'Just as I thought! You're here under duress, aren't you? Well, you're not alone in that, my dear.'

Chapter Six

Next morning, and with the dread of a second stint at Woodside to look forward to that afternoon, Lizzie was tempted to stay in bed and pull a sickie. Many a time when she'd been a child she had fooled Mum into thinking she was at death's door and couldn't possibly make it to school. Once, to give extra credence to her story, she had persuaded Luke to pretend he'd gone down with the same bug and they'd spent the day wrapped in their duvets on the sofa watching back-to-back episodes of *The Simpsons*.

But fooling Mum in this instance was never going to work; it would be too obvious a ploy. And anyway, an element of pride compelled her to prove that she could present herself at Woodside for another five hours of voluntary work, and do it with a smile on her face. If only because she knew everyone doubted she would see it through.

There had, of course, been no way of stopping Mum once she had the idea in her head that Lizzie should sort of cover for her at Woodside while she was busy at home with Freddie, and while it was the last thing she wanted to do, she felt she owed it to Mum to fall in line. So before she knew it, she had been interviewed by Jennifer Hughes, the matron in charge, and the rigorous checks insisted upon in order to do any kind of work with the young, old or vulnerable had been carried out and she was all signed up and ready to be a befriender.

Hearing the sound of footsteps pattering across the landing, she turned over to see Freddie peering round her bedroom door. Dressed in his blue and white stripy pyjamas and with sleep-tousled hair and rosy cheeks, he couldn't have looked cuter. 'Hello, sweetie,' she said, 'have you brought me a wake-up cuddle?'

He grinned and hopped comically from one foot to the other, then scooted off in answer to Mum calling him. Seconds later there was a knock at the door and this time it was Dad with a mug of tea.

'Have you been up for hours with Freddie?' she asked, sitting up.

'No, he only woke a short while ago.'

Her father set the mug down on the bedside table, then went over to the window, side-stepping the bin bags and boxes of her things, and pushed back the curtains. 'I'm happy to report that it's another fine day in paradise,' he said. 'I think I might cut the grass this morning.'

Lizzie smiled at her father's words. Even when it was pouring with rain and blowing a gale, he'd greet the day with, 'It's another fine day in paradise!'

He turned around from the window. 'What are your plans, then?'

'I'll do some more job-hunting online this morning, ring round a few people and then brace myself for another afternoon of fun at Woodside.'

He came and stood at the end of the bed. 'Did you hate it very much yesterday?'

'Hate would be too strong, but I don't think I was much use, or that I'll be asked to stay on. Don't tell Mum, but I very nearly managed to tip one old dear out of her wheelchair.'

He smiled. 'You'll get the hang of it, and it's not as if you'll be doing it forever. A new job will soon come along for you.'

As ever, she was touched by her father's eternal optimism and belief in her capabilities. She knew he was doing his best to make her believe that this really was another day in paradise, and that just around the corner was her very own crock of gold at the end of the rainbow, or whatever the saying was.

'I can't help but think I would be better suited to looking after Freddie than running the risk of harming some poor old person,' she said.

Her father shook his head. 'You don't want to be stuck at home all the time, not in your situation. Better to be out and about and meeting people. Fresh perspective and all that.'

'You're beginning to sound like Mum,' she said with a frown.

'Don't be too hard on yourself, first days are always tricky.'

'That's what the old lady said yesterday before I nearly jettisoned her into a flowerbed.'

Again he smiled. 'But the good news is that she survived to tell the tale.'

'Well, she was certainly alive when I left her.'

He laughed, then, presumably imagining that he had imparted sufficient optimism for her to believe her life was about to be restored to its former glory, he left her to drink her tea alone. Listening to him whistling 'Oh What a Beautiful Mornin'' as he went downstairs, she thought how wonderful it must be to be her father. A large-hearted man who was incapable of harbouring a grudge or a negative thought, he took everything in his stride, his whole attitude one of easy-going cheerfulness. Which didn't mean he was insensitive to her situation; he simply believed that everything would come good for her.

What he didn't know, and which she didn't have the heart to tell him, was that she was staring into the bleak abyss of another day that would once more smack her in the face with the reality that there were no jobs to chase, and any phone calls she made would yield absolutely nothing. To put it bluntly, she would get more luck out of a PPI nuisance call.

Every contact she had tried so far had drawn a blank. Not a single radio station in London was looking for a researcher right now. If they were, they were using interns who they didn't have to pay.

Ironically, working for Starlight Radio had been one of those lucky breaks which Dad claimed always came along. Previously she had been doing a variety of jobs that hadn't really given her the satisfaction she'd been hoping for since graduating. Unlike Luke, who had studied Law and had known before going to university that he wanted to be a lawyer, she had chosen American Studies with History almost at random, seeing the next three years as time in which to decide what she wanted to do when she graduated. But before she knew it, the three years had vanished in a blur and she entered the job market with no clearer idea about the kind of career she wanted to pursue. Following a year off which she spent travelling with her friend, Rachel, she returned home and signed up to an agency in London as a temp, doing mostly admin or reception work. One of those temporary jobs led to a full-time post in the HR department of a Swiss bank, which couldn't have suited her less, but the money was good. From there she moved to a PR company on a permanent basis, and it was while working on a campaign for an American crime author promoting her latest novel and doing the rounds of the commercial radio stations in London that Lizzie learned of a vacancy for a researcher at Starlight. In need of a change, she applied for the job and started work there four weeks later. With the station aggressively chasing a larger share of the audience market, she found herself researching a wide variety of subjects – one minute she could be interviewing a woman about her experience of living in India as a child and how she rode to school on an elephant with her brother and sister, and the next she could be ringing the manager of a boy band that had aspirations of being the next big thing. She loved the high-energy atmosphere in the studio and being a part of a team that made the three-hour programme possible. Curt used to like saying, 'Guys, we know it's all smoke and mirrors, but let's go make some banging magic!'

He was great like that, he could really enthuse the team,

make everyone want to do their best to produce the best pro-gramme they could. Of course it was all about the listening figures and satisfying the owners and ensuring the advertisers were happy. Big kudos to Curt – under his management the listening figures were up by 30 per cent. 'I bet everybody wanted to be your best friend at school, didn't they?' Lizzie once teased him.

'Nah, they all hated me.'

'They were jealous of you?'

He'd laughed. 'Jealous was the last thing they were. They were terrified of me.'

'Why?'

'Let's just say I was a big lad from an early age and could land a blinding punch when provoked.'

Snuggled up to him in the bar where they'd been having this conversation, she'd said, 'I shall have to be careful never to provoke you, in that case.'

'Punch a lass?' he'd said with a shake of his head. 'That's for cowards.'

'I'm glad to hear it.'

Remembering that evening so clearly, how safe yet at the same time how alive he'd made her feel, a flash of desperate need to be in Curt's reassuring presence came over Lizzie, to hear him say the magical words that made her heart leap – *I love you.*

Whenever he uttered the words, she felt as though the rest of the world no longer existed; it was just him and her, and whatever problems they faced they would face them together. He was like a hypnotist in that respect, he could look deep into her eyes and sweep away any doubts she had. He was not a man who doubted, he frequently said. When he wanted something, he made it happen.

She wished he was with her now to encourage her to believe everything was going to be all right; that she'd soon have a job as good as the one she'd been fired from, if not something better.

The only contact she'd had with Curt since leaving London was by email; his were always sent when he was at work and were far too brief to satisfy her need of him. Lizzie pictured him furtively writing them on his laptop at his desk, at the same time looking over his shoulder, checking that nobody could see what he was doing.

It had been hard enough hearing so little from him, but now she had to endure total radio silence while he was on holiday in Crete with his wife and daughter, a holiday that had been planned months ago and which he said he'd had no choice but to go through with. The thought of him lazing by a hotel pool drinking cocktails with his wife was driving Lizzie mad with jealousy. Was it wrong of her to hope that being cooped up 24/7 with a wife he no longer loved would give Curt the courage to come clean with her?

Was it also wrong to want to hear from him so desperately? It was a need so strong that just thinking it had her reaching for her mobile on the bedside table. One little text would be all right, wouldn't it?

Her hand wavered. She had promised Curt she wouldn't, that she would think of the bigger picture and let him sort things out his way, in his own time. He had a child to think of, after all.

Lizzie had only ever seen one photo of his daughter; it had showed a cute four-year-old girl who had corkscrew blonde curls and a happy, smiling face. Her name was Layla and although it scared Lizzie to imagine winning over this little girl, she knew she would have to do it. In time it was very likely Layla would end up being a playmate for Freddie.

But before any of that happened, there was the small matter of Curt meeting Lizzie's family. She hoped that would be soon, because then it would feel as though the worst of the madness was behind them.

Part of that madness was the effect her relationship with Curt had had on her friendship with Rachel. She and Rachel had been best mates since university, but after Lizzie had told her about Curt – after their affair was discovered – things had changed between them, to the point where it wouldn't be exaggerating to say Rachel now all but shunned her. To be fair, Lizzie could understand why – adultery was a touchy subject for her friend ever since she had found out that Steve, her husband of two years, had been having an affair. It was one of the reasons why Lizzie had kept quiet about Curt.

'How could you do it?' Rachel had asked her, furiously. 'Didn't you ever stop to think of his poor wife?'

The honest answer was no, no she hadn't. 'The love had gone out of their marriage long before we met,' she'd said instead.

'Oh, you idiot, that's what they all say!'

Knowing there was no point in pursuing the subject, Lizzie had had no choice but to let Rachel believe what she needed to about Curt.

With Steve having promised that his straying had been no more than an office fling that had got out of hand, he and Rachel were trying hard to make things work, but what Rachel didn't understand was that what Lizzie and Curt had was so much more than just a fling. This was real between them, real and lasting.

Rachel wasn't the only one to stand in judgement of Lizzie. Work colleagues at Starlight, those she'd thought of as friends, had suddenly become abnormally censorious and turned their backs on her. Luke said it was to be expected; they were scared of management tainting them by association and had distanced themselves from her.

She finished her tea and, hearing Freddie scampering about on the landing trying to evade Mum as she insisted it was time for him to get out of his pyjamas, she pushed back the duvet. Freddie wasn't the only one who needed to get dressed.

Chapter Seven

In her ground-floor room with its pleasant view of the garden through the open French doors, Clarissa was straining her eyes to peer towards the wooded perimeter of Woodside. She was sure that she'd spotted Ellis and Artie there a few minutes ago. If only her legs weren't so uselessly shaky, she would haul herself out of her armchair and go in search of them.

This habit of theirs of popping up when she least expected it was so typical of them; they had always done it. Back then she had taken it in her stride, but now, now that she looked far from her best, she wished they would show her the kindness of giving her a little advance notice. She wouldn't need long, just enough time to put on a nice dress, do something with her hair and maybe add a dab or two of perfume.

It was ridiculous to be so vain at her age, of course, especially as Ellis would see straight through any attempt to make a silk purse out of a sow's ear. She smiled; dear Ellis, such a blunt, outspoken man, but scratch the surface and there, beneath that smooth, toughened exterior, was a sensitive soul hiding a guilty secret.

Secret ... The word echoed in her head, nudging at her to remember something. Something important. Now what was it? *Secret* ... Oh yes, that was it, she had to keep her friends' visits a secret, she mustn't tell anyone about them.

But why?

She struggled to think why, teasing out the threads that had started getting tangled in her mind. How tiresome it was when this happened. Mostly she could be entirely sure of what she was thinking and then, quite suddenly, it was as if somebody had switched television channels without telling her and she would find herself thinking about something altogether different.

She forced her brain to cooperate, tried to follow the line of thought, but it was no good, it was lost to her. Well, whatever it was she was supposed to keep secret, it was quite safe because she couldn't remember what it was.

With her eyes beginning to water with the strain of watching for Ellis and Artie, she closed them and leant back into the chair, welcoming its familiar softness. The chair was an old favourite of hers; she'd brought it with her when she'd moved here. Woodside had a policy of encouraging its residents to bring with them some favourite possessions and furniture from their old homes to help settle them in. Clarissa had deliberately not brought too much with her, if only to make things easier for when she died – she wanted to leave behind her the minimum of mess for others to deal with. She hated the idea of inconveniencing anyone, and favoured disappearing quietly without trace, like footsteps in the sand washed away by the incoming tide.

A knock at the door roused her. 'Yes,' she responded, 'who is it?'

'It's me, Lizzie.'

Clarissa repeated the name in her head. *Lizzie*. Did she know a Lizzie? *Lizzie*. Wait a minute, wasn't that the girl who had started volunteering here yesterday, the one who turned out to be the daughter of that nice woman who came in to play the piano? There, she thought, pleased with herself, she had remembered that perfectly well, hadn't she?

'May I come in?' came the voice from the other side of the door.

'Please do,' she said. 'So you've returned to finish off what you failed to achieve yesterday, have you?' Clarissa said when Lizzie stood before her.

'Finish what off?' asked the girl with a frown.

39

'To finish me off. What plans do you have for me today, a dunking in the pond, perhaps?'

The girl's face flushed almost to the same colour as her pink tabard. 'I'm sorry I was so cack-handed yesterday,' she said. 'I hope I didn't hurt you.'

'My dear, I wouldn't have made it to this great age if I couldn't survive a few knocks and bumps; I'm not made of china, you know. Now then, I presume you've been sent to my room with a purpose in mind – what precisely is it?'

'I'm here to do whatever you'd like me to do. Unless,' she added with a small smile, 'you'd rather I went and irritated somebody else?'

Liking the teasing tone of her voice, Clarissa said, 'Good lord no, I couldn't possibly inflict you on the others here, I'd never forgive myself if they came to any harm.'

'In that case, your wish is my command. So what's it to be?'

'It's such a beautiful day again; let's venture out to the garden, shall we? But perhaps we should fix some L-plates to the wheelchair. What do you think?'

'I think I'll try to do a lot better today.'

To Lizzie's relief they made it out to the garden without mishap and, after Mrs Dallimore had requested she take her to sit in the rose arbour, she asked if there was anything else she could do for her.

'Why don't you sit with me for a while?'

Surprised at the suggestion, Lizzie hesitated. She knew that a key part of her role here at Woodside was to chat and form relationships with the residents, to view them as individuals and not as just another anonymous old person. But what could she chat to this old lady about? What did they have in common?

Her hesitation did not go unnoticed. 'But if you're too busy,' Mrs Dallimore said, 'you can run along. I shall be quite happy left on my own.'

Suddenly Lizzie felt sorry for this dignified old lady who seemed so frail a gust of wind might carry her off. The poor woman, was she so lonely she was prepared to make do with Lizzie's far from scintillating company? But then she thought of how different things would be if she had been sent here in her capacity as a researcher. If that were the scenario, she would have any number of questions ready to ask, but more importantly, she would be ready to listen, for, as she'd learnt, it was in listening that you discovered the most about a person, or a subject. And wasn't it true that all old people, if given the chance, liked nothing better than to reminisce? All she had to do was ask the right question and sit back and listen.

So, flicking away a scattering of pink rose petals that had fallen onto the wooden seat next to Mrs Dallimore's wheelchair, she sat down. It was while she sought to think of a suitable opening question that Mrs Dallimore asked one of her own.

'I'm not exactly an expert in these things,' she said, 'but would I be right in thinking that you're new to this type of voluntary work?'

'Do you ask that because I'm so obviously rubbish at it?'

'Not at all. You just seem … a little out of your depth.'

Lizzie couldn't help but smile at the understatement. 'I think you're being kind,' she said politely.

'Perhaps I am, but I don't see that as a bad thing. What job were you doing before you came here?'

Lizzie turned to look more closely at this strangely inquisitive woman, thinking that, as physically insubstantial as she appeared, there was nothing lightweight about her personality. 'You ask a lot of questions, don't you?' Lizzie said.

'Wouldn't you if you were in my shoes and had nothing better to do?'

Lizzie smiled again. 'I probably would. And to answer you, I was a researcher for a radio station in London.'

'That sounds interesting – what made you leave?'

'It's a long story.'

'Long stories are always the best kind. Tell me more.'

'Let's just say I did something which, with hindsight, wasn't the smartest of things.'

'Were you sacked?'

Direct with it, thought Lizzie, amused. She nodded. 'Yes, I'm afraid I was. Unfairly so, in my opinion.'

'Goodness, what did you do?'

'You'd be too shocked if I told you.'

The old lady visibly bristled. 'Please don't make the mistake of thinking that what you see before you now is what I've always been. I've experienced more shocks than you could possibly imagine.'

The abrupt intensity to Mrs Dallimore's voice took Lizzie by surprise and made her try to picture her as a much younger woman. But try as she might, she failed hopelessly. All she could see was this small, vulnerable woman whose slight body was failing her, whose bony hands were covered with a layer of skin so thin it resembled translucent parchment and whose face, pale and unblemished, was etched with a tracery of lines.

Sensing she had inadvertently caused some kind of offence, she changed the subject and started to explain about having to move back home and her mother volunteering her services here as a befriender. 'Mum believes strongly in keeping me busy until I find myself a proper job,' she finished by saying.

'You might want to rephrase that; for a lot of people what you're doing here is a proper and very worthwhile job, more so because it's unpaid.'

Realising how clumsy she'd been, Lizzie apologised. 'You're right, but I keep lapsing into feeling sorry for myself.'

'Young lady, from what I can see you have everything going for you, so let's have no more self-pity. After all, you could be sitting where I am, and think how miserable that would make you.'

Once more Lizzie changed the subject. 'Do you mind me asking how old you are?'

'I don't mind at all, but how old do you think I am?'

'Umm … eighty-five?'

The old lady laughed. 'Try adding another ten years.'

'Ninety-five? No! You can't be.' Lizzie was genuinely surprised; she didn't think she'd knowingly met anyone as old.

'I assure you I am, and you know, until not so long ago I subscribed to the view that there was plenty of time yet for me to grow old, but it pains me to admit that the spectre of old age has finally caught up with me.'

Quickly working out when she must have been born, and all the changes this woman had lived through, Lizzie's inner researcher sprang into life. What sort of life had she led? Had it been a happy and fulfilled life? Had she done anything she regretted? Was there anything she wished she had done?

Her curiosity fully piqued, and resorting to a question she had found to be both an icebreaker and revealing when carrying out an interview, Lizzie said, 'Mrs Dallimore, can I ask you a personal question?'

'You may.'

'Would you say there had been a defining moment in your life, a moment when you knew that your life was never going to be the same again?'

The woman fixed Lizzie with a long hard stare from her faded blue eyes, but then, as though distracted by something out of the corner of her eye, she turned to look towards the trees in the distance. Seconds passed, during which a radiant smile swept over the old lady's face – a smile that magically transformed her features, stripping away the years and giving Lizzie a glimpse of what she hadn't been able to imagine before.

Then, as if remembering she was still there, Mrs Dallimore slowly turned to face her again. 'I was nineteen years old when my life changed forever,' she said. 'Would you like to know how?'

'Yes,' Lizzie said simply. 'Yes, I would.'

Chapter Eight

April 1939, Boston, America

On a chilly spring morning and wearing her favourite red coat with a cream beret and silk scarf tied at her throat, Clarissa stood between her parents' graves to say goodbye.

It was 1939 and she was about to embark on the unknown. Her mother's approval was implicit; Fran had always urged her to take her courage in both hands and fear nothing. 'Uncertainty sees only obstacles,' she had told her from a young age, 'hope and courage will help you to soar on wings of faith.'

It was a message that Clarissa would hold dear to her heart the day after tomorrow when she would board the SS *Belle Etoile* and cross the Atlantic to England. She was making the journey, in part, to right a terrible wrong, but also because she had always known that one day she would leave to discover her roots in a country she had only ever heard about, lovingly described by her mother in the greatest of detail. 'Remember,' she used to say, 'you're as English as you are American.' Actually Clarissa felt more English than American, mostly because her mother had been such an enormous influence on her, even insisting that she spoke with an English accent.

Her mother had been brought up in England, the only child of Charles and Lavinia Upwood of Shillingbury in Suffolk where there had been Upwoods since the days of the Crusades. They were a family who cared deeply about appearances and their standing within society, so when Fran ran off to France with Nicholas Allerton, an American soldier she had met at the end of the First World War when she'd been working as a nurse, her family were furious at her scandalous behaviour and threatened to disown her if she didn't come to her senses. But Fran remained where she was and revelled in her bohemian life on the Cote D'Azur in France where Nick started work on the novel he wanted to write.

The only son of a prominent Boston banker, Nick was able to afford a comfortable existence for the two of them on an allowance provided for him by his parents. But that allowance was abruptly stopped when, back in Boston, Franklin Allerton and his wife, Ethel, received a letter from their only child announcing that he was soon to be a father and was planning to marry. It was bad enough that their son was playing at being a writer instead of joining the bank as was expected of him, but now to flaunt a child conceived out of wedlock was too much for their Roman Catholic sensibilities. A telegram was despatched demanding he return at once to Boston. 'Under no circumstances are you to marry!' he was instructed. 'Do so and we will cut you off.'

It was the last communication he received from them until five years later when he was informed that his father had died. Not without a sense of duty, Nick now knew the time had come for him to relinquish the dreams he'd had for himself and return to Boston with his wife and young daughter, Clarissa. It was a bitter pill to swallow, but he was tired of the daily struggle to scratch a living together from his writing – to his shame, his earnings allowed for only the basics, a roof over their heads and a very meagre diet which Fran supplemented by growing vegetables in the terraced garden at the back of the house and keeping chickens.

From the moment they arrived in America, Nick became a different man, weighed down with the responsibility now thrust upon him. He started work at the bank – the bank his grandfather had founded – and against his every instinct threw himself into the role that had been carved out for him since his birth. It was a role that made him thoroughly miserable, so desperately miserable he shot himself soon after the Wall Street stock market crashed in October 1929. He left a note for Fran in which he apologised for his cowardice, begging her to forgive him, but he simply couldn't go on.

His death brought about an unexpected change in Clarissa's grandmother, Ethel. As if suddenly realising Clarissa was the only link to the son she had lost, Ethel took it upon herself to show more of an interest in her granddaughter. She showered Clarissa with gifts and summoned her to visit where she lived alone in regal splendour, an army of servants at her beck and call.

When she was twelve years old Ethel informed Clarissa that she was to be sent away to school. 'You are to attend Noroton Convent of the Sacred Heart,' her grandmother explained. 'It's the school I attended when I was your age. Your education,' she went on, 'including vital religious instruction, is woefully lacking, and I feel it my God-given duty to make good the damage that has thus far been inflicted upon you.'

When Clarissa went home and told her mother that Grandma Ethel was anxious to save her mortal soul, Fran was livid. It was the only time Clarissa could recall her mother being so angry. 'You'll go to that school over my dead body!' she fumed. 'And the only soul in danger right now is your grandmother's!'

There followed a protracted period when Clarissa didn't visit her grandmother's gloomy mansion; instead her Saturdays were taken up with playing tennis with a group of school friends and learning to play the piano. But then one Sunday afternoon Grandma Ethel turned up unannounced at their apartment. The sight of this imperious woman hovering awkwardly in their sitting room, refusing all offers to sit down or to have a drink, made Clarissa think that the decision to visit had not been an easy one. She observed her mother trying to make polite conversation and waited for the purpose of the visit to be revealed – was she to be forced to go to the school her grandmother believed would save her from the flames of hell?

It turned out that she was to be spared an education at the hands of nuns dedicated to the cause of lost souls, her grandmother promising to forget all about it if she could just be allowed to spend time with her granddaughter again. She claimed she missed the young girl's company. To prove her love for the child, she explained that she had created a trust fund for Clarissa – when she reached the age of twenty-one she would become a wealthy young woman.

With this new level of mutual respect achieved, Fran decided to try again with her own parents. To her disappointment she received nothing in response to her letter.

It was that same year, with Clarissa's thirteenth birthday just around the corner, that she and her mother were invited to spend the summer with Grandma Ethel at her summer house in Hyannis Port on Cape Cod. Nick had often spoken of his childhood holidays spent at the beach and, although curious to see where he had played as a boy, Fran declined the invitation as she couldn't take that amount of time off work. For the sake of her sanity, and much to Ethel's disgust – she was firmly of the opinion that a lady of proper standing in the community should apply herself to nothing more taxing than charity work – Fran had found herself a job writing a weekly column for a magazine.

The piece was a light-hearted take on family life from the perspective of an upper-class English woman living in America. It was called *The Vicissitude of Lady Cordelia Fanshawe* and was growing in popularity. But Ethel insisted that she should come, and that if she brought her typewriter with her, she would be able to work as much as she needed and her column would be taken to the office personally by Brodie, the chauffeur. It would have been churlish to refuse the offer, and so Fran and Clarissa packed their things and joined Ethel for the month of August. The same thing happened the following year, and from then on it became a tradition. Fran's only concern was that she strongly suspected Ethel now saw these summer vacations as a means to draw Clarissa into a world where she would meet a suitable future husband, a husband of Ethel's choosing from amongst the sons of her fine upstanding friends. However, there was one family with whom she would have nothing to do, and she made it very clear that Clarissa was to avoid socialising with any of the Kennedys, who, in her opinion, were entirely the wrong sort and had brought nothing but havoc to the neighbourhood since buying a house there.

It was shortly after Clarissa's seventeenth birthday, while staying at Hyannis Port, that Fran admitted she had been feeling unwell for some time with excruciating headaches. Ethel sent for her own personal physician who immediately admitted Fran to hospital for tests. The diagnosis was not good; there was a tumour pressing down on Fran's brain and an operation was out of the question. She wouldn't see Christmas.

In the unbearably sad final weeks of her life, when Clarissa rarely left her mother's side as she slipped in and out of consciousness, Fran's memory repeatedly drew her back to her childhood in England, in particular to the simple pleasures she had enjoyed while growing up – of autumn walks breathing in the smell of burning leaves, of filling her pockets with shiny conkers, of eating blackberries picked from the hedgerows, of summer picnics, of lying in the grass listening to the song of a skylark. They were all things her mother wished she had been able to do with Clarissa.

Then out of the blue she made Clarissa promise that she would go to England. 'Make things right with your grandparents,' she said, 'and before it's too late. Succeed where I failed. Promise me you'll do that.'

Clarissa had made the promise willingly.

Her mother's death meant that she had to go and live with Grandma Ethel in her large and gloomy mansion. Although she had become attached to her grandmother, Clarissa did not enjoy living with her. She disliked the house and saw it as a suffocating prison from which she longed to escape.

On her nineteenth birthday she announced her intention to sail to England and meet her grandparents. Ethel was completely against the idea. 'I forbid it,' she said, adding, 'You're too much your mother's daughter, headstrong and stubborn.'

Any word of criticism of her mother was not to be borne. 'If I'm my mother's daughter then you must know that I shall simply defy you and run away,' Clarissa retaliated. 'After all, I have the money my mother left me which I can use. I don't need anything from you.'

The more her grandmother resisted her desire to go to England, the harder Clarissa pressed to go, even when she read in the newspapers that there was talk of war brewing in Europe. In the end, Ethel gave in and took control of the situation. She booked a first-class passage on the SS *Belle Etoile* and insisted that Clarissa travel with a chaperone, a friend who happened to be embarking on a tour of Europe.

Her parting words to Clarissa were: 'You must at all times be on your guard against those who will take advantage of you, assuming that for one so young you have no social sense. Do not, whatever you do, let me down.'

Still standing between her parents' graves, Clarissa said one final goodbye to them and turned away, knowing that it would be a long time before she returned. She needed to be free, and she couldn't be free if she stayed in Boston with her grandmother dictating the terms of her life. She had no choice but to go.

Chapter Nine

'The next day I set sail for Plymouth from New York and so that, my dear, was the defining moment of my life, as you put it.' Mrs Dallimore smiled. 'And I can assure you that from then on nothing was ever the same again.'

Lizzie shifted in her seat to move into the shade. She had been so absorbed in Mrs Dallimore's story she hadn't noticed the sun had climbed higher into the sky and had become quite hot. Checking that the old lady wasn't in too much sun either, she said, 'You were only nineteen and yet so much had happened to you already. It was a lot to cope with,' she added after a moment's reflection.

'I never saw it that way. I simply got on with life, just as my mother had. Now then, after all that talking, could I trouble you to fetch me a cup of tea, please?'

Wishing she could stay put and hear what happened next to Mrs Dallimore's nineteen-year-old self, Lizzie reluctantly stood up. 'Of course,' she said. 'How about a biscuit to go with it?'

'A nice piece of shortbread would be lovely, thank you.'

With Freddie strapped into his pushchair, Tess hurried along the main street of the village in the direction of Orchard House. She had noticed Lorna's car driving by when she'd been buying a loaf of bread in the community shop and had been seized with the sudden urge to speak face to face with Lorna. It was ridiculous that their friendship should be jeopardised because Lizzie and Simon had split up – they'd been friends before their offspring had met, so why shouldn't they continue to be friends?

But even as she told herself this, rattling the pushchair along the rough surface of the road where the pavement ran out, she feared Lorna might not view things in quite the same way. Lorna could be sharp when she chose to be. Tess had once overheard her giving her gardener a thorough dressing-down over the way he'd pruned the wisteria. On the other hand, she could be incredibly generous, and had given Tess some gorgeous presents over the years, which if she were really honest had made her feel just the teensiest bit uncomfortable because Tess had never been able to afford anything so extravagant in return. Most of the presents she gave people were home-made – scarves she'd knitted or crocheted; pots of jam, marmalade and chutney; traybakes of cookies and muffins; patchwork cushion covers and her latest creative project: hot-water bottle covers. All of which looked a little shabby when compared to the beautifully wrapped gifts Lorna treated her to. 'Think nothing of it,' Lorna had said when Tess had hinted at the disparity between the gifts they exchanged.

Orchard House, a beautiful stone-built Georgian property with a garden of almost two acres, was one of the largest and most attractive houses in Great Magnus. Normally Tess would go round to the back door, but today she rang the bell at the front. To calm her nerves – how stupid that she should be this nervous! – she bent down to Freddie and stroked his cheek and was instantly rewarded with one of his endearingly sweet smiles. Surely her adorable grandson would soften Lorna's heart and make things right between them again? Who could stay cross on the receiving end of such an angelic smile?

Hearing the door being opened behind her, she stood up and tried to ignore the guilty truth of what she was doing – shamefully using her grandson as a shield to hide behind in the hope of brokering peace, or at best negotiating a truce.

Lorna's kitchen was as familiar to her as her own. It was never other than showroom smart, everything tidily put away or artfully placed, as though styled ready for a glossy magazine photo shoot. Tess knew better than anyone that it didn't happen by chance; those colour-coordinated hand and tea towels didn't arrange themselves, nor did those shiny vintage copper pans lined up along the shelf above the Aga polish themselves. Nor were they ever used. It was an idyll of restrained domestic splendour, in which previously Tess had loved to spend time.

Now as she sat at the waxed farmhouse table overlooking the garden – a view framed by spectacularly expensive Jane Churchill curtains – she sensed that its very perfection again highlighted the disparity in their friendship. Life at Keeper's Nook, with all its haphazard clutter, was very much the poor relation. No matter how hard she tried, Tess could never achieve order of this magnitude.

With Freddie on her lap and watching Lorna adding milk to their mugs of coffee, she noticed with a stab of catty satisfaction a cobweb draped across the bunch of dried hydrangea flowers hanging from the hook driven into the beam above her friend's head.

'I'm afraid I don't have any fruit juice for Freddie,' Lorna said, turning round. 'Is water all right?'

'That'll be lovely, won't it, Freddie?' Tess said, giving him an affectionate squeeze. His answer was to wriggle out of her arms and slide down from her lap to go and investigate the tiered wicker vegetable baskets labelled *Oignons*, *Pommes De Terre* and *Carottes*. Feeling exposed and vulnerable without the warmth of his small body acting as a human shield, Tess gave a forced laugh. 'He's always enjoyed playing with those baskets, hasn't he?' she said, watching him rootling around in a basket of pre-washed, marble-sized new potatoes. 'Remember when we found him trying to eat a raw onion?'

A brittle smile appeared on Lorna's face. 'He's grown since I last saw him.'

'Yes,' agreed Tess enthusiastically, 'he's shooting up like the proverbial weed. He'll be at full-time school before we know it.'

'You're lucky to have him,' Lorna said, passing Tess's coffee to her.

She took the mug and the implied slight – *now that Lizzie has split with Simon, heaven only knows when I will become a grandmother*. Not that Tess would admit it, but the thought of Lizzie ever being responsible enough to have a child of her own did stretch the bounds of belief. For that matter, Simon was hardly the sort to be champing at the bit to be a father; it was one of the many things that he and Lizzie had been in agreement about. But then Luke and Ingrid had thought the same, and look how they'd changed their minds.

In many ways Lizzie and Simon had been an unlikely match, but once they'd come together, it had been one of those relationships that just seemed right. It was their shared sense of humour that had been at the heart of their love, Tess had always believed. They'd met here at Orchard House at a Boxing Day party Lorna and Keith had thrown six months after moving in. It was during those six months that Tess and Lorna had become firm friends.

A plate of Duchy stem ginger biscuits was placed now on the table, along with a china Peter Rabbit mug of water. Lorna had bought the mug especially for Freddie's visits with Tess – garish primary-coloured plastic rubbish wasn't welcome here.

With her bulging waistline a snug fit against the waistband of her trousers, Tess knew she shouldn't succumb to what was on the plate, but she needed something to do and eating one of the future King of England's finest biscuits would have to suffice. Predictably Lorna abstained – her slim body, the result of good genes, she claimed, but which Tess knew was the result of hours spent at the gym – was as enviable as her smooth complexion and hair that was treated to weekly visits to the hairdresser. Tess's own hair was lucky to see the inside of a salon every three months, and even then she coloured it herself with, it had to be said, varying degrees of success. *Well, we can't all be as perfect as Lorna*, a snippy voice whispered in her ear.

Shocked at how nastily she was behaving, if only inside her head, she took a sip of her coffee. 'Mmm ... lovely, just what I needed; it's been a busy day. What have you been up to?'

Lorna shrugged. 'Oh, you know, the usual, this and that.'

Snatching at something to say, Tess said, 'Did you know the vicar's organising a food bank?'

'Here in the village?'

'Not *for* the village, obviously, but for wherever it's needed. We were talking about it in the community shop. Suzy was joking that everybody will be hunting through their cupboards to offload anything that's past its sell-by date. I said I'd have nothing left in my cupboards if I was to do that.' Tess gave a strained laugh.

Without comment, Lorna raised her mug to her lips, but stopped before actually drinking from it. 'Freddie,' she said, 'don't put that in your mouth, please.'

Tess glanced over to where her grandson was sitting on the floor, sinking his teeth into a carrot. 'He won't come to any harm with it,' she said.

'I'm sure he won't,' Lorna said coolly, 'but I want those carrots for tonight's supper.'

Determined not to rise to Lorna's pettiness, Tess picked up the plate of ginger biscuits. 'Freddie, how about one of these nice biccies?'

His face lit up, and with the carrot pushed back into the *Carotte* basket, he came and helped himself from the plate.

Biting into the biscuit, he dropped crumbs on the oak floor as he went back to the baskets of vegetables, and the silence between Tess and Lorna continued. Such was her desperation for something to say, Tess asked after Simon.

'Busy with work,' Lorna answered. 'I heard Lizzie's back at home with you.'

'That's right,' Tess said brightly, 'she's covering for me at Woodside, while I look after Freddie for Luke and Ingrid. Freddie's nursery flooded and had to close, so it's been all hands to the pump, so to speak.'

Lorna's gaze intensified as she looked at Tess above her mug of coffee. 'I also heard the reason why Lizzie's back here.'

'Yes, it's hit her badly being made redundant; she loved her job at the radio station.'

'Is that what she told you, that she was made redundant? I heard that she was sacked after she was found having sex with her boss on his desk. The married boss with whom she'd been having an affair.'

Tess's jaw dropped.

'You must be so very proud of your daughter,' Lorna added. Her words dripped with pure spite.

'I don't know where you heard such a vile thing,' Tess murmured, struggling to keep her hands from slapping the smug look off Lorna's face, 'but I can assure you it's quite untrue. Lizzie would never do anything like that.'

'Simon told us,' Lorna said matter-of-factly. 'He heard it from one of Lizzie's ex-colleagues at Starlight Radio.'

'And naturally Simon has no axe to grind,' Tess said tersely, 'so he'd be totally unbiased in anything he told you about Lizzie.'

'Are you accusing my son of lying?'

'Better than accusing my daughter of – of—' Tess floundered.

'Of being a slut?' said Lorna. 'Is that the word you're looking for?'

Tess banged her mug down on the table, not caring that she'd splashed coffee onto its waxed surface. 'No! No, it is not.' She rose quickly to her feet. 'Freddie darling, it's time we were going. We're clearly not wanted here. I really don't know why I thought we would be.'

'I couldn't have said it better myself,' Lorna said, also on her feet.

In her haste to escape, Tess almost broke into a run with the pushchair. How could Lorna have said such a disgracefully vile thing? Was she really so petty that she had to come up with something so sordid?

But even as Tess tried frantically to believe that it was a malicious lie that Lorna had invented for her own purposes, the nagging voice of her subconscious said it was true. Hadn't she and Tom said all along that there was more to Lizzie losing her job than she'd let on? And hadn't Luke said it would be better to leave well alone, that pleading a case of unfair dismissal might be counterproductive? Which of course meant Luke had known what Lizzie had done and had helped cover for her. Oh, how could Lizzie have done it! How could the girl do such a stupid, *stupid* thing!

'Nana go faster!' Freddie sang out merrily, leaning forward in the pushchair. 'Faster, Nana!'

'I am, Freddie,' she panted breathlessly, 'I am.'

Her mind anywhere but on where she was going, Tess didn't see the rut in the road and the next thing, like a cannonball fired from a cannon, Freddie flew out of the pushchair straight onto the tarmac verge. Horror-struck, Tess realised that in her fury to get away from Orchard House, she had forgotten to strap Freddie in.

They arrived back at Keeper's Nook with poor Freddie's face horribly grazed and his T-shirt smeared with blood and dirt. 'How could I have been so careless?' Tess sobbed to Tom when he heard her calling to him for help. 'I'll never forgive myself. What if a car had been passing?'

'There wasn't,' he said firmly, disentangling a bemused Freddie from her iron-like hold. 'And Freddie's just fine, aren't you, old chap?'

Freddie drew his eyebrows together and wobbled his head.

Then he suddenly grinned. 'Lizzie!' he said, catching sight of Lizzie coming round the side of house. 'Lizzie, Lizzie, Lizzie!' he chanted happily, clapping his hands.

'There,' said Tom, 'nothing wrong with him at all. Nothing that a wash, a change of clothes and a plaster or two won't sort out.'

Once a month Tom met up with a group of men from the village for a drink at The Bell. Of the two pubs in Great Magnus, this was his preferred choice as it served proper beer and wasn't ashamed to sell packets of pork scratchings at the bar. Despite it being a pleasantly warm evening, they were seated in the panelled snug where they always sat. Keith was the only one missing from the gathering. Nobody knew why, although based on what Tess had told Tom of her visit to Orchard House this afternoon, Lorna had probably put her foot down and insisted he stay at home – there was to be no fraternising with the enemy.

Privately Tom had always been suspicious of Lorna's slightly superior air over Tess, as though Tess should somehow be grateful for the attention paid to her. He'd bet any money you liked that, at school, Lorna was the one who had called the shots; the one everybody else was expected to gravitate towards. In fairness, though, a lot of friendships were like that – unbalanced, with one side dictating the terms to the other.

Only half listening to the banter around the table, Tom took a long, satisfying sip of his beer and let his thoughts stray to his daughter. He'd be lying if he said he wasn't shocked by Lizzie's admission that what Lorna had told Tess was true, but he knew there was nothing to be done and that he and Tess had to do what Lizzie was doing: put it behind them. But in the history of mad moments committed by Lizzie, she had perhaps outdone herself this time.

The challenge ahead, Tom thought, was how he was going to be able to look Curt in the eye when they finally met. It was a bridge he would have to cross when the time came. But by God, the man had better be worth the trouble he'd caused. And was continuing to cause.

Chapter Ten

When Luke had come off the phone last night after speaking to his mother and hearing that Freddie had taken a tumble out of his pushchair but there was nothing to worry about, he was perfectly all right, Ingrid's first thought was to drive straight over and fetch Freddie home.

Had she done that, Luke would most certainly have accused her of overreacting. So rather than go down that particular route, which would have led to her being accused of being overly protective and Luke dragging up yet another tale about the scrapes he and Lizzie had got into as children and how they'd survived perfectly well, she had gone to bed and quietly seethed, snapping out the light and pretending to be asleep when Luke had joined her.

Seriously though, was it an overreaction to be so concerned about her son? Wasn't it the job of a loving parent to care? Or, more specifically, the job of a loving mother? It was beyond her that Luke could have such a cavalier attitude towards their son. But that, she supposed, was because he was a man and had the ability to switch off his emotions when he needed to. Plus he had much the same DNA as his sister, so, when push came to shove, he was always going to have a more relaxed mindset.

Not for a second did Ingrid believe the ridiculous story Tess had told Luke about her forgetting to strap Freddie into his pushchair. Tess might be a bit of a scatterbrain at times, but when it came to Freddie she *never* forgot things, she was as reliable as day follows night; it was why Ingrid had entrusted her precious son to her mother-in-law.

No: the real story, and nothing would convince her otherwise, was that Lizzie had been left in charge of Freddie, and surprise, surprise, he'd come to harm in her care. And how typical that the family should cover for that useless girl!

To stop herself from dwelling on Freddie and the daily battle of guarding him, Ingrid switched her thoughts to the battlefield which she could take command of far more effectively than the one which existed at home.

In front of her on her desk were the notes she'd made regarding a negligence case against a GP who had failed to refer a patient for cancer investigations. In this instance the patient had been a five-year-old girl whose mother, a young single woman in her mid-twenties, had repeatedly told the GP she was convinced her child had something seriously wrong with her. She had been labelled a neurotic mother and told not to bother the doctor who was a very busy man. As a result, the child was now dead.

Don't ever tell me a loving mother doesn't know best, Ingrid thought grimly as she gritted her teeth and got down to work.

Chapter Eleven

Given the heavy tension in the house, and knowing she was at the centre of it, if not the source, Lizzie opted not to ask her parents to give her a lift to Woodside, but to dig out her old bicycle from the garage and cycle to work. After pumping up the tyres and squirting some oil onto the chain, and her father insisting she wore a safety helmet, she was finally on her way. Enjoying the sun-warmed breeze on her bare arms and legs, she was suddenly filled with the kind of devil-may-care exhilaration that had caused her parents so much consternation over the years.

It was her lack of coordination that had always been the problem, the left hand blindly and wilfully oblivious to what the right was getting up to. When she was thirteen she'd flown head first into a ditch, resulting in a dislocated shoulder and five stitches to the side of her head. The tumble had led to her parents laying down the law that, unless she was wearing a cycle helmet, she was going nowhere.

Whizzing along now, she loosened the strap of her helmet that was cutting into her chin and sped on. Passing the community shop on her right, she spotted Lorna's charcoal-grey juggernaut of a four-by-four coming towards her. Knowing that she was public enemy number one for Lorna and as good as had a bullseye target stamped on her chest and back, Lizzie kept her gaze firmly on the road to avoid the danger of their eyes meeting. As a precautionary measure she swerved closer to the kerb, just in case the red mist came down for Lorna and she succumbed to an overpowering need to satisfy a mother's urge for revenge.

The car passed smoothly by without incident, and with her legs pumping faster than ever, Lizzie pressed on until the outskirts of the village with its verges of cow parsley and willowherb were behind her and she was on the open road with the sun-bleached wheat fields either side of her. The beauty of the day was quite at odds with the ugly anger now simmering inside her after seeing Lorna.

Lizzie would never have thought Simon's mother could behave so vindictively. Her rudeness to Mum yesterday was beyond belief, and it made Lizzie glad there was now no danger of the woman ever becoming her mother-in-law. But what did Lorna hope to achieve by being so nasty to poor Mum? For heaven's sake, anyone would think Lizzie had murdered Simon the way his mother was carrying on! Mind you, she had to admit she was tempted to do just that after him stirring things up. She wondered who had spilled the not-so-pleasant beans to him. Odds on it had filtered through from Cal at Starlight, whose girlfriend worked at the same IT technical support company that Simon did.

Until yesterday Lizzie hadn't appreciated things were so bad between Mum and Lorna; it just hadn't occurred to her that Lorna would take umbrage to the extent she obviously had, or behave so pettily. The more Lizzie thought about it, and how upset Mum had been, the angrier she became. She was particularly annoyed because she had tried her best to protect her parents from the knowledge of what she'd been sacked for – they absolutely didn't deserve to have that embarrassment thrust upon them.

Putting her anger to good use, she channelled it to fuel her legs, and by the time she reached Woodside, her breath was ragged and she was hot and sweating. She looked in the mirror in the staff room where she slipped on her hideously pink tabard and saw that her face was near enough the same colour. It was not a good look. Not by a very long way.

She was putting her things away in the locker she'd been allocated when the door of the staff room opened and a man peered in. He was dressed in faded jeans and a T-shirt with the collar of a shirt and tie printed on it; his thick light brown hair was either naturally lightened by the sun or dyed a golden colour. He was, Lizzie realised, the first man she had seen at Woodside who was about the same age as she was. Seeing her, he hesitated in the doorway.

'Can I help you?' she asked.

There was an awkward moment when he didn't say anything, he just stood there giving an impression of a man processing an unpleasant situation and working out the best way to deal with it. 'I'm not sure,' he said at last. 'Can you?'

'That rather depends on what it is you need help with,' she said.

'Who said I did?'

'Did what?'

'Need help.'

Oh, so he was one of those clever types, was he, thought Lizzie, a show-off who liked to play games instead of answering a straight question with a straight answer? Well, he needn't waste his ammunition on her! 'You had that look about you,' she said.

He drew his brows together and scratched his unshaven chin. 'Then I must do something about that. I can't be going around with a face that makes out I'm helpless.'

Skirting round him to get to the door, she said, 'Perhaps you should, it might save you from any further offers of well-intentioned help.' And before he could get the last word in, she pulled open the door and legged it fast.

After two hours of serving cups of tea, and then getting out the board games in the main lounge while the care staff dealt with the inevitable toilet relay race for those who needed assistance, Lizzie was told by matron that Mrs Dallimore was asking for her.

Uh-oh, she thought, what had she done wrong? Nothing, she told herself firmly as she went to find the old lady.

Yesterday they'd parted company on perfectly good terms; in fact, Mrs Dallimore had said how much she'd enjoyed chatting with her. Maybe she wanted to chat some more about her life when she left America. Lizzie hoped so; she was intrigued to know more about the young woman Mrs Dallimore had once been, suspecting that she had probably been quite a character. Not unlike Grandma Wendy. Lizzie hadn't really known her other three grandparents – they'd died when she and Luke had been young children – but Dad's mother had been a larger-than-life character and fiercely independent right up until the day she died four years ago of a heart attack while on a coach tour travelling through Germany. Although Lizzie scarcely knew Mrs Dallimore, there were definitely moments when she was reminded of Grandma Wendy.

She found the old lady on the terrace in the garden, her wheelchair positioned in the shade of a large parasol over a circular wooden table. There were two other ladies sitting at the table, both of whom were fast asleep and snoring gently. One of them must have just had her hair done by the visiting hairdresser, for she had a fluffy white hairdo that had something of the bichon frise about it.

Seeing Lizzie, Mrs Dallimore lowered the book she was reading and, indicating her sleeping companions, put a finger to her lips. 'I would welcome a change of scene,' she whispered, and tapping the arm of the wheelchair, added, 'Care to have another go at steering this confounded thing?'

'Practice makes perfect,' Lizzie whispered back with a smile. 'Where do you fancy going?'

Mrs Dallimore pointed across the lawn towards the rose-covered arbour where they had sat yesterday.

Determined not to let her charge come to any harm, Lizzie steered the wheelchair across the lawn with concentrated care. Thanks to the hot, dry spell, the ground was hard and the grass short.

Looking back from the arbour they had a view of the entire garden and the house, along with the red-brick modern extension that was considered an eyesore by both staff and residents alike. It housed the medical wing of the care home from which, according to Mum, the residents liked to keep a healthy distance for fear of never leaving in an upright state. The original house had been built of honey-coloured stone, but the walls were now so thickly draped in ivy they were all but hidden. There was another extension to the building, a large Victorian-style conservatory known as The Orangery, and it was a much more attractive addition. Residents who were gardening enthusiasts were encouraged to potter in there and tend to the plants.

'Tell me some more about yourself,' Mrs Dallimore said, indicating the chair next to her. 'And don't worry about thinking you're neglecting the other residents, I cleared it with Matron. Her precise words were, "Mrs Dallimore, if it keeps the rest of the residents safe, you have my blessing to keep Lizzie with you as long as you can."'

Lizzie was about to remonstrate that she was being un-fairly cast in the role of Dr Shipman when she saw the ghost of a smile quivering at the corners of the woman's pale lips. 'Mrs Dallimore,' she said, 'I'm beginning to think you're not half as nice as I thought you were.'

'Then you were labouring under a gross misapprehension,' the woman replied with a laugh. 'Come on, amuse me, tell me something wildly interesting about yourself.'

'I wish I could, but really I just don't—'

Mrs Dallimore tutted. 'If you dare to say you haven't done one single interesting thing in your life I shall be very cross with you, not to say deeply disappointed.'

'But it's true.'

'I refuse to believe that. For instance, you mentioned yesterday that it was a long story why you were sacked from your last job. What happened there?'

Lizzie shook her head. 'You *so* don't want to know.'

'What an absurd thing to say! Why else would I have brought it up if I didn't want to know?'

'It was a figure of speech.'

Mrs Dallimore tutted again. 'More like a figure of prevarication.'

'Do you ever take no for an answer?'

'Do you?'

It was Lizzie's turn to laugh. 'Not if I can help it.'

'And yet you expect me to. I can't abide double standards. Is it because I'm so ancient you have me written off as some old dear who doesn't have a clue about the world you inhabit?'

Lizzie didn't want to be unkind, but really there wasn't a hope in hell of this woman having the slightest inkling of what went on at Starlight Radio. For that matter, Lizzie was beginning to feel she no longer had an inkling of that world. She hadn't been living back at home for that long, but already her London life, even Curt, now that she hadn't heard from him while he was on holiday, was dissolving into a hazy memory. In the blink of an eye it was as if she'd become institutionalised, with the village of Great Magnus, Keeper's Nook and Woodside becoming the sole focus of her life. All that had gone before seemed to be a faraway landscape seen through the wrong end of a telescope.

'You haven't answered my question,' Mrs Dallimore said, interrupting her thoughts. 'Was that because you were trying to find a tactful way to agree with me without hurting my feelings?'

'If you knew me better you'd know tact isn't exactly my strong suit.'

'A lack of tact is the prerogative of the young – the acquiring and employment of it comes later in life, and then there comes a point when one realises there simply isn't time to beat about the bush.'

Thinking there was something Oscar Wilde-ish about the remark, Lizzie listened to a pigeon cooing and a woodpecker drilling in the woods. Aware of the silence around her she began to feel uncomfortable; she wasn't used to long silences.

She was used to noise, lots of noise. The constant energising buzz of people talking, of traffic roaring by, of people always in a hurry, jostling and barging, voices raised. With a pang she thought of London and how much she missed it. Which, of course, led her to think of Curt. Oh Curt, she thought miserably, I miss you so much. The wait to hear from him was unbearable. She'd never known a misery like it.

And still the silence went on, punctuated by the woodpecker. She pictured the bird hell-bent on drilling its way through a large, unyielding tree. She glanced at Mrs Dallimore, wondering if she had fallen asleep. She hadn't; she was staring intently into the distance, into the leafy shade of the trees, as if she were looking for something. Or someone. Lizzie hoped she wasn't about to suggest they went for a meander into the woods; it would be hard going with a wheelchair.

'Would you tell me what happened to you when you left America and came to England all those years ago?' she asked, hoping the request would distract the woman, just in case she did have a bee in her silvery bonnet and wanted to go on a woodland walkabout.

Getting no response to her question, Lizzie was about to repeat it when the old lady turned to look at her with her pale, watery blue eyes. 'Do you really want to know, or are you just humouring me?'

'I'm not humouring you,' Lizzie replied adamantly, realising how awful it must be to think that you weren't being taken seriously, that everything said to you was banal and insincere, no more than a feeble attempt to make conversation for the sake of it. 'I really would like to know what happened to you when you arrived in this country,' she added. 'But, please, only tell me if you'd like to.'

The old lady stared sceptically at her as though still unsure that Lizzie's interest was genuine. 'I wouldn't want to bore you,' she said.

There was something so sadly stoic and dignified in her

expression that, without thinking, Lizzie put a hand on the old lady's thin arm. 'Please, Mrs Dallimore,' she said, 'if what you told me yesterday is anything to go by, you could never bore me. And after Matron said you had asked for me this afternoon, I was hoping you'd tell me some more about your life.'

A slow and tentative smile spread over Mrs Dallimore's face. 'Well, if you're sure.'

'I am. Really I am.'

'In that case, I shall start at the beginning, when I stepped on board the *Belle Etoile*.' She sighed. 'Oh, what a ship it was! I've never seen anything like it before or since.'

Chapter Twelve

12th April 1939, SS *Belle Etoile*

The *Belle Etoile* was considered by many to be one of the most spectacular ocean liners ever built, and from the moment Clarissa set eyes upon it she could well believe the claim.

The chaperone arranged by her grandmother saw things quite differently, and had declared the French-owned ship to be far too big and the interior design with its Art Deco style so modern and lavish as to be utterly vulgar. 'But then what could you expect from the French?' Marjorie Boyd-Lambert opined in a voice that, to Clarissa's ears, had the power to carry from one end of the vessel to the other, all 1,020 feet of her. She would, she further maintained, preferred to have travelled with the Holland America line, or Cunard. 'One always knows where one is with Cunard White Star,' she informed Clarissa, who knew where she would like the tiresome woman to be, and that was left standing on the pier. To put it bluntly, Majorie Boyd-Lambert was a pretentious snob who was determined not to enjoy herself, or allow anyone else to have any fun.

Little wonder her husband had not stayed for a drawn-out farewell. Instead, due to 'an important meeting with a client', he had deposited his wife and Clarissa at the pier, having found them a porter, and then hastened away to his office. Clarissa privately suspected he couldn't wait to be rid of his wife and was already relishing her two-month absence.

As for Clarissa's grandmother, warned by her friend, Marjorie – 'Ethel, the crowds are simply ghastly!' – she had cited a dread of crowds and the risk of the palpitations consequently induced and had flatly refused to make the journey from Boston to Manhattan to see Clarissa off.

Marjorie's foghorn voice was coming through the wall that divided their first-class cabins as she instructed the immaculately dressed *garçon de cabine* where to put the flowers her husband had bestowed upon her, as well as telling him how to unpack her clothes. Travelling with five trunks in all, four of which had been stored elsewhere, she had piously pointed out that she was an extremely light traveller and would require only the one trunk while crossing the Atlantic. In contrast, it had taken the steward assigned to assist Clarissa a mere few minutes to unpack her things and without any instruction. There were no flowers for her, but there was a telegram from her grandmother wishing her well for the voyage.

Seizing the opportunity to explore the vast ship while her chaperone was otherwise occupied – the poor steward was being told to make dining-table and deckchair reservations – Clarissa slipped quietly away. She didn't want to wave goodbye to America in the company of Marjorie Boyd-Lambert, she wanted to savour the moment alone and without her thoughts continuously interrupted by the ghastly woman's incessant babble on the horrors of travelling abroad. If she hated leaving America so much, why was she making this trip?

But solitude appeared to be nigh on impossible to find. The ship was chaotically full of people buzzing around, many of them visitors who were allowed on board to see families and friends off. Through open cabin doors Clarissa caught noisy snatches of bon voyage parties in progress, with canapés and glasses of champagne consumed amidst laughter and gaiety. It all looked so much fun, but brought home to her that there was no one to throw a party for her. Fun, she reflected, would be in very short supply throughout the crossing unless she could escape the clutches of her chaperone.

For now, though, she *had* escaped, and losing herself in the ebullient throng of passengers and visitors she took pleasure in the knowledge that, for Marjorie to find her, it would take all the skill of locating a very fine needle in a very large haystack.

After she'd wandered aimlessly, taking in the dazzling splendour of her surroundings – vulgar be damned! – she decided to go up to the sun deck. Many others had had the same idea, but eventually she found a small space against the rail. She was staring down at the packed pier and the Manhattan skyline in the afternoon sunshine when the order was given for all visitors to disembark. A murmur of eager anticipation ran through those gathered around her – at last, they would soon be on their way! It was impossible not to succumb to a rush of exhilaration, and Clarissa happily gave in to the thrill of not knowing what awaited her in England. Another girl her age, and in her shoes, might have been fearful, but the way she saw it, she was sailing to freedom. No more would she be answerable to Grandma Ethel – or anyone else for that matter.

Her first priority, once she had made it to London, was to make arrangements to travel to Suffolk. She knew that her grandparents were still alive, but she had no idea if they had read the letter she'd sent, or if they would agree to meet her. She was determined, however, to do everything she could to see where her mother had spent her childhood. Nothing would stop her from trying; it was what her mother had wanted, her last wish for Clarissa.

A sudden shove from behind jammed Clarissa painfully

against the rail. She turned to see who or what was the cause, at the same time clasping her handbag tightly to her – amongst many of Marjorie's warnings had been to be on her guard against pickpockets, who gained access to the ships for the sole purpose of stealing from the wealthy, unwary passengers. 'It's easy pickings for them, like shooting fish in a barrel,' Marjorie had said.

Looking back at Clarissa, or rather looking haughtily down his long straight nose at her, was a tall man in a cream sweater and grey flannel trousers. The expression of disdain on his arrogant face, particularly in his unnaturally green eyes, implied that it was she who was in the wrong and therefore she should be the one to apologise. She stared back at him defiantly before turning away. She knew his type; she had met many of them at Hyannis Port during the summers – the self-important born into families of great wealth and taught from an early age to have a colossal sense of entitlement. Out of the corner of her eye, she watched him walk on by. She was disappointed he hadn't said anything; she would have enjoyed putting him in his place and telling him what a rude man he was.

A loud blast from the ship's whistle made her jump and once more visitors were urged, with greater insistence, to disembark.

Thirty minutes later the whistle was blown again, and with tugboats nudging at the bows, Clarissa felt the first thrill of the great ship beginning to slide away from the pier. All around her passengers leaning against the rails began waving goodbye to loved ones, and although she had no one to wave to, she felt compelled to raise her hand and join in. Fixing her gaze on an unknown couple – the man was waving his hat in the air, the woman a handkerchief – she unexpectedly found herself pulling off her own hat and waving it with all her might.

Before long the figures on the pier were no more than a

blur – not just because of the distance between the ship and the pier, but because there were tears filling Clarissa's eyes.

'Goodbye,' she said under her breath. 'Goodbye.'

On returning to her cabin, Clarissa found Marjorie waiting for her, the connecting door between their cabins wide open.

'Where on earth have you been?' the woman demanded. 'I've been frantic with worry! Another few minutes and I'd have asked for the purser to put an emergency call out for you!'

An overreaction, surely, thought Clarissa. 'I was on the sun deck watching our departure,' she said. 'I would have asked you to join me, but I knew you were busy and wouldn't welcome me disturbing you.'

'I'd sooner be disturbed than be left fretting about you,' Marjorie replied stiffly. 'What if you'd fallen overboard?'

Clarissa laughed. 'I think that's highly unlikely, don't you?'

'As a woman one can never be too careful when travelling to foreign parts,' said Marjorie darkly.

'I'll bear that in mind,' Clarissa replied. 'Shall we go for afternoon tea now?' she added with a conciliatory smile.

'First you'll have to do something about your hair,' the woman sniffed. 'And you can't possibly wear that dress. You must change. Please be quick about it.'

Tea was served in the Petite Salon and service was well under way when they were shown to a side table that to Clarissa's delight afforded them a grandstand view of the salon's comings and goings. For Marjorie it gave her the opportunity to complain about the draught sweeping in through the Lalique glass doors every time they swished open. She complained also that they were placed too far away from the quartet playing in the furthest corner of the room to hear the musicians properly above the noise of rattling crockery and overly loud chatter. 'I shall have a word with our steward and ensure that we are appropriately seated tomorrow,' she declared, sending the waiter away with a wave of her hand, having stressed that the water for their tea must be hot and the cream cold.

While they waited for their waiter to reappear, Clarissa gazed around the beautiful room that was hexagonal in shape, with columns at each point and adorned with bronze statues in various states of undress. Potted palms and white lilies added to the sumptuous luxury.

'Oh my, just look who's walked in,' said a plump, matronly woman arrayed in an abundance of pearls at the nearest table to them. Clarissa turned to see who the woman was referring to, which immediately earned her a ticking off from Marjorie for staring.

But Clarissa *did* stare. She even let out a little gasp. 'It's Elfin Effie!' she said in awe.

'Clarissa, *please,* keep your voice down! Do I need to remind you again that the vulgarity of curiosity does you a great disservice?'

The woman next to them chuckled and leant in towards Clarissa. 'I shouldn't worry, Effie Chase is more than used to people gawping at her. After all, people have been doing it since she was ten years old.'

Clarissa smiled. 'I've seen every one of her movies.'

'Me too,' said the woman. 'She's a real beauty, isn't she? Look at that peachy complexion! What I wouldn't give for that at my age ...'

'My favourite movie of hers is *You're My Gal*,' said Clarissa wistfully. 'I thought she was wonderful in that. She sang with such feeling she made me cry.'

'They say she's given up films to concentrate on stage work now.'

The two of them, along with most others in the salon, watched the former child star – at twenty she was now considered too old to play juvenile roles – being shown to a table. She wasn't alone. Her father and stepmother were with her. Clarissa had seen photographs of her father's wedding in a magazine earlier that year; it was a much talked-about event, mostly because the stepmother was twenty-five, only five years older than Effie.

'She's taller than I imagined,' Clarissa whispered to the woman beside her.

'That's because Elfin Effie is all grown up now. By the way, my name's Betty. Betty Dolores Lowe, if we're gonna be formal.'

Clarissa held out her hand. 'Clarissa. Clarissa Allerton. And please, let's not be formal.'

'Well, I'm real glad to make your acquaintance, Clarissa. And is that your grandmother with you?'

Marjorie, who had until now been staring resolutely in the opposite direction, gave a snort of indignation. 'I most certainly am not!' she declared. Good manners prevented her from saying anything more when their waiter reappeared with a large tray. With white-gloved hands, he carefully set everything on the table – a tiered cake stand loaded with dainty sandwiches, scones and pastries; a silver teapot with matching cream jug and sugar bowl; bone china plates, cups and saucers, and all monogrammed with SS *Belle Etoile*.

While Marjorie instructed the waiter as to how better to arrange things, Betty winked at Clarissa. 'You gotta real live one there, then,' she said in a low voice.

Smiling back at her, Clarissa rather hoped this jolly woman might prove to be an entertaining ally. 'Perhaps you'd like to join us for a cocktail before dinner this evening?' she said.

'Why, honey, that would be just swell.'

'I don't drink cocktails,' Marjorie said, the waiter having now left them, 'and nor should you, young lady.' Then, casting a glance in Betty's direction and perhaps thinking it was time she took charge of the conversation, she said, 'I'm Mrs Boyd-Lambert; Miss Allerton's travelling companion for the duration of this voyage. I've been entrusted with the task of seeing her safely across the Atlantic before I embark on a trip around Europe.' That said, she took hold of the silver tongs and dropped two cubes of sugar into her tea.

Betty smiled again at Clarissa, then looking round the salon, she said, 'I wonder who else is travelling with us? The last time I was on the *Belle Etoile*, the Duke and Duchess of Windsor were on board. Mercy, you should have seen the quantity of luggage they travelled with! You know, it's said they never go anywhere with less than eighty pieces of luggage. Another trip I made, Marlene Dietrich was on board and—'

'You're obviously a woman who travels regularly,' Marjorie interjected brusquely, 'and are presumably quite used to your own company. So we won't intrude upon you any longer.'

Shocked as she was by Marjorie's rudeness, Clarissa knew better than to make the situation any worse, so she gave a discreet smile of apology to Betty and helped herself to a salmon and cucumber sandwich. She was onto her second when she spotted somebody else making an entrance through the glass doors. It was the ill-mannered man with the emerald-green eyes. Alongside him was a pale, slim man with horn-rimmed glasses and thick dark hair that was swept back from a broad expanse of forehead. There was a careless, rumpled appearance about him, as if he'd dressed in a hurry. Tucked under his arm was what looked like a large notebook with pieces of paper sticking out of it. The man with the emerald eyes muttered something to him and strode purposefully across the salon, the other man following behind at a slower pace.

They came to a stop at the table where Effie Chase was seated. When she saw the man with the emerald eyes, a dazzling smile lit up her face and she sprang to her feet and offered her cheek for him to kiss. After a brief exchange with her father and stepmother, a waiter was summoned and another table organised for Effie and the two new arrivals.

All this Clarissa watched in shameless fascination, as did

most others, including Betty. '*Quelle surprise*!' she said, sotto voce.

'Why's that?' Clarissa whispered back.

'I'll tell you later over cocktails.'

Chapter Thirteen

Dinner that evening was served in the largest dining room Clarissa had ever seen. The splendour of the vast space was quite extraordinary, and everywhere she looked there was something to catch the eye – marble urns, bronze relief plaques set against lacquered walls of gold, immense black marble statues of half-naked muscular men appearing to support the weight of the coffered ceiling, where Lalique light fittings cascaded like waterfalls casting a soft glow over the tables. Apparently the light produced had been designed to flatter the skin of female diners.

Yet for all its extravagance there was a streamlined simplicity to the Salle à Manger. What gave it an atmosphere of theatricality, Clarissa decided, was its occupants – waiters moving between tables like well-rehearsed actors on a stage, and diners beautifully dressed, the men in formal black tie, the ladies in stunning gowns and adorned with exquisite jewellery. Clarissa was wearing one of the silk evening dresses which she had had specially made for the voyage and a pearl necklace her mother had given her.

With diners making their entrance from the top of the wide staircase that led down from the Grand Salon to the Salle à Manger, Clarissa was enjoying herself watching people arrive. Suddenly there was an abrupt hush and what amounted to a visible parting of the waves when Effie Chase made her appearance at the top of the staircase. Wearing an apricot silk bias-cut gown that clung to her body like a second skin, she looked like a Grecian goddess. Draped around her shoulders was a snow-white fox fur, and at her throat was a diamond necklace that sparkled in the soft light. She was a vision of perfection and could not have resembled less the orphaned tomboy character of Elfin Effie she had played in so many of her movies – movies which Clarissa had watched with her mother, often crying and laughing together. Never had Clarissa thought that she would one day be in the same room as her film idol.

There was no sign of Effie's father and stepmother, but to her right, his arm slipped through hers, was the rude man with the emerald eyes. To her left, and looking discernibly ill at ease, was the man with the horn-rimmed spectacles.

Once an actress, always an actress, thought Clarissa as she watched in fascinated admiration as Effie soaked up the moment of her entrance, waiting for every head to turn and notice her. Plainly her companion, who was scowling and radiating irritation, wasn't prepared to play along and, taking the lead, he jerked her forward down the stairs. Effie's response was to laugh and fall in step with him.

'What did I tell you about the vulgarity of curiosity,' Marjorie admonished Clarissa. 'If you must stare, couldn't you do so with a degree of subtlety?'

'Sorry,' Clarissa said mechanically, barely listening. They had been at sea for six hours now, and she had reached the conclusion that every time Marjorie chided her for some imagined wrongdoing she would simply apologise. She reasoned it would be the best way to get any peace.

'And where, I want to know, is the captain?' demanded Marjorie. 'Surely he should be here? I dined on the captain's table the last time I made this crossing. But of course that was on the *Queen Mary*. A very different class of ship.' She went back to studying the guest list, no doubt searching for passengers of worth, those with whom she wished to socialise.

'I expect he's busy stoking the boilers,' Clarissa muttered, her gaze still on Effie as she glided down the stairs in their direction, 'or doing whatever else it is captains must do.'

'Don't be ridiculous, child, it's not the captain's job to stoke the boilers.'

'I know. It was a joke. A poor one, I'll admit.'

Marjorie tutted, then rolled her eyes as she followed the direction of Clarissa's gaze.

'What I fail to understand is what all the fuss is about,' she said, returning her attention to the passenger list. 'The girl is nothing but an overdressed clothes horse. What makes her worthy of so much attention?'

She made no attempt to lower her voice, and her words could be clearly heard just as Effie and her entourage were a few feet from their table. Clarissa was mortified. More so when she realised that the man at Effie's side had slowed his step and was glaring at them, his mouth twisted into a grimace of withering disdain. Instantly Clarissa's cheeks were aflame. Oh, let the ground swallow her up! Or, failing that, let the ship sink!

A little drastic, she told herself when, to her relief, the party of three walked on without a word exchanged. Hiding her scorching face behind her menu, and needing to vent her humiliation at being tainted by association, she hissed at Marjorie, 'What was that you were saying about subtlety?'

Marjorie bristled. 'I speak as I find.'

'But could you not have done so when they were out of earshot?' So much for trying to keep the peace!

Whatever reprimand the dreadful woman was about to make, it was cut short by another entrance into the dining room. This time it was Betty Dolores Lowe, and in a voluminous gown of pale grey silk she sailed down the flight of stairs like a large billowing cloud.

She scanned the Salle à Manger, spotted Clarissa and came over with a beaming smile on her face. 'So sorry, my dears,' she said, all breezy cordiality. 'What must you think of me? I was all set to meet you as arranged for a cocktail, but mercy me, wouldn't you just know it, I'd clean forgotten I already had an invitation to attend the captain's cocktail party? And he's such a dear man, the absolute personification of Gallic charm; I could hardly not go, could I? Not when he had gone to the trouble to write to me personally last Christmas to thank me for the donation I – well, never mind all that. Do please say you forgive me!'

Clarissa heard the sharp intake of breath from Marjorie and worked hard to keep from smiling. Oh, what a slight it must be to know that Betty was so firmly in cahoots with the captain. 'Of course you're forgiven,' Clarissa said. 'Did you meet anyone interesting at the party?'

Betty leaned in closer, her jolly face just inches from Clarissa's. 'I met the divine Effie Chase. She couldn't have been sweeter. I must introduce you, seeing as you're such a big fan. I'm sure she'd love to talk to somebody her own age.'

Thinking that meeting Effie was about as likely as her jumping overboard and swimming across the Atlantic to England, especially after Marjorie's offensive comments, Clarissa invited Betty to join them for dinner. 'Unless, of course, you've already made other arrangements?'

'My dear,' she said, 'I would deem it an honour to dine with you.' As if by magic, a waiter materialised from nowhere and pulled out a chair for Betty. When she was settled, she placed her bejewelled hands on the table. 'I can see we're going to be the best of friends. I always make friends on these trips. How about you, Marjorie? Do you make friends when you travel?'

Marjorie's face was as tight as a drum. 'It depends what you mean by friends.'

What a joy it was to have Betty's company for the evening, if only because Clarissa knew Marjorie's snooty nose was so comprehensively put out of joint. Such was her annoyance she barely ate a thing, grumbling that the vichyssoise soup wasn't to her liking, and picking at the fillets of turbot, and the duck a l'orange, although she relented slightly when presented with a hot, light-as-a-feather soufflé to finish with.

'Oh mercy me,' groaned Betty when the waiter removed the empty dessert dishes and replaced them with coffee and petits fours. 'I shall need a tender all to myself when it's time to disembark!'

Clarissa laughed. 'Is it my imagination, or is the boat pitching more than it was?'

'It's a ship, not a boat,' Marjorie corrected her with a weary shake of her head.

'I think you're right,' Betty said, 'the captain did mention we'd be heading towards some rougher weather before bedtime.'

'Oh dear, I hope it won't be too rough, this is my first time at sea and I'm not sure how good a sailor I'm going to be.'

'Then perhaps you should have thought about that before you ate and drank so much, young lady.'

With no polite response at her fingertips for Marjorie, Clarissa sipped her coffee and quietly plotted her revenge. Later that night, when all was quiet, she would sneak into Marjorie's cabin, smother her with a pillow, then push her scrawny body overboard – *splash!* – never to be seen again.

It was a satisfying fantasy, but really Clarissa wasn't the murdering kind. Unlike Effie's friend who, twice now, had looked as if he could have cheerfully murdered Clarissa on the spot. Not that he gave the impression of ever experiencing a cheerful emotion. She glanced discreetly over to where he was sitting with Effie and his bespectacled companion. The latter, Clarissa observed, was polishing his spectacles with a napkin. Next to his coffee cup was the notebook she had previously seen tucked under his arm. *Was he a writer?* she wondered. He looked as if he could be; there was an intellectual air about him. Across from him, and with one elbow resting on the table, his body inclined towards Effie so that his shoulder was almost touching hers, the rude, scowling man was drinking from his wineglass and listening to something Effie was saying while she checked her face in a powder compact. Such was the tableau they created that

82

it seemed to Clarissa the three of them were cut off from everybody else, as though an invisible screen was positioned around their table.

Remembering the *quelle surprise* comment Betty had made earlier during tea, Clarissa turned to ask her to explain, but was prevented from saying anything by Marjorie rising from her seat and announcing it had been a long day; it was now time for bed.

'But I haven't finished my coffee,' Clarissa said. 'And besides, I'm not in the least bit tired.' The only tiredness she felt was from this ghastly woman treating her like a child!

'Hey, Marjorie,' Betty interceded, 'if you're keen to get some beauty sleep, I'd be real happy to sacrifice an hour or so to deputise for you and look after Clarissa. I'll personally see her back to her cabin. What do you say?'

'I couldn't possibly put you to so much trouble,' Marjorie replied stiffly.

'Nonsense, it's no trouble at all. I have nieces and god-daughters aplenty and know what it is to worry about them, so you can sleep real easy knowing Clarissa's in safe hands.'

'I'll be fine,' Clarissa said, taking her cue. 'And I promise not to stay up too late or disturb you when I go to bed.'

'I should hope not indeed,' Marjorie replied. 'Very well, but I shall expect to see you bright and early for breakfast.'

'Of course.' Watching her tormentor walk away, and waiting until she was out of earshot, Clarissa thanked Betty. 'You really don't have to babysit me, you know.'

'I know I don't, and I don't intend to. But oh Lord, that woman needs to loosen up. Do you suppose she's ever known a moment's fun in her life?'

'If she has, I expect it was fleeting. But never mind, Marjorie, tell me some more about meeting Effie Chase at the captain's cocktail party. What was she really like? And what do you know about her two companions?'

Betty laughed. 'You sly girl, you! You have your eye on one of them, don't you?'

'Certainly not!' Clarissa remonstrated.

'Well, I'd steer clear of Ellis Randall if I were you; he's too handsome for his own good and has been raised with an extremely exaggerated sense of his own cleverness.'

'Is he the one with the unusually green eyes?' Instinctively Clarissa knew the answer would be yes.

Betty nodded. 'He's the heir to Randalls Paper Products and is exactly the type of young man any mother would warn her daughter to avoid – but of course, that only increases his attractiveness.'

After a pause, Clarissa said, 'You mean, Randalls as in "The toilet paper that's soft and firm, and leaves you fresh and dry"?'

'One and the same.'

Clarissa laughed at the irony of the heir to the biggest toilet paper company in the US looking like he had a bad smell permanently under his nose.

'What about the other man,' she asked, 'the serious-looking one?'

'Ah, now he's a very different kettle of fish. His name's Artemis Bloomberg and he's—'

'Do tell me he's a writer!' Clarissa burst out.

'Why, as a matter of fact he is. Or rather he's an aspiring author. He's only twenty-one, the same age as Ellis Randall. They were at school together and of the two, he's by far the brighter.'

'How do you know so much about them?'

She shrugged. 'I know so many people,' she said airily, 'and I take an interest in those around me. And you, my dear girl, are somebody who interests me greatly. I predict you have a very intriguing life ahead of you.'

'What on earth makes you think that?'

'You're strong-minded, independent and searching for adventure, aren't you? Why else would you be making this journey?'

Clarissa laughed and suddenly felt a poignant closeness to

this friendly woman, a woman she had known for no more than a few hours, but with whom she felt able to talk so freely. 'I'm so pleased we've met,' she said.

Betty patted her hand. 'Me too. And before our voyage is over, we must be sure to exchange addresses, because I'd love to stay in touch. And who knows, you might need my help one day, which I'd gladly offer.'

Her friendly kindness, so at odds with Marjorie's coldness, was almost too much, and needing to change the subject, Clarissa said, 'Why were you surprised to see Effie and her companions having tea together this afternoon?'

'Was I?'

'You said "*quelle surprise*" when they sat down.'

'Oh that!' Betty said with a smile. 'You obviously haven't been keeping up with the gossip magazines, have you? If you had, you'd know that it was hotly rumoured that Effie was about to announce her engagement to the film producer Roddy Campbell.'

'But he's ancient!'

'More or less the same age as Daddy Chase.'

'So what happened?'

'Daddy Chase put a stop to things, claimed she was only involving herself with Roddy Campbell to get at him for marrying somebody so young and so soon after the death of Effie's mother, whom she adored. And apart from that, Daddy Chase would much rather his daughter married a wealthy heir her own age, somebody like Ellis Randall who she's known for a year or two now. I suspect Daddy Chase may have ensured they were travelling to Europe at the same time.'

Together they glanced across the dining room to where Effie and her companions were now on their feet and preparing to leave.

'Come on,' Betty said, taking hold of Clarissa's hand, 'I'll introduce you.'

Chapter Fourteen

'I'm sorry my dear, but it looks very much like you're needed elsewhere.'

So captivated by the scene Mrs Dallimore had created for her on board the *Belle Etoile*, Lizzie had to take a moment to think where she was. The woman really was an amazing storyteller. Seeing Jennifer, the matron, on the terrace up at the house gesticulating to her, she grudgingly got to her feet. 'I suppose I'd better go,' she said, wishing she didn't have to. 'Will you tell me what happened next when I see you again?'

The old lady smiled. 'If you'd like me to, yes. But not if it means you'll get into trouble for spending too much time with me and not enough with the others. Now off you trot before Matron sends for reinforcements to drag you away.'

Thinking she might be lucky and have only a quick task to carry out before being able to escape back to Mrs Dallimore and her story, Lizzie sprinted across the lawn towards the terrace. She was just rounding the largest of the flowerbeds when she suddenly found herself flying through the air before landing flat on her face with a thud. There was a moment, at the point of impact, when the world turned black and she felt every last breath sucked out of her and her body go as limp as a rag doll. When she opened her eyes she saw a face she recognised, but couldn't place.

'Are you okay?' the person asked.

'I'll let you know when I've checked in with my body,' she wheezed, fighting to get her breath back.

'Take it easy, you're probably a bit winded.'

Feeling for anything broken, she flexed her jaw, wobbling

it from side to side, and ran a finger down her nose. She then rubbed at the grass stains on her knees.

'It was pretty impressive what you did. You took off in fine style.'

Lizzie looked up at the person talking to her and, with sufficient brain cells now in communication with each other, she said, 'You're that bloke from the staff room.'

He wiggled one of his eyebrows. 'Depends how many blokes you've seen in there. I'd hate for there to be a case of mistaken identity.'

'No chance of that,' she said. 'You're definitely one and the same.'

He offered her his hand to help pull her up.

Ignoring it, she hauled herself into an upright position. 'So is it your fault I hit the deck? What did you do, rugby-tackle me?'

'I'll tell you if you promise to keep it to yourself.' He made a play of looking around them, as though checking for eavesdroppers hiding in the bushes. 'I launched you into orbit using my superpowers,' he whispered.

She gave him a long hard look and spontaneously took a step back from him. Ooo-k*aaay*, so he was a full-on crazy. A full-on crazy gardener, she then thought, noticing the collection of gardening tools on the ground behind him, along with a wheelbarrow. Had he tripped her on purpose? she suddenly wondered. Then remembering that Jennifer had needed her for something, she said, 'I have to go.'

'See you around,' he called after her. 'But remember, no telling anyone what I told you.'

'Why, will you lose your superpowers if I do?'

Ignoring her sarcasm, he put a finger to his lips.

Yeah, I'll give you *Ssh!* thought Lizzie, limping up to the terrace. If he had deliberately tripped her, just for the fun of it, there'd be hell to pay.

She went in search of Jennifer and found her in her office. 'Sorry I took so long,' she said.

'That's all right,' the other woman said. 'Did Mrs Dallimore not want to part with you? I think she's enjoying having you around.'

'No, it wasn't that. I – I fell over something in the garden. Who's the gardener? I haven't seen him before.' What she really wanted to ask was whether he was a lunatic, and if so, perhaps he shouldn't be allowed to be anywhere near the elderly and vulnerable.

'His name's Jed and it's his first day. Mr and Mrs Parks are trying out a new contractor because the firm they were using before wasn't reliable enough. But as one of the residents has pointed out, he's rather easy on the eye, isn't he?' She smiled and turned to look out of her office window to where the subject of their conversation was hard at work in the flowerbed where Lizzie had left him.

Easy on the eye or not, he was a menace as far as Lizzie was concerned.

It wasn't long before the warmth of the afternoon sun took its effect and Clarissa's eyelids closed and she succumbed to the drowsy sensation of escaping the confines of her tired old body. Happily, and like a feather caught on a breeze, she floated back to where her thoughts had been when Lizzie had been sitting with her.

What a dreadful woman Marjorie Boyd-Lambert had been, but what a blessing Betty had proved to be, and how much poorer Clarissa's life might have been had their paths not crossed.

Funny how sharp and clear most of her reminiscences were, but how others had become faded and worn thin like the threads of an old tapestry. She couldn't decide if they had lost their clarity through constant use, or had become so tangled in the myriad memories stored away in her head, they were now beyond loosening free.

But one memory would never be lost to her: the moment Betty had introduced Clarissa to Effie and her companions. 'I can't apologise enough for the awfulness of what the woman sitting next to me at dinner said about you,' she had said to Effie. 'I've only known her a short while, but already I'm plotting her demise, preferably in the most despicable manner possible.'

'Oh, think nothing of it,' Effie responded with a small shrug. 'I hear that kind of thing all the time. And usually from Ellis here.' She laughed and indicated the scowling man next to her. He made no attempt to deny or confirm the comment, just stared intently at Clarissa while putting a lighter to the cigarette in his mouth.

To her amazement, Betty had been right when she'd said Effie would welcome the company of another girl the same age as herself. 'You must join us for a drink,' Effie had urged Clarissa. 'You cannot imagine how tedious it is having only these two boys to talk to.' Then turning to the man in horn-rimmed glasses, she'd said, 'Artie, this couldn't be more perfect, you now have the most divine partner for when we go dancing later. You do like to dance, don't you, Clarissa? Please say you do, or I'll have to divide myself between the two of them and I'm sure I shan't have the energy for that.'

'Of course she dances,' Betty had said before Clarissa had a chance to say that, according to her dance teacher at school, she was in possession of two very clumsy left feet. It was one of the reasons she had resisted all her grandmother's efforts to throw her into the many social dances that she deemed so important for a young woman of her background.

'Good! That's settled then.' And linking her arm through Clarissa's, Effie had sashayed her way towards the staircase of the Salle à Manger. When they'd reached the top, she murmured in the softest of voices in Clarissa's ear, 'Now you must turn and look back the way you've just come, for a true performer never leaves her audience without giving them one last glimpse. There,' she'd giggled when they'd passed through the doors with Ellis and Artie following behind. 'You're a natural star!'

Clarissa had always found that memories often had a life of their own; they chose when to surface and when to lie dormant. Just as true was the danger of a muddled memory becoming a truth. Was it a muddled memory now to think that she knew in her heart during those days on board the *Belle Etoile* that Effie, Ellis and Artie were to become so dear to her? Surely that could not have been the case? Yet now, more than seventy years later, she would swear that it was true.

At the sound of rustling in the trees to her right, Clarissa opened her eyes. She smiled. 'Ellis, is that you? Have you come back to correct me on my facts? You always did like to put me right, didn't you? But you had me all wrong that first night, just as I had you all wrong.'

It wasn't Ellis, though; it was Artie, and at the sight of his caring face a familiar aching pain clenched at Clarissa's heart.

'Hello, Artie,' she said. 'Why don't you come and sit with me?'

But no sooner had she uttered the words than, and at the sound of what could have been something cracking underfoot, he vanished like a puff of smoke. Disappointed, she turned to see what had caused the noise and gave a start. A few yards from her was a stranger staring back at her.

'Sorry,' the man said, 'I didn't mean to startle you.' He narrowed his eyes and peered into the darkness of the trees. Clarissa felt her face flush. Had he heard her speaking to Artie?

'Are you looking for somebody?' she asked, rattled by his intrusion.

'No, just going about my business.'

'And what business would that be?'

'Gardening business. The sort that involves these.' He held up a pair of secateurs and a large black bucket, which until then she hadn't noticed. 'I thought I'd deadhead the roses on the arbour,' he said. 'That's if you don't mind. I could come back later if you'd prefer.'

'No, no, that's quite all right,' she said, her composure reinstated, 'so long as I'm not in your way.'

'I'll work round you. And if you like,' he added with a wink, 'I'll give your hair a trim while I'm about it.'

She watched him get to work, wondering when was the last time a young man – a well-spoken, handsome young man at that – had winked at her.

Snip went the gardener's secateurs.

'Don't mind me,' he said abruptly. 'If you want to continue talking to your friend in the woods, I won't listen in.'

Her cheeks flushed again. 'You frightened him away,' she blurted out. Immediately she wished she'd kept quiet. He was bound now to think she was gaga.

'It seems to be my day for frightening people off,' he said. *Snip*. 'It must be my ugly mug.'

She sneaked a look at his face and thought that he was being modest; he was far from ugly.

'Who else have you frightened today, then?'

'Well, not exactly frightened, but I certainly annoyed her. She works here, as a matter of fact. Don't ask me her name, but she managed to trip over me while I was weeding. She came hurtling round the corner of the flowerbed where I was kneeling, and literally flew right over my back. Then she had the cheek to blame me.'

Clarissa thought about watching Lizzie running up the lawn in answer to the matron's summons. 'I think I know who that might have been,' she said. 'Was she about your age with dark hair tied up in a ponytail?'

'Yeah, that sounds like her. Bit of a bolshie madam, between you and me, and zero sense of humour.'

'I expect you'll find you simply got off on the wrong foot with her,' Clarissa said. 'It's the easiest thing in the world to leap to the wrong conclusion about a person.'

Once more she was reminded of Ellis, and how she had taken such a strong dislike to him before getting to know the man he really was.

Chapter Fifteen

April 1939, SS *Belle Etoile*

'I'm afraid I'm a terrible dancer.'

'Are you? I hadn't noticed. You're doing just fine.'

Clarissa smiled at Artie's kindness, at the same time trying not to lose her rhythm – *back, back, sidestep, together, back, back, sidestep, together*. She had never danced in a bar before, and she dreaded to think what Marjorie and Grandma Ethel would have to say if they could see her here in the glamorous setting of the Rhapsody Bar.

But at least her chaperone and grandmother needn't concern themselves with any impropriety when it came to Artie – his behaviour was as perfect as his dancing prowess. 'Where did you learn to dance so well?' she asked, as he gently but expertly manoeuvred her to avoid colliding with another couple.

'My brother and I had no choice but to submit to our mother's desire to turn us out in a manner she perceived as socially well equipped. If nothing else, she believed we'd be able to dance our way out of trouble.'

'And have you put that skill to the test yet?'

'So far I've managed to keep out of trouble, but who knows what the future holds.'

Who indeed, thought Clarissa, casting a glance over to the bar, where Ellis was scowling deep into a glass of whiskey as though searching the bottom of it for something he'd lost. His bow tie untied and drooping around his neck, he looked absurdly dashing. There was no sign of Effie; perhaps she had gone to powder her nose.

'I know I've only just met you all,' she said, 'but Ellis doesn't strike me as being a particularly happy man.'

'Don't be fooled by that morose way of his, it's a well-honed act.'

'Have you been friends for long?'

'Long enough to know that there isn't anything I wouldn't do for him.'

At the intensity of his words, Clarissa raised her eyes to look at her dancing partner more closely. Beneath thick hair parted to the right and a broad sweep of forehead, dark, sensitive and intelligent eyes stared back at her from behind the lenses of his spectacles. 'He's lucky to have you as his friend, in that case,' she said. 'I can't think of anyone who would say that about me.'

'Maybe you just haven't met the right friend yet. But you're wrong, it's not Ellis who's the lucky one; it's me. He befriended me at college when others shunned me.'

'Why were you shunned?'

'Because of my surname, Bloomberg,' he said simply.

It was a few seconds before she understood what he meant. She then wished she could snatch back her question. How gauche he must think her! And what would he think if he knew that her grandmother habitually ranted about Jews taking over the country?

'Prejudice has no place in a civilised society,' she said, trying to make good her clumsiness.

'You're right, but prejudice is on the march. Nowhere is it more obvious than in Nazi Germany, where many believe there is no future for German Jews.'

'Is that really true?'

He nodded. 'A friend of mine saw for himself what happened on Kristallnacht last November when Hitler's thugs waged war on the Jewish people. Do you know what Goering said after that awful night of mass murder? He grumbled at the cost of replacing so much smashed glass. He said that more Jews should have been killed and less glass broken. For some, that's the world they want to live in.'

Clarissa shuddered at Artie's words, words uttered not with angry outrage, but with quiet, unnerving conviction. She had heard about the Night of Broken Glass in Germany, but to her shame she hadn't fully taken it in; she had been too preoccupied with her mother's death. Now Artie made her realise just how little she knew of the world beyond her sheltered upbringing.

'I'm sorry if I've spoilt the mood of the night for you,' Artie said, just as the music came to a stop and they let go of each other to applaud the band. 'Ellis often grumbles that I'm too serious.'

'You haven't spoilt anything,' she replied, 'far from it. But you have made me think, and that's good.'

The band started playing again. It was an Al Bowlly song, one of Clarissa's favourites – 'Love is the Sweetest Thing'.

'If I promise not to become too serious again, would you dance with me once more?' Artie asked her.

'I'd love to,' she said with a smile.

'If you don't mind me saying,' he said, after he'd taken her in his arms again, 'you don't seem very American.'

'That might be because my mother was English and I was born in France, but my father was American, so I'm what you'd call a mixed bag.'

'That would explain it, then. My maternal and paternal grandparents are a mixture of Polish, Hungarian, Austrian and German, so I'm the same as you, a mixed bag.'

She smiled. 'Betty told me that you're a writer – what sort of thing do you write?'

'I'm going into journalism after my visit to Europe, but writing a novel is what I really want to do.'

'My father wanted to be a novelist, but unfortunately his family had other ideas.'

'Did he ever have anything published?'

'Short stories and pieces for magazines and the newspapers

when we were living in France. He died some years ago. He – he shot himself.' Clarissa swallowed, shocked at what she'd revealed. As laid down by Grandma Ethel, it had been a strict rule that the manner in which Clarissa's father died was never referred to. 'And you're the first person I've ever told that to,' she said in a low voice.

'I'm sorry.'

'Looking back on it,' Clarissa continued, 'he must have been so very unfulfilled. He wanted a different life to the one expected of him. I hadn't thought of it before, but maybe that's part of why I'm making this trip. I have to go where my heart leads me.'

Artie nodded thoughtfully. 'I'd recommend you never lose that simple sense of purpose. Always follow your heart.'

'I intend to. Which is what my mother did when she left England and married my father. Funnily enough, she also wrote, and in many ways she was more successful than my father.'

'Tell me more.'

Clarissa told him about the weekly column Fran had written, and of her death last year and the main reason for making this trip. Artie Bloomberg was, she realised, so very easy to talk to.

When once again the music came to a stop, he put a hand to the small of her back and steered her away from the dance floor. 'See,' he said, 'you relaxed perfectly while we were talking and had no problem in dancing with me.'

'That's because you were such a good teacher,' she replied with a smile.

He smiled too and led her to where Ellis was still standing at the bar.

'What a fine couple you make,' Ellis said, raising his glass at them. 'But when, I want to know, am I to be rewarded with a dance with the lovely Clarissa? Why does Artie get to dance with you all the time?'

Artie laughed. 'Two dances, Ellis; how does that manifest itself into "all the time"?'

'Feels that way, stuck here as I have been on my own.'

'Where's Effie?' asked Artie, looking around them.

'Her father wanted a word with her,' Ellis said with a roll of his eyes. Then, draining his glass and putting it down on the bar, he thrust out his hand to Clarissa. 'Care to risk a canter around the dance floor with me?'

'Only if you're patient enough, or maybe brave enough, to cope with my two left feet.'

'Challenging my courage, are you? I'll let you into a secret: we'll have four left feet between us, which makes us a perfect match, I'd say.'

Once they were on the dance floor, he took hold of her and not at all in the same gentle way Artie had.

'Tell me three interesting things about yourself that you think I should know,' he said abruptly.

'Goodness,' she said, trying to sound nonchalant, '*only* three things interesting about me?' Darned if she could think of a single one!

'Don't prevaricate,' he said tersely, tightening his hold on her, and at the same time stepping on her foot and not apologising. 'I can't bear it when people do that.'

Feeling the strength of him through his hands, anger seized hold of her. How dare this appallingly self-satisfied man think he could tell her what to do? 'The first thing you need to know about me,' she said, drawing on all her skill to sound offhand, 'is that I bruise tremendously easily, so please don't step on my toes again.'

'It would help if you didn't get them in my way,' he replied.

'Do you ever apologise?' she asked.

'Only when I deem it absolutely essential.'

'And barging into me on the sun deck earlier today didn't warrant an apology?'

He leaned back from her, his green eyes seeming to glow

in the subdued lighting. 'It's how I get beautiful girls to notice me. And you did notice me, didn't you?'

'You arrogant swine, you!'

He laughed. 'That's more like it; it's good to see some real emotion from you instead of a cool, buttoned-down reserve. I can't stand artifice in a person.'

'There's an awful lot you can't stand, isn't there?'

'For which I feel the need neither to apologise nor justify. Ah, I see Effie's finally shaken off her father and returned to the fold.'

Following his gaze, Clarissa saw Effie going over to join Artie at the bar. Without thinking, she said, 'Effie's so beautiful, isn't she?'

'Oh, please, don't go all starry-eyed on me, anything but that. And don't do it around Effie. She has enough people bolstering her ego as it is. What she needs are real friends who tell her the truth, no matter how painful; friends she can rely upon.'

'And are you a real friend to her?'

'I like to think so, yes. I'm the sort to say to her, "Effie, darling, much as we love you, we're all tired of struggling in the glare of your brilliance when underneath it all you're just plain old Effie from Baltimore."'

Yes, thought Clarissa, she didn't doubt for a minute this blunt-speaking man wouldn't hesitate to be brutally honest and remind Effie of where she'd come from. Effie Chase's humble beginnings had been well documented over the years, as had her parents' determination that she would one day be a big star.

'Tell me what you're going to do when you arrive in England,' Ellis said, after once more their feet collided.

'I shall take the train to London and stay with my god-mother, who I've never met before. She was my mother's best friend while growing up and we've kept in touch.'

'And what will you do in London? Enjoy the life of a socialite?'

Was he making fun of her? Condemning her as being incapable of doing anything of any real worth or purpose? 'I shall find a job and do something useful with my—'

'A *job*?' he interrupted with heavy sarcasm. 'What sort of job? What are you trained to do, other than travel first class aboard one of the finest ships ever built?'

'I don't know yet,' she retorted sharply, 'but I can promise you I will not spend my time in England being idle. I plan to do something worthwhile with my life.'

'Good for you, well said!'

'I assure you I don't need your approbation.'

'I'm certain you don't,' he said, with what she saw was a glint of amusement in his eyes, 'but perhaps in a rare moment of idleness you might like to have dinner with me when I'm in London. I don't know when that will be as yet, but I shall be staying at the Ritz in Mayfair.'

'I might, if I'm not too busy,' she replied coolly. Then wanting to play him at his own game, she said, 'In the meantime, why don't you tell me three interesting things about yourself which you think *I* ought to know.'

'Aha, turning the tables, I see. Well, there's only one thing you have to know about me and that is that it's people who matter to me. Not the charlatans of this world who suck up to a fellow because he has a few dollars in his pocket, but true friends who'd be your friend with or without the dollars.'

'Like Artie?'

He narrowed his eyes and stared at her. 'Yes. Exactly like Artie.'

The next morning, when the ship was pitching and heaving as if trying to tip its passengers overboard into the grey, roiling sea, Clarissa discovered she had a cast-iron stomach. It was Marjorie – the self-lauded seasoned traveller and expert sailor – who woke victim to what she referred to as a touch of *mal de mer*.

'I've never suffered like this before,' she told Clarissa after breakfast had been brought to their cabins by their steward. 'All I can conclude is that this dreadful ship is not up to the task of providing a smooth passage. Or,' she added with a sickly grimace, staring at her untouched tray of breakfast, 'I ate something last night which did not agree with me. Perhaps you would be so good as to summon the doctor.'

The doctor's verdict was that, along with many other passengers, the rough Atlantic had got the better of Marjorie's well-travelled stomach; he recommended she stay in bed and, if possible, try to eat an apple.

He congratulated Clarissa on having a fine pair of sea legs, and went on his way. She was smiling at the remark when she went for a walk on the sun deck.

With a headscarf tied firmly under her chin to keep her hair from whipping at her face, and her coat buttoned up to her neck, she stared out at the savage swell of the sea, forcing herself to face it, fighting the instinct to turn away from the thrashing cauldron that was as grey as the stormy sky that was swallowing up the horizon. Tempestuous waves as big as buildings crashed violently against each other, spewing out eruptions of foam that were sent flying in the ferocious wind. After a while it became almost mesmerising to watch the turbulence, as though she were staring death in the face, defying it to do its worst.

How strange it was to be quite literally in the middle of nowhere, she reflected, and with no more than a handful of other passengers on deck with her, none of whom had the slightest notion who she was. The same would be true when she arrived in England. With this thought came the unexpected idea that she could reinvent herself – she could be anybody she wanted to be. She could shake off the old Clarissa Allerton of her childhood and become a woman of her choosing. Just as Effie had reinvented herself from the girl from Baltimore to Effie Chase, famous child star.

The more she thought about it, the more she liked the

prospect of deciding on a new persona for herself, a persona she would have in place by the time she reached London. She would be more sophisticated, and more assertive and confident. That way she would be regarded as a strong, independent young woman who knew her mind. But wasn't that what Betty had said of her last night during dinner? Maybe that was how people already saw her. If that was true, then she had to start believing it herself.

By coincidence she found herself standing in the exact same spot where she had stood yesterday afternoon when she had waved goodbye to the Manhattan skyline. But now she felt no sadness, only the thrill of all that lay ahead for her in England.

Hearing her name being called above the crash and roar of the sea, she turned to see the slight figure of Effie, coming towards her swathed in a fur coat, battling against the wind. 'I thought it was you,' she said breathlessly, when she staggered to a stop next to Clarissa. 'Isn't this a hoot!' She had to shout to be heard above the wind.

Clarissa nodded. 'It's breathtaking. Quite literally.'

Effie smiled and grabbed hold of Clarissa just as the ship gave a violent pitch and roll. 'I love it because it makes me feel so insignificant. I'm no more than a scrap of puny flesh and bones, while out there,' she raised a gloved hand to point into the stormy distance, 'nature reigns supreme.' She turned to Clarissa, her eyes bright. 'It's important to be reminded of that sometimes, isn't it?'

Clarissa nodded her agreement. 'It's good to be reminded that we're all mortal,' she shouted back and then, with a laugh that was whipped away on the wind, she added, 'Although maybe Ellis is the exception to that.'

Effie smiled at her. 'How clever of you to understand his god-like status already. He walks among us mere mortals, but he's made of very different stuff. He likes you.'

'You say that as though there's a reason he shouldn't.'

'Ellis is very selective when it comes to making friendships.'

'I don't know whether to be honoured or concerned.'

'Be neither. He's a soft-hearted bear beneath the claws and teeth. He's the way he is because of his horrid mother. She's a monster with a heart of stone. But then, so many are. I guarantee you'll grow to love him, just as Artie and I do.'

'You're assuming I'll see him again.'

'You will. I know it. Just as I know we're going to be the best of friends. Do you have someone in whom you can confide all your darkest secrets?'

Clarissa shook her head.

'Me neither. I've always—' But her words were snatched away by a powerful gust of wind that buffeted them together, nearly knocking them off their feet. Holding onto each other, they threw back their heads and laughed. Clarissa couldn't remember the last time she had laughed so freely or so happily.

Chapter Sixteen

On her way home from Woodside and freewheeling down a long, sloping stretch of clear road, the warm breeze against her face, Lizzie was surprised by how much she had enjoyed her afternoon shift. Okay, she could have done without tripping over that idiot gardener, but any day that ended with cake was not a bad day in her book.

It had been the newest resident's eighty-ninth birthday, and with everybody gathered in the sitting room to sing happy birthday to Mr Sheridan as Mrs Park brought in an impressively large cake decked out with a gazillion candles, Lizzie had to admit that she'd been oddly moved by the sight of the old gentleman eagerly blowing out the candles; he'd looked to be having such a good time. No one from his family was there – both of his sons and their families lived overseas, but they had sent plenty of cards and presents.

When the cake was cut Jennifer had suggested Lizzie take a piece out to Jed, the gardener, saying it was a tradition that all members of staff shared in the celebrating of a resident's birthday.

'You haven't poisoned it, have you?' Jed had asked, regarding the plate suspiciously.

'You'll have to try it and see,' Lizzie had said, at the same time trying to figure him out. Clearly Jennifer didn't think he was a madman, but Lizzie was yet to be convinced.

'Oh well,' he'd remarked with a shrug, taking a mouthful of cake, 'here's to living dangerously.' The first mouthful eaten, he'd said, 'Just in case I die in the next five minutes, I'd like my last words to be an apology. I'm sorry I was flippant when you fell over me earlier. You'll have to excuse my sense of humour; it can be a bit off sometimes. Are you all right now? No bones broken?'

'Nothing broken,' she'd replied.

'So, apology accepted?'

'Apology accepted,' she'd confirmed, before turning to go back up to the house.

The downhill slope now behind her, Lizzie resumed pedalling, passing the golden fields of wheat either side of her. She had just followed the bend in the road that would take her to Great Magnus when she heard her mobile ringing from inside her rucksack. Her heart leapt – *Curt!* She immediately stopped pedalling and squeezed hard on the brakes. Oh, please let it be Curt and not some automated voice informing her that she was entitled to a grant to insulate her loft.

Jumping off her bike, she wrenched the rucksack from her back and rummaged inside for the phone. When she saw the caller ID, she could have danced for joy; it *was* Curt! And at the sound of his voice, she couldn't stop a rush of questions tripping off her tongue. 'How's your holiday going?' she asked. 'No! Don't tell me, I don't want to know! Just tell me how you are. Are you missing me?'

'Hey, back up there and give me a chance to get a word in edgeways,' he said with a laugh. 'Look, I can't talk for long, but I'm back in London now.'

'You are, why? What's happened?' But in a flash she saw it all and her hopes soared. This was it, then, this was what she'd been waiting for: he'd told his wife that he didn't love her any more and that he wanted a divorce. Naturally, after a bombshell like that, they would have cut short their holiday. Her mouth suddenly dry with the shock of it all, she inhaled deeply. It was happening, just as Curt had said it would! Hadn't he said that she just had to be patient and trust him?

'I need to see you,' he said, his voice serious.

'I need to see you, too,' she said, forcing her own voice

to match his, warning herself that this was no time for jubilation; his marriage was ending, which meant serious repercussions would inevitably follow. 'I've missed you so much. When do you want to get together? And where?'

'Can you come to London tomorrow?'

She was about to ask what time, when she remembered she'd agreed to be at Woodside all day tomorrow. 'I'm sorry, I can't,' she said. 'I'm working.'

There was a pause from Curt. 'I thought it was only voluntary stuff you were doing? You can get out of that, can't you? The old folk probably won't even notice you're not there.'

Lizzie's pride surfaced. It wasn't that insignificant, what she was doing. And some people might miss her.

'Sorry,' his voice crackled, 'I'm losing you. Hang on, I'll cross the road to get a better signal … Is that better? Can you hear me?'

'Yes,' she said. 'Can you hear me?'

'Loud and clear. So what about tomorrow, can you meet me?'

'Why don't I get the train when I've finished work tomorrow afternoon and we can have dinner together?'

'A great idea, but the evening's no good for me, I have to be at home. Let's have lunch the day after if that works better for you.'

Cycling the rest of the way home, Lizzie felt like singing at the top of her voice. She could not be happier.

Tess was in the kitchen getting supper ready when Lizzie walked in humming to herself.

'Hiya, Mum,' she said, tossing her rucksack onto a chair, a reminder of when she and Luke had been children just home from school. 'What's cooking?'

'Lasagne. You sound very jolly.'

'I am.'

'Good day, then?'

Lizzie smiled. 'The best yet. Where's Dad and Freddie?'

'In the shed. I was told it would be men's stuff going on out there and I wasn't to disturb them.'

Lizzie laughed and went over to the cupboard for a glass. She ran the tap, then drank thirstily. Tess was glad to see her daughter was looking and sounding more like her usual self, but a small, unworthy part of her resented the light-hearted manner in which Lizzie was behaving, when in her wake lay a trail of devastation.

Still stinging from Lorna's awful behaviour yesterday afternoon, Tess had had to endure a phone call from Ingrid at lunchtime today, effectively cross-examining her on how Freddie had come to fall out of the pushchair. It didn't matter how many times Tess reiterated how sorry she was that she had forgotten to strap Freddie in and that it was just one of those terrible little accidents, she could not shake off the feeling that not only would Ingrid never forgive her, but she was as good as accusing Tess of wilful neglect.

'Shall we have supper outside in the garden?' asked Lizzie. 'I'll lay the table.'

'If that's what you'd like,' Tess said absently.

When Lizzie had sorted out the table on the patio, she came back into the kitchen. 'You okay, Mum?' she asked. 'You seem a bit down.'

'I'm fine,' she lied.

'Are you sure? You're not still upset by what Lorna said, are you?'

'Of course not,' she said lightly, unable to bring herself to admit that she had been dreadfully hurt by Lorna's comments. Hurt, too, that she had lost her closest friend in such a horrible way. 'I'm just a bit tired,' she said. 'It's all the running around after Freddie.'

'Well, I want you to know that I really am sorry for the way things have turned out between you and Lorna. It's not right that she's having a go at you over my decision to end things with Simon. If she wants to have a go at anyone, it should be me. It was cowardly what she did yesterday.'

Tess looked at her daughter in grateful surprise. But also with some guilt for the less than supportive thoughts she had been having towards her. Lizzie, she told herself, could not be held accountable for the extent of Lorna's bitchy pettiness; that was all down to Lorna. 'You're wrong,' Tess said. 'Lorna shouldn't need to have a go at anyone. She simply needs to accept that what's done is done and to stop behaving like a child.'

Lizzie crossed the kitchen and hugged her. 'You're the best, Mum,' she said. 'You know that, don't you?'

Wherever this softer and more sympathetic side of her daughter had come from, Tess welcomed it. No, that wasn't quite fair. Lizzie had always had a softer side to her; she just didn't always show it at the right moment. 'What's brought all this on, then?' Tess asked. 'What's put you in such a good mood?'

'It's Curt,' Lizzie said with a smile that brightened her face, 'he's asked me to have lunch with him in London the day after tomorrow.'

'I thought you said he was away on holiday?'

'He's come back early.'

'Did he say why?'

'He didn't have time, but I think it's pretty obvious why: he's talked things over with his wife and there didn't seem much point in going through with the rest of the holiday after that. I just hope it didn't get too awful for him; it couldn't have been easy what he had to do.'

Keeping to herself that it couldn't have been easy for Curt's wife, Tess said, 'So when do your father and I get to meet Curt?'

'Soon, Mum. Very soon. And I know you're going to just love him.'

Chapter Seventeen

Lizzie cycled to Woodside again the next morning.

Yesterday anger at the way Lorna had treated Mum had powered her legs; today cheerful optimism, and the knowledge that she would be seeing Curt in just over twenty-four hours, was the source of her energy. Had Curt not been in such a hurry yesterday, and had the mobile connection been better, she would have loved to have chatted with him for longer, if only to reassure him that she would do everything she could to make the difficult time ahead as stress-free as possible.

She wasn't without sympathy for Natasha, Curt's wife; after all, having finished with Simon, Lizzie knew first-hand how tough it was to accept that a relationship was over. But when it was over, it was necessary for one party to find the courage to cut the tie; it was the only way.

'You're looking very chipper this morning,' Mr Sheridan greeted Lizzie in the large sitting room at Woodside. Jennifer had asked her to spend some time with him. 'I think he's a bit down in the dumps this morning,' she'd said. 'I know I always feel that way after a birthday. If you could think of something to cheer him up I'd be grateful.'

'Well, since you mention it, Mr Sheridan,' Lizzie said brightly, noting that he did indeed look glum, 'I do feel rather chipper. Very chipper, in fact.'

'Good for you, there's nothing that cheers the heart of an old man more than a pretty popsy with a smile on her face.'

'Popsy?' she repeated with a laugh. 'That's a new one on me; I've never been called that before.'

'I suppose a word like that isn't allowed these days, is it?' he said, his fantastically bushy eyebrows drawn together in a deep frown. 'Disrespectful to women and all that PC nonsense.'

'I've been called worse things,' she said, 'so please don't let it bother you. Do you fancy a game of Scrabble?'

He shook his head. 'Can't stand the game. If I'm honest, I'm a rotten speller.'

'Me too. How about a game of cards?'

Again he shook his head. 'Not really in the mood.'

'A jigsaw?'

Now he chuckled gruffly. 'Good Lord, it's come to something when I'm asked by a pretty girl if I'd like to do a jigsaw. Time was when I would have—'

'When you would have had your ears boxed by your mother for being so bold!'

They both turned to see Mrs Dallimore in her wheelchair peering round from behind a wing-back chair a few yards away in the bay window overlooking the garden.

'Good morning Mrs Dallimore,' said Lizzie, 'I didn't see you there. Can I get you anything?'

'No thank you.'

'Would you like to join us?' asked Mr Sheridan.

'If it will stop you embarrassing the poor girl, then I see it as nothing less than my duty.'

Mr Sheridan pulled a face and lowered his voice. 'She's a tartar when she wants to be, isn't she?'

'I presume I was meant to hear that,' Mrs Dallimore responded sharply as Lizzie went over to manoeuvre her wheelchair to join them.

'I was checking to make sure there's nothing wrong with your hearing,' Mr Sheridan said with a wink at Lizzie. 'I can't bear having to repeat myself.'

'How very considerate of you.'

'That's me. And putting your hearing to one side, I was about to ask Lizzie why she's looking so pleased with herself.'

Mrs Dallimore tutted. 'It wouldn't occur to you to mind your own business, then?'

'No more than it would to you, I'll be bound.'

Listening to their bickering, and seeing how Mr Sheridan had perked up, Lizzie was tempted to slip away and leave them to it, content in the knowledge that she could tell Jennifer that she had done exactly what she'd been asked to do. But no sooner had she turned to go than Mr Sheridan stopped her.

'Oh no you don't,' he said. 'No leaving without telling us what's put such a spring in your step.'

'Ignore him, Lizzie,' Mrs Dallimore said. 'Don't give in to his bullying.'

'Bullying be blowed! It's called taking an interest.'

'It's called poking your nose in, I think you'll find.'

'Saints preserve us and save me from censorious women!'

Lizzie laughed, and such was her good mood she was more than happy to share the cause of it. 'If you must know,' she said, 'I'm going to see my boyfriend in London tomorrow. We haven't seen each other for ages.'

'A boyfriend?' said Mr Sheridan. 'Well, and there was me thinking if I played my cards right I might be in with a chance with you. So what's this chap got that I haven't, eh?'

'She wouldn't know where to start on such an exhaustive list of deficiencies,' said Mrs Dallimore with a shake of her head. 'There again, being made aware of one's deficiencies is no bad thing, so maybe you should tell him, Lizzie.'

At this Mr Sheridan let out an explosive laugh, which seemed to catch him unawares and set off a rattling coughing fit that caused his face to turn an alarming shade of red and his eyes to bulge. He pulled a handkerchief from his pocket to cover his mouth and when he'd managed to get his breathing back under control – and Lizzie was sure he was all right – she fetched him a glass of water. But when she'd returned, he'd gone.

'He suddenly remembered it was time for his appointment

over at the medical wing,' Mrs Dallimore said.

'There's nothing seriously wrong with him, is there?' asked Lizzie anxiously.

'Not that I know of, but mercifully he isn't the sort to share his every medical detail with all and sundry. Oh, look,' she said, her attention caught by something outside, 'there's that young man who's recently started doing the gardening here.' She gave Lizzie a sidelong glance. 'I heard you wrestled him to the ground yesterday.'

Lizzie watched Jed pushing a wheelbarrow across the lawn, his head bobbing in time with whatever music it was he was listening to through a pair of headphones. 'If I *had* wrestled with him he wouldn't be well enough to strut around like a prancing peacock,' she said coolly.

'He strikes me as a little unconventional,' said Mrs Dallimore thoughtfully, 'but not what I would call a peacock.' Then: 'Tell me about this boyfriend of yours. What's his name and is he very handsome?'

Amused that Mrs Dallimore had no compunction in questioning her about Curt, but Mr Sheridan had been accused of nosiness when he had, Lizzie sat down next to her. The honest answer was that Curt wasn't what you'd call obviously handsome; the balance of his face was off-centre, his nose was slightly crooked having been broken when he was a teenager, and his chin protruded with a forcefulness that reflected his eagerness to get hold of life and wring from it all that he wanted. For Lizzie, his attractiveness lay in the dynamism of his energetic personality. 'He's good-looking in an unconventional way,' she said in answer to the question.

'And does this lucky boy have a name?'

The thought of Curt hearing himself described as a boy made Lizzie smile. 'His name's Curt and he's forty-two, so far from being a boy.'

'An older, more experienced man … well, that has its attraction, doesn't it? And what does Curt do?'

'You sound like my parents writing out a potential

son-in-law application form,' Lizzie said. 'He works at the radio station where I used to; he was my boss.' Then, reluctant to go into any more detail about Curt, particularly his marital status – the old lady might not approve of that – Lizzie changed the subject and asked Mrs Dallimore to continue with her story of her life on board the *Belle Etoile*.

Chapter Eighteen

April 1939, SS *Belle Etoile*

Of course, this wasn't the first time Clarissa had crossed the Atlantic. She had made the journey with her parents from France to New York when she was five years old, but her memories of the trip were scant and muddled. This time she would remember everything about her time on board the *Belle Etoile*; not a single detail would she forget.

With only one day left until they arrived in England, Clarissa was conscious that she was going to miss the company of her new friends, especially Effie, who was so much fun to be around and was always rounding them up to play some game or other.

This morning it was deck quoits, and after Clarissa and Effie had soundly beaten Ellis and Artie, much to Ellis's annoyance, Clarissa was now teasing him for being a poor loser and sulking.

'Ignore him, Clarissa,' Effie said. 'He's full of spit and vinegar and so used to getting his own way, he can't abide giving ground to anybody else. Isn't that so, my darling?'

'I guess that makes us two of a kind.' He scowled at Effie and tightened the woollen scarf around his neck. 'I need a drink,' he said, staring out at the sea. 'All this sea air is making me thirsty.'

Effie drew her pretty, well-defined brows together and pouted. 'You're always thirsty.'

Ignoring her, he pushed his hair back from his forehead, shoved his hands deep into the pockets of his cream flannel trousers, then sauntered off without another word.

They watched him walk away. 'What's wrong with him today?' Effie asked Artie. 'Why's he such a misery? He's no right spoiling our fun!'

'He received a cable this morning, but wouldn't say what it was. All I know is that after he'd read it his mood altered.'

'Was it from his parents?'

Artie nodded. 'I believe so.'

'I suppose they're on at him again about not staying in Europe for too long.' Effie turned to Clarissa. 'His mother's a vile woman who wants to marry him off to an equally vile creature of her choosing, the daughter of one of her vile friends. I've a good mind to marry him myself just so he can be free of his mother's clutches.'

'That's a little drastic, don't you think?' Artie said.

'If that's what it takes to make him happy,' she replied with a shrug. 'And he does love me, doesn't he?'

'But do you love him?' asked Clarissa.

'Of course I do. We're all madly in love with Ellis. Even you, and you've only known him a couple of days. Isn't that true?'

The blood rushed to Clarissa's face, making her blush. Flustered, she said, 'I wouldn't say that, exactly, I only—'

Artie came to her rescue. 'But she's not crazy enough to want to marry him on a whim,' he said lightly.

Effie disregarded his comment and held onto her hair, which was being blown about by the wind. 'Come on,' she said, 'let's go find Ellis and get to the bottom of what's troubling him and then we'll go for lunch.'

Clarissa looked at her watch. 'I'd better not,' she said. 'I promised Marjorie I'd have lunch with her.'

'Oh, really? But I don't want to lose you for a single second today, not when it's our last full day together. Artie, make Clarissa change her mind.'

'It's my experience that only a fool attempts to change a woman's mind,' Artie said with a small smile.

'In that case, let's kidnap her! How does that sound, Clarissa? What ransom shall we ask for you?'

'As fun as that sounds, I fear Marjorie probably wouldn't offer you a dime in exchange for me.'

'Then if she's so mean, why have lunch with her?'

'Because she's a well-brought-up girl who doesn't want to offend or appear impolite,' Artie suggested.

'But what about offending me?' Effie retorted.

Artie laughed. 'Go on, I dare you to stamp your foot to emphasise your displeasure.'

Effie pouted. 'Artie Bloomberg, I never thought I'd say this, but you're becoming more and more like Ellis.'

'Does that mean you might want to marry me one day?'

'And becoming much too clever into the bargain,' she said with a roll of her eyes. 'Well then, in the time we've stood here debating the point, we could have found poor Ellis and cheered him up. Clarissa, come seek us out the minute you can, or perhaps we'll come and rescue you. Yes, that's what we'll do, we'll mount a rescue mission!'

It hadn't taken any time at all for Clarissa to understand that Effie was used to getting her own way, just as Ellis was. Clarissa didn't mind; she quite understood that for a star of Effie's stature it was all part of who she was, or what she had become through fame coming to her at so young an age.

Reminders of Effie's fame were never far away. Passengers would often stop to talk to Effie and ask for her autograph, or have their photograph taken with her. To her credit, Effie never disappointed; she willingly signed their scraps of paper, or menu cards that people brought to her table while she was eating. It was usually Ellis who would eventually drive them away with one of his fearsome looks that said, very plainly, enough was enough, that Effie was entitled to some privacy.

He would, Clarissa surmised as she located Marjorie in the dining room for lunch, make an ideal husband for Effie: he would protect her and keep her grounded – as much as anyone could.

'You haven't changed your dress,' Marjorie greeted her disagreeably.

This was a familiar refrain from the older woman who, along with many other passengers, changed her outfit for every meal. Clarissa had opted to take a less ostentatious stance and change only for dinner. Just as Effie did.

'I didn't want to be late,' she said, allowing their waiter to pull out her chair for her and acknowledging the other passengers around the table, a number of whom were new to her. Since surfacing from her *mal de mer*, Marjorie had made it her business to surround herself with a rota of dining companions she deemed appropriate, or worth knowing. Without exception they were all as dull as ditchwater.

'Well, you failed in that instance,' Marjorie said. 'I make you late by a good ten minutes.'

'I apologise; I was playing deck quoits. Have I delayed things very much?' Clarissa knew she hadn't; there were plenty of empty tables in the dining room and nobody was eating yet. Marjorie was tediously early for everything.

'I suppose you were cosying up to that Effie Chase again, weren't you?' Marjorie said accusingly, her voice lowered while their fellow diners chatted amongst themselves and studied the menu. 'I hope you realise you'll have gained yourself a reputation for being a hanger-on. I would strongly recommend you be a lot more circumspect in the friendships you make when you're in England. I really do wonder what your grandmother was thinking when she agreed to let you travel on your own.'

'She must have believed it would be good for me, a means to broaden my horizons,' Clarissa replied equably, though she knew this was far from the truth. And to prevent me from becoming as boring and narrow-minded as you, she thought, turning her attention to the menu, while at the same time listening to Mr Lockwood across the table from her. A New York stockbroker, he was saying that in his opinion all the talk of war looming in Europe was greatly exaggerated;

moreover, he believed that Germany was to be applauded for what it was doing for its people and the economy of the country.

It was when their soup had been brought to the table that Clarissa spotted Effie make her appearance in the dining room. As always, Ellis and Artie accompanied her, but Betty was also alongside. Understandably, Betty had not repeated the experience of dining with Marjorie again, but Clarissa had enjoyed her company outside of the dining room many times. They had swapped contact details and Betty had made her swear to stay in touch. 'I want to know all about the adventures you get up to in England,' she'd said. 'Not a detail is to be left out!'

To Clarissa's surprise Effie came towards their table. 'There you are, Clarissa,' she said. 'I've been looking all over for you.' Then adopting one of her most dazzling smiles, she turned her focus to Marjorie and the others around the table. 'I have the teeniest of favours to ask of you,' she said with a flutter of eyelashes and a breathy voice that had the instant effect of reducing Mr Lockwood to a state of open-mouthed awe. 'My father has requested Clarissa join us for the gala dinner tonight. In any other circumstance I wouldn't dream of being so rude as to make such a request, but it's our last night and it would be just wonderful for us to spend it together. What do you say, Marjorie? I can call you Marjorie, can't I? Please say yes, I'll be utterly heartbroken if you say no.'

'Very well,' Marjorie replied, doubtless sinking under the weight of expectation from not just Effie, but their fellow diners who, to a person, gave the impression that they would love nothing better than to dine with Effie themselves.

'Say, why don't we all meet for cocktails beforehand?' suggested somebody.

The man received a withering glance of disapproval from Marjorie. 'You're forgetting the captain's cocktail party, Mr Shaughnessy,' she said firmly.

Once again Effie applied the full charm of her smile. 'Why, that's even better, we'll see you there later then. Toodle-pip,' she added with a flutter of her fingers, 'it was just swell to meet you all.'

A first-rate performance, thought Clarissa with a smile as she picked up her soup spoon. She wondered how easy it would be for her to employ some of Effie's tricks when she arrived in London and unpacked her new, more confident self.

The captain's cocktail party was an event that Marjorie had been looking forward to, despite grumbling constantly that she had scarcely set eyes on the man throughout the crossing, and that when she had been invited to sit at the captain's table he had been otherwise engaged. But now her moment had arrived and, as Clarissa watched her wait her turn to shake the elusive man's hand as they entered the Pole Star Lounge where the party was already in full flow, she wondered whether the dreadful woman would harangue or flatter him.

It turned out she was able to do neither because no sooner had she grasped the poor man's hand than he deftly moved her along to the purser on his left and was shaking Clarissa's hand and engaging her in conversation. 'I believe you are a friend of Madame Betty,' he said in a rich French accent. 'Such a charming woman. Have you enjoyed your stay on board the *Belle Etoile*?'

'I've had a wonderful time, thank you,' Clarissa replied, surprised that he was so well informed.

'Madame Betty said that you were born in France, is that true?'

'Yes, my parents lived there for a time.'

'Maybe one day you will return.'

'Who knows,' she said, trying to sound enigmatic, 'perhaps I will.' And conscious, not just of the guests behind her waiting to meet the captain, but of Marjorie's icy glare on her, she moved on.

'If your grandmother could see you now, such shameless and improper behaviour!' Marjorie hissed when they'd stepped away from the receiving line. 'Monopolising the captain like that when he has so many other passengers to speak to – you have a lot to learn, young lady!'

Indeed I have, thought Clarissa happily, spotting Betty waving to her. Dressed in a vermilion creation with a matching turban, she stood out magnificently in the crowded room. 'Seeing as I'm such a vulgar disappointment to you,' Clarissa said, 'I'll spare you the embarrassment of spending any time with me and leave you to your friends.' And before Marjorie had a chance to express her outrage, she sped off towards Betty, grabbing a cocktail from a waiter as she went.

'I don't care what it is,' she said to Betty, raising the glass to her lips, 'but it's got to be less bitter than Marjorie's acid tongue. I swear if she disembarks the ship alive tomorrow, it'll be a miracle!'

'And a very grave mistake!' Betty laughed.

They were still laughing when Effie sashayed over in an ivory silk gown that trailed the floor. Taking care not to step on the dress, Ellis and Artie followed behind, both dressed in tuxedos and looking devastatingly handsome.

'Good gravy, don't you all look glamorous,' Betty cried, 'I'm not fit to be seen in your company!'

'Oh, stuff and nonsense!' Effie replied, slipping her arm through Betty's. 'Now you *are* joining us on our table for dinner, aren't you? I absolutely insist. I won't take no for an answer, Betty.'

'In that case, I shall be honoured.'

'Excellent. We shall be quite a party. What a hoot we'll have!'

The evening proved to be tremendous fun and, as with previous nights, culminated in the Rhapsody Bar. Clarissa knew that she had drunk more than was good for her, but she was enjoying herself too much to care.

'I think I like you better when you're a little drunk,' Ellis said when they were dancing and he held her tightly against him.

She laughed gaily and wagged her finger at him. 'I'm tipsy. Not drunk. There's a distinction.'

He smiled. 'And how would a well-brought-up girl like you know a thing like that?'

'Because I'm not as well-brought-up as you believe! And you know, I think I like myself a little better when I'm tipsy. I should drink too much more often.'

'I wouldn't recommend it.'

She tapped her forefinger against the starched front of his dress shirt. 'I shall do as I damn well like, thank you very much!'

His eyes widened. 'I can't decide whether to slap you for your behaviour or kiss you.'

'Be warned, if you slap me, I shall slap you back.'

His lips curled into a smile of amusement. 'In that case you leave me no alternative.'

Chapter Nineteen

'Good gravy, as Betty would have said, don't tell me you let that scoundrel take such a liberty with you, Mrs Dallimore?'

The old lady laughed at Lizzie's question. 'I most certainly did, my dear.'

'You saucy minx, you!'

'Who's a saucy minx?'

It was Mr Sheridan, shambling in with what Lizzie now recognised as his customary air of rumpled affability.

'Just someone I used to know,' said Mrs Dallimore, giving Lizzie a small conspiratorial smile. 'What's that you have in your hands?' she asked Mr Sheridan.

'A list of activities and outings for the coming weeks that I picked up on my way back from the medical wing. There's a trip to the theatre in Cambridge planned, fancy it?'

'I don't think so.'

'Oh, come on, Mrs D, live a little. Don't you want to escape Woodside for a few hours? We could even sneak off and enjoy an illicit drink together. What do you say?'

'I'd say my sneaking-off days are well behind me; why don't you try one of the younger, more sprightly ladies?'

'What, and have them run me ragged? I'd sooner take my chances with you.'

If they were sixty years younger Lizzie would have been inclined to tell them to get a room, but leaving them to their amusing banter, she went to find out what needed doing next.

Stripping beds and room-cleaning was the answer. With one of the cleaners off sick, Matron had asked if Lizzie would help them out for the day. 'I know it's not what you volunteered to do, but I'd be enormously grateful if you would help,' Jennifer had explained. Armed with a trolley of bed linen and a ton of cleaning things, including a vacuum cleaner with a snaky hose that had a mind of its own, Lizzie set to work.

The first room she had to clean was Mrs Dallimore's and as she stripped the bed, she thought of a tipsy Mrs Dallimore smooching on the dance floor with a green-eyed man she'd only known a few days. *What further liberties had the young Mrs Dallimore allowed the badass bounder to take?* Lizzie wondered with a smile. And if any man threatened to slap her, even in jest, he'd get short shrift and make no mistake!

The bed made, she moved on to vacuuming the room, and, not that she would have skimped in another person's room, she did find herself taking extra care because it was Mrs Dallimore's, pushing the end of the vacuum cleaner as far under the furniture as she could reach. There'd be no dustballs on her watch!

Woodside prided itself on running a 'relationship-centred' care home – a description Lizzie had previously dismissed as no more than marketing hype, but now, and although she had only been here a few days, she had a sense of already having formed a relationship with Mrs Dallimore. Over the years Mum had often spoken about the residents she had got to know and how upsetting she found it when they died; on more than one occasion she had come home in tears. Lizzie had once asked her mother why she put herself through the torment when there were plenty of other voluntary jobs she could do that wouldn't be so upsetting. Mum's answer had been that the privilege of getting to know these people far outweighed any sadness she experienced.

Lizzie was beginning to get a glimmer of that feeling herself. These people mattered. They'd experienced all manner of life's ups and downs, joys and disappointments, and all had their own stories to tell. They weren't just faceless nobodies, as she'd previously thought: they were real people who counted.

She was pushing the hose of the vacuum cleaner under the bed when it bumped against something hard. On her hands and knees, she took a look and saw a small old-fashioned brown leather suitcase. Pushing it to one side, she carried on and with her head near the noisy end of the vacuum cleaner, she didn't hear the door open. It was only when she was reversing away from the bed that she started. She wasn't alone; Mrs Dallimore was there in her wheelchair, the door closed behind her.

Lizzie switched off the vacuum cleaner. 'How did you get here?' she asked, knowing that the old lady didn't have the strength in her arms to wheel herself round.

'Mr Sheridan kindly gave me a push.'

'I think you've won an admirer there,' said Lizzie with a smile.

'What nonsense.'

'Not nonsense at all, he's definitely sweet on you.'

'I think the excitement of seeing your boyfriend tomorrow has gone to your head. I'm surprised to see you cleaning, I didn't think befrienders did that.'

Lizzie explained she was doing it as a favour to help out. Getting to her feet, and smoothing out the wrinkles in her jeans at the backs of her legs, she suggested she came back later to finish.

'No need for that,' Mrs Dallimore replied. She turned to the small bookcase on the wall next to the French doors. 'I have a sudden urge to reread something I loved as a young girl, *Little Women*. My mother used to read it to me. And that, before you dare to think it, does not mean I'm reverting to being a child.'

'I wouldn't dream of thinking such a thing,' said Lizzie, going over to manoeuvre the old lady nearer to the bookcase. She then picked up a cloth and set about dusting, trying hard not to appear as though she was snooping and checking out the woman's few possessions. Next to the bed was a very old leather photograph frame, the sort that contained two photographs and could be folded shut. It took all her powers of restraint not to study the faded black and white pictures in detail. From what she could see there were two young boys in one photograph and an even younger little boy in the other. She would have loved to ask who they were, but in view of all the rooms she had to clean she didn't dare prompt a conversation she wouldn't want to stop.

'You can ask me who they are, you know,' said Mrs Dallimore. 'I shan't mind.'

'Sorry,' Lizzie said, 'I didn't mean to pry.'

'I know that. I like curiosity in a person; it shows an interest in something other than oneself. The boy on his own is Nicholas, my son, and the other two are Thomas and Walter, two boys who I looked upon as sons.'

Mrs Dallimore stopped the obvious question on Lizzie's lips – where were those boys now? – in its tracks. 'I'll tell you about them another time,' she said firmly. 'For now I mustn't keep you. But if I could trouble you to open the French doors and push me outside to the patio, I'll sit there out of your way.'

Lizzie did as she said, then went back to her cleaning, but not before taking another look at the black and white photographs of the three boys. She sensed that whatever Mrs Dallimore told her about them, a happy ending would not be forthcoming.

Chapter Twenty

How wonderful it was to be back in London. 'Here I am, everyone!' Lizzie wanted to shout. 'Have you missed me? Because I've missed you!'

She fairly bounced along Shoreditch High Street to where Curt had asked her to meet him. It was a bar she'd never been to before, a mile or so away from the building Starlight Radio had been broadcasting from since its creation eight years ago. They had always been careful where they'd met for their secret rendezvous and though a part of Lizzie had felt guilty, the thrill that they were escaping into a world that existed only for them had always accompanied their moments together. Initially she would have been happy for the secrecy and exclusion to go on forever, enjoying having Curt all to herself as well as fooling her friends with enigmatic answers to their questions about what she was getting up to when she wasn't seeing them, but then, out of the blue, had come the need to share Curt with her friends, to show him off. 'See,' she'd wanted to say, '*this* is the reason I've been so secretive lately, isn't he fantastic? Don't you just love him?'

She took a deep breath to quell her excitement at seeing Curt again, an excitement that was tinged with apprehension because this was an important and defining moment between them, she was sure of it. Maybe from today there would be no more secrecy; no more would she be branded *the other woman*. She made no apology for descending to the depths of Hallmark card thinking – every bit of her was convinced that this really was the first day of the rest of their lives together.

A quick scan around the bar revealed that she had arrived

before Curt. Which gave her time to nip into the ladies and make sure she was looking her best. After a cursory touch-up of lippy and a brush through her hair, she went back out to the bar, ordered herself a glass of Merlot and took it over to a corner table as far away from the window as possible. It had always been one of their many rules when meeting: no window seats. But perhaps after today the old rules would no longer apply.

With its over-the-top kitsch glam and a generous side order of Alice in Wonderland thrown in, the bar could not have been further removed from the kind of place Curt generally favoured. She smiled at the incongruity of him sitting here with her and wondered if his choice was somehow symbolic. Of what, she couldn't really say.

Tess was in the kitchen baking. With Lizzie in London for the day and Tom and Freddie out feeding the ducks, the house was filled with a much-needed quiet calm. It reminded her of the days when Luke and Lizzie were babies and she'd relish the time while they napped. Goodness, how she'd filled those minutes, squeezing into them as many chores as she could – hanging out the washing, preparing the evening meal for when Tom returned from work, flicking a duster round and doing whatever else it was that needed doing. Invariably, Lizzie would be first to wake and more often than not just when Tess had sat down with a cup of coffee. If she was lucky she would have Lizzie fed and her nappy changed by the time Luke woke.

She often thought she was better organised back then than she was now, when, to all intents and purposes, she had all the time in the world. Or was that an illusion, the mind play-ing games with the memories, filtering out the worst of the mayhem of living with twins? Tom called it the pick-and-mix of selective memory.

She certainly wished she could be selective with the mix of emotions she felt towards Lorna. The pettiness of the woman wouldn't be out of place in the school playground. After dropping Lizzie off at the station this morning, Tess had called in at the community shop on the way home and while she was waiting in the queue to pay for some milk, Marian Bainbridge came in.

A bossyboots woman, Marian had long since seized autocratic rule over the village, a despot who loved to take command and offload the work onto the shoulders of others and then take all the credit. Increasingly, when yet again she had fired off a volley of orders and diktats for some village cause or event, she instilled in Tess the ludicrous desire to stick out her tongue behind the woman's back.

Not surprisingly the woman had been clutching a bundle of papers in her hands – she was either distributing leaflets or, more likely, on the prowl for others to do it for her. With no avoiding her (the shop was much too small for that), Tess had put on her best positive face and braced herself.

'Ah, just the woman I was looking for!' announced Marian. 'Harvest Supper rota. You can add your name to the list of helpers, either to cook or serve.'

'It's a bit early to start planning for the supper, isn't it?' Tess had replied. 'It's ages away.'

'Preparation is all. Now then, I imagine you'll want to do the same as last year. But you'll have to find a new partner, Lorna's signed up to wait on tables with Rosamund Beccles.'

There was no question as to whether Tess wanted or indeed was available to help – there never was – and suddenly the arrogant presumption of the woman had filled Tess with the horrifying urge to tell Marian exactly where she could stick her Harvest Supper rota. Fearing she might do exactly that, she had marched straight out of the shop, forgetting all about the milk she had gone in for.

With the finishing touches to the lemon drizzle cake now complete, Tess felt ashamed of her behaviour towards Marian. The woman might be the bane of many a life in the village, but she didn't deserve to be on the receiving end of such rudeness – rudeness triggered by the hurt Tess had felt at learning that Lorna had chosen to partner Rosamund Beccles and not her. Lorna could not have made her feelings or intentions clearer had she posted a sign on the village noticeboard.

And it was all thanks to Lizzie.

The thought slipped out treacherously, wholly unbidden, and Tess shooed it away guiltily. Lizzie may have triggered the situation in which they now found themselves, but it was Lorna who was taking things to an absurdly spiteful level.

It was with considerable effort that Tess now made the decision, no matter how tempting and instinctive it was, that she wouldn't stoop to the tactic of two-can-play-at-that-game. She was better than that. Well, she probably wasn't, but she would take the coward's way out and engineer things so that she and Tom were otherwise engaged for the evening of the Harvest Supper.

That decided, she turned her attention to this evening, when Luke and Ingrid would be joining them before taking Freddie home for the weekend. She still felt guilty about the tumble Freddie had taken from his pushchair through her carelessness, and was at pains to prove to Ingrid that her precious son had come to no real harm. Or more importantly, that he was perfectly safe in his grandmother's care.

The potatoes peeled, and at the sound of Freddie's cheery sing-song voice chattering away to Tom as they came round the back of the house and into the garden, Tess wondered how Lizzie was getting on in London. It had been good to see her with such a bright and happy smile on her face, but with a mother's instinct to protect and cherish, Tess hoped her daughter wasn't underestimating the difficulties ahead if Curt really was about to leave his wife for her. There was no getting away from the crucial fact that the consequences of such a decision, though not insurmountable, would last forever because there was a child involved – a little girl who would effectively become a second grandchild to Tess and

Tom if things progressed the way Lizzie hoped they would. Tess hadn't previously considered the prospect of this with any real seriousness, but now she knew she ought to.

'Sorry I'm late,' Curt said, pulling out the old wooden school chair across the table from Lizzie. He removed the large leather bag that was slung across his chest and shoulder and dropped it on the floor next to his feet. 'It's been a bugger of a morning; Cal's driving me mad with his constant whinge-ing. Sorry, forget I said any of that: the last thing you want to hear is shop talk.'

Lizzie smiled; he could recite the phone book to her and she'd be deliriously content. 'I want to hear everything,' she said. 'Give me all the gossip, leave nothing out!' She shook her head and the smile turned into a laugh. 'It's so fantastic to see you. I've missed you so much. I've missed being *us*. If you know what I mean.'

'Yeah, I know what you mean,' he said. He turned to look around them. Old habits, thought Lizzie, he's checking for anybody here who might know him. The bar had filled up since she'd arrived and revealed itself to be a popular hangout for hipsters; it was wall-to-wall beards and skinny jeans. 'I've missed you too,' he said, his gaze now back on her. 'Work isn't as fun without you there.'

'I should hope not,' she said, sliding her hand across the table, the tips of her fingers meeting his. Touching him after so long, even so slight a touch, was enough to send her senses reeling. That was the effect he'd always had on her: he made everything seem that much more intense and vibrant. As if knowing the effect he was having on her, he lifted his hand, placed it firmly over hers. 'I want you to promise me something,' he said, staring directly into her eyes.

Suddenly her chest felt tight and her throat constricted. This was it. This was the moment she had been waiting for. She willed herself not to look too jubilant, to bear in mind how difficult this must be for him. 'Go on,' she murmured.

'I want you to promise that you won't overreact,' he said, 'that you'll try and understand what I'm about to tell you.'

At the seriousness of his voice, a chill ran through her. 'What are you about to tell me?' she managed to say.

'Promise me first,' he said. 'Promise you won't get upset.'

'Why would I be upset?' she asked, her heart beating double time.

'Because, Lizzie, it has to end between us. I can't see you again. Not ever.'

She swallowed. She tried to say something but failed. But inside her head a voice was screaming a deafeningly loud *Nooooo!*

'I'm sorry,' he said, 'and please believe me, it's not what I want.'

'Curt,' she finally said, 'you're not making sense. If you don't want it to end between us, then don't end it, it's as simple as that.'

He leant forward. 'It's not simple, Lizzie. It's anything but simple. Come on, don't make this any more difficult for me than it already is; you're an intelligent girl, surely you can see it from where I'm standing.'

'What's changed? You told me you were leaving your wife, that you just needed time to prepare the way. You said you needed space to get things sorted. You came back from your holiday early because you'd told your wife that your marriage wasn't working, that you wanted a divorce.' Now that she had found her voice, it had risen sharply and was in danger of rising further.

'You promised you wouldn't get upset,' Curt muttered, his eyes darting anxiously towards the nearby tables.

'I didn't promise anything! And pardon me, but I think I have a perfect right to be as upset as I want. What's more, you haven't answered my question. What's changed?'

'My wife's pregnant.'

When Lizzie didn't respond, and as if thinking she might not understand, he said, 'She's expecting our second child.

So you see, I can't leave her. It's just not possible. You understand that, don't you? Another child changes things. That's why we came back from Greece earlier than planned. She wasn't feeling well, turned out she was pregnant and not suffering from some bug she thought she'd picked up at the hotel.' He frowned. 'And I don't know where you got the idea that I'd told my wife while we were away that I wanted a divorce.'

Her mind spinning, and like a drowning person, Lizzie reached out to the only solid fact within her grasp. 'You told me you weren't sleeping together.'

He lowered his gaze to the wedding ring on his finger. 'Don't be naive, Lizzie, and really, I shouldn't have to explain myself; she is my wife, after all, we do share the same bed.'

'And what am I? Or more to the point, what *was* I? Your mistress? Your easy bit of stuff on the side? The stupid idiot you could shag on your desk when the mood took you, when perhaps your wife wouldn't oblige?'

His eyes narrowed. 'Don't try that one with me. You were up for it as much as I was. You knew I was married. You knew what you were getting into, just as I did.'

'But you said you loved me! You said you were going to leave your wife. None of that was true, was it? You didn't love me at all, did you?'

'Would it make it easier for you if I said I did? Would it really make any difference?'

She stared at him in disbelief. 'Easier?' she repeated, stunned. 'You bastard! You cold-hearted bastard. I really never knew you at all. All the time I had you down as a man who cared. A man who felt things passionately. But I got that wrong. You don't care a stuff about me. You don't care that because of you I've lost everything. *Everything!*'

He shook his head. 'Don't be melodramatic, Lizzie, it doesn't suit you. Besides, you've found yourself another job without too much trouble, haven't you?'

This was too much for her. 'I'm a volunteer in an old

people's home! Do you think that's what I want to be doing? Do you? Do you really?'

Again he looked around him. 'Keep your voice down. At least try and behave like the adult you're supposed to be.'

'I don't believe I'm hearing this. *You're* lecturing *me* on how to behave. Unbelievable!'

'Come on, Lizzie, keep it together, for God's sake. Just accept that it was good while it lasted, but now we need to part on amicable terms.'

'Do we? Why?'

'Because it would be so much better if we did. And think about it, I can't be that much of a bastard if I've gone to the trouble to end it with you face to face – a lesser man would have done it by text. Can't we part in a civilised fashion?'

She sat back in her chair and contemplated this ruthless stranger before her. Where had he sprung from? This wasn't the Curt she knew, the fun Curt she had fallen in love with. Or had she got him wrong from the start? Had she deceived herself as much as he had deceived her? Had she really been that dumb?

'Lizzie? I said, can't we part in—'

'I heard you,' she said abruptly, suddenly seeing things clearly. 'You want us to part on good terms, maybe even with a handshake, and for no other reason than you're terrified I'm going to make trouble for you, aren't you? You're worried I'm going to turn into some kind of crazy stalker determined to make your life a living hell.'

He narrowed his eyes. 'I wouldn't advise you to do that.'

'Why not?'

'You're not that sort of a girl.'

'Maybe you've turned me into that sort of a girl; a nutjob bunny boiler. Frankly after what you've done to me, I'd be perfectly justified in turning up on your doorstep one day when you're at work and letting your wife know what you get up to behind her back.'

He planted his hands firmly on the table and leant across it. 'Do that and you'll regret it.'

'Ooh, scary Curt,' she said mockingly. 'Why, what will you do to me?'

'It's not what I'd do; it's how you'll end up making yourself feel: cheap and full of bitter self-loathing.'

'And you think I don't already feel that?'

He shook his head wearily, as though he were dealing with a recalcitrant child. 'I expected more from you, Lizzie.'

'I bet you did. Well, go home to your wife and adorable daughter and tell them what a wonderful husband and father you are. I hope you can live with yourself.' She picked up her glass and, delighting in seeing him flinch, added, 'Don't worry, I wouldn't waste a drop of good Merlot on you, you're so not worth it.'

She raised the glass to her lips and drained it in one satisfying swallow. Putting the glass down on the table with exaggerated care, she stood up.

No stumbling, she warned herself as she made it towards the open doorway and out onto the street. And no tears. Do not, on pain of death, give him that satisfaction.

Chapter Twenty-One

Oh, for pity's sake, thought Ingrid, was she the only one who wasn't surprised by this turn of events? A married man ending a sordid fling in favour of not leaving his pregnant wife? Who'd have imagined such a thing! Really, when was Lizzie going to grow up and stand on her own two feet? Would she ever stop running home to her family, expecting them to make everything better for her?

None of this Ingrid actually said aloud, but if she had to listen to any more histrionics from Lizzie she might literally burst with the superhuman effort it was taking to keep her mouth shut. The best she could do was offer little nods of sympathy while the diatribe rocketed on, seemingly without end. Yes, yes, *yes*, she wanted to shout, we heard you say it the first time, the man's a liar and a cheat and played you for a fool, there's no need to keep telling us!

An hour later and with a fresh torrent of tears now streaming down Lizzie's face, Ingrid had had enough. Thankfully so had Freddie. For the most part he had been shielded from the drama by either Ingrid or Tom playing with him in the garden, but now that he was overtired and beginning to play up, Ingrid knew she could get away with calling a halt to proceedings and say it was time they were going.

Driving away from Keeper's Nook Freddie said, 'Lizzie sad. Lizzie crying.'

'Yes she's very sad at the moment,' Luke answered him, 'because she heard something very upsetting today. Perhaps we could make her a card tomorrow to cheer her up, would you like to do that?'

Freddie thought about this for a moment. 'Big card,' he said at length and in a sleepy voice. 'With a atterpeer.'

'I'm sure she'd love a card with a picture of a *caterpillar* on it,' Ingrid said. 'After all, that will make everything better for her, won't it?'

Her comment was met with a silence from the back of the car as Freddie's eyes were now shut, but next to her in the front, Luke gave her a sidelong glance. He said nothing, but she knew what that look meant.

Minutes passed – perhaps Luke was waiting to be sure Freddie was properly asleep – then he said, 'You really could make more of an effort, you know.'

'What do you mean?'

'You know exactly what I mean. You made no attempt to show any genuine sympathy and understanding for what Lizzie's going through.'

'That's not fair. I'd defy anyone to have got a word in edgeways with you all rushing to console her.'

Luke's gaze flickered from the road to Ingrid again, then back to the road. 'Couldn't you just once try looking at something subjectively?' he said. 'You're always so detached. It's as if you're incapable of—' He broke off abruptly.

'Go on,' she said. 'What am I incapable of?'

He shook his head. 'Forget it. It's nothing.'

'It clearly isn't, or you wouldn't be gripping the steering wheel the way you are or looking so furiously uptight.' And why am I pressing him? Ingrid wondered, knowing that to continue any further with the conversation would serve no purpose other than to dig herself into a deep hole from which there might not be any way out.

Once more, minutes passed. Then: 'Why do you have to have such a downer on my sister? What has she ever done to annoy you so much?'

'What an absurd thing to say,' Ingrid replied. 'Of course I don't have a downer on Lizzie.'

Luke said nothing.

Again, like that sidelong look he'd given her, Ingrid knew his silence spoke volumes – she was being judged, and unfairly so in her opinion. Righteous indignation made her want to defend herself. Nothing infuriated her more than Luke's steadfast loyalty to his sister, a loyalty that precluded him from seeing Lizzie's manifest faults. It appalled Ingrid that he could be so blind. Yet what appalled her more was suspecting Luke might not feel the same loyalty towards *her*.

'Just once,' he muttered, as he was forced to slow down behind a tractor on the winding lane in front of them, 'it would be nice for you to think well of Lizzie.'

The battle to rein in her indignation was lost. 'Are you sure this is a conversation you want to pursue?' Ingrid asked.

'I wouldn't have raised it if I didn't think it was time we did.'

'Sometimes elephants in rooms are best left ignored.'

'So that's your answer, is it, a flat refusal to be honest with me?'

She sighed, exasperated. 'Luke, just leave it, will you? You're turning something that is really quite trivial into something needlessly confrontational. What's got into you?'

'I saw you roll your eyes when Lizzie was crying, that's what's got into me. It was seeing how little you cared. Or more precisely, how little you care for her.'

'Oh, this is ridiculous! Yes, I admit I found her reaction tiresome, because so what that she's been dumped by a man who'd lied to both her and his wife. Shouldn't you be only too pleased that she's rid of him? If I were in her shoes I'd be celebrating.'

'But that's just the point, you don't seem able to put yourself in her shoes. Rightly or wrongly, she was seriously in love with the man and is now heartbroken.'

'Nonsense, she was in *lust* with him.'

'I don't think you, or I, can speak for Lizzie when it comes to what she felt for Curt.'

'She'll get over it. We all do. Who hasn't made a bad

choice and then had to pick themselves up and shake themselves down? And, frankly, it would have done Lizzie more good if you'd taken that line with her instead of pandering to her – to her childish need always to be at the centre of any drama.'

The tractor turned off to the left and Luke sped on. 'Well,' he said, 'I'm glad we have that cleared up.'

'You asked for my honesty, Luke, so please don't now complain about it.'

For all the self-assurance of her words, Ingrid felt anything but sure of herself. The righteous anger she had felt before had now been replaced with grave misgivings at the wisdom of speaking so plainly. Why couldn't Luke have left well alone? And how ironic was it that she, who preferred to take the direct approach, should now be the one wishing Luke had stuck to the Moran script of tiptoeing round what needed to be said.

Chapter Twenty-Two

Saturday morning, and Lizzie was trying to do what she knew was expected of her, and that was attempting to pull herself together, but as it was not yet twenty-four hours after seeing Curt, there were too many parts of her that were resistant to the idea to make it a reality.

She was crushed. Her mind, body and heart were shattered into so many pieces she didn't think she would ever feel the way she used to. The shock of what Curt had done to her had turned her stomach to a queasy, fluttering hollow. Whenever Mum tried to tempt her to eat or drink something, the very thought of it set off the queasy fluttering and made her rush to the bathroom. She had never known a feeling like it. She was sick at heart. Bereft. She would never love or trust anyone ever again.

It staggered her now to think how cool she had played it yesterday with Curt. She didn't know where that strength had come from. It was as if a different person had been sitting at the table opposite Curt while he ruthlessly dispensed with her. How pathetic she now seemed, so eager to see him, so full of happiness that he was going to tell her what she so desperately wanted to hear, that he was leaving his wife.

She had no idea now how she had made the mistake of thinking that was the reason he wanted to see her. Over and over she replayed the conversation they'd had when she'd been on her way home from Woodside and he'd phoned her. But not one word he'd uttered could she now interpret as suggesting things were about to change between them. Certainly not the way she had imagined, or indeed the way it had turned out. Idiot that she was, she had allowed her elation at hearing from him to fill in the blanks of her hopes and desires. It was a mistake she would never make again. Not ever.

Standing at the open window of her bedroom, she looked down at the garden where her father was mowing the lawn. Up and down he went, stripe after immaculate stripe bringing satisfying order to the garden. With tears filling her eyes, she marvelled at the simplicity of her father's life. And her mother's. They lived ordinary lives, but were so happy. By the time they were her age, they'd been married a few years and she and Luke were born. She had never before envied them their lives, but she did so now. How wonderful it must be to have lived through all the major dramas of life and now simply enjoy themselves.

Except now, she realised, she had dumped her problems onto them, and that was wrong. Because of her, Lorna had frozen Mum out and Keith was probably under orders to do the same with Dad. She should never have come back here. But where else could she have gone? And at the time she had truly believed it would be a short-term solution until Curt left his wife.

Had he ever really intended to do that? Lizzie didn't think so. He'd probably lied all along to her. Maybe he'd lied yesterday when he said his wife was pregnant again. He might have said that just to shut her up.

Some of the things he'd said had been downright cruel. He had almost threatened her at one stage – *Do that and you'll regret it*, he'd said when she'd suggested she might talk to his wife. Admittedly that had been the voice of revenge speaking and was something she would never do, but was that the kind of man Curt really was, a man who dished out threats?

What did it matter anyway? She was never going to see him again, so that was an end to it.

Downstairs in the kitchen she found a note on the table that Mum had left for her. Typical Mum! Even though Dad was here to explain her absence, she'd gone to the trouble to let Lizzie know that she was at Woodside helping out with a craft session.

'*I hope you're feeling a little better this morning,*' she'd written. '*Much love. X PS Scotch pancakes in the bread bin, your favourite honey in the usual place.*'

Twenty-four hours ago Lizzie might have laughed at her mother's note for treating her like a ten-year-old, but now the thoughtfulness touched her deeply; it tapped into her inner child who wanted to be wrapped in a great comfort blanket of parental love and be told everything was going to be all right.

She was just thinking that perhaps she could manage a pancake when from nowhere she thought of Simon. Was this how he had felt when she'd dumped him? She hoped not. She really did. Nobody deserved to feel this way.

Or maybe some people did. People like her, for instance. Was this her punishment for treating Simon so badly? Do unto others, blah, blah. It really hadn't felt that bad at the time, the way she'd finished with Simon, but now she knew better. Now she could see how wantonly heartless she had behaved when she'd ended their relationship. In her defence she had been so high on the euphoria of her affair with Curt that all that mattered was that she was free to be with the man she loved. She hadn't really understood that Simon would be desperately upset, for in her selfish need to think only of her own happiness, his had barely figured. He would get over it, had been her view.

But now a sickening and humbling shame crept over her and gave momentum to a fresh and far stronger wave of nausea. With a hand pressed to her mouth, all thoughts of pancakes were forgotten as she rushed to the downstairs loo.

Chapter Twenty-Three

Clarissa had remembered why she had to keep her friends' visits a secret. It was because if she were ever to breathe a word about them she would, in the blink of an eye, be shipped off somewhere else, somewhere a lot less appealing. For Woodside, as caring as it was, did not cater for those whose minds had slipped over the edge into the abyss from where there was no return. And though she reluctantly accepted that she experienced periodic lapses in memory and the occasional muddled confusion, she hoped that so long as she was able to keep a relatively firm grip on what was what, she would be safe. As a test, she reminded herself that she knew what day of the week it was – it was Monday and she was due to see the chiropodist later this afternoon.

But, and it was a considerable but, while knowing full well that her dearest friends were long since dead, when they appeared to her they seemed as real as her own reflection did when she looked in the mirror. They weren't ghosts; she was convinced of that, moreover she could not bring herself to believe in ghostly apparitions. Which left the only plausible possibility: they resided solely in her head.

'Is that what you really think?'

Startled, Clarissa turned sharply to see Ellis leaning nonchalantly against the side of the rose arbour where she was sitting. 'Yes,' she said, 'I do.'

He shrugged. 'Suit yourself.'

'I will. Just as you always did.'

'My, but you're snappy today.'

'As snappy as you always made me feel.'

'Good to know I'm not losing my touch.'

'Oh, you'll never change; you'll always be the same old Ellis. I must say, I might have expected death to mellow you a little.'

'Surely you wouldn't want me to be any different?'

Clarissa laughed. 'No, I don't suppose I would.'

He drew nearer to her, his green eyes as bright as emeralds in the brilliant summer sunlight. 'If I were any different you wouldn't love me, would you?'

'I think it's safe to say I'll always love you,' she said softly, 'just as Artie and Effie always will.'

He stared off into the distance, across the lawn to some faraway point. He began to hum. It was a refrain from so long ago, yet at the same time felt so near and tangible she could reach out and grasp it within her hands.

'*Love is the sweetest thing* ...' she sang along with Ellis, her eyes closed, her body swaying to the music she could hear in her head, and picturing herself dancing with Artie as she had that night on board the *Belle Etoile*, '... *what else on earth could ever bring such happiness to everything as love's old story?*'

She was halfway through the second verse when she felt the coolness of a shadow fall across her. She opened her eyes to find not Ellis standing in front of her, but Lizzie.

'That was nice,' the girl said, 'but it sounded sad. Is it a sad song?'

'It can be whatever you want it to be,' Clarissa said, disconcerted. She turned to see where Ellis had gone. There was no sign of him.

'At the moment everything seems sad to me,' Lizzie said with such feeling that Clarissa stopped thinking about Ellis.

'Oh dear,' she said, 'that doesn't sound good, not for a young girl like you. I've missed you these last few days. Where have you been?'

'I had the weekend off feeling sorry for myself,' she said morosely. 'But never mind me and my knack for attracting trouble. I came to ask if there was anything you needed.'

'I don't need anything, thank you, other than to see you back to your normal happy self,' Clarissa said, noting how pale the poor girl looked. She patted the seat beside her. 'Why don't you sit down and tell me what's wrong? The last time I saw you, you were going to see your boyfriend. How did it go?'

The girl visibly shuddered. 'Not well. Not well at all. And if I told you what happened you'll tell me I've been the biggest fool on the planet. You'll say there's no bigger fool alive.'

'I hate to contradict you, but I think you'll find plenty of us who can equal, or outdo, whatever foolishness you think you're guilty of. What have you done?'

'You'll tell me I should have known better,' Lizzie said as though Clarissa hadn't spoken. 'I guarantee it.'

'What flummery and tomfoolery! Stop telling me what I'll think or say and get on with it. At my age I haven't the time for unnecessary prevarication.'

Lizzie frowned. 'If you're going to be so impatient with me, I'm not sure I want to share anything with you.'

'Fair enough, but just so as you know, I'm not in thrall to childish histrionics.'

'That's not very sympathetic of you.'

'Ah, so it's my sympathy you want, is it? You should have said. How's this for my best sympathetic face?' Clarissa tilted her head to one side and fixed her features into an exaggerated expression of empathy and compassion.

Lizzie smiled. 'Stop it, you're scaring me.'

Clarissa smiled too. 'That's better,' she said. 'Now shall we talk about something else, or do you want to unburden yourself? Yes or no?'

'Please don't ever think about a career in counselling, will you? I'm not sure it's quite your forte. But if you really want to know what a mug I've been, here goes. My boyfriend, my *so-called* boyfriend, was married and after promising he was going to leave his wife, he dumped me on Friday. Apparently his wife is expecting their second child. And I know what you're thinking, that I had no business having an affair with a married man and that I got what I deserved.'

Clarissa tutted. 'As I said before, I do wish you'd stop telling me what I must be thinking or what I'm going to say. Now, as far as I can see, the most important aspect in what you've just told me is this: do you still love the rotter?'

Lizzie smiled faintly. 'Rotter ... what a delightfully quaint way to describe Curt.'

'Is there a term you'd prefer to use?'

'Plenty, none of which I'd dare utter in your presence. But to answer you, I don't know what I feel about him right now. Other than blind anger.'

'Anger's the start on which you can build constructively, so use it wisely. But don't let it rule you. Did you love him very much?'

Lizzie nodded. 'Crazily so,' she murmured. 'I hadn't experienced anything like it.'

'Well, that's a good thing, isn't it? To have known something so extraordinary.'

'It doesn't feel good.'

'No, it won't. For now you'll be feeling wretched and mostly because you're blaming yourself for getting involved with a man whose true colours you can now see all too clearly.' Clarissa reached out and patted Lizzie's hand. 'Things will get better, they always do. Trust me on that. I haven't lived to this great age without learning that the heart mends itself surprisingly well, no matter how deep the cut, or how severe the pain.'

The girl inhaled deeply, before letting her breath out in a long weary sigh. 'I hope you're right.' Then: 'Will you tell me some more about your life, when you were young and came to England?'

Clarissa smiled. 'If it will help take your mind off things, yes, of course.'

Chapter Twenty-Four

April 1939, London, England

The *Belle Etoile* reached the south-west of England two hours later than scheduled, the time lost to the mid-Atlantic storm never having been made up. Clarissa had been warned that the luxurious days spent on board the magnificent ship would remove all sense of reality and when she stepped off the ship at Plymouth she was brought up short by the truth of this. In an instant the real world eclipsed all that had gone before, and confronted with a busy and boisterous crowd going about the business of dealing with the arrival of so many people, she was sorely tempted to turn tail and flee to the comfort and security of the *Belle Etoile*. Standing alone on the dockside with a sharp wind tugging at her hat, nothing could have made her feel more isolated as she prepared to fight her way through the throng.

Eventually, and with the help of a porter, she boarded the Great Western Railway train bound for Paddington and took her seat in one of the Super Saloon coaches surrounded by fellow passengers heading for the same destination: London. No sooner had the whistle been blown and the train began pulling out of the station than she felt the absence of her newly made friends who'd stayed behind for the final leg of the journey to Le Havre. Marjorie had remained on board too, and her farewell to Clarissa could not have been cooler, or more censorious.

'I shall be writing to your grandmother to say that I have carried out her wishes to the best of my ability,' she'd intoned, 'but I shall make it plain that I fear for your safety from here on, if for no other reason than you seem determined to act against every ounce of common sense with which you were born.'

Glad to be rid of the woman, Clarissa had departed from her as good-naturedly as she could before rushing off to find Effie and the others. They had kissed and hugged her goodbye with promises made to visit her in London just as soon as they could. The only person not to promise to see her again was Ellis. 'I never make promises I can't be sure I shall be able to keep,' he said, his hands pushed deep into the pockets of his trousers and leaning against the rail.

'Take no notice of him,' Betty had said, moving in again to hug Clarissa one more time. 'Of course he'll see you in London. We all will!'

Her first impression of England was that it was not the dreary, waterlogged place Marjorie had claimed it to be; instead it more than lived up to her mother's fond description of a landscape as beautiful as any in the world. And certainly, as Clarissa watched from the window of the carriage, taking in the softly undulating countryside and the lovely villages glimpsed in the distance – thatched cottages with gardens pretty with spring flowers and pink and white blossom, ancient stone churches and endless fields of green – she was filled with an eagerness to explore this country, to feel the earth beneath her feet, to breathe in the cool refreshing air.

Despite her excitement and the desire to absorb every minute of the train journey, lack of sleep from the previous night when she hadn't got to bed until nearly three in the morning inevitably got the better of her and she slept heavily until she was woken by the woman in the seat opposite tapping her gently on the arm.

'We're in London now, honey,' the woman said.

Momentarily disorientated, Clarissa blinked hard and peered out of the window. Sure enough, there was a large sign with *Paddington* written across it. The platform was busy with people milling around, and she pressed her face to the window hoping to spot the woman who had been her mother's oldest friend. With no luck, she gathered up her things and followed behind the couple with whom she'd shared the carriage.

It was some time before she was reunited with her luggage and while a cheery porter took care of it, she straightened her hat and looked up and down the platform for her godmother. No, she wasn't there.

'Where to then, miss?' asked the porter.

She hesitated. Should she find some sort of tearoom and wait, or maybe find a taxi? After all, she had her godmother's address.

'I'm not sure,' she said at length. 'Somebody is supposed to be—' She broke off at the sound of a silvery voice ringing out clearly above the melee of activity on the platform.

'Yoo-hoo! A thousand apologies! What must you think of me turning up late like this? You've crossed the Atlantic and all I've had to do is cross London!'

The woman striding towards her was tall and strikingly dressed in a pair of grey flannel trousers and a silk blouse with a close-fitting jacket. Perched on her head was a pale grey hat that was tipping precariously to one side – the large dent to it at the front suggested it might well have recently fallen off and been trodden on.

Before Clarissa had a chance to say anything, the woman looked at her hard. 'How perfectly extraordinary,' she said, 'you really are the absolute spit of your mother, I'd know you anywhere! Which is just as well, as otherwise I could have made a frightful ass of myself!'

Wondering if she would ever get a word in edgeways, but remembering the promise she had made to reinvent herself when she made it to England, at the same time recalling how effortlessly Effie could slip into character, Clarissa stuck out her hand confidently. 'And you must be Polly Sinclair,' she said. 'You look just like you do in the photograph you sent me. I'm so very pleased to meet you at last, I hope it wasn't too much trouble for you to come for me.'

'Nonsense, it's the least I can do. Have you had a dreadfully tedious journey?'

'Quite the contrary, it's been fun and very enlightening.'

'Excellent! I do so hate a poor traveller, especially Americans, who complain of simply everything. And before you take offence, I don't regard you as American. You're Frannie's daughter and that makes you as English as me. Now come along, I have my car parked outside.' She paused to look at the trolley of Clarissa's luggage and the porter who was patiently waiting for his instructions. 'Hmm ... this little lot will have to be sent on separately.' She delved into her handbag, pulled out some money and gave the man her address.

Doubtful that she would ever see her luggage again, Clarissa matched her stride with that of Polly's and hurried out of the station. The car that awaited them was the smallest she had ever seen and, once installed inside, Polly drove it as though she were being chased by the devil himself.

'Don't be nervous,' she said above the roar of the engine, and presumably noting Clarissa's hands gripping the sides of her seat. 'I'm a perfectly safe driver, never once had an accident. Although there's always a first time,' she added with a gay laugh.

After much honking of horns and looks of angry disbelief from other drivers, they drew to a breathtakingly abrupt halt outside a row of white-painted houses. On the other side of the road was what looked to be a gated garden. Clarissa was still taking in her surroundings when Polly sprang out of the car and came round to open the door for her.

'I don't know what you're used to in Boston,' she said, 'but I guarantee you're going to find things very different here, chez moi. Probably a lot smaller. All the Americans I meet are always saying how everything in the States is so much bigger and better. To which I say, if that's the case, then why bother coming here at all?' She laughed, and slipping her arm through Clarissa's, guided her towards the house nearest to where they were parked, a house that seemed identical to all the others. From her handbag she withdrew a bunch of keys and let them in. From there they went up two flights of stairs to a spacious landing where a cat could be heard meowing from the other side of a door with a small brass plaque declaring it to be 16b.

'I hope you don't mind sharing my humble little abode with Valentino,' Polly said, inserting the key into the lock. 'In the absence of a husband or any children, I'm afraid I rather spoil him and treat him as my baby.'

'I'm sure we'll be the best of friends,' Clarissa said equably.

There was nothing remotely humble about Polly's 'little abode', and at once Clarissa felt how very English it was. Panelled walls were home to large oil paintings, mostly portraits of rather severe-looking men and women interspersed with a number of landscapes. Scattered atop a marble fireplace were framed photographs and a number of cards, which Clarissa guessed were invitations. To the right of a tall sash window was a grand piano, its polished surface so flawless the vase of roses sitting on it was reflected in the light coming through the window. A stately grandfather clock struck the hour, informing Clarissa that not only was it six o'clock, but that she hadn't eaten since breakfast and she was suddenly aware how ravenous she was.

'Now you're to make yourself at home,' Polly instructed her from behind one of the two chintz-covered sofas where she appeared to be selecting something to drink from a row of bottles and decanters on a console table. 'How about a Manhattan,' she asked, holding up a glass, 'in case you're feeling homesick?'

'I'm not feeling in the slightest bit homesick,' Clarissa said, bending down to Valentino, a large fluffy white Persian cat who was wrapping himself around her ankles. 'And I rather overdid it last night and have taken a vow of abstinence for a few days.' She was quite pleased with the nonchalance of her remark. Maybe this reinventing business was going to be easier than she'd thought.

'Good for you! In that case, I'll have a straightforward G&T and then see what Mrs Haines has left us for supper. I'll hazard a guess that it's shepherd's pie. Which brings me to the house rules, of which there are only two. Firstly, Mrs H runs my household like clockwork and is to be obeyed at all times; she's a genuine find and I wouldn't be without her, so no upsetting her.'

'I wouldn't dream of it,' said Clarissa. 'And the second house rule?'

'No grumbling about the plumbing, just accept that, like me, it's wildly unpredictable and you'll get along fine with it. Now, let me show you to your quarters, which I do hope won't fall too short of the high standard you're probably more used to with your grandmother. I've put you in the room overlooking the garden in the square, that way you get a lovely view of all the comings and goings. I'll give you a key tomorrow so you can sit in the garden, if you like. Take your time having a wash and brush-up and I'll see what's what in the kitchen. How does that sound?'

'It sounds more than I deserve.'

'The daughter of my oldest friend deserves all I can give her. Not to mention that you're my god-daughter whom I now have the chance to spoil. Such a pity it's only now that we've met. I blame that rotten family of Frannie's – talking of whom, there's a letter for you from them.'

'Really?'

'Well, I have a confession to make. I wrote a stinker of a letter to them to say you were coming to stay with me and that if they had a shred of decency they would do the right thing.'

'You said that?'

'I could have said an awful lot more, but let's just say I was feeling generous. Ah, there's the doorbell, that must be your luggage.'

Left on her own in her 'quarters', Clarissa sat on the bed and mentally caught her breath. She could see that staying with Polly was going to be enormous fun, but it was also going to be exhausting. The woman was an absolute whirl-wind of energy.

She had just removed her hat and was looking in the mirror, trying to do something with her hair, when she noticed the letter on the dressing table. Curious to know how her mother's parents had reacted to Polly's missive, she wasted no time in tearing open the envelope.

Chapter Twenty-Five

Shillingbury Grange,
Shillingbury,
Suffolk.
12th April 1939

Dear Clarissa,

   *It has been brought to my notice that you will shortly
be in London staying with a friend of your mother's.
In the circumstances I feel it incumbent upon me to
make your acquaintance and therefore suggest you visit
Shillingbury Grange at your earliest convenience.*

   Regards,

There was a signature at the bottom of the page, but it was
so illegible that Clarissa had no idea who had written the
letter. Man or woman, it was impossible to tell. After repeated readings she concluded that the formality of the lan-
guage was that of a man. So now, four days after Clarissa's
arrival in London, during which time Polly had taken her
on a whirlwind of non-stop activity to see the sights, spend
evenings at the theatre and shop till her feet cried out to rest,
she sat down to reply to the invitation to meet her English
grandparents. There was a rebellious streak fighting within
her to refuse the invitation, to pay them back for what they
had done to her mother, but she knew Fran would not have
wanted her to do that, and in truth it was not what she

wanted herself; after all, her main objective for coming to England was to see if she could put right a great wrong.

Two days later, and while Polly was at work, Clarissa received a reply to her letter; again the signature was illegible. Nonetheless, the matter was settled: the following morning she would take the train from Liverpool Street and be met at the station in Shillingbury.

It was a sparklingly bright morning when Polly waved Clarissa goodbye, and it was not without a degree of trepidation that she sank into her seat and watched London disappear from view in a cloud of steam. This time during the train journey she did not sleep, nor did she look at the *Picture Post* magazine Polly had given her to keep her amused. Rather she kept her gaze on the passing countryside, marvelling at the prettiness of everything she saw. Fran had always described herself as a country girl at heart and Clarissa was beginning to think she was the same. She supposed those childhood years in France had left their mark without her really knowing it. Some of her earliest memories were of her mother digging in a garden and of showing Clarissa how to plant lettuce seeds. One day, if she ever had children of her own, she would teach them the same simple pleasures.

Or maybe, like Polly she would never marry and have children, but instead she would have a job and do something worthwhile just as Polly did. And hadn't she told Ellis that that was what she would do in London, find something useful to do with her life? Perhaps she could do something worthwhile at the agency where Polly worked, an agency that sought sponsorship and homes for Jewish children fleeing those parts of Europe where it was feared they were no longer safe. Before leaving America, Clarissa had had no idea such things were going on, and had thought all the talk of war was just that, talk. First Artie had opened her eyes to what was really going on, and now so had her godmother.

The door of her compartment slid back and a ticket

collector asked to see her ticket. 'Another twenty minutes and we'll be at Shillingbury,' he said, tipping his cap to her. 'Pretty place, that. Stopping there long, are you, miss?'

'Just the one night,' she said.

'Well, I hope you enjoy your brief stay.'

Time will tell on that score, she thought when the man had left her.

True to his word, they arrived at Shillingbury twenty minutes later and with only the one bag and her handbag to carry, Clarissa stepped onto the platform and followed behind a handful of other passengers. Once outside the station, and after giving her a long hard look with a pair of steely grey eyes, a man in a cap and rough workman's trousers, his shirtsleeves rolled up to his elbows, approached. 'Yow be far Shillingbury Grange?' he asked, his thick accent unlike anything she'd heard before.

'I am,' she replied politely.

'Thought yow moight be. Oi be Jimmy and I bin sent ter fetch yow.'

She looked around for a car, but all she could see was a horse and trap next to a wooden post.

'The motorcar ain't warking too well,' the man said by way of explanation. 'But Apollo 'ere, even though he can be a bit of a rascal when provoked, will sartinly get yow where yow nid to be jest as well.' With a strong, callused hand, he helped her up into the trap. Once they were both settled, he gave the reins a sharp snap and muttered something to the horse that was incomprehensible to Clarissa. After a few yards he said, 'Truth to tell, miss, ain't much warking too well these days at the Grange. Nothing's what it used to be.'

His voice held all the lightness and warmth of an Old Testament prophet predicting the end of time, and filled her with foreboding. Was this really such a good idea? Could anything positive come of such a visit?

With no ready answer at her disposal, she could do nothing but hang onto the hope that she would do all she could within her power to undo the harm caused by years of stubborn pride. To do that she was going to have to rely heavily on her new self – the new, confident Clarissa who had stepped off the *Belle Etoile* would rise to the occasion and take the encounter in her stride, just as Effie would.

To her delight, Clarissa had received a letter from Effie in yesterday's post. She was in Paris with her father and stepmother and claimed to hate the city, saying she couldn't wait to leave because Ellis and Artie weren't there with her; selfishly they'd gone on to Biarritz without her. '*If only they, or you, were here with me, then I'm sure I would love Paris,*' she'd written. '*I miss you so much, my dearest new friend.*'

The sound of a vehicle approaching from behind had Clarissa turning round. A red, open-topped sports car bearing down on them coincided with a blare of car horn, which startled the horse and made it speed up at an alarming rate. Beside her Jimmy cursed and tightened his hold on the reins. 'Whoa there!' he shouted. 'Whoa there!' But the horse paid him no heed and galloped on, its tail swishing, its hooves clattering noisily. To Clarissa's consternation, the driver of the car revved its engine and overtook with a loud honk of its horn, missing them by inches and causing Clarissa to let out a cry of fright.

But worse was to come. As the car shot by, Apollo's head went down and, with his ears back, he galloped faster and faster, dragging the trap behind him, making it sway perilously from side to side. Ahead of them, Clarissa saw a tractor emerge through a gap in the trees and turn to join the road, just where it narrowed into what appeared to be a small stone bridge. 'Whoa there!' the man beside her shouted; he was on his feet now, pulling on the reins, the muscles of his forearms straining hard. Fearing for her life, Clarissa gripped the rail in front of her and prayed with all her might that the horse would slow down. Just as Jimmy's efforts went unheeded, so did her prayer and disaster was unavoidable. The violent collision of horse and tractor catapulted her through the air, and the last thing she was conscious of was a feeling of dreamlike weightlessness before landing with a heavy thud with the sound of a hundred banshees screaming nightmarishly in her ears. On and on went the terrible noise, until suddenly it ceased and in the blessed silence she succumbed to the sensation of weightlessness again, and felt herself drifting away from the body that had once been hers.

The next thing she knew she was staring into a whiteness, a whiteness that was so bright it hurt. She closed her eyes, wanting to slip back into the dream she'd been having, of floating on the silky softness of a vast cloud.

'Can you hear me?' asked a voice. It was a voice she didn't recognise. A man's voice. 'Open your eyes if you can hear me.'

Go away, she thought drowsily. Whoever you are, leave me alone. She pictured herself trying to hide from the man, her mind conjuring up the image of a child slipping behind a heavy velvet curtain and holding her breath till he was gone.

But the man wasn't playing fairly, he was calling to her, insisting she show herself. She didn't like him very much. He was the bossy type who would be determined to spoil her fun. Just like Marjorie.

Marjorie.

Where did that name come from? she wondered. Who was Marjorie? And for that matter, where was she and why did her head hurt so much? Stepping out from behind the curtain, wanting to have her curiosity satisfied, she opened her eyes. Above her a circle of faces stared down at her with concerned expressions. 'Who are you?' she asked, shrinking back from them – a woman and two men.

'I'm Dr Rutherford,' one of the men said. He had thick bushy eyebrows the colour of ash and a large nose that was home to two extraordinarily cavernous nostrils. In his hand was a black object, which he suddenly pointed at her face; once more she was blinded by a white light shining directly into her eyes. She turned her head away sharply, but then gasped at the pain the movement brought with it. 'I'd advise you to keep still, young lady,' said the man with the bushy eyebrows.

'Why?' she asked. 'What have I done? And where am I?' They seemed reasonable enough questions, but judging from the expression on his face and, come to think of it, on the faces of the other two people peering down at her, she had cause to wonder. As she did so, she stared back at the other two – a man and a woman, neither of whom she recognised. The man seemed absurdly small, no taller than a young child. But then she realised he wasn't standing; he was seated in a chair. No, not a proper chair but one of those ...? She forced her brain to think of the word she was looking for. A chair with wheels and a wicker back. Invalids used them. Oh, what was it called? She cudgelled her brain to summon the word, but was distracted by the woman speaking.

'You're at Shillingbury Grange.' The woman was softly spoken with a strained air about her. 'You came to see us,' she went on. 'Yesterday.'

'Did I? Why?' Then a thought struck her. 'Are you Marjorie?'

The woman frowned. 'No, I'm your grandmother. Lavinia Upwood.'

'My grandmother,' she repeated. Something about that rang a bell. She mulled it over. 'If that's the case, why don't I know you?'

'You've never met me before. This is your grandfather, Charles Upwood.'

The man in the chair moved towards her. 'Have you and I met before?' she asked.

'No,' he said gruffly, at the same time dabbing his mouth with a handkerchief. On closer inspection she could see that his face had a strange lopsidedness to it, as though one side was being dragged down by an invisible weight.

The doctor spoke again. 'You were involved in an accident

on your way here yesterday.' He then turned to speak to the woman called Lavinia. 'Obviously the blow to her head has left her with amnesia. I've seen this before and usually the memory returns bit by bit. As far as I can see, she's—'

'Did you say yesterday?'

The man returned his attention to her. 'Yes. You've been drifting in and out of consciousness since you were brought here.'

'Who brought me here?'

The man in the chair spoke now. 'You were found by a neighbour of ours.'

'Was I alone?'

'Can't you remember anything of the accident?' he asked, again dabbing one side of his mouth.

'Nothing.'

'Then for your sake I hope it stays that way,' he muttered.

'You must be hungry,' the woman who claimed to be her grandmother said. 'Dr Rutherford, will it be all right for her to eat something?'

'I don't see why not. Unless it causes nausea. Keep it light, though, nothing too heavy.'

'May I ask another question, please?'

Three faces turned to look at her again.

'Of course,' the doctor said. 'What do you want to know?'

'What's my name? Who am I?'

Whatever the answer was, she didn't hear it, for her eyelids suddenly drooped and, as though her body was flooded with a powerful drug, she sank into a deep, deep oblivion.

Chapter Twenty-Six

April 1939, Shillingbury Grange, Shillingbury

While she flitted in and out of a restless sleep, she was conscious at times of not being alone, of somebody watching over her in the darkness. During one brief instance of wakefulness, she observed the woman who said she was her grandmother sitting in a chair beside the bed where she lay. On her lap was a book, but the woman was asleep, her head tilted back, her jaw slack, causing her mouth to open, from which emitted an occasional snore from the back of her throat.

When finally she rose to the surface from the depths of a chaotically dream-filled sleep and roused herself into a sitting position, she experienced the first faint stirrings of recall and understanding.

Her name was Clarissa.

Clarissa Allerton.

And she had been staying with somebody in London. Who was that somebody, though? And if she had been staying in London, where had she been before? Where was home?

It was no longer dark and she was quite alone, the chair by the side of the bed empty. From somewhere beyond the room she could hear noises. Voices. A dog barking. A door slamming. Through the gap in the heavy chintz curtains a shaft of sunlight reached across the rug on the floor and onto the pale green counterpane on the bed. Her gaze moved around the room, taking in the dark mahogany pieces of furniture – wardrobe, chest of drawers, dressing table, low stool, lamps. Everything had a worn and uncared-for appearance. The more she looked at each item, the shabbier it revealed itself to be. The walls and ceiling were full of cracks and in places the wallpaper was coming away. Parts of the cornice were missing. This was not a wealthy household, she concluded. But once upon a time it must have been, for the proportions of the room befitted those of a sizeable house.

As she watched the dust motes dancing in the beams of light against a backdrop of damask roses scrambling their tangled way up the curtains in a manner that mirrored the confusion of her thoughts, she tried to piece together how she came to be here. Like Hansel and Gretel she followed the scant crumbs available to her. There was a train journey involved, from ... from a large and busy station and somebody was saying goodbye to her. A nice woman. Next there was a man with a horse. The horse had a name. But as the horse's name remained out of her reach, it was replaced by the image of a red sports car followed swiftly by a tractor. Something told her the tractor was important, but as she pursued its significance, she simultaneously recalled hearing a terrifying noise and her brain veered away from the image, like a horse refusing to jump a hedge.

She still had no memory of how she had actually arrived here, and looking down at the nightdress she was wearing, she recognised the delicate embroidery and mother-of-pearl buttons. She remembered packing it, along with a change of dress and underclothes. She remembered too the anxiety she had felt as she packed her case, that the journey she was about to make was a leap into the unknown.

That leap had taken her far deeper into the unknown than she could have possibly imagined. Although she didn't feel the same anxiety now, for it had been replaced by a determination to solve the mystery of why she was here in this strange house with two complete strangers who claimed they were related to her.

She was contemplating getting out of bed to go in search

of a bathroom when the door opened. It was the woman who'd sat by her in the night. A ghost of a smile lifted the tiredness from her face. 'You're awake,' she said. 'That's good. How do you feel?'

'Better. But I need the lavatory,' Clarissa said, pushing back the bedclothes.

'Let me help you.'

'There's no need, I can manage.' But the second she put any weight on her feet and felt the room spin slightly, she realised she couldn't manage alone.

'Here,' the woman said, 'put your arm around my shoulder.'

Fearing the woman wasn't strong enough to take her weight – she looked too thin to bear more than a shadow – Clarissa did her best to accept the help, but sparingly. Once she was inside the bathroom and the door was shut and she had used the lavatory, she leaned tiredly against the basin to wash her hands. It was then that she saw herself in the mirror above the basin and gasped with shock. It wasn't so much the sight of her heavily bandaged head that shocked her as the bruising to her face. She looked awful. The skin around her eyes was swollen and blackened, and her right cheek was twice the size it should be and hideously bruised. Heaven only knew what was going on under the bandages. In her current weakened state she didn't dare lift anything to find out.

With the woman's help she made it back to bed and sank gratefully into its welcoming softness. 'I'm sorry to be such a bother to you,' she said.

'Please don't feel you have to apologise. There's really no need.'

'But I'm putting you to all this trouble.'

A great sadness filled the woman's face. A moment passed before she spoke. 'You're so very like her,' she said quietly.

'Like who?'

'Your mother. It wasn't until I set eyes on you that I

realised the harm we've done, all that we've missed. All these years ...' Her voice caught and she looked away. 'I'm sorry,' she said, when she'd composed herself. 'I was so sure I wouldn't feel anything. But I was wrong. Oh, so very wrong.'

Confused by the woman's words, but seeing how upset she was, Clarissa pointed to the chair by the side of the bed. 'Please, will you sit with me and explain what you've just said, because none of it makes any sense to me.'

The woman shook her head. 'No, first you must have something to eat. You must be ravenous after all this time.'

'Will you talk to me after that? Maybe it will help more of my memory to come back. There are so many things that are all jumbled up inside my head.'

'Very well, if you believe it will help. But I don't want to exhaust you. Or upset you,' she added in a voice so tremulous Clarissa was suddenly filled with a wave of compassion for her.

An hour later, after she'd eaten a small bowl of soup and a slice of bread and butter, it wasn't Clarissa who was upset, but this woman called Lavinia who, it seemed, really was her grandmother. Tears ran down the poor woman's face as she spoke, all the while alternating between wringing her hands on her lap and wiping her eyes.

'But how could you have done that?' Clarissa asked, shocked at what she'd heard. How could this couple cut off their only daughter, and all because she'd fallen in love with a man not of their choosing? 'What had my mother done to deserve such a punishment?' she asked.

'It was pride, pure and simple,' Lavinia said, not quite meeting Clarissa's eye, 'I see that now. But at the time we believed it was the right course of action. Never did we think our beloved daughter would defy us, and when she did, we had no choice but to hold firm in the hope she would see the error of her ways.'

Of course you had a choice, Clarissa wanted to argue, but she let it go, pondering on what she'd been told about this woman called Fran, who was her mother, a mother who had married an American. It was America where Clarissa had lived all her life, apart from some years spent in France. But like quicksilver, anything more detailed that came within a whisker of her grasp slipped away, and all she was left with was the disbelief that this story she'd just heard involved her – that these people had not only shunned their daughter, but her. Until now.

'What made you want to see me after all these years?' she asked.

Lavinia nodded. 'When I received word that you would be in London I knew then that I had to see you and make amends in some small way for what we did. I knew also that it might be my only chance to do so.'

'Does your husband ...' Clarissa found it difficult to refer to the man as her grandfather '... share your feelings?'

'Charles is not a well man. He had a stroke a number of years ago, which has left him greatly altered. Some days are better than others.'

'You haven't answered my question.'

'I'm sorry. I didn't mean to appear evasive. What I was trying to say is that some days Charles feels enormous regret for what we did, and other days his stubborn old self dictates his mood and he's compelled to justify it. I didn't tell him I'd written to you, for the simple reason I didn't know how he'd react. But seeing how badly hurt you were when you were brought here, I think the shock of it softened his heart. I know I have no right to ask this of you, but I hope you won't think too badly of us. Not now.'

Clarissa didn't know how to respond. She needed time to think. She didn't want to judge these people harshly, or condemn them, not when that was precisely what they had done to her mother. 'I think I should like to sleep now,' she said.

'Of course. I'm sorry if I've tired you out. Is there anything else you need?'

'No thank you.'

'Dr Rutherford said he'd call in to check on your progress.'

'Let's hope he brings a magic potion with him that will restore my memory,' Clarissa said lightly.

Left alone, Clarissa didn't sleep. She couldn't. She was too agitated. She didn't want to be stuck here in bed in a house she didn't know. She wanted to be up, actively searching for all that she had lost. But eventually she slept and as she did so, a jumble of memories bubbled up from the depths of her consciousness – the colour of a summer frock her mother used to wear; an expression on her father's face as he kissed her goodnight; a stern word from her Grandma Ethel; a pair of emerald eyes; a garden with lettuces growing; a house overlooking the ocean; a large and very beautiful ship; a dark and gloomy house, her mother working at a typewriter; a long train journey; a man in shirtsleeves with a peculiar accent; a sports car; a tractor; a narrow stone bridge and terrible agonised shrieks.

She woke with a start, her heart pounding with the feeling that she had almost remembered what had happened. So near, yet so far, she thought. She had no idea if all those memories were in any sort of order, or whether it was merely a kaleidoscope of recollections thrown together at random.

She tried to glean some encouragement from what she'd dreamt; she had to believe that with each new cataract of light that had been shone into the darkness, more memories would be illuminated as a consequence. She had to treat each newly learned piece of information as a stepping stone to the next. The challenge she faced was somehow to try and piece it all together into something that made sense. What she currently had was akin to a photograph album interspersed with blank pages.

Her head began to ache, and so she leant back against the pillows and closed her eyes. Forcing the memories would not help, she told herself; better to let them form in their own good time, just as they had while she slept. But it was so frustrating not to be able to stand back and see the whole picture in one go. All she could manage was to see bits close up and in isolation, which didn't help. For all that she knew her name was Clarissa and she was nineteen years of age, and that she had travelled across the Atlantic to this country, it didn't help her know exactly who she was. She was as good as a stranger to herself. Worse than that, a lost stranger.

She was drifting off to sleep again when she heard the ring of a doorbell; a long, sonorous tone that brought forth slow, unhurried footsteps. Whatever words were exchanged, Clarissa couldn't hear them, but minutes later there was a knock at her door and in came a young girl in a maid's uniform.

'Beggin' your pardon, miss, but there be some people to see you. Shall oi show them up?'

'Is it the doctor?'

The young girl shook her head. 'No, it not be 'im, miss.'

'Where's Lavinia, Mrs Upwood?'

'She's gone out. She'll be back soon, and Mr Upwood is having his afternoon nap. There be no one else 'ere. So what about them visitors, do you wants to see 'em? They say they're friends.'

With such a hideously bruised and battered face Clarissa didn't want to see anyone, but if there was a possibility these supposed friends might help her in some way, then she ought to see them. Besides, if they were kind enough to call, then it showed they cared.

'Did they say who they are?'

'Oi didn't think to ask, miss. Shall oi go and find out for you?'

'That's all right,' Clarissa said pessimistically. 'I don't expect I shall know who they are anyway.'

*

Her prediction wasn't entirely correct.

'Forgive me,' she said when her visitors were standing at the end of the bed and staring down at her, 'I know you, but – but I don't know *why* I know you. I'm told I have amnesia.'

The woman came round to the side of the bed and sat on the edge of it, her face full of concern. She was very smartly dressed and on her head she wore a hat the colour of amethyst, with a diamante pin pushed through at the front where there was a small dent. Something about the hat rang a bell. But only faintly.

'I'm Polly. Polly Sinclair,' the woman said, 'your mother's oldest friend. I'm actually your godmother. You were staying with me in London before this awful accident.' She took hold of Clarissa's hand and squeezed it gently. 'I put you on the train. I wish now I hadn't. This is all my fault. I shouldn't have meddled by writing to your grandparents. I should have kept you safe with me in London.'

'How did you know I'd been involved in an accident?'

'Lavinia sent me a telegram. She thought I ought to know. I was on my way here when this charming fellow turned up on my doorstep enquiring after you.'

Clarissa turned to look properly at the pale, slightly built man still standing at the end of the bed. He had thick black hair that was pushed back from a broad forehead, and behind horn-rimmed spectacles earnest dark brown eyes stared back at her. In the breast pocket of his jacket was a pen. 'I know you,' Clarissa murmured, 'I really do, but—' Suddenly it was all too much for her, the knowing, and the not knowing. What if she stayed like this forever, a prisoner of a mind that would never be the same again? She began to cry; great gulping sobs that caught in her throat. The woman called Polly put her arms around her and held her close.

'There, there, you poor thing,' she soothed, 'what a terrible ordeal this must be for you. But you go ahead and cry all you want. Just let it all out. Don't mind us for a single moment.'

For what felt like forever, Clarissa did exactly that and when finally a calmness settled on her, she took the handkerchief the man offered her. She blew her nose and corralled her emotions. 'Will you tell me your name, please?' she said to him. 'And how we know each other?'

He sat in the chair next to the bed. 'I'm Artie Bloomberg. We met on board the *Belle Etoile*.'

'Go on,' Clarissa said, when he seemed to think that was sufficient information.

'I was with Ellis Randall, and Effie Chase was on the ship, too, with her father and stepmother. We got friendly with another woman called Betty.'

'Was I travelling alone?'

'No. You were being chaperoned by an awful old dragon. You spent most of your time trying to avoid her.'

'Marjorie!' Clarissa blurted out. 'Was her name Marjorie?'

He smiled. He had such a lovely smile, she thought. 'Yes. And you hated her. She was about as much fun as a raincloud on a sunny day.'

Whether or not it was the distraction of his smile, but something else fell into place. 'Marjorie was a friend of my Grandma Ethel, wasn't she? Yes, yes, I remember! And I remember somebody with the most unusually green eyes. Who was that?'

'That would be Ellis. Everybody always remembers his eyes; they're very distinctive, as he is himself.'

'Yes, I do remember him, but he was so very conceited!' As soon as the words were out, Clarissa covered her mouth with a hand, embarrassed. 'I'm sorry, that was perhaps rude of me. Is he a good friend of yours?'

Artie laughed. 'He is – and he is also an exceptionally conceited man. I shall bring your comment to his attention when I see him next.'

As he was speaking, Clarissa watched the woman called Polly remove the hat she was wearing. Something roused itself inside her. 'Do you have a pale grey hat,' she asked, 'one with a dent in the side of it?'

'I'm afraid all my hats have dents in them,' Polly said with a smile. 'I'm forever dropping or sitting on them. But there you are, there's something else we've helped you remember because I do indeed have a pale grey hat.'

'You wore it when … when you met me at the station, didn't you?'

'And I was inexcusably late.'

'I was anxious,' Clarissa said with a frown. 'I didn't know whether to wait for you or look for a taxi. Oh, how strange that I should be able to recall something as inconsequential as your hat, and it then awakens other memories for me.'

'The mind's a complicated piece of machinery,' Artie said. 'You need to be patient with it. Everything will eventually fall into place for you. You've survived quite a serious accident, I'm surprised you're not being cared for in hospital.'

'A doctor's seen me, so I suppose the Upwoods decided I wasn't that badly hurt.'

'Nothing that a good long rest won't cure,' joined in Polly. 'I'm all for staying away from hospitals, ghastly places. No, take it from me; you're better off here, so long as they're looking after you well. Although if the state of this house is anything to go by, I have my doubts. Goodness, it could do with a good clean. I can't remember seeing so many cobwebs. Now, far be it from me to get above myself, but I shall leave you here with Artie while I go in search of that maid and see if we can't rustle up something to drink. I'm appalled she hasn't offered something already. This really is the slackest of households. Or better still, maybe you should go, Artie, I'm sure you could charm her into providing us with some refreshments. No, better leave it to me; I suspect I'll have more authority about me than you. You're much too sweet a man to boss her about.'

When Polly had sailed out of the room, Clarissa looked shyly at Artie. 'I think she meant that as a compliment.'

'That's all right. I'd only been in Miss Sinclair's company a few minutes before I realised what an extraordinarily energetic woman she is. I'm just glad I'd changed my plans and decided to leave France to come to London when I did.' He leaned forward and fixed his kindly brown eyes intently on hers. 'I was so worried about you when Miss Sinclair told me the news.'

At the intensity of his expression, Clarissa felt an emotion stir within her. It made her wonder what sort of a friendship they had, if from what she understood they'd only met very recently. Had she, she wondered, fallen in love with him? He would be an easy man to love, she thought. 'What do you and Polly actually know about the accident?' she asked.

He looked doubtful. 'I'm not sure I should tell you.'

'You must! I need to know. Why should everybody else know but me? Where's the fairness in that?'

He put a hand out to her. 'Please,' he said, 'don't upset yourself. I'll tell you what I've been told if you insist, but only if you think it will help.'

Chapter Twenty-Seven

30th April 1939, Hotel du Palais, Biarritz, France

Clarissa, trust you to be so careless and have an accident within days of being in England.

Get well soon, I don't want to have dinner at the Ritz in London with an invalid, it would be very undignified!

Ellis Randall

1st May 1939, Hotel Negresco, Nice, France

My dear Clarissa,

I heard the news of your terrible accident from Effie, what rotten luck for you my dear girl. Is there anything I can do? Just say the word and I shall do whatever I can to make things better for you.

If you were able to travel I'd suggest you come and join me in Nice – heavens to Betsy it's such fun here!

Take care and get well very soon,
Betty

While bored to tears with the regime of enforced daily bed rest, as laid down by a ruthlessly authoritarian Dr Rutherford, it did mean that Clarissa had been able to spend time getting to know her grandmother.

In contrast, her grandfather was still no more than a distant figure that she saw little of. Lavinia had explained that the effort involved for her husband to climb the stairs was too much for him – only on exceptionally good days could he rely on his legs to support him. Ironically, the afternoon of Clarissa's arrival had been a good day when he had, with assistance from his wife and Lily, the housemaid, managed the stairs and his cumbersome wheelchair was then carried up. Clarissa frequently heard him shouting to the dogs, or to Lily. He sounded a short-tempered man, but perhaps it was frustration that fuelled his temper.

As the days passed, as predicted, the amnesia cleared bit by bit until finally Clarissa's memory was fully restored. She now remembered the days spent on board the *Belle Etoile*, as well as the dreadful Marjorie who, no doubt, would say Clarissa had brought the accident upon herself with her wilful behaviour. However, there were moments when Clarissa wondered how she would ever know if there remained any lost segments to her memory. What if she had forgotten some important detail about who she was?

What had also returned to her was the full horror of the accident. She now knew that the calamitous screaming that had haunted her was the sound of Apollo, the horse, dying in agonising pain. Jimmy, who had been in the trap with her, had been thrown clear and had landed in the relative softness of the hawthorn hedgerow. Clarissa had not been so lucky; she had been jettisoned from the trap straight into the road, where she had narrowly missed being crushed by the horse as it fell to the ground. Mortified at what had happened, the driver of the tractor, with Jimmy's help, and along with a man from the village who had been passing, had lifted her onto the back of his trailer and taken her to where she had now resided for two weeks.

At Lavinia's invitation Artie and Polly had stayed for several nights at Shillingbury Grange in the belief that their presence would help Clarissa recoup that much faster, and it was with some sadness that she had said goodbye to them. Polly had wanted to stay longer, but she was needed back in London – the agency for finding homes for Jewish children was working at full tilt and couldn't do without her any more. She had spoken at length with Clarissa and Artie about her work with the Kindertransport, and with friends and relatives in Berlin, Prague and Vienna, Artie was keen to learn all he could. He had written to his friends entreating them to flee, but to his consternation they said they couldn't leave their families or homes. He had now returned to France to meet up with Ellis and Effie on the Riviera.

Thankfully, the worst of Clarissa's bruises had subsided and the stitches to the side of her head had been removed. Today she was enjoying her first full day out of bed and relished the freedom. It was wonderful to have a change of scene, other than the miserable four walls that had so far imprisoned her. Being able to move about meant that she now had a better idea of her surroundings.

In the drawing room, sitting by the French doors, she watched Charles Upwood being pushed across the lawn by Jimmy. To give him his full name, he was Jimmy Pharr and was one of Lily's many uncles. Apparently, and in Lily's own words, you couldn't move in Shillingbury for tripping over members of the Pharr family. Clarissa had grown quite fond of the girl, perhaps because Lily was just two years younger than she was. She was also quite a spirited girl beneath her thin veneer of polite duty and wasn't afraid to say what she thought when provoked. On one occasion, when yet again she presented a tray of unappetising food to Clarissa, she had apologised for it and told her that Cook, Mrs Kent, was a fearsome tyrant in the kitchen and no matter how bad the meals were that she produced, Mrs Upwood never dared criticise her, knowing as she did that she would never find anybody else to work for such poor wages.

It was an echo of what Polly had said during her brief stay. 'Standards have certainly slipped since I stayed here as a young girl,' she had told Clarissa. 'Time was when this was one of the smartest houses in the area with a whole army of staff running about the place. It's a shadow of its former self. Too depressing for words.'

The house was uncompromisingly large and set in grounds that spoke of years of neglect – the tennis court was full of weeds, the kitchen garden wildly overgrown and the lawns home to rabbits and moles. Many of the rooms were closed off, their doors shut, the furniture covered with dustsheets, and although it was spring and the sun was shining, little warmth penetrated the walls.

From conversations with Lavinia, Clarissa had learned that in recent years Charles's investments had not been soundly made and they were now paying the price of a combination of poor judgement and the far-reaching effects of the Depression. It would have been easy for Clarissa to say that it served her grandparents right, that this was their punishment for their cruelty towards Fran. But she believed that guilt, and the subsequent shame of losing their standing within the community, had punished them enough without her wishing to further compound their pain. And they were in pain; that much was obvious to Clarissa. Every time she looked into Lavinia's heavily lined face and watched her habitually wringing her hands, her thin shoulders hunched, she saw sadness and regret.

'Never could I have foreseen that our lives would become so dismal, or that we'd be reduced to such an impecunious state,' Lavinia confessed to Clarissa. The raw honesty of this admission touched Clarissa, and more and more she found herself wanting to do something that would improve their lot. But what? What could she do?

The next day the postman brought two letters for Clarissa, one from Polly and another from Artie. She opened his first.

He was still on the Riviera, he wrote, but would soon be leaving to return to London, where he hoped to secure a job with Reuters as a news correspondent.

I cannot in all conscience accompany Ellis and Effie with their plans to continue travelling in Europe when catastrophe is about to strike. I don't say this lightly; I believe it with all my being, the clouds of war are gathering pace and anyone who thinks otherwise is a fool. The menace of Hitler's Germany is becoming ever more threatening and it's time people acted.

Which brings me to the main point of my letter. Polly will be writing to you shortly with a formal request, and though I know I should leave matters to her, I cannot help but add my weight to her request. I have known you for so short a time and therefore have no right to ask anything of you, but I know you to have a good and generous heart, so if you could find a way to persuade your grandparents to agree to what Polly will ask of them, I would forever be in your debt.

Here is something else I don't say lightly, and really I should have stated this at the top of my letter, but you are in my thoughts daily and I sincerely hope that you are now feeling more like the delightful girl I met on board the Belle Etoile. We never know who we are going to meet next, or indeed what the consequences of that meeting will be, but I'm convinced our paths were meant to cross, and in that I consider myself the most fortunate of men to have made your acquaintance.

Oh, dear God, I sound so absurdly archaic! So before I say anything else foolish, I shall sign off.

Yours affectionately,
  Artie

PS I'm mailing this to Shillingbury in the hope you're still recuperating there.

Clarissa hurriedly read the letter through one more time, then opened the one from Polly, intuitively knowing what it would be about. No sooner had she absorbed the information than she heard Lavinia calling to her.

'Is this your doing?' her grandmother demanded when she entered the drawing room and handed her a piece of typewritten paper.

'Not at all,' Clarissa replied after reading the letter. She then explained about her own letter from Polly.

'Well, whoever concocted this ill-conceived plan, it's out of the question,' Lavinia said emphatically. 'We simply wouldn't be able to cope. Charles certainly won't stand for it, not for one second. He needs peace and quiet, not the chaos of an army of foreign children invading the house.'

'I'm sure it wouldn't be like that,' Clarissa said, although in truth she had no idea what it would be like. 'It won't be an army of children, only one or two,' she went on, 'and they might not be here for long.'

Lavinia tugged on the cardigan draped around her shoulders. 'Please don't think I don't have sympathy for the poor wretches, but is it really our problem? We have difficulties enough of our own. Besides,' she went on, wringing her hands, 'we're not equipped here for children. So that's an end to it. I shall reply to that letter accordingly. Polly Sinclair always did go chasing after some cause or other. If she'd married and had a family of her own she wouldn't have time for all this nonsense.'

'I don't consider her work nonsense,' Clarissa said quietly. 'But can we really stand back and do nothing? Would we ever forgive ourselves if the situation worsened for these people?'

'*We?*' Lavinia repeated stiffly. 'Where do you come into this?'

'I'd like to stay on and help if you'll let me,' Clarissa said. It was suddenly clear to her that she wasn't meant to go back to London. She had been led here for a specific reason and it was now staring her full square in the face. Never could she have imagined that this would be the consequence of her travelling across the Atlantic, but never had she felt more certain that this was where she was meant to be. This was her being the new, confident person she had planned to become when she stepped off the *Belle Etoile*, the confident young woman who would do something worthwhile with her life.

Slowly rising to her feet, and with the zeal and instinct of one possessed of the righteous belief, as prompted by Polly in her letter, that this act of generosity would in some way atone for what Lavinia and Charles Upwood had done to their daughter, she set about convincing her grandmother that Shillingbury Grange should be a temporary home for no more than two children in need of a safe haven from the Nazis. Hardly drawing breath, she systematically dismissed every objection put forward – the house was in no fit state to take in children; Cook wouldn't like it and would resign on the spot; Lily would leave as well at the extra work; Charles would never get any rest; and the children wouldn't speak English and would run amok and create endless havoc. Then Clarissa produced the trump card she had kept up her sleeve, saying she would not only stay and help, but she would use some of the money her mother had left her to absorb the additional cost of looking after the children.

'I suppose this is how you Americans do things, isn't it,' Lavinia said with a weary shake of her head. 'You bulldoze your way through until you get what you want.'

'I suppose we do,' Clarissa said happily, then to be absolutely sure of removing every last trace of doubt and potential argument, and knowing that her grandmother had taken to Artie, she explained that it would be a personal favour to Artie for Lavinia and Charles to take the children in, that their plight troubled him profoundly.

'If it's that important to Artie, why doesn't he help by arranging to send them to America?' asked Lavinia.

'Because their parents don't want them so far away,' Clarissa replied, and without thinking she added: 'As a mother you can understand that, surely?'

At the stricken expression on Lavinia's face, Clarissa feared she had inadvertently gone too far. She was about to apologise when her grandmother straightened her shoulders. 'Very well,' she said. 'I can see that you're every inch your mother's daughter and not prepared to give ground one iota. I shall discuss the matter with my husband and reply to Miss Sinclair that we shall take in two children. No more, mind. I don't want you, or her, running away with the idea that just because this is a large house we can accommodate every ragtag and bobtail that's going.'

'Thank you,' Clarissa said. 'Thank you so much.' And in a rush of delighted spontaneity she hugged her grandmother. It was the first time she had done so since arriving. Initially Lavinia froze at her touch, as though repulsed by it, but then the stiffness went from her body and she hugged Clarissa back.

'And for the record, I'm not wholly American,' Clarissa said when she let go of her grandmother. 'I'm half English, and my mother never let me forget that.'

A hint of a smile lifted the downward slope of Lavinia's mouth. 'I'm pleased to hear it.'

Clarissa smiled, then remembering something that had been bothering her for some days, she said, 'Can I ask you something?'

'You may.'

'What should I call you? Lavinia, as I have done so far, or—'

'Lavinia will suffice in the circumstances,' the woman said, resorting once again to rigid formality, 'unless you feel uncomfortable with that?'

'No, no, that's fine. I just want to do what feels right for you.'

'Well then,' the woman added in a warmer tone of voice, 'if there's nothing else, I shall go and see Cook and discover what new horror awaits us for lunch. Is there anything I can bring you?'

'No, I have everything I need, thank you.'

It was after lunch that a boy from the village arrived on a bicycle with a telegram for Clarissa from Grandma Ethel.

Duty-bound to keep her grandmother in America in the picture, Clarissa had written to say she'd been involved in an accident, but there was nothing to worry about as she was in good hands and staying with her grandparents in Suffolk.

'*You are to come home as soon as you are well enough to travel*,' was the stern instruction. '*You are needed here*.'

Chapter Twenty-Eight

At the intrusively loud noise of a strimmer starting up nearby, Mrs Dallimore's unfolding story came to a stop. 'I think, my dear, we'll have to leave it there; my voice is no match for Jed's horticultural administrations, and apart from that, I've rattled on quite long enough.'

Disappointed, Lizzie looked over to where Jed was neatening the edges of a flowerbed. Concentrating on what he was doing, a pair of ear defenders clamped on over a red and white bandanna tied around his head, he gave the impression of being blissfully unaware of the racket he was causing; he seemed in a world of his own. Just as Lizzie had been. She had been listening so intently to Mrs Dallimore, she had lost track of time and where she was. But Jed had brought her back down to earth with an almighty thump, she thought irritably. What was more, during the spell cast by Mrs Dallimore, Curt had not featured in her thoughts, but now he probably would again. Unless she could keep herself fully occupied. Reluctantly, she stood up. 'Would you like me to take you inside, or fetch a drink for you?' she asked Mrs Dallimore.

'No, I'm quite content to sit here, thank you. I'm sorry if I've bored you.'

'You haven't at all,' said Lizzie, quick to dismiss such a thought, 'you truly haven't. You did what nobody else has managed to do: you took my mind off the mess I've made of my life, and I couldn't be more grateful to you.'

The old lady looked at her sternly, her silvery-white brows drawn together. 'Whatever mess you think you've made of your life, I assure you it's no more than a temporary hiccup.

Now run along and see to somebody more in need than me.'

With Jed and the strimmer getting nearer, Lizzie had to raise her voice. 'Will you carry on where you left off another time, please? Tomorrow, perhaps?'

Her reply lost in the din, Mrs Dallimore nodded.

As she walked past him, Jed looked up at Lizzie and raised his hand in a mock salute. Be nice, she told herself, it's not his fault he has a knack for popping up at the least convenient of moments. She flashed him a salute in return and hurried on up to the house where the smell of lunch cooking made her queasy stomach flip. That was something else that had been calmed while sitting with Mrs Dallimore; the butterflies that had taken up residence in her stomach had settled, not a flicker had they given her. Until now. It was stress; she knew that. She'd experienced something similar years ago at university when she'd realised she was doing the wrong course. For weeks she'd stuck with it, hoping that the course would suddenly fall into place for her. It hadn't. It had got worse and worse, and she'd grown miserable figuring out how to extricate herself without looking like she had once again failed. With that misery came the queasy stomach and the loss of appetite. It was perhaps only her pride that had stopped her from giving up and walking away, and yet again admitting defeat.

Failing seemed to be her speciality. Here was something in which she could claim to be an expert. Here was her great achievement in life, the one thing she could do to the highest standard. Come to think of it, she could write a self-help manual, *How to Succeed at Being a Spectacular Failure*. Except she couldn't even do that because she didn't know why she kept messing up, it just seemed to happen to her. Wrong choices, she supposed. Like Curt. He could not have been a more wrong choice.

When it was time for her to go home she went in search of Mrs Dallimore to say goodbye and to tell her that she would see her again tomorrow, and that she hoped to hear what the old lady had done all those years ago when she'd been summoned back to America by Grandma Ethel. Did she disobey the summons and stay on at Shillingbury Grange, or do as she was told? Lizzie reckoned the smart money was on her staying right where she was.

It was difficult to think of Mrs Dallimore, with all her frailty and loss of independence, being the same person as the young, headstrong Clarissa. Lizzie wondered if the woman herself felt the same way.

She found the old lady in the sitting room where she was fast asleep, a cup of tea untouched on the table at her side. In the chair opposite, Mr Sheridan was also sleeping soundly. Their heads inclined towards each other, they could have been an elderly married couple sitting companionably by the fireside in their twilight years.

Quietly taking away the cups and saucers, Lizzie placed them in the dishwasher in the kitchen and went to the staff room to remove her tabard. She then signed out and went to collect her bike, thinking as she unlocked it that she was in no hurry to go home. Not because she didn't want to be with her parents, but because she knew that with nothing constructive to do she would end up thinking about Curt.

She had got as far as the end of the drive when she saw a familiar figure leaning against one of the gateposts, a bike propped against the opposite post. It was Jed, the red and white bandanna from his head now tied around his neck.

'Fancy going for a drink?' he asked, stepping out and blocking her way.

She braked hard and came to a stop just inches from his feet. 'You'll get yourself run over doing things like that,' she said.

'I'll take my chances. How about you? Fancy taking a chance on accepting my invitation?'

'If that was some kind of gauntlet thrown down to challenge me, you'll have to do better than that.'

'Always happy to raise my game,' he said, 'especially if I can learn something. So what's it to be? Stand here for a game of verbal ping-pong, or do the same over a drink in some enticing beer garden? If you're nice I might even throw in some crisps.'

'I don't do *nice*.'

He smiled. 'Yeah, I thought that might be the case.'

What did she have to lose? Lizzie asked herself when, half an hour later, and after she'd texted home to say she would be late, she was settled at a table in the garden of the Riverside pub while Jed was buying their drinks.

When he returned from the bar with their beers, he also had a copy of a broadsheet tucked under his arm. Hmm, so he was anticipating such a boring time with her, he'd grabbed a newspaper to read, had he?

'Any good at crosswords?' he asked when he was sitting on the wooden seat next to her and folding the paper into the desired shape.

'Do I look that kind of a girl?' she replied.

'You look the kind of girl who could do anything she wanted. Got a pencil in that bag of yours?'

After a rummage, she found an old work biro with the words *Starlight Radio* stamped in black along the length of it. 'Thank you,' he said, taking it from her. He clicked it a couple of times, then took a mouthful of his beer. 'Here we go then, first clue: intriguing girl who scowls a lot. Five letters.'

'Not funny.'

'No, that would be three followed by five.' He tapped the pen against his mouth. 'Yes, I reckon I know what it is.' He clicked the pen and began filling in a row of squares. 'There,' he said, showing her what he'd written. It was her name.

'All right, I get the message,' she said irritably. 'But just because I agreed to have a drink with you, it doesn't mean I have to be the life and soul of the party.'

'Did I say that's what I expected?'

'No, but you probably think your special brand of charm will disarm me. But you've picked the wrong girl. Right now I'm off men.'

'Nice to know I have a special brand of charm. I must remember that.' He put the newspaper down, laid the pen on top of it. 'I'm glad we're sitting here being civil.'

'Your standards must be pretty low if you settle for civil.'

'Quite the reverse, I'm too choosy for my own good. So I'm told. Personally I prefer to call it discernment.'

Lizzie took a long sip of her beer. Followed by another. And another, all the while keeping her gaze on the river and studying the reflection of the willow trees and the sky in the still surface of the water.

'I'm perfectly happy to sit here in silence, if that's what you want,' Jed said, lifting his right leg up onto his left knee, then flicking at some dried grass stuck on the hem of his jeans, 'but I do so hate a lost opportunity.'

She turned to look directly at him. 'By that you mean you intend to keep digging away until you've learnt all you think there is to know about me? Is that it?'

'Wow, a real live person who believes the world really does revolve around her; I'm impressed. But I'm prepared to talk about anything, and anyone, other than you, if you'd rather. For instance, I've noticed you spending a lot of time with Mrs Dallimore. What do you reckon to her? Harmless old lady, or sagacious wit?'

'My, my, that's a big word for a gardener.'

He narrowed his eyes. 'And that's a very prejudiced thing to say, if you don't mind me saying. Because I cut lawns, you've got me down as a thicko, is that it?'

Lizzie had shocked herself. She put down her glass and briefly covered her face with her hands. 'I'm sorry,' she murmured, 'that was a pretty low shot. Maybe I should just go, before I say anything worse.'

'No, don't go, I'm curious to see just how rude you really

could be if you tried. I suspect we've only tickled the top of the iceberg so far.'

She frowned. 'Why are you so determined to get to know me?'

'Maybe I fancy you.' He smiled. 'But there again, maybe I don't.'

'You're just a little mad, aren't you?'

'That's the cross I have to bear in life, not to be taken seriously.'

'If you behaved with a bit more gravitas, then people might take you seriously.'

'And I'd die of utter boredom in the process. Is that what you want for me?'

'Right now I'd settle for—'

'Back to settling again!' he interrupted her, his voice breaching the quiet of the beer garden and causing a few people to look their way. 'I want none of it, I want to sing and dance on the tables of life!'

Oh hell, he was a full-on crazy! 'I'm warning you,' she hissed, 'if you start dancing on the tables here, I'm off.'

Quick as a flash, he banged his glass down on the table and stood up.

She groaned. 'Please don't!'

As quickly as he'd leapt to his feet, he sat down again. 'Had you going there for a moment, didn't I?' To those around them who were still looking, but pretending they weren't, he said, 'Nothing to see here, move along, please.'

In spite of everything, Lizzie smiled.

'Finally, at long last, I've made you smile.'

'It won't happen again. Now, please, will you try and behave yourself and let me enjoy my drink without having to worry that you're about to do something crazy? You're worse than my two-year-old nephew.'

'I wouldn't have had you down as the easily embarrassed sort.'

'How could you possibly have any idea of what I'm like?'

He shrugged. 'Instinct, I guess.' After a small pause, he said, 'And what does your instinct tell you about me?'

She looked him dead in the eye. 'It tells me there's something fake about you.'

He nodded. 'Interesting. In what way?'

'Well, you're certainly not fooling anyone with your simple gardener routine. You're a posh boy who for some reason is deliberately choosing to underachieve. What did you do, go on an extended gap year and never quite get it together again?'

'And if I did, would that be such a crime?'

'The crime is ... is that ...' Her voice trailed away. She was firing off salvos for no real reason, but somehow she couldn't bring herself to say anything pleasant. 'Forget I said anything,' she muttered.

'Sorry, no can do. You've got some injustice buzzing around inside your head and right now I seem to be on the receiving end of your anger and resentment.'

She frowned. 'You do know you speak a lot of nonsense, don't you?'

'Fair maiden,' he said, raising his glass to her, 'I am the pedlar of bombast, the jester of jocularity, the nonny of nonsense, hyperbole is my game! So come on, get it off your chest, whatever it is that's giving you cause to hate me.'

'I don't hate you.'

'Yeah, you do. You took one look at me and decided I had all the charisma of a cockroach.'

'I wouldn't rate you that poorly.'

'A rat, then?'

She rolled her eyes and drank some of her beer. 'Funny you should have chosen that particular animal, because love rat is my most hated species at the moment.'

'Ah, so you've had man trouble recently, have you?'

'You could say that.'

'What did the swine do?'

'Lied. Cheated. Betrayed. You name it, he did it.'

185

'He sounds a sweetheart.'

'Do you take anything seriously?'

'Only the serious stuff.'

'And having your heart broken isn't serious?'

He stared at her hard. 'You look fine to me. Your heart isn't broken. Not by a long way. Besides, do you want him to have that honour? Was he worth it? Nah, he was a tosser. You're better off without him.'

'Is life always that simple in your world?'

'Life is as simple as you want it to be,' he said with a shrug.

'So that's why you're working as a gardener?'

He frowned. 'What is it with you and denigrating what I do?'

Lizzie let out a long sigh of resignation. Or more precisely, surrender. The fight had gone out of her. 'I'm sorry,' she said gloomily. 'But the truth is, I'm tired of people not being who they say they are, and with everything that's gone wrong for me recently, I guess you're an easy target. It's nothing personal.'

'Glad to be of use, in that case. So what else has gone wrong for you? Anything I can help you with?'

'If you could wave a magic wand and find me a proper job like the one I used to have, that would be a good start.'

Chapter Twenty-Nine

Dusk was settling when Lizzie cycled home through the village, the cool evening air scented with honeysuckle and freshly mown grass. All the way from the pub she had warned herself not to get her hopes up. Jed was probably exaggerating the strength of his relationship with the friend who worked at Skylark Radio, a commercial radio station that covered East Anglia and which Mum occasionally listened to. He was probably just trying to impress her, because frankly, it was too much of a coincidence that he should know somebody who might be in a position to offer her a job. She couldn't be that lucky.

Not so long ago she would have laughed at the pitiful prospect of working for a commercial radio station outside of London – the backwater of radio doom – but now here she was, hoping against hope that there might be an opening for her. Even if she had to make do with making tea and running errands, she would do it just to get herself back in the game. She needed to be out there again in the real world before she became as institutionalised as some of the residents at Woodside had become.

She was passing the church when she did a double take. Driving towards her was a Mini Cooper, and at the sight of the familiar charcoal-grey car with black trim her immediate thought was to hide. But there was nowhere to hide, no convenient tree or car to slip behind. As thoroughly exposed as she was, all she could do was hope that her cycling helmet was sufficient disguise for Simon not to recognise her. Lowering her head with all the focused intent of a Tour de

France cyclist, she pedalled on, her gaze fixed determinedly on the pavement to her left. It meant she had no way of knowing if Simon had spotted her, and while she knew he wasn't the sort to revel in another's misfortune, there was no getting around the fact that he had told his mother the real reason for her being sacked. And, let's face it, he wouldn't be human if he wasn't just a little bit pleased to know she had fallen from grace so spectacularly. Who didn't like to see the villain get their comeuppance? But what concerned her most was, what if word had gone round that she had been royally dumped by Curt? How satisfying would that be to Simon? Yet surely, unless Curt blabbed, nobody in London would know about that. But really, what did any of it matter? Her shame was complete whichever way she looked at it.

Earlier that afternoon Mrs Dallimore had advised her to use her anger in a constructive manner, that she shouldn't let it rule her. In view of how vile she'd been to Jed, she could safely say she hadn't heeded that advice in the slightest. She had said some terrible things to him, all of which reflected her own pathetic self-judgement. How many times had she been told by Mum that judging others always said more about oneself than the person being judged? She had, after a second drink, apologised unreservedly to Jed for her rudeness and tried to explain why she was acting the way she was. She told him about losing her job and being forced to return home to her parents, and that being dumped was the last straw. 'None of which excuses my being so nasty to you,' she'd said, 'but I am sorry I've been so horrible.'

'And there was me thinking your default setting was bitch-queen,' he'd said lightly. 'I'm almost disappointed: I was getting to quite like that side of you.'

She'd asked him again if he ever took anything seriously. 'Seriously enough,' he'd said. 'Tell me some more about the job you lost.'

Once she had relaxed and lowered her guard, she had found it surprisingly easy to talk to him. He was like her brother in that respect: a good listener. He had an open face with blue eyes that held her gaze while she spoke and she could tell he was listening properly to her, not just feigning interest.

They'd just finished their second drink when his mobile had rung. 'Sorry,' he'd said, after speaking no more than a few words to whoever had rung him, 'but I'm going to have to go.' They'd parted in the pub car park, he'd turned left and she right in the direction of Great Magnus.

Home now, she put her bicycle in the garage, shut the door and went round to the back door. Mum and Dad were in the kitchen. They had that look on their faces, the one that said they had something to say, but didn't know how to go about it.

'But why?' asked Lizzie. 'What on earth possessed Simon to come and see you?'

'He was on his way to see his parents for a couple of days and called in here first to apologise.'

Lizzie looked at her father in disbelief. 'Why, what has he done?'

'He hasn't done anything; in fact, he couldn't have been nicer.'

'He's embarrassed by the way his mother's carrying on,' Mum said hotly. 'And rightly so. She's behaving like a very spiteful child.'

'You didn't say that, did you?'

'Of course not,' her mother said indignantly. 'Unlike other people, I know how to behave.'

'It was good of him to care about our feelings,' Dad said, 'but I can't help thinking he came here hoping to see you as well.'

'I doubt that very much. Unless he came to gloat.'

Lizzie's father shook his head. 'I think you're doing Simon a grave injustice. There was nothing in his manner to suggest he wished you ill. Quite the opposite, he was most solicitous in asking after you.'

189

'What did you tell him?'

'We told him the truth,' her mother said, 'that Curt was now out of the picture.'

Inwardly groaning, Lizzie sank into the nearest chair. Anything but the truth, she thought miserably, as the last remnants of her tattered pride disintegrated.

Chapter Thirty

The next day after lunch, when Lizzie had set off to Woodside on her bike, Tom took Freddie to feed the ducks. He was glad to be out of the house. Today was one of those days when he had to step away from Tess and give her some space; she wasn't easy to be around right now. It was an admission, even if it was just to himself, that didn't sit well with him. He and Tess rarely disagreed; neither of them liked confrontation, which meant at times they weren't entirely honest with each other.

Tom certainly hadn't been honest yesterday with Tess about Simon. In his opinion, her blurting out to Simon that Curt was not leaving his wife for Lizzie, and had probably never intended to do so, had not been fair to Lizzie. He suspected Tess had said what she had because she would like nothing better than to have things as they once were – life pre-Curt Flynn. If Tom were honest he'd like the same, but he doubted Lizzie would see it that way. And how could life return to how it had once been? Too much trust had been destroyed in the last few weeks for that to be possible, not just on the part of Lizzie and Simon, but between Lorna and Tess. Could their friendship ever be repaired? Tom doubted it. In contrast, he and Keith would most likely be able to smooth things out between themselves, if only because they would deliberately never speak of the matter, but Tess and Lorna were a different kettle of fish.

It wasn't often Tom was lost for words, but when he'd opened the door yesterday and seen Simon on the doorstep, he'd been at a loss to know what to say. There had been a split second when the sight of Simon had been so wholly familiar, he had very nearly welcomed him inside just as he always used to when the lad had practically been family. It was, he'd realised after checking himself, the first time they had seen each other since Lizzie had turned the world upside down. It had been a close-run thing as to who had looked the more awkward of the pair of them, but with nothing else for it, Tom had ushered Simon inside and taken him through to the sitting room where Tess had been reading to Freddie before taking him upstairs to bed. It had been Freddie who had saved the day for them all by taking the book from Tess's hands and showing it to Simon, excitedly pointing to the picture of a monkey and throwing in a few monkey noises for good measure. To Simon's credit he had responded perfectly and pointed to a lion and asked Freddie what noise it made. There had then followed all manner of animal noises with Freddie jumping off the sofa to bounce around the room like an over-excited kangaroo. There was nothing like a small child to act as an icebreaker, and with the mood slightly eased, Simon had come right out with the purpose of his visit: to apologise for the way his mother was behaving. 'I don't know what's got into her,' he'd said, 'but there's no need for her to be taking things out on you two. The four of you were friends before Lizzie and I got together; there's no reason you shouldn't remain so.'

Tom had tried graciously to accept the apology, at the same time shrugging it off by resorting to clichés and saying it was all a storm in a teacup and time would heal once the dust had settled, but Tess had leapt in and accused Lorna of not having any idea how badly they felt and how upset they were since she had all but blamed and vilified them. Tom had tried discreetly to signal to his wife to stop speaking, but unusually for her she was giving vent to her feelings and saying it wasn't for Simon to apologise, that it was Lorna who should be expressing regret. Worried that Tess was about to undo the good Simon had come to do, Tom had offered him a drink and after politely refusing, Simon had asked how Lizzie was. That was when, once again, Tess had said more than was appropriate.

A short while later, when they'd got Freddie to bed and Lizzie arrived home, the truth of his concern was made all too apparent.

'Why, Mum?' she'd groaned. 'Why did you have to tell Simon about Curt?'

'Why not?' Tess had answered back, her tone defensive. 'It's true, isn't it?'

'True or not, I'd rather you didn't feel the need to share with Simon my every failure.'

Tom hated knowing that Lizzie saw her life so bleakly. He wished he could do something to cheer her up, but what could he do? What she needed was a massive boost to her self-esteem, and he was damned if he knew how to provide that.

At the duck pond now, Tom unstrapped Freddie from the pushchair and took him to the edge of the pond. With eager hands Freddie took the bag of breadcrumbs Tom gave him.

'Now remember to throw just a little bit each time,' Tom said, knowing full well the instruction would be ignored. Sure enough, Freddie began flinging handfuls of bread in all directions. At once a squadron of ducks swam over to where they were standing, inciting squeals of delight. The nearer they got, the more animated Freddie became – he was now at the stage of stamping his feet he was so excited.

How easy children are at this stage, Tom thought nostalgically, remembering Lizzie and Luke at a similar age. He remembered also how Lizzie just naturally demanded more of their care and attention than Luke ever did. Luke was born lucky, Tess used to say; everything just fell into his lap. The fact that they never had to worry about him was just as well: worrying about Lizzie was quite enough to contend with.

A splash followed by a shrill cry and a squally chorus

of quacking jolted him out of his thoughts. To his horror, Freddie must have taken a step too far towards the water's edge and tumbled in.

If Tom had been able to smuggle Freddie in and change him into some dry clothes without Tess knowing, he would have gladly done so. But as it was, the whole of the village probably heard Freddie's cries as Tom hurried home with him, his socks and shoes squelching with pond water with every step. He blamed himself, of course; if he hadn't been so distracted, he would have kept his eye on his grandson.

Before he'd even got round to the back of the house, Tess came running towards him. 'What's happened?' she cried, her hands outstretched to take Freddie from the pushchair.

'Don't fuss, it's nothing!' Tom snapped back at her, unstrapping Freddie and carrying him inside the house, but not before seeing the stricken expression on his wife's face.

'It doesn't sound like nothing,' replied Tess, following behind him. 'Tell me you didn't let him fall in the pond!' Her voice was raised – it had to be above the awful din Freddie was making – and Tom balked at the stinging accusation contained within her words.

'He just got a bit wet, that's all.'

'A bit wet?' she remonstrated. 'He's soaked to the skin from top to toe! Here, give him to me. I'll calm him down, then you can tell me what on earth you've done. Heaven only knows what Ingrid will say!'

In that precise moment, nothing would have made Tom relinquish his grandson to Tess. He rounded on his wife. 'Why do you always have to make such a big drama out of everything? And why is it that you can have an accident with Freddie and I can support you, but when it's me, you do nothing but make out I'm some kind of blithering fool?'

She stared back at him, stunned. 'I don't make a drama out of everything. And I'm not blaming you.'

'You *are*!'

Their angry exchange had the effect of silencing Freddie and, looking first at Tom, then at Tess, he gave a long juddering sniff and stuck out his lower lip. 'Sorry,' he murmured. 'Freddie very sorry.'

In the sudden silence, Tom blinked and swallowed hard. Unable to speak, he handed his grandson over to Tess and bolted back outside to the garden, his body shaking with a spasm of impotent regret. How had it happened? How could he have been so furiously sharp with Tess? What had got into him?

Thinking of his little grandson apologising, he could not have felt more ashamed of himself.

Chapter Thirty-One

Enjoying the peace and quiet of her usual spot in the rose arbour, Clarissa watched Lizzie on the terrace helping Mr Sheridan – or Gordon, as he insisted she call him. From what Clarissa could see he was asking Lizzie to reposition his chair so he could sit directly in the sun – *Pah, skin cancer at my time of life be damned!* was his battle cry when advised to sit in the shade, as they all were. What a silly old goose he was. But, of course, she understood all too well that his flouting of the advice was his way of maintaining a sense of autonomy. They all did it to a degree, a digging in of heels here, a refusal there. Clarissa's small act of defiance was to feed the birds outside her room – they were told not to in case it encouraged rats.

Observing how attentive Lizzie was being, Clarissa very much hoped that Jed had been astute enough not to let on to Lizzie that it had been her idea for him to ask the girl out for a drink. She also hoped that Lizzie had been gracious enough to accept the invitation. Her world seemed so very gloomy for her at the moment, and a little lightness, even if it was fleeting and no more than a distraction in the form of a young man who had got off on the wrong foot with her, would be no bad thing in Clarissa's opinion. It was what everybody needed, something a little unexpected to provide a respite from an excess of disappointment and the grinding monotony of a dull routine.

Clarissa had had many highs and lows in her life, but she could never lay claim to a dull life. Was that a state of mind, she wondered, or a highly selective memory at work? Even as a child she couldn't recall being bored, she could always find something to do, but perhaps that was down to her being comfortably, though not exclusively, self-contained. She enjoyed the company of others, but was quite happy to be alone.

Not being allowed to be alone was one of the things she had feared most about her intention to end her days here at Woodside. Cutting that final tie and selling her house had represented not just the throwing in of the towel, but an acceptance that she would have to face the inevitable loss of her individuality, maybe even her personality, and more importantly, the right to enjoy her own company. However, her worst fears had not materialised and she was enormously relieved and grateful for that.

Funny really how she had ended up here when there were dozens of homes to pick from in Suffolk. Unlike some of the other residents here, she had had no previous connection with this particular village, or immediate surrounding area, it really had been a matter of chance. But then, so much in life was. There had also been an element of choosing somewhere new to live, her last hurrah, you could say, her swansong.

Still watching Lizzie as she tried to persuade Mr Sheridan to wear his sun hat, Clarissa thought how much she enjoyed talking to the girl. There had been no opportunity yesterday to chat with her and initially that had annoyed Clarissa. Then she had chided herself for turning into what she had always vowed she never would, a selfish and demanding old woman. There were other people here with whom Lizzie could spend time, not just her.

But there was no getting away from it, the girl intrigued Clarissa; she so blatantly wore her heart on her sleeve, yet probably believed she did the complete opposite. Just as Clarissa had thought she had done as a young girl.

She was touched how genuine Lizzie's interest in her life was; she didn't feign interest because that was what was expected of her – the occasional question asked purely for the sake of appearing as though she cared. Admittedly it was self-centred of Clarissa to enjoy Lizzie as a sole audience, but she liked reliving the past: going into things in such detail brought it all vividly alive for her. It also brought back memories she hadn't thought of in a very long time. Strange how it was all there, it just needed the right prompt for it all to come flooding back and in the smallest and seemingly insignificant detail. The more she told Lizzie, the more she wanted to share with her, perhaps because she knew this chance to relive the past would never come her way again.

Up on the terrace, Lizzie waved to her. Mr Sheridan – *Gordon* – was now absorbed in his newspaper and very likely harrumphing at most of what he read, denouncing it as nothing but governmental whitewash or media manipulation. With Lizzie miming the actions of drinking a cup of tea, Clarissa nodded, happily.

Ten minutes later and with her captive audience now making her way across the lawn to her, Clarissa readied herself for telling the next part of her story.

Chapter Thirty-Two

May 1939, Shillingbury Grange, Suffolk

With what felt like alarming speed, the children arrived less than a fortnight after Clarissa had convinced Lavinia that she should offer her home to two children desperately in need. Charles had said little on the matter to her, other than to abnegate all responsibility and involvement.

'Not my bailiwick,' he said gruffly over dinner the evening before the children's arrival, as though to reinforce what he'd said before. 'I'll have nothing to do with the blighters, and if they annoy me they'll be sent packing.'

'I don't think it works quite like that,' Lavinia had said quietly. 'They can't be sent back because they're a bit of a nuisance.'

Lavinia might have resisted Clarissa's initial request to host a couple of children, but she had come round to the idea, and while she wasn't as willing a champion of the cause that Polly, and now Clarissa, believed in, that as many children as possible had to be rescued and found homes as soon as possible, she was doing her best to do what she clearly saw as 'the right thing'.

The stories coming out from not just Nazi Germany, but Nazi Europe, were terrifying. Artie kept Clarissa regularly updated by letter, as did Polly, both of them adamant that Europe was sleepwalking into a vision of hell. Clarissa's biggest regret was that she couldn't persuade Lavinia to take in more children – after all, the house was plenty big enough. But it wasn't Clarissa's house to throw open the doors of, and she had to content herself with what she had achieved so far. She had also to bear in mind that, strictly speaking, she was a guest in her grandparents' home, and should therefore abide by the protocol expected of her. But whenever she thought she might be overstepping the mark, she reminded herself that these people had a debt to pay, and she had no qualms in extracting every last ounce of it.

Grandma Ethel in America was furious that Clarissa had refused to return home. '*It isn't safe to be in Europe right now*,' she telegraphed. '*I NEED you here.*'

Clarissa could think of no real reason why Grandma Ethel would need her – she had a platoon of servants at her beck and call and any number of friends – and so she wrote once again to cajole the old lady into accepting that, for now, her home was in England. 'I have work here to do,' she informed Grandma Ethel, somewhat grandly. 'Please let me stay.' Acceptance was reluctant, but it came, as did a generous increase in the allowance her grandmother gave her, which Clarissa put to good use.

After what must have been a bewildering journey from Berlin, the children arrived at Harwich and were then put on a train to Liverpool Street station where Artie, since he was in London, met the boys and accompanied them on the train to Shillingbury.

They spoke no more than a handful of words in English – *hello*, *please* and *thank you*, which the eldest, a boy of eight years of age, blurted out in a confused rush on meeting Clarissa when she went to fetch them at Shillingbury station. His name was Thomas and his younger brother, Walter, not yet six, refused to let go of his hand. 'He's done that all the way,' Artie told Clarissa quietly.

She bent down to the two boys and looked them kindly in the eye, turning her head from one to the other. Smiling to put them at ease, she told them her name. 'Well then,' she went on, 'you must be tired and hungry; shall we go and see what we can find for you to eat?'

She had no way of knowing if they understood her, but in a clipped polite voice, Thomas said. 'Thank you, please, miss.'

Clarissa led the way from the station to where Jimmy was waiting for them with a rickety old cart, a replacement for the trap that had been all but smashed to pieces in the accident. Apollo had been replaced by the most docile of horses that went by the name of Jack. He was a large, bored-looking animal and, unlike Apollo, didn't scare easily, so his previous owner claimed.

The two boys took one look at Jack and visibly tensed, the younger emitting a small gasp. 'They're city boys,' Artie said under his breath, 'more used to cars and trams.'

'A horse and cart is a lot more fun for two young lads,' Clarissa said brightly, hoping that Jimmy wouldn't terrify them with one of his notorious grimaces – when he chose to, he had a grimace that could drive rivets through steel.

She helped Artie lift the boys into place in the cart. When they were all settled, Jimmy ordered the horse to move on and they set off at an unhurried pace. Lavinia and Charles did own a car, but since Jimmy was terrified of it, and Charles could no longer drive, it hadn't been used in a long time.

As they progressed slowly along the open country lanes, Jack plodding unhurriedly as if he had all the time in the world, the children spoke quietly in German to each other. Dressed identically in good-quality clothes – shorts, shirts and pullovers, beneath thick overcoats and with polished brown leather shoes on their feet – each carried a small suitcase that bore a manila label with his name written on it. The sight of those suitcases, presumably packed by their anxious parents with clothes and one or two precious things to help them feel at home wherever they ended up, brought a painful lump to Clarissa's throat. To distract herself, she leant forward to the two boys and suggested they removed their overcoats; it was, after all, a warm day.

They shook their heads simultaneously and shrank away from her.

'I think they're scared of losing what little they've come with,' Artie said. 'I would imagine their parents told them to be careful and wary of anybody trying to take things from them.'

'Poor lambs,' murmured Clarissa, 'they must be so confused and upset. I hope they'll realise before too long that they're quite safe with me.'

Artie turned to look at her, his expression serious. 'They may not appreciate what you and your grandparents are doing for them now, but one day they will. As will their parents. For now you'll have to make do with my gratitude.'

'I'm only doing what any right-minded person would do.'

He smiled and took hold of one of her hands. 'If it hadn't been for your persuasiveness, I don't believe your grandparents would have agreed to do this.'

'Perhaps not,' she said, conscious of the pleasant warmth of his skin. 'But other host families would have been found for these boys.'

'Maybe so. But I appreciate what you're doing. Staying in Shillingbury for a protracted length of time wasn't really part of your plan, was it?' he continued. 'It was London where you wanted to be.'

She smiled. 'But here I am in Shillingbury, and I wouldn't want to be anywhere else.'

'I wish I could stay with you.'

The colour rose to her face, but before she could respond, he let go of her hand. 'So I could help you with the boys,' he said quickly, as though needing to clarify himself.

'Of course,' she said evenly. 'When do you start work?' she asked in an attempt to ease his discomfiture. Instead of working for Reuters as he'd originally planned, the offer of being a European reporter for CBS had come up and Artie had grabbed it without a second thought.

'Sooner than I thought,' he said. 'Next week. I'll be based in London initially, and then ... and then we'll see.'

This was the way a lot of people were now speaking; there

was so much uncertainty in the air. Although from what Polly and Artie had shared with her, war with Germany seemed as certain as night following day. Just recently she'd heard on the wireless that farmers were now required to plough as much grazing pasture as possible to increase home-produced food in case there were shortages of imported food, if war did break out. There was talk also of children being evacuated from London.

'I know it might sound fanciful, but staying in Europe as a reporter is what I believe I'm meant to do,' Artie said, after a moment's silence had passed, during which Clarissa had dug around in her handbag for the chocolate she'd brought for the children.

'I understand exactly what you mean,' she said. 'It's why I believe I was meant to come to this country and visit my English grandparents when I did, so that I could do something meaningful with my life.'

The chocolate bar found, she tore away part of the wrapper, snapped off a couple of pieces and held them out to the boys. They looked unsure, but at Artie's encouragement, they each took a piece. Within seconds they looked less solemn. But at no stage did Walter let go of his brother's protective left hand. Passing over the bridge – the scene of the accident, the memory of which still gave Clarissa nightmares – it struck her that maybe Thomas was gaining as much strength and reassurance from holding hands with his little brother as Walter was.

Lavinia was waiting for them when they reached the house. With her hair tied back in the severe way she often wore it, and her dignified demeanour stiff with apprehension, she did not exactly present a kindly welcome as she stood in the large hallway. She tried to shake hands formally with the two boys and Thomas acquiesced, but Walter was having none of it and hid behind his brother.

'Perhaps you'd like to show them up to their room,' Lavinia said awkwardly to Clarissa, 'while I ask Cook to rustle up something to eat. Mr Bloomberg, please make yourself at home in the drawing room. Charles is in there.'

Indicating to the boys that they should come with her, Clarissa took them upstairs to the small room next door to hers. Lavinia had said they could have a much larger room at the other end of the house where their noise could be annexed and contained, but Clarissa had said the boys would feel they were more a part of the household if they weren't effectively isolated.

The boys stood in the middle of the room, still holding hands, and looked solemnly about them. Clarissa had tried her best to brighten the room to make it feel more cheerful and welcoming. With Lily and Jimmy's help she had painted over the existing wallpaper and found a rug from another room that was less threadbare than the existing one had been. Lily had revealed a talent for sewing and, after Clarissa had ordered some blue and white cotton gingham, the two of them had made some new curtains to replace the original heavy velvet ones which had produced clouds of dust when taken down. Clarissa had also ordered two new single beds and a chest full of toys from London – a train set, building bricks, a cricket bat and ball, a set of soldiers and a wooden castle with a drawbridge and some books. She had also purchased a pair of desks for the children to sit at – she had pictured them writing home to their parents while looking out of the window at the garden.

Secretly she had been rather pleased with the changes she had wrought; pleased, too, to have had something positive to do, but now as she watched the boys silently surveying the room with its shabby attempt to make them feel at home, she wondered at her conceit. How arrogant of her to think they would be thrilled with their new surroundings, when all they would want was to be with their parents. The older boy turned his solemn face to her. 'Thank you, please, miss.'

'I'm afraid it was the best I could do in the circumstances,' she said, wishing with all her heart she could convey to these forlorn little boys that she would do all in her power to lessen the pain of their separation from all that they knew and loved. Moreover, she wanted them to know that they would be well cared for here, she would see to that herself. They would want for nothing … other than their home and parents.

Chapter Thirty-Three

June 1939, Shillingbury Grange, Suffolk

The boys had only been with them for a week and already they were picking up English at an impressive speed. The learning process had so far involved a lot of gesticulating on Clarissa's part, or resorting to sketching on paper. Usually Thomas would pick up the word or phrase first and then explain it to his brother. They were still inseparable but Walter no longer held onto Thomas's hand in the way he had when they arrived, though he had yet to sleep in his own bed. Lavinia had pulled a face when Clarissa had made the discovery on their first night that Walter was fast asleep in bed with his brother, the pair of them clutching two small teddy bears.

Today Clarissa was taking them to meet the schoolmistress of the village school, a Mrs Russell. To explain where they were going, Clarissa had drawn a rough picture of children sitting at rows of desks looking up at a blackboard. Neither of the boys had expressed any enthusiasm for the idea, and now, as they approached the centre of the village, passing the blacksmith's on their left where a man in a leather apron and shirtsleeves was bent over an anvil and swinging a long-handled hammer, the boys slowed their step alongside a stone water trough and pump. They might have been genuinely interested in watching the blacksmith at work, but more likely it was a delaying tactic, just as they had taken forever standing on the bridge over the river and looking out for fish. Hurrying them along, she had tried to explain that they could do that on their return.

She indicated they move on and shortly came to a garage where a man in overalls was filling a car with petrol. He tipped his cap at Clarissa and smiled at the boys. From there they followed the curve in the road and passed the wheelwright's, then on towards the baker's shop where a woman was placing a tray of iced fancies in the window. Next door was the butcher's and then the post office.

A little further on and they came to the village green. It was ringed with a higgledy-piggledy assortment of pink and white cottages, some steeply thatched, others with slate-tiled roofs. Their windows were small and diamond-paned and their front doors so low most people would have to stoop to enter. It was a delightfully picturesque scene that Clarissa marvelled at each time she saw it; she loved the sheer quaintness of it. How different it was to what she'd left behind in Boston.

She indicated to the boys that they had to cross the road and, after passing the church, they walked the short distance up the hill to the school. A mixture of brick and flint with a small playground to the front, the school looked a good deal more inviting than the imposing edifice Clarissa had attended. It wasn't long since she had left school herself, but as she pushed open the wooden gate, it felt a lifetime ago.

With Thomas and Walter looking hesitant and lagging behind, she smiled encouragingly at them and held out her hands to them both. They had never taken her hand before, but they did so now. 'There's nothing to worry about,' she said. 'It'll be all right.'

Mrs Russell was waiting for them in her office, a room that was about five feet square with no window and a desk pressed against one wall. It seemed to be doubling up as a storeroom as the other walls were covered in shelves laden with books and a whole host of classroom paraphernalia. Mrs Russell was by no means small and when she rose from the chair in front of the desk, she dominated the cramped space, towering over not just Thomas and Walter, but Clarissa too.

'Your reputation goes before you, Miss Allerton,' she said warmly. 'I've heard a lot about you.'

'Really?' asked Clarissa, taken aback.

'Not that I indulge in gossip, but in a village of this size word soon goes around when a wealthy American heiress moves in amongst us.'

Clarissa smiled. 'I'm half English, let's not forget that.'

The woman laughed. 'I apologise. Well then, tell me about these fine young boys.'

Clarissa nudged them forward. 'Thomas is eight years of age and Walter will be six in a month's time.'

'How much English can you speak?' Mrs Russell's question was directed at Thomas and accompanied with a kindly expression to put him at ease.

'A leetle,' he replied.

The woman smiled. 'Enough to understand the question, so that's an excellent start.'

'I've been teaching them a few words of English since they arrived,' Clarissa said, 'but obviously the more they mix with other children, the faster they'll learn.'

'I'm afraid they will have to learn fast. We're only a very small school here – I just have two other teachers who help me – but I'm sure we'll manage. I would suggest the eldest boy starts off with his brother in the youngest group. If he's a bright lad, he'll soon pick up sufficient English to move in with the older children.'

It was agreed they would start school the next morning.

That evening, after Clarissa had said goodnight to the boys, she went downstairs to the drawing room, all set to listen to the usual grumbles from her grandfather.

His complaints were always the same: how their lives had been turned upside down since Thomas and Walter had arrived, and how everything revolved around them. And not *you*, Clarissa was always tempted to add. In that respect Charles Upwood had a lot in common with Grandma Ethel.

But as she took her place in the chair beside her grandfather and picked up a book she was reading, he appeared to have forgotten to make his protest. Progress, she thought, as he remained silently absorbed in the newspaper he was reading. Every day he scrutinised it for news about the situation in Europe; like Artie, he was convinced war was inevitable, that it was time for somebody to stand up to Hitler. He frequently referred to Chamberlain, the prime minister of England, as a fool with about as much backbone as a jellyfish.

For five minutes the only sound in the room was the ticking of the clock on the mantelpiece and the occasional rustle of the newspaper, or Charles clearing his throat. Clarissa was quite comfortable with the silence and didn't in any way find it uncomfortable; time spent with Grandma Ethel had taught her that much.

Lavinia appeared just then, and remembering Artie's most recent letter to which she had yet to reply, Clarissa asked her grandmother if she could use her writing desk.

'Of course,' Lavinia said absently, going over to the wireless to switch it on.

After fetching her writing things and making herself comfortable at the desk, Clarissa had written no more than *Dear Artie*, when Lavinia, who seemed more restless than usual, drifted across the room to her. 'I'm afraid life here must be so very dull for you,' she said.

'Not at all,' responded Clarissa, surprised.

'I can't think why you should want to stay with us.'

Clarissa put down her pen. 'Are you saying you'd rather I left?'

'Of course not. But I do wonder at what you've got yourself into, marooned here with us and two young boys you don't know from Adam. Why, you're not very much older than they are.'

'I'm not a child, far from it,' asserted Clarissa.

'Even so, it's hardly what you could have imagined your visit to England would entail.'

'I had an open mind when I arrived, which is something my mother taught me. That, and to follow my instinct.'

Lavinia frowned, and drawing her cardigan around her shoulders in what Clarissa recognised as one of her numerous and habitual gestures of unease, she said, 'How like Fran that sounds.'

Later that night, shortly after she had got into bed and was thinking about the next morning when she would take Thomas and Walter to school, Clarissa heard an unexpected noise through the open window. She couldn't be sure, but it sounded like some sort of engine. Was it an airplane flying low over the house? But as the noise grew louder, she recognised it as the engine of a motorcycle. She glanced at her alarm clock on the bedside cabinet – it was ten forty-five. Her grandparents had long since gone to bed, so who on earth would be calling on them at this hour?

She slipped out of bed, found her slippers and pulled on her dressing gown and quietly opened her door. Crossing the landing to the front of the house, she parted the curtains at the window and peered into the moonlit darkness at the driveway below. Sure enough, there was a motorcycle, and standing by the side of it was a tall man. Raising his chin to undo the strap on his helmet, he looked up at the house, provoking Clarissa to gasp with amazed recognition. She sped down the stairs to prevent him from yanking on the wrought-iron bell and having its echoing clamour wake the household.

'Ellis, what in the world are you doing here?' she asked when she had the door unlocked and open.

'I was just passing and thought I'd call in to say hello.'

'Just passing!' she exclaimed. 'At this time of night?'

He tilted his head back and laughed. 'That's not exactly the welcome I was hoping for, but I guess it'll have to do in the circumstances. Any chance of something to eat? I'm starving.'

Impressing upon him the need to keep quiet, she led the way to the kitchen in the darkness. Once there, she closed the door and switched on the light, its harsh brightness reminding her that she was in her nightclothes. Self-consciously she tightened the belt on her dressing gown.

Ellis observed her. 'Don't worry, your sacred honour is quite safe with me,' he said with a smirk, 'so long as you hurry up and give me something to eat, or I may have to resort to eating *you*!'

'Goodness, I had forgotten how appallingly rude you could be.'

'Your amnesia was good for something, then. Artie, your greatest advocate, says you're fine now, is that true?'

In spite of herself, she blushed at his description of Artie, and before she could say anything, Ellis lifted the lid on a large crock, pulled a face and lowered the lid. He then looked about the kitchen, taking in the shabbiness. The kitchen had become such a mess; Clarissa supposed it was beyond Mrs Kent's capabilities, or will, to sort it out. It was one of the many things Clarissa longed to take in hand. If it were down to her, she would get rid of Mrs Kent and employ a new cook, paying her a decent wage to ensure loyalty and good service.

'I'll make you a cheese omelette,' Clarissa said, moving round the large table to get to the pantry. Mentally she crossed her fingers that there were enough eggs and sufficient cheese that would be palatable to a man as particular as Ellis.

'You seem very at home here,' Ellis remarked a short time later when he was sitting at the table and tucking into the omelette. 'Is this you doing something *worthwhile*?'

Her hackles went up. 'Yes,' she said. 'What are you doing that's worthwhile?'

He finished what was in his mouth. 'Well, I've been rocketing around the Riviera with Effie, followed by London on my own to see some folks my parents insisted I visit. By the way, Effie sends her love and says she misses you more than words can say, which we both know is an exaggeration, but that's Effie for you. Hyperbole is second nature to her.'

'So why aren't you still in London, what are you doing here?'

'Visiting *you*, of course. When I realised you probably weren't going to meet me for dinner in London, I thought there was nothing else for it but to make the journey to see for myself where you'd dug yourself in. It doesn't really look your kind of place, if you don't mind me saying.'

'I do mind you saying, actually.'

The omelette now eaten, he pushed the plate away from him. 'I love it that you're so defensively prickly with me. I don't suppose you're like that with Artie, are you?'

'No I'm not, but then he's so much nicer than you.'

Ellis laughed. 'You're right. But what you get with me is good old-fashioned honesty. Has Artie been honest with you?'

'I'm not aware of him being *dis*honest with me.'

'It's always what isn't said that you have to listen to most closely. Got any bourbon?'

'No,' she said, stifling a yawn. 'Ellis, as pleased as I am to see you, it's late. Do you think we could continue this conversation tomorrow?'

He looked at her. 'You don't sound at all pleased to see me. In fact, I'd go so far as to say you sound distinctly put out.'

'I'm sorry. It's just ...'

'It's just what?'

'I feel so wrong-footed. It's how you—' She hesitated, reluctant to admit he'd had this effect on her from the moment they met. 'It's what you delight in doing, isn't it,' she said instead, 'making people feel ill at ease?'

'Thank God for that! I was beginning to worry I'd lost my touch and you were indifferent to my unique allure and devilish good looks.'

She laughed. 'Trust me, Ellis, nobody could ever be indifferent to you.'

'Since we have that cleared up, are you going to offer my weary body a bed for the night?'

She looked at him, shocked. 'Aren't you booked into an inn nearby?'

'No. This was an entirely spontaneous desire of mine. There I was staying in London with some exceedingly dull friends of my parents when I thought, to hell with it, I'll get myself a motorcycle and cheer myself up by seeing you.'

'I'm flattered that you should think me capable of doing that.'

'Now don't go fishing for compliments, just point me in the direction of a comfortable bed for the night.'

'But it's not my house. You're putting me in a very difficult spot.'

'The hell I am! A close friend of yours turns up unexpectedly, why wouldn't your grandparents offer me a bed for the night? Are they that mean-spirited?'

'Come on, then,' she said. 'But heaven only knows what they'll say in the morning when they learn they have an uninvited guest.'

'They'll be perfectly British about it and pretend to be delighted to meet me.'

'I wouldn't count on it.'

Chapter Thirty-Four

June 1939, Shillingbury Grange, Suffolk

Clarissa woke early the following morning.

From the bedroom next door came the sound of voices. These were not the voices she was now used to hearing – the quiet murmurings in German of two anxious boys – no, this was exuberant chatter that included a man's voice. *Ellis!*

At the sound of laughter, she got out of bed and hurriedly dressed. Trouble lay ahead with her grandparents, and she had to do her best to minimise the damage.

The door to the boys' room was ajar and, pushing it further open, her gaze fell upon Thomas and Walter in their pyjamas playing on the rug with the wooden toys. They were not alone: dressed in his clothes from last night, Ellis was lying on his side on the floor with them and saying something in German. Seeing her, all three went quiet; the happy smiles from the boys' faces gone in a flash.

'Guten Morgen,' Ellis greeted her brightly, as if there was nothing out of the ordinary in him being here and playing with two German boys.

'You never mentioned you could speak German,' she said.

'You never asked,' he replied. He sat up. 'What's for breakfast? The boys tell me the cook here is terrible.'

'I'm inclined to agree with you, but if you want to be fed, I'd keep that to yourself. And do keep the noise down; Charles doesn't want to be disturbed at any time of the day, let alone this early. Can you tell the boys they need to get dressed, please?' She pointed to the two piles of neatly folded clothes she had put out for them at bedtime last night. 'It's their first day at school. If you can do that for me, I'll go and find Lavinia to explain about your presence here.'

'Say nice things about me, won't you?' he called after her.

'I'll try,' she said, glancing back at him, 'but it won't be easy.'

He smiled and turning to the boys, addressed them in German. At once their faces resumed the happy expressions of before and they smiled and nodded their heads.

'What did you just say to them?' asked Clarissa, curious. She was pretty sure it had nothing to do with getting dressed.

'I asked them if they didn't agree with me that you were the kindest and most beautiful girl in all of England.'

Clarissa flushed. 'You shouldn't tell lies in front of children,' she said.

'For your information, Fräulein Prim, I'm not lying. They were telling me earlier, before you so rudely interrupted our fine game, that they wished they could thank you properly for your kindness, but didn't know how. I told them I wished you were half as nice to me.'

She smiled. 'Perhaps if you were as well behaved as they are, that might be possible.' To the boys she tapped the watch on her wrist. 'Breakfast in ten minutes,' she said in a clear voice.

Now to explain things to her grandmother and assure her no impropriety had taken place under her roof.

Clarissa didn't know what shocked her more, that Lavinia greeted Ellis with impeccable politeness, or the impeccable manner of Ellis's behaviour in return.

His apology for arriving at such a late hour last night, and without invitation, was so fulsome and so utterly devoid of his customary disdain and arrogance that Clarissa could scarcely believe it was the same man sitting at the table beside her. Over breakfast he explained about his friendship with Artie and that he'd wanted the opportunity to see for himself that Clarissa was quite recovered from her accident, as he was required to reassure another mutual friend – none other than Effie Chase – that Clarissa was not at death's door. Clarissa could tell that her grandmother didn't have a clue who Effie Chase was, but was much too polite to say so.

'What a lot of friends you have who are so concerned about your welfare,' she said to Clarissa, 'but really, I'm appalled you didn't wake me last night so I could ensure proper arrangements were made for Mr Randall's stay.'

Evidently thoroughly charmed by Ellis, Lavinia went on to insist he stay for lunch, as she was sure Charles would value chatting with him – he was in his room eating his breakfast alone. 'It makes a refreshing change for my husband to have some male company,' she said. 'We see so few people these days. He enjoyed having your friend Artie here.'

Throughout the exchange, not once did Lavinia wince at the noise of Thomas tapping his teaspoon against his saucer, or reprimand Walter for helping himself to too much jam for his toast. Being a stickler for table manners, mealtimes were a minefield of irritations for her, but this morning she was as good as oblivious to the children's presence so absorbed was she in talking to Ellis.

'Time to go now,' Clarissa said to the boys when she heard the grandfather clock behind her chime.

Without her asking him to, Ellis spoke in German to them, presumably translating what she'd just said. Thomas replied to him and, turning to Clarissa, Ellis said, 'He's asked if I can come with you. Better still, let me take them to school on the Norton.'

Not daring to think what he might want to do to impress two young boys with his motorcycle, she said, 'I think walking will be safer.'

The bell was being rung by Mrs Russell in the schoolyard when they arrived.

'Just let them go in on their own,' Ellis said in a low voice, when Clarissa started to walk with the boys towards the entrance of the building. 'You can't be with them during the day, so you might just as well let them get on with it.'

She knew he was right, but it didn't lessen the anxiety she felt at abandoning the two lost souls to whom she already felt so attached. If it were allowed for her to spend the day in the classroom watching over her young charges, she would. But dragging their feet they slowly joined the throng of children and went through the open door without a backward glance.

'That was brave,' said Ellis quietly.

'Yes,' she said, 'they were very brave.'

'I didn't mean Thomas and Walter, I meant you, letting them go. You do realise, don't you, that you're going to have to resist the emotional need to protect them and fight their battles for them.'

'It's not a *need*,' she said, without looking at him and turning to walk home. 'It's a desire. There's a big difference.'

He scoffed. 'You're not fooling me, Clarissa. Mothering two orphans is more or less the perfect way to satisfy your urge to prove yourself in the world. This is your big worthwhile moment in life, isn't it?'

'They're not orphans,' she corrected him, quickening her step, 'and I do wish you'd stop telling me what I'm supposed to be thinking or doing.'

He ignored her chastisement. 'From what I hear, I'm afraid there's every reason to believe they soon will be,' he said, his voice suddenly grave, 'if they aren't already.' He came to a stop alongside her.

They were standing on the edge of the village green, waiting for a tractor to trundle slowly by. When it had gone, Clarissa said, 'I hope you haven't been expressing that opinion to Thomas and Walter.'

'Of course I haven't, what do you take me for? But they're not stupid, especially not Thomas. He was telling me earlier some of what he's witnessed at home in Berlin, and what he's experienced personally, the bullying at school for being

Jewish, not just from other children, but from teachers, of being made to sit alone at the back of the class, and finally being banned from even attending school last November. He told me of the neighbours who threw stones at him and his brother, and worst of all, he told me what he witnessed during Kristallnacht when Stormtroopers ransacked the family shop while a braying mob looked on. He saw his father and grandfather taken away and returned some days later, badly beaten. So, Clarissa, he knows that his parents are in the greatest of danger and you can't protect him from what he knows already.'

'But I *can* do my damnedest to lessen the nightmare,' Clarissa said, her heart beating rapidly at the horror of what Thomas and Walter had escaped. 'Is that so very wrong?'

Ellis smiled and slipping her arm through his, walked on. 'You're a special girl, Clarissa – promise me you won't ever lose your zeal for doing good.'

She waited for a sarcastic sting in the tail of his remark. When none came, she said, 'Don't be absurd, you're making me out to be some kind of saint.'

'I'm damned if I pay you a compliment and damned if I don't. I can't win with you, can I?'

'Is it that important to you that you do?'

'I *always* win, Clarissa. Remember that, won't you?'

'And in this instance, what exactly is it you think you'll win?' She had a sudden recall of kissing him while less than sober on board the *Belle Etoile*, and didn't like the association of thought.

He threw his head back and laughed. 'That remains to be seen. How do you fancy a ride on the Norton? You could show me round some of this delightfully English countryside, then maybe we could stop at a small quaint inn and sample a glass of this warm soapy beer I've yet to develop a taste for. The English really have no idea when it comes to beer, do they?'

'Not possible, I'm afraid. I have to return here at lunchtime

218

to walk the boys home for lunch. Plus Lavinia is rather keen for you to spend some time with my grandfather.'

'To hell with that, I haven't come all this way to spend time with some bad-tempered old boy who'll talk down to me. I get enough of that back at home.'

'I knew all that charm you were laying on so thick this morning was fake,' Clarissa said with a smile. 'You really are a fraud, aren't you?'

'We're all frauds, Clarissa. Even you.'

'And what's that supposed to mean?'

'You're not honest enough with people. You don't share your true feelings. You've built yourself a wall to hide behind.'

'Does anyone show their true feelings? Look at the performance you put on for my grandmother's benefit at breakfast.'

'I had a reason for my duplicity: I wanted to spend time getting to know you, the *real* you.'

That, thought Clarissa, was the biggest mystery of all. And why did he appear to know her better than she knew herself? Or more precisely, better than she was prepared to admit about herself?

Ellis's visit to Shillingbury extended to a further night, during which time he never faltered in his genial performance, the result being he had both Charles and Lavinia hanging on his every word. He was a surprisingly good raconteur, but also paid Charles plenty of notice by listening to him attentively. Charles mostly spoke of his conviction that war was imminent and that the government should be doing more. With several large glasses of whisky consumed, he spoke bitterly of his financial losses during and after the Depression.

Before Ellis left to return to London, Clarissa's grandparents extracted a promise from him to return again, and soon.

'You've quite cheered us up,' Lavinia said with a soft,

girlish smile that lifted the corners of her customarily downward-sloping mouth and made her seem younger and more carefree. Seeing her grandmother so transformed touched Clarissa; it made her realise that the woman could be happy if the circumstances were different. It made Clarissa want to see her smile more often.

No sooner had this thought passed through her mind than she pictured Ellis raising an accusing eyebrow at her – *Something else to add to your growing list of worthwhile things to do?* she imagined him sneering.

But even she had to admit that it had been fun having Ellis around. Thomas and Walter had thoroughly enjoyed his company and had needed no encouragement to climb onto his motorcycle with him and go for a ride, the two of them, at Clarissa's instruction, holding on tightly, and laughing happily. The day after he left, Thomas came and found Clarissa in the kitchen where she was trying to bring some order to the chaos of Mrs Kent's domain on the cook's afternoon off. Handing her a picture he'd drawn – it was of Ellis standing beside the motorbike – he'd said simply, 'For you.'

What surprised her most was not that Thomas thought she would want a picture of Ellis, but the quality of the drawing. For an eight-year-old, it was exceptionally well executed, to the point that he'd caught the likeness of Ellis remarkably well; the tilt of his head, the directness of his stare, the confidence of his stance – it was unmistakably Ellis.

A week after Ellis had left them, Clarissa received a letter from him saying he was on his way to Florence to rejoin Effie and her father and stepmother. He asked Clarissa to say hi to Tommy and Walt, as he called them, and asked how they were getting on at school. His interest in the children surprised her. She hoped it was genuine, and not some ruse to endear himself to her.

The answer to his question was that after a few difficult

days the boys seemed to be settling in well at school. They were now perfectly happy to walk to and from school on their own, including coming home for lunch. To Clarissa's amazement they were making rapid progress with learning English and were happy to sit with her in the garden while she tested them on what they knew. To balance things, she encouraged them to teach her a few words in German. They thought it terribly funny when she made a hash of pronouncing something that tripped off their tongue.

Often, as they sat on a blanket on the lawn, she would read to them from the children's books she had bought. She sensed they enjoyed listening to her even if they didn't understand all of it. She knew as a child she had loved her parents reading to her, and had derived great comfort from the soothing sound of their voices. Walter would often move in closer to her while she read, until finally he would be so close he could seamlessly manoeuvre himself onto her lap.

Walter was an easy child to love and his vulnerability pulled on Clarissa's heartstrings. He was small for his age, anxious and liable to start at sudden noises. His hair was as dark as his brother's, but his blue eyes were paler and often resembled pools of sadness. At bedtime when she tucked him in – he was now sleeping in his own bed – he would kiss her cheek and hug her close. Of the two boys, he was the one who craved physical affection and Clarissa willingly gave it to him. Her experience of young children was practically nil, and it surprised her just how comfortable she was with these two young boys.

Just as they were learning to adapt to their new life, she was doing the same and knew not to overwhelm Thomas with her desire to make him happy. It could not be forced. She could tell that he was naturally a quiet and reserved boy, and courteous to a fault. Clarissa was no expert, but she wondered if he believed that any display of emotion from him towards Clarissa or Lavinia would seem like an act of disloyalty to his mother. Polly had explained to her that this was frequently the case. Polly had also supplied some limited background information about the family, that they weren't practising Jews so there was no need to worry about that side of things. 'Like so many,' Polly had explained, 'the parents see themselves first and foremost as German; religion doesn't come into it.' To Clarissa, this made their plight seem altogether worse.

Despite Thomas and Walter writing to their parents every other day, there had been only the one letter to arrive from Germany for them. Judging by the postmark on the envelope, it must have been mailed almost immediately after Thomas and Walter had boarded the train from Berlin. Clarissa didn't know its contents but it seemed both to cheer and sadden the two boys.

Chapter Thirty-Five

August 1939, Shillingbury Grange, Suffolk

The days and weeks passed and before Clarissa knew it, it was August and she'd been at Shillingbury Grange for three months. Somehow they had all adapted in their different ways to the changes thrust upon them. Some days were easier than others, and it felt as though the household had never known any other routine.

The days Clarissa found difficult were those when tempers and frustrations flared. Like the day when Thomas had come home from school and angrily shut himself away in his room and refused to come out. With gentle encouragement, from both Clarissa and Walter, he had eventually opened the door and, with eyes brimming with tears, he had told her in faltering English of the taunts he'd received at school that day. Clarissa dealt with it swiftly the next morning by speaking to Mrs Russell. The thought that Thomas had escaped persecution in Germany only to be treated badly here in England incensed Clarissa. She had known from reading the newspapers that there were plenty in England who were pro-Fascism and anti-Semitic, just as there were people in America who were equally blinkered, but she'd be damned if she would stand back and do nothing about it. To her credit, Mrs Russell dealt with the matter firmly and threatened dire punishment to anybody who indulged in name-calling, whatever the reason. It transpired that the taunts had been as a result of Thomas coming top for the third time running in an arithmetic test. He was obviously a bright child of above average intelligence and that, of course, made any child a target, irrespective of culture or nationality.

But today, as the hot summer continued and with the school holidays still stretching languidly ahead of them, there were no angry tears of frustration to deal with. Today the garden echoed to the sound of what any observer might think was an ordinary family having fun. At lunch Charles had deemed it essential that Thomas and Walter should be taught to play the game of cricket, and now, while Clarissa and Lavinia watched from the terrace where they were shelling peas they had picked from the vegetable garden, she listened attentively to the instructions being given. She was as much in the dark as the children when it came to the rules, and knew that to compare the game to baseball would infuriate her grandfather. She had fond memories of her parents each extolling the merits of the game with which they had grown up.

'This is what will make you truly English,' Charles told them sternly as he handed Walter a bat and Thomas a ball. 'Master this and you'll have no trouble living in this country.'

Clarissa could see that teaching the boys to play, and all from his wheelchair, brought out a new side to Charles; it was one of those rare moments when she saw him truly involved in something and enjoying himself.

'He always hoped he'd have a son to play cricket with,' Lavinia said quietly to Clarissa as they watched Thomas swinging his arm ready to throw the ball at his brother.

'And perhaps then a grandson?' replied Clarissa with an enquiring look. 'If I had been a boy maybe that would have brought about a reconciliation sooner for him.'

'He's had a lot of disappointment in his life,' Lavinia murmured in a faraway voice, without answering Clarissa's question. 'We both have. A lot of which we've brought on ourselves, I can see that. I don't think the regret of what we did will ever leave me.'

Clarissa laid a cautious hand on her grandmother's arm.

'It's not too late to enjoy life now, you know. Or to accept forgiveness.'

'Do you really forgive us?' Lavinia asked, her voice little more than a whisper.

Clarissa nodded. 'It's obvious that you've suffered enough; it would be needlessly cruel of me not to forgive you.'

'It's more than we deserve,' Lavinia said, now staring at her husband leaning out of his wheelchair to show Walter the correct way to hold the cricket bat. 'I don't say this lightly,' she went on, 'but one way or another you've brought us back to life. Your mother would have been proud of you.'

'And she would have been proud of you, giving three strangers a home.'

Lavinia twisted her head round to look at her, her brow creased. 'You're not a stranger.'

'I was when I first showed up here. I could have been anyone. But you made me feel welcome despite all that had gone before. That couldn't have been easy for you, I do understand.'

'For one so young, you have a wise head on those shoulders of yours, and a compassionate heart. It's a rare combination.' She went back to shelling peas, but then, at the sight of Charles beckoning to Clarissa, she said, 'I see that it's now your turn to be instructed on the finer points of cricket.'

'I'll play if you do,' said Clarissa boldly.

'Me?' The expression on her grandmother's face – the face of a woman of unimpeachable respectability and of an age when wielding a cricket bat was as likely as growing wings and taking to the skies – was one of startled horror.

Clarissa rose to her feet. 'Why not?'

'But I'm ... I've never ... I mean I couldn't possibly—'

'Even more reason to try now.' And taking her grandmother's hand, they crossed the lawn together. It was then that Clarissa had the idea to enlist the help of Jimmy and Lily. 'From what I can see, the more players we have, the better,' she said when she put forward the suggestion.

Charles smiled. 'Capital idea! It'll be just like in the old days when I was a boy and my father used to round up the servants to join in.'

Lily and Jimmy could not have looked more shocked, but once they'd recovered themselves, Charles divided everyone into two small teams – Thomas was captain of his team, which was made up of Clarissa and Lily, and Walter captain of Lavinia and Jimmy. It soon became apparent that Lily was a demon bowler, having grown up playing the game on the village green with her brothers. In his element, Charles delighted in shouting out the scores and what they were doing wrong. But the high point came when Lavinia took a wild swing with the bat and struck the ball with such force, she sent it flying over the beech hedge and straight through the roof of the glasshouse.

Charles roared with laughter and applauded her. 'You couldn't have done that if you'd tried!'

When she was finally bowled out by Lily, and Charles declared Thomas's team the victors, Lavinia went over to her husband. With her cheeks glowing and her grey hair, always so sharply pulled back, tumbling loosely around her face, the hairpins she used to hold it securely in place lost on the lawn somewhere, she knelt on the grass in front of him. The look that passed between them was so tender and intimate that a lump formed in Clarissa's throat and she had to look away.

With Jimmy now gathering up the stumps and cricket bat and ball, Clarissa asked the boys to come inside with her and Lily to help bring out the tea things. At the mention of food, their faces lit up and they raced ahead, Walter's shorter legs struggling to keep pace with his brother's longer strides.

As of last week, after Mrs Kent gave notice to leave Shillingbury and go and live on the Norfolk coast, they now had a new cook. Amusingly, her name was Mrs Cook and she was Lily's aunt on her mother's side of the family. She had recently moved back to the village following the death of her husband – the threat of war also a deciding factor in her moving out of London. A jolly woman with a rotund shape that put Clarissa in mind of a barrel balanced on a pair of stout legs, she was a breath of fresh air and took to the household with enthusiasm, lavishing delicious, well-cooked food on them, especially Thomas and Walter, who she adored on sight. Charles would occasionally mutter about the extravagant cost of the meals now being served, but Lavinia hushed his grumbles and told him not to be such a misery.

The truth was, and Lavinia didn't want Charles to know this, but Clarissa was paying Mrs Cook's wages. As she had planned, Clarissa was helping with the household finances. Lavinia had been against the plan, but she was no match for Clarissa's determination that since she had talked her grandparents into taking in Thomas and Walter, contributing financially was the very least she could do.

There were other changes she had gradually made to the running of the household, such as organising the cleaning of all the curtains. Then, while they were down, with Lily's help she had washed away years of sad neglect from the windows and polished the glass until it gleamed.

From the garden, and from the areas that Jimmy had managed to keep under his control, Clarissa picked roses and sweet peas and placed them strategically in vases to scent the house. She filled decorative bowls with rose petals and lavender picked from the straggly border beneath the dining room window and placed them where anyone passing by would smell the summery fragrance. On walks across the meadows with Thomas and Walter she would return with bunches of wild flowers to put in pretty china jugs. Sometimes Jimmy would accompany them, and in his gruff, and at times incomprehensible, East Anglian dialect, he would teach them the names of the wild flowers and insects they came across.

Clarissa was sure on one outing that he was pulling their legs when he pointed to a ladybird and called it a bishy-barnibee. His heavily lined face darkened with a fearsome scowl when she asked him if he was joking. Without answering her, he'd gone on ahead, muttering and shaking his head. From that day on she didn't doubt another word or explanation from him, and did her best to absorb as much of his knowledge as she could. She learnt that a crow was a dunbilly, a hedge sparrow was a hedge-Betty, a nightingale a barley bird, an owl a jilly-hooter, a robin a ruddock and a skylark was a lavrock. The skylark had become Clarissa's favourite bird; she loved to hear it sing, there was something so wonderfully joyful about its song.

Under her guidance, the house was slowly regaining some of its shine. Or a shine that Clarissa imagined the house had once had in the days when its occupants had been happy. Some nights she would go to bed and wonder at the turn her life had taken. Grandma Ethel was still demanding she return home, but Boston no longer felt like home; Shillingbury did. Maybe it wouldn't always be home, but for now it was. She was needed here. Whatever lay ahead for her, this was where she was meant to be right now. In her long and frequent letters to Grandma Ethel, she tried to explain that for the first time in her life she believed she was doing something useful.

In the kitchen, Mrs Cook had everything for tea waiting for them. 'And don't even think about pinching one of those jam tarts or gingerbread men,' she warned the boys as she filled the teapot with water from the kettle – or the betsy, as she called it. 'You know I have eyes in the back of my head. Now wash your hands and be quick about it!'

Her sternness never caused Thomas and Walter to feel anxious; they had quickly learned that her bark was worse than her bite and that she didn't have a mean bone in her body, for frequently, after any warning or scolding given, she would chuck them under the chin and shoo them off with a beaming smile and usually a boiled sweet, from a jar which she kept on the shelf of the dresser. The kitchen was almost unrecognisable under her command; she kept it as neat as a shiny new pin and liked nothing better than to have an audience while she cooked. Thomas and Walter could often be found there, either watching her making something, or helping.

Mrs Cook had confided in Clarissa that with all the talk of war she deemed it prudent to start getting in an extra stock of what she called 'essentials' to store in the larder. 'I remember the First World War and all the shortages,' she told Clarissa, 'so with your permission, miss, I'll ask the grocer for a few extras, you know, tins of corned beef, salmon, peaches, powdered milk, cocoa, tea and sugar. I'll show you all the receipts and that way you'll know what's what.'

'Please do as you think best,' Clarissa had replied, 'but perhaps keep this between us for now; I don't want my grandparents alarmed in any way. I'll settle the grocer's bill as usual.'

The teapot filled and hands washed and dried, with Lily setting the table for her and Mrs Cook to sit down with a cup of tea together, Clarissa gave Thomas a plate of sardine paste sandwiches to carry out to the garden and Walter a basket of freshly baked scones, their fruity fragrance filling the warm kitchen.

The atmosphere in the house had changed considerably since the departure of Mrs Kent and Mrs Cook's arrival. A well-fed person was a happy person, was the latter's motto, and as Clarissa carefully carried the heavily laden tea tray out to the garden, it seemed the gem of a woman was on a mission to prove that sentiment true.

The next morning the sun shone down from a cloudless sky and once breakfast had been eaten and the boys had tidied their room, Clarissa took them for a walk across the meadows. With Thomas and Walter scampering on ahead – Walter's cries for his brother to slow down for him going unheeded – Clarissa wandered behind at a more leisurely pace, enjoying the beauty of the landscape. A skylark flew overhead, its cheerful call blending harmoniously with the dazzling beauty of the day. Life could not be any better than this, she thought.

And yet, if the newspaper reports were true, and what was being said on the wireless by the BBC Home Service, precious days like this were numbered; it was only a matter of time before the skies would be filled with airplanes and bombs and not birds. Two of Lily's brothers had recently enlisted, as had several of their friends from the village. Change was on its way.

Polly had written from London to say that some people just wanted war to be announced, that the knowing would be more bearable than the *not* knowing. Polly's letter had also contained the advice that if Clarissa wanted to return to America, she should do so now before it became too risky to cross the Atlantic. But Clarissa had no intention of leaving England, or Shillingbury. How could she? How could she leave her grandparents and Thomas and Walter? They were, to all intents and purposes, her new family.

Later that day, as though to underscore this realisation, the boy from the post office arrived on his bicycle with a telegram for Clarissa.

It was from the lawyers in Boston: Grandma Ethel had suffered a heart attack and wasn't expected to live much longer.

Chapter Thirty-Six

September 1939, Shillingbury Grange, Suffolk

Clarissa had decided to return to America right away when she heard about her grandmother but she was strongly advised by the lawyers in Boston that, with the threat of war imminent, it would be extremely unwise to cross the Atlantic now.

Then on the 3rd of September, as the long, hot summer showed no sign of ending, the news that everybody had been waiting for finally came: Britain was at war with Germany. The announcement on the wireless came as no surprise, but nonetheless it had the instant effect of casting a sombre atmosphere over the house.

'I knew all along this would be where we'd end up,' Charles kept muttering to no one in particular that evening, and rarely strayed from the wireless in case he missed some fresh piece of news.

The following day there were news reports that a passenger liner, the SS *Athenia*, bound for Halifax in Canada, had been torpedoed. As they took in the horror of the attack, Lavinia and Charles both urged Clarissa to heed the advice she had been sent from Boston, that she should stay in England. Two weeks later, on the 17th September, the day the HMS *Courageous* was sunk in the Atlantic, Grandma Ethel died.

Shocked at how upset she was over her grandmother's death, Clarissa threw herself into keeping busy, applying blackout fabric to all the windows of the house with Lavinia's help, and learning from Mrs Cook how to bottle produce from the orchard and vegetable garden as well as how to knit socks for the troops. It was better to be busy than dwell on her grandmother's death and the fear of what the reality of going to war really meant.

Down in the village there was a false sense of jollity. It seemed to Clarissa that whenever she went to the shops people were arming themselves with a veneer of British Bulldog spirit, of laughing in the face of adversity. Many claimed the war would be over practically before it had started.

But it wasn't long before that spirit turned to scepticism and the war was seen as a phoney war, nothing more than scaremongering. Not a single bomb had been dropped and yet they weren't supposed to leave the house without a gas mask. Nor were they able to use their motor vehicles, as petrol was now rationed, and just as horses and carts and traps became a common sight along the roads, so too did a stream of military vehicles when work began on reinstating the old airfield just two miles north of the village. The news that there would be an influx of RAF servicemen on their doorstep had been met with great excitement, particularly amongst the girls in the village; it was all they could talk about, so Lily told Clarissa.

However, the mood began to change when the cost of everyday groceries went up: people were furious and not afraid to speak their minds. There were two grocery shops in the village; the one Mrs Cook preferred was Leek's, whereas Mrs Kent had shopped at Howell's, where her nephew worked. 'Them lot at Howell's would cheat you soon as look at you,' Mrs Cook claimed, thoroughly disgusted by what she referred to as the daylight robbery prices Mr Howell was expecting customers to pay.

One morning as Clarissa walked into the village she slowed her step outside Howell's to allow a young mother with a pram to pass by. Through the open door she heard angry words being exchanged. 'If you don't like the price, you can push off and buy your spuds elsewhere!' shouted Mr Howell at the customer, a woman who Clarissa had made it her business to avoid since getting more involved with village life. Her name was Virginia Charlbury and she had a ferociously haughty manner. She had been, so Lavinia had told Clarissa, one of the first in the village to cut the Upwoods off socially when it became known they were as poor as church mice. Recently appointed the billeting officer for Shillingbury, she was in charge of finding homes for evacuees. Which gave nearly everybody in the village reason to dread a knock on the door from her.

'Ain't you 'eard, there's a bleeding war on,' Clarissa heard the irate Mr Howell yell at the woman. 'That's why everything costs more!'

'Don't you talk to me like that, you dreadful little man!'

'Go on! Get your uppity self out of my shop! And don't think you can come crawling back anytime soon when nobody else will serve you!'

'I'm speechless at your insolence!'

'Gawd, if only that were true! Do us all a big favour if you *were* speechless!'

'You're nothing but a scoundrel and I have a good mind to report you to Constable Fairweather.'

'I think you'll find Constable Fairweather's got more important things to worry about than the price of my ta'ers.'

'We'll see about that!'

Moving on, Clarissa reached her destination, the haberdasher's. There she encountered a similar, but mercifully less heated exchange. The price of blackout fabric was now a third as much again as it had been last week. Black card was being offered as an alternative. Noticing that the usual girl who served her wasn't around, Clarissa asked where Joan was. Mrs Strange who owned the shop sighed. 'Joan's only gone and joined the Land Army. Can you imagine such a thing? I never heard anything so daft in all my life.'

Clarissa couldn't imagine it either. With her painted nails and pert, made-up face, Joan simply didn't seem cut out for working on a farm.

Her purchase of grey sock wool completed, and back out on the street, Clarissa debated whether to treat herself to a coffee at the Primrose Tea Rooms. This was one thing she did miss from America; the coffee here just wasn't as good. But at the Primrose they made a passable cup, so spying an empty table in the bay window, Clarissa pushed open the door and went in. No sooner had she closed the door behind her when she saw she was out of luck: a man was just removing his hat and sitting down at the last available table, the one in the window. He caught her looking at him and her face must have given away her disappointment for he immediately stood up. 'Please,' he said, 'have the table.'

'No, no, you had it first. I'll wait for another.'

'We ...' He hesitated. 'We could always share. If ... if that doesn't sound too forward.'

Slightly built and only a little taller than Clarissa, he was fair-haired and smartly dressed in a well-cut suit. At his feet on the floor was a brown leather briefcase. A businessman passing through, she surmised.

'Why not?' she said. 'So long as you're sure I'm not intruding.'

'You're not.' He pulled out a chair for her, but in so doing managed to bump the table and upset the sugar bowl. While he made a poor attempt to tidy the mess he'd made, she stowed her basket of shopping on the floor beside her chair, along with her gas mask. 'Sorry about that,' he said. 'I'd like to say it was out of character, but that would be a lie. Mother's always complaining how clumsy I am.'

'That is unquestionably the prerogative of a mother: to point out our flaws,' replied Clarissa with a friendly smile.

He returned her smile and attracted the attention of a waitress. When the girl had taken their order, Clarissa stared out of the window and saw the five minutes past ten bus

234

lumber into view. It was exactly on time and slowed to a stop outside the post office where a handful of people got off, many of whom Clarissa recognised.

One of them was Dr Rutherford's wife and, spotting Clarissa through the window, she waved. Behind Mrs Rutherford were the elderly Finch sisters who were as bird-like in appearance as their name suggested. The spinster sisters lived in a tiny cottage on the green in genteel penury, but would rather die than admit how bad things were. Clarissa had a soft spot for them, as she did for most of the inhabitants of the village.

Next to step off the bus was Molly Shaw, the vicar's wife, a pretty and vivacious woman whose husband, much to the horror of some, was fifteen years her senior. They had no children of their own, but on either side of her were two girls, their blonde hair pulled back into pigtails, their floral dresses perfectly pressed, their socks pristine white and their sandals polished. They had arrived in the village with a dozen other children evacuated from London. Molly had told Clarissa how the girls – four-year-old twins and not yet at school – had stepped off the train with their heads crawling with lice and their clothes little more than dirty rags. With no idea how to use a knife and fork, they'd told Molly they'd always eaten with their hands, a fact they'd been most proud of. Watching them now as they skipped along beside Molly in the late September sunshine, it was hard to imagine the transformation that had been wrought at the vicarage. Molly, being nearer to her in age than most of the other women, was the closest Clarissa had to a friend here.

When the bus drove off, leaving behind a cloud of black exhaust fumes, the man across the table from Clarissa spoke. 'Do you live here in the village?' he asked. 'Only you don't sound local. I'd hazard a guess there's something of the American about you. Or perhaps Canadian?'

'I'm half Yank, half Brit,' she replied with a smile, just as their waitress appeared with their drinks. 'And I'm staying with my grandparents for what could be described as an indeterminate time,' she continued when they were alone. 'What about you, I haven't seen you around here before?'

'I'm visiting a client.'

'In what capacity?'

'I'm a solicitor. A country solicitor, so all jolly dull, I'm afraid.'

'I wouldn't have thought that was necessarily the case. Do you enjoy your work?'

'It has its moments, certainly.'

'Is there something you'd rather be doing?'

He lowered his gaze and stirred his tea.

'Go on,' she said, unable to resist getting an admission out of him.

His tea now stirred, he put the spoon neatly in the saucer, then looked at her shyly. 'Promise you won't laugh?'

She put a hand to her chest. 'Hand on heart.'

'I would have loved to have been an actor, but my parents wouldn't hear of it. Not quite the done thing in their eyes.'

It was on the tip of Clarissa's tongue to say she knew a famous American actress, but she held back for fear of sounding as if she were showing off.

Effie and Ellis had returned to America on board the *Belle Etoile* the day Germany invaded Poland. Effie had written to Clarissa to say there had been a horribly melancholy atmosphere throughout the journey, and when they arrived in New York the general feeling was one of relief.

I worry about you stuck there in England, Effie had written, *you should have come home with us. Now you're stuck there until the war is over, however long that will be.*

I worry about Artie too. I don't know why he had to take a silly old job as a war correspondent in Europe when he could be a reporter here in America. I don't know why he wants to be a hero by staying there. Unless it's to make Ellis feel a coward for returning home.

Please write soon to reassure me you're safe and well. And tell me all that you're getting up to; I so enjoyed your last letter, hearing about the wonderful Mrs Cook and how she's taught you to knit. Do you suppose she could teach me? She would have to have the patience of a saint!

Did I tell you I'd been approached to play the part of a nun in a movie with Robert Montgomery? What a hoot! Me as a nun! Ellis thinks it's the funniest thing ever, that it's the worst case of miscasting he's ever heard of, which makes me all the more determined to do it. I'll be the best nun he's ever seen, just you see!

Dearest Clarissa, I miss you more than words can say. In those few days we spent together, I sensed in you somebody with whom I can be completely honest. With everybody else I have to pretend to be something I'm not.

A thousand kisses to you, my darling!
Effie

PS Being a friend of mine is not always easy – just ask Ellis! – but please stay in touch!

Clarissa loved receiving letters from Effie; they always read as though they had been written at breakneck speed with not a moment to be lost.

'I suppose you think the same,' the fair-haired man said when Clarissa hadn't said anything.

'Not at all,' she responded quickly, remembering what he'd said. 'I was just thinking of somebody I met recently. My advice to you is if there's something you really want to do, you should go ahead and do it.'

He stared back at her with a baffled frown, as if he'd never heard anyone say such a thing. 'You mean blow convention and all that?'

'Oh, especially that!'

He gave a short laugh. 'Perhaps that's one of the many differences between you Americans and us British, you're more gung-ho.'

She smiled. 'I wouldn't say that exactly, but I for one am determined not to live my life in a half-hearted manner just to conform to some perceived right way of doing things.'

He shook his head. 'What a wonderfully spirited young woman you are. May I have the pleasure of knowing your name?'

Charmed by his formality, she said, 'It's Clarissa. Clarissa Allerton. And who might you be?'

He held out his hand to her. 'I'm Henry Willet, and I'm very pleased to make your acquaintance.'

It wasn't until they had finished their drinks and were preparing to leave the Primrose Tea Rooms that the coincidence of their meeting became apparent – the client Henry Willet was on his way to see, and for the first time, was none other than Clarissa's grandfather, Charles Upwood.

A week after his visit to Shillingbury Grange, Henry wrote to Clarissa asking if he might see her again. She agreed, and the following week he picked her up in his car, a black Morris 8, and drove them to Bury St Edmunds. It was a cool but sunny autumnal afternoon and he took her for a walk around the abbey gardens. He voiced his surprise when she said she'd never been to Bury St Edmunds before, let alone the abbey ruins.

'I just haven't had time to go anywhere,' she explained, 'I've been so busy. And there hasn't been anyone with whom I could explore,' she added.

'In that case,' he said, 'if you'll permit me, I shall be your guide and give you a potted history of the town. But you must stop me if I'm boring you.'

Afterwards they went for a drink at the Angel Hotel. The place was a sea of air force blue and it took Henry a while to push through the crowd of RAF personnel to get served. Once they had their drinks they retreated to a corner and sat down. Every now and then loud cheers and boisterous laughter made conversation impossible, and sensing Henry was regretting his choice of where to have a quiet drink, Clarissa tried her best to show him she was perfectly happy and having a good time. Which was true, she was. It had been quite a novelty for her, leaving Shillingbury and spending the afternoon with somebody who had such an extensive knowledge of the town and its history, going right back to the seventh century when a small religious community was established by King Sigeberht on the site where the abbey ruins now stood.

While he fiddled with his glass of whisky, turning it this way, then that way, his plaintive blue-grey eyes downcast, she suddenly thought how forlorn he looked and that, almost like a child, his eagerness to please was equal to his fear of disappointing.

Eventually he seemed to relax and she asked him to tell her about his family and how he became a solicitor. 'My father was a barrister and the expectation was that I would become one, too,' he told her. 'I've let them down badly in that respect. Mother thinks I've settled for second best.'

'I'm sure that's not true,' Clarissa said, thinking that *Mother* should jolly well keep quiet! 'What does your father say?'

'He's not around any more. Dead. Dicky heart. But let's not talk about me, I'm much more interested in you. Tell me all about yourself and your family.'

And so she did.

'Compared to you I've led a very quiet life,' he remarked in a subdued voice when she'd finished. He drained his glass of whisky. 'But I hope that will change before too long. I've decided to enlist and join the RAF.' He looked longingly over towards the bar and the men in their smart uniforms. 'For now, though,' he said, turning to look at her, 'here I am having a wonderful time with a beautiful girl who I very much hope will agree to see me again.'

'I think she might well agree,' Clarissa said with a smile.

They met twice more before Clarissa began to suspect that Henry wanted to go beyond being just friends, which she now knew was all she was prepared to be.

After he'd dropped her off following a gruesome afternoon spent having tea with him and his ghastly mother – a domineering woman who made no attempt to disguise her disapproval of Clarissa – she waved him goodbye with a sense of relief. Her mind was made up; she wouldn't be seeing him again.

That evening, when she was reading a bedtime story to Thomas and Walter, who now had a sufficient grasp of English to enjoy the books she read to them, Thomas interrupted her to ask if she was going to marry Mr Willet.

'Heavens!' she exclaimed. 'What put that idea into your head?'

'Because ... because you keep spending time with him and not us. Do you like him a lot?'

'He's just a friend,' Clarissa said firmly. 'And I promise you, I'm not going to marry him.'

'What about Ellis?'

'What about him?'

'Do you like him better than Mr Willet?'

'Yes,' she said simply.

'And Artie?' This was from Walter, and he was looking at her anxiously with his large, sad eyes.

'I like Artie too. Now then, shall I continue with the story?'

Ignoring her, Walter said, 'But who will you marry?'

'I may not marry anybody. Maybe nobody will want to marry me. Have you thought of that?'

'But you will marry, I know you will, and then you will leave us. And I don't want you to leave us. Not *ever*!'

'Oh, Walter,' she said, taking the little boy in her arms, 'as long as you need me, I'll never leave you, and that's a promise.'

There had been no further word from the boys' parents. Thomas would occasionally hang around the hallway when he thought the post would be delivered. Clarissa had tried to explain that now Britain was at war with Germany, it made it impossible for any letters to be sent. She didn't know whether this was entirely true, but Thomas accepted the explanation.

After she'd kissed them goodnight, she went downstairs. Charles and Lavinia were in the drawing room listening to the wireless. There was yet more talk of food rationing. Everybody knew it wasn't so much *if* there would be rationing, as *when* it would happen. The thought of all the food Mrs Cook had stored away in the larder should have been a comfort, but it wasn't; it made Clarissa feel guilty to have so much when others might have so little. 'It's only what anyone with any sense has done,' Mrs Cook had said when Clarissa had voiced her concerns about their hoarding.

Seeing her come into the room, Charles cleared his throat and put aside the newspaper he was reading. 'I've been thinking,' he said. 'It's time we did more to help. But stuck as I am in this confounded wheelchair, I'm as good as useless.'

'Don't say that, darling,' Lavinia said, getting up to turn off the wireless.

'But it's true!' he said, banging his fist on the arm of the chair.

'What have you been thinking about?' asked Clarissa quietly. It was never wise to contradict her grandfather.

'We have all this space around us,' he said, 'a garden we hardly use. And a meadow. The land should be used for growing vegetables and maybe crops.' He pointed to the discarded newspaper. 'If the Germans are successful in blockading the Atlantic and preventing merchant shipping from getting through, there won't be enough food to go round, that's the plain fact of the matter. There's nothing else for it but for us as a country to grow our own, just as they've been saying on the wireless and in the newspaper.'

'But we already have Jimmy doing his best in the garden,' Lavinia said. 'There's only so much he can do.'

'We need to think bigger than that. We could have a productive market garden here. Don't look at me like that, Lavinia; I haven't lost my marbles, quite the contrary. I have nothing else to contribute to the war effort, other than the land I own, which is currently doing nothing. With a bit of effort, or rather, a *lot* of effort, we could really do something positive with it.'

Clarissa sat in the chair next to her grandfather. 'How would we do the work on our own?' she asked. 'I'm willing to learn and do as much as I can, but there's a limit to what I can do.'

'We'd have to get some of those Land Army girls. Or maybe a refugee – I hear they make good workers.'

'And where would they live?' asked Lavinia, wringing her hands.

'There's the barn and those outbuildings with nothing in them but junk that should have been jettisoned years ago.'

'Charles, we can't expect them to live in the barn. There are bound to be rats there.'

'There are the attic rooms,' Clarissa said, warming to her grandfather's idea. 'We could clear them out; I'll gladly do that. Jimmy and Lily will help. And don't forget Thomas and Walter – they can lend a hand too. I'm sure Thomas would be a dab hand with a paintbrush.'

'You've both gone completely mad,' Lavinia said faintly.

A smile on his face, Charles squeezed Clarissa's hand. 'Mad as hatters, the pair of us, aren't we? But better that than starved to death by that bloody Hitler.'

Chapter Thirty-Seven

Shillingbury Grange,
Shillingbury,
Suffolk.
11th May 1940

Dearest Effie,

It's been a while since I last wrote to you and my only
excuse is that life has been so busy for us all here.

Had you seen Shillingbury Grange six months ago,
you wouldn't recognise it now – the garden has been
totally transformed. Moreover, the whole of Shillingbury
has been transformed – everybody who is able to has dug
up their garden and planted it out with vegetables. We're
all Digging for Victory!

Charles is also a man altered beyond recognition
and spends every hour he can outside in the garden.
Occasionally he complains that he's not doing enough
to help, stuck as he is in his wheelchair, but I always tell
him that he's the brains behind everything we're doing.
He's also the one who has to deal with the red tape from
the Ministry of Food. 'Ministry of this, ministry of that,'
he mutters, 'won't be long before we won't be able to
sneeze without applying to the appropriate ministry for a
blasted permit!'

The glasshouse has been restored and Jimmy has built
a pathway for Charles to come and go to that part of
the garden unaided in his wheelchair – he's in charge of

growing seeds in there, something he can easily do.

Jimmy is now a member of the Air Raid Wardens' Service and is our local air raid warden. He's on duty three nights a week and much to our amusement regularly lectures us on the importance of obeying blackout regulations – as if we need reminding!

As for me, I spend all the time I can digging, weeding and willing everything we've planted to grow – I'm quite a sight to behold in my shabby overalls and hair tied up with a scarf, it is far from a glamorous look! Even Lavinia puts on a pair of boots and helps, something I never thought would happen. We have potatoes sprouting up nicely in well-earthed trenches, and also onions, cabbages and carrots. A couple of young lads from the village come in to help now and then, but they both say the moment they turn eighteen, or can pass for that age, they'll enlist, so that'll be the end of their help.

Charles's original plan to plough up the meadow and plant sugar beet has been put on hold for now, which secretly I'm rather pleased about as it means Thomas and Walter and I can still go for walks there. Yesterday it was warm enough to take a picnic down to the meadow and while the boys were playing a game of hide and seek, I lay on the grass listening to the skylarks singing. I was almost drifting off to sleep when the birds were drowned out by the rumbling roar of a squadron of Wellington bombers flying over in formation – it was such a stirring sight I lost count of how many there were. We've become surprisingly blasé about the presence of airplanes filling the sky, but I must say, the airmen from RAF Shillingbury do make a rather dashing sight in the village!

From the beginning of March we've had a Polish refugee living with us. His name is Leon and he's wonderfully hard-working, which Charles approves of greatly. He's a shy young man with a sensitive face, and before he fled Poland he was an engineering student. His parents made him leave Poland just before Germany invaded and ever since he left he's had no word from them. He comes from a farming background, so he's very hands-on with growing and fixing things. I don't know what we'd do without him. Thomas and Walter have taken to him enormously and are already teaching him all the East Anglian expressions they've learnt from Jimmy and Mrs Cook – one of my favourites is when Mrs Cook says Walter has got why-wiffles; it means he's fidgety and can't stay still.

Lily is still with us, but I fear she might have ideas to sign up to go and do some sort of war work. I don't blame her, but I hope she doesn't leave as I shall miss her. Between you and me, I'm hoping she and Leon might form an attachment.

We had some hens given to us by Brian Coddling, a neighbouring farmer. The boys are in charge of looking after them – every morning they feed and clean them out before going to school. Mrs Cook is very glad of the eggs and has risen magnificently to the challenge of food rationing; somehow she keeps us all fed without a word of complaint.

Last week I heard from the lawyers in Boston. According to the date of the letter, and the postmark, it had been delayed by nearly two months, which is not surprising, given what's going on in the Atlantic with German U-boats torpedoing Allied shipping as well as neutral vessels, and killing any number of innocent people. The letter was to tell me that Grandma Ethel's affairs have now been finalised and that, being the sole beneficiary of the will, I will, when I turn twenty-one, become ... well, let's just say I'm in a state of shock. I suppose I had always known my father's family had been well off, but this was wildly beyond anything I had imagined. It's been decided by the lawyers that the bulk of the money should be kept in trust in America, where they believe it will be safer than here in England.

I haven't heard from Artie in quite some weeks, have you? I do hope he's all right – I miss hearing from him. The last letter I had from him was from Paris. With Germany invading Denmark and Norway, and now Holland and Belgium under attack, everybody here is worried about France. I hope Artie gets out before anything awful happens.

Write as soon as you can, Effie, I so enjoy receiving your news – I loved hearing about you working with Robert Montgomery! I know there's a danger of our letters ending up at the bottom of the Atlantic, but as Mrs Cook says, we have to carry on as normal or we'll go mad. So please write!

   With all my love,
      Clarissa

PS With so much news to share with you I almost forgot to mention the most important news here – as of yesterday Winston Churchill became Prime Minister. The general feeling is that he's the man to put Hitler in his place. Even Charles, who rarely has a good word for politicians, is full of optimism that Churchill will save the day. I hope he's right!

> The Plaza Hotel,
> 768 5th Avenue,
> New York.
> 18th April 1940

Dear Clarissa,

Can you believe it's a year since we met? And good gravy, what a lot has happened to you in that time! With every one of your letters I have to catch my breath in admiration for all that you've taken on, you truly are an inspiration.

What we read here about what's going on in Europe chills my blood. It's a terrifying thing to say, but at the rate things are going there won't be a country left in Europe that won't be at war. I've read about the awful food rationing that you're now enduring, if there's anything I can send you, just say the word!

You'll never guess who I ran into last month – none other than Marjorie Boyd-Lambert! I had just been to see the magnificent Queen Elizabeth *make her arrival here in New York after her secret maiden voyage across the Atlantic – just too appalling to think of the beautiful liner zigzagging her way to safety from England while German U-boats lurked wickedly beneath the surface of the water. There was a large welcome party here for her, but I must confess that to see such a beautiful ship painted in battleship grey did make my heart sink a little. She's now moored alongside her sister, the* Queen Mary, *and the* Normandie *and our dear old friend the* Belle Etoile. *Imagine what a sight they make!*

It was when I was preparing to leave the dockside that I spotted Marjorie, and I couldn't resist breezing over to say hello. The horrified expression on the old sourpuss's face was priceless. She was there with her husband to whom she reluctantly introduced me – mercy, the poor man looked like a timid mouse trapped in a corner by a scorpion! I invited them to join me for a drink at The Plaza where I'm staying for an indefinite period of time – indefinite because I'm still trying to find the perfect new home and can't make up my mind where I want to be, so for now The Plaza is home. Who knows, maybe I shall never leave! Anyway, while Mr Boyd-Lambert seemed inclined to accept my invitation, Marjorie was having none of it and took him by the arm declaring they had a prior engagement. I'll wager they had no such thing, but who cares!

Well, enough of my rattling on, I must wrap things up and get this in the mail to you and pray that it not only reaches you, but finds you well.

My fondest love,
Betty

San Antonio,
Texas.
20th April 1940

Dear Clarissa,

Who knows if this letter will eventually reach you, if it does, you'll be pleased to know I'm following your lead – heck, if you and Artie can do something worthwhile, so can I! So be impressed – I've enlisted in the Aviation Cadet Program in Texas, in six months I'll graduate. Who knows, I might end up in Europe bombing the hell out of those Germans!

Take care,
Ellis

PS Thanks for your last letter – how about knitting me some socks? I think it's the least you could do.

Heaven help the Germans, Clarissa thought with a smile after she'd read Ellis's brief letter which had come in the second post, along with Betty's.

She was taking a break from working in the garden and enjoying a welcome cup of tea in the kitchen on her own while Mrs Cook was on her afternoon off and Lily was upstairs cleaning. Lavinia was at the village hall for a Women's Institute meeting – she'd recently joined after it became known that Virginia Charlbury had stepped down from the role of president, for reasons yet to be revealed, which had everybody highly intrigued – and Charles was in the drawing room going over some papers with Henry Willet.

Initially when Clarissa had put some distance between herself and Henry he had pushed to know what he had done wrong. 'You didn't do anything wrong,' she had explained, going on to say that she really couldn't spare the time to go gallivanting off when her grandparents needed her. He'd dismissed her explanation by pointing out that they'd managed perfectly well on their own before she'd arrived in Shillingbury. Annoyed that he was pressing her, she'd said that the war had changed things, and besides, her time was her own and she didn't need to justify to anyone what she did with it. Such was the sting of her rebuke, he pursed his lips angrily and left without saying goodbye.

A week later he wrote to apologise for his less than gentlemanly behaviour and begged for forgiveness. '*For all the world I would never want to offend you or cause you a moment's distress*,' he'd written. '*I admire you greatly and do so hope that we can remain friends*.'

She'd replied saying there was nothing to forgive and politely added that of course they would stay friends. Even so, she usually tried to be out of the house, or engineered to be busy in the garden, when he came for one of his visits with Charles. The last time he'd called, she had not been so lucky and had endured a conversation with him during which he had shared with her his disappointment that he'd been turned down by the RAF after failing the medical. 'It turns out I've inherited my father's dicky heart,' he'd said mournfully. 'Just my confounded bad luck!'

Hearing voices in the hall – Henry's meeting with her grandfather must have come to an end – Clarissa quickly went through to the scullery, then out to the back porch where she'd left her boots. Pulling them on, she beat a hasty retreat to the garden to join Leon and Jimmy before Henry came looking for her.

Chapter Thirty-Eight

June 1940, Shillingbury Grange, Suffolk

It was the first week of June, and with cottage walls and outbuildings covered in scrambling roses and honeysuckle, the lanes and hawthorn hedges frothing with cow parsley and may flowers, as well as harebells, yarrow, red campion, hollyhocks and foxgloves popping up wherever they'd managed to get a foothold, summer had well and truly arrived.

It was Saturday afternoon, and that evening there was to be a dance at the village hall. Many a girl's heart was aflutter at the prospect of dancing with the airmen from the airfield and much effort was being put into preparing the hall for the event; nobody – not even Virginia Charlbury – wanted to be accused of not putting on a good show for all concerned. Initially Virginia had opposed inviting the airmen on the grounds of encouraging 'immoral consequences', but had caved in when it was put to her that the dance would be a much-needed morale booster, especially for the brave pilots who risked their lives every time they took to the skies.

Morale was lower than Clarissa could recall since war had been declared. The evacuation of Allied forces on the 4th June from Dunkirk had been a bitter blow, but now that France seemed in imminent danger of falling to Germany, Clarissa had extra cause to worry. She still hadn't heard from Artie, and had no idea if he was still in France as a war correspondent for CBS, or whether he was now reporting from somewhere else. But worry, as Mrs Cook always told her, was like a rocking chair, backwards and forwards it went without ever getting anywhere. The remedy, as Clarissa knew all too well, was to keep busy.

All yesterday she had been at the village hall helping to give it a thorough spring clean in readiness for the dance, and then this morning she and Molly had volunteered to set out the trestle tables and cover them with tablecloths before the ladies of the WI took over in the afternoon to decorate them with wild flower arrangements and, more importantly, lay out plates of food.

Now back at home and walking through to the kitchen, Clarissa could hear Lily joking that she was going to get dressed up to the nines and bag herself a husband at the dance. 'Trouble is,' she said, 'oi don't have a dress that's loikely to catch the eye of a good-lookin' man.'

'You could borrow something of mine,' Clarissa said, hanging her gas mask case on the back of the door. 'We're about the same size, so take your pick.'

Lily looked at Clarissa in astonishment. 'Oi couldn't! Oi really couldn't.'

'Yes you could. I insist. So long as it's not the dress I intend to wear,' she added with a smile.

'I shouldn't look a gift horse in the mouth, Lily, my girl,' said Mrs Cook. 'You won't be the only one with their eyes out on stalks looking for a likely husband, so you'd best be prepared for some competition. And I don't want to hear of no fighting amongst you sharp-clarred cats!' She gave Lily a wag of her finger.

From outside, through the open window, voices could be heard and shortly afterwards Leon came in with Thomas and Walter. Standing either side of him, dressed in shorts and dusty gumboots, the boys both had large grins on their faces, as well as a few earthy streaks across their cheeks. They appeared to be hiding something behind their backs.

Playing along, Clarissa put her hands on her hips and gave them a long searching look. 'You look like you've been up to no good,' she said. They giggled under her scrutiny. 'What do you think, Mrs Cook?'

'I'd say they both look a proper pair of scants,' she replied, 'as sly and guilty as a pair of rabbits caught with carrot stains down their fronts.'

Walter could keep quiet no longer and from behind his back, and with a triumphant flourish, revealed a small bucket of potatoes. 'Look! Look what I've got!'

Thomas then showed the bucket he was holding. 'Leon taught us how to do it,' he explained earnestly, 'to dig carefully so the fork doesn't hurt the potatoes.'

'Well done, boys, and well done, Leon,' Mrs Cook said approvingly. She bent to inspect the haul; they were the first of the potatoes to be harvested and were about the same size and shape as hens' eggs. Leon had told Clarissa yesterday that he thought it would be nice for Thomas and Walter to have the honour of lifting the first of the early potatoes.

'They'll go nicely with the pie I'm making for lunch,' said Mrs Cook. 'But first we need to wash them. Would you boys like to help me?'

Thomas shook his head. 'Leon says we can help him dig up some more, the ones to be sold. We have to be very careful with those potatoes.'

'But only if that is all right with you, Miss Clarissa?' Leon interjected.

'Of course it is,' Clarissa said, wishing that he would stop calling her 'miss'. It didn't matter how many times she asked him not to, he refused to drop the formality. She took the buckets from the boys. 'I shall wash these little gems myself for Mrs Cook.'

'Well, 'afore you go rushing back outside, sit you down and I'll put the betsy on for a cuppa,' Mrs Cook said. Not only did she cluck around Thomas and Walter like a mother hen, she now did the same with Leon. When he'd first arrived he'd been as thin as a reed, and even with the rationing imposed on them, Mrs Cook had managed to put some weight on him. A selection of clothes had been found for him, care of the WVS, and when he wasn't in his work clothes for the garden, he polished up pretty well.

Over their mugs of tea – and home-made lemonade for the boys – and after Mrs Cook had teased Lily again about finding herself a husband at the dance, Lily asked Leon if he had a date for the evening.

His face instantly turned a deep shade of red. 'I shall not be going,' he said quietly.

'Why not?' Clarissa asked. 'Just about everyone else from the village is going.'

He looked at her shyly before his glaze flickered towards Lily. 'I have no one to go with. And—' He broke off.

'And?' prompted Mrs Cook.

He smiled ruefully. 'And I cannot dance. Not a step.'

Lily laughed. 'Nor can most folk round 'ere, but it won't stop any of 'em from going.'

'Please do change your mind,' Clarissa urged Leon with a smile. 'I'm sure dancing won't be compulsory.'

'Not unless there's a new Ministry of Something or Other that's passed a law that says we all have to dance from now on!' Mrs Cook said with a hearty laugh.

The dress Clarissa had chosen was a deep shade of coral and was neither too dressy nor too plain. She had deliberated over what to wear for some time, trying to look as though she had made the effort but had not tried too hard. The dress she'd chosen had been one of the day dresses she had worn on board the *Belle Etoile*, and at the time Effie had remarked how well the colour suited her. 'Don't you think Clarissa looks beautiful in that dress?' she had asked Ellis.

'Don't play those games with me,' Ellis had answered her with a snarl.

An expression of mock innocence on her face, Effie had said, 'I don't know what you mean.'

'Sure you do. If I say it suits her, you'll accuse me of some kind of bias, and if I say nothing, you'll accuse me of something far worse.'

'Such as?'

'Of feigned indifference.'

'Indifference or artifice is not something any of us could accuse you of,' Artie had stepped in. 'Come on, Clarissa,' he'd added, 'let's leave these two to it and have a game of quoits.'

More than a year on since she'd crossed the Atlantic and met them, Clarissa still did not know how Ellis and Effie really felt about each other. Was their sparring no more than an elaborate act of courtship before finally accepting they were – and always had been – perfectly suited? She really wouldn't be at all surprised one day to receive a letter from them saying, '*Guess what, we're married!*'

With a light cream wrap and her gas mask case hooked over her shoulder, her lipstick and a handkerchief tucked inside, she hurried downstairs to the drawing room where she could hear Charles and Lavinia talking in low voices; they were talking about her. And Leon. They turned abruptly when they realised she was in the room and had probably heard what they'd been saying.

'Please,' she said, when they looked at her with embarrassment, 'you really don't have to worry about Leon's intentions towards me.'

Lavinia's face was grave. 'We know things have changed dramatically with this wretched war,' she said, 'and the normal conventions seem to be a thing of the past, but do you really think it was wise of you to ask Leon to walk you down to the village for the dance? What message will it give to people?'

'You should know me well enough by now to know that I don't give a toot what people will think,' Clarissa said, trying to keep her voice light. 'Besides, Leon isn't interested in me, it's Lily for whom he has a soft spot.'

'Are you sure?' asked Lavinia.

'Yes, that's why I wanted him to go to the dance, so he can spend some time with Lily. It's just a pity she went home to change, as otherwise I would have proposed he escorted her.'

Charles frowned. 'Is that such a good thing, the two of them becoming – becoming overly friendly with each other?'

'I think whatever moments of happiness people can find for themselves in these difficult times should be grabbed with both hands. Enjoy your evening,' she said with a bright smile.

Leon was waiting for her in the kitchen where Mrs Cook was fussing with a brush at the shoulders of his second-hand jacket. His anxious eyes implored Clarissa to make the woman stop.

'Ready to go?' she asked him.

He nodded, but his expression was that of a man bound for an experience far worse than anything Mrs Cook was capable of inflicting.

It was a lovely evening, and as Clarissa and Leon walked along the lane to the village, the sound of birdsong filled in the silence between them, the light and busy chatter of sparrows and the chirpy refrain of blackbirds underpinned by the lower cooing of woodpigeons.

Leon was a man of few words at the best of times and, like Clarissa, he seemed perfectly content to let the quiet stillness between them continue. They had reached the entrance to Brian Coddling's farm – Shillingbury Farm – when Clarissa decided that, given Leon's extreme shyness, he might need to be given a little encouragement when it came to Lily this evening. She was about to offer some words of advice when he asked, 'Do you believe Lily is serious when she says she hopes to find a husband tonight?'

Clarissa chose her words with care. 'All the girls in the village will have been joking today about finding a husband, but it's nothing more than talk. Really what they want is to enjoy themselves, and maybe a man to hold them close and perhaps kiss them.'

Leon nodded his head and appeared to think about it. 'You think that is what Lily wants?'

'Yes. If this were in the village where you lived back in Poland, wouldn't it be the same? Wouldn't the girls there behave in the same way?'

He suddenly looked very sad, as though thinking of home was too painful for him.

'I'm sorry,' she said, 'that was clumsy of me. You must miss your home so very much.'

'I do. I miss my family. And my friends. But you are all so kind to me here. I will never forget that. Sometimes I cannot imagine that I will ever return to my village. For what shall I return to? And what will poor Thomas and Walter go back to in Berlin?'

'We none of us know the answer to that,' Clarissa said. 'All we can do is take one day at a time.'

'And live for the moment. That is what everybody says we must do, is it not?'

'It might seem shallow, but what is the alternative? We have to live as best we can and with a heart full of hope.'

He nodded once more and they continued on in silence. At the post office he paused to pull a letter from his jacket pocket and without a word slipped it into the post box. Clarissa wondered to whom he could be writing; not that it was any of her business.

They arrived on the dot of seven, the official start of the dance. Such was everybody's eagerness to get the evening started there was already a sizeable and voluble crowd in the hall. The men – and a few WAAFs – from the airfield were much in evidence, their smart blue uniforms contrasting greatly with the small gathering of young men from the village whose clothing had definitely seen better days. The stark contrast also highlighted just how few young men were now left in Shillingbury; so many sons, brothers and even fathers had joined up. In a small village like this, their absence, should they not all return, would be hard to bear.

Spotting Lily on the other side of the hall with a group of girls who all appeared to be admiring the pale green satin dress she was wearing, Clarissa smiled. Now, *how to get Leon to go over and chat with Lily?* she wondered. Perhaps some Dutch courage was the answer.

'Let's see what there is to drink,' she said to Leon, taking him by the arm to where George Stamford from the butcher's was busy pouring out drinks with Vera Hubbard from the baker's.

'Oi've elderflower wine, gooseberry wine, blackcurrant cordial, rum punch, or lemonade,' George said to Clarissa. 'Oi should warn yew 'bout the rum punch, its kick'll knock yew ter Ipswich and back!'

'I think there's nothing else for it but to see if that's true,' Clarissa said cheerfully. 'What about you, Leon, will you risk it? Shall we live for the moment?'

He hesitated. 'Why not?' he said at length, and with the briefest of smiles.

George Stamford had just handed them their drinks when Lily came over. 'Thanks again for the dress, oi niver felt such a proper lady 'afore. The girls bin a-larfin' at me for me lah-di-dah finery.'

'Ignore them, Lily, you look wonderfully elegant,' Clarissa said, thinking how grown up Lily suddenly seemed. 'Doesn't she look lovely, Leon?'

He took a gulp of his drink. 'You look beautiful, Lily,' he said.

Lily laughed. 'An' yew din't look so bad either.'

The poor man blushed and took another gulp of his rum punch.

Seizing the moment, Clarissa said, 'Lily, why don't you take Leon over to meet your friends?'

Lily didn't need telling twice. 'C'mon, Leon,' she said, grabbing his hand, 'yew can say hello to my friends, and bless me if we then can't find them dancin' legs of yours.'

Minutes later, the band on the raised platform struck a chord. In response a cheer went up, and within no time the middle of the hall was filled with foxtrotting couples. To Clarissa's delight one of those couples was Lily and a terrified-looking Leon. No guesses for who had taken the initiative to dance, she thought with a happy smile.

It was good seeing so many people enjoying themselves – Jimmy was there in his ARP uniform, looking very official, while his friends from the village looked much more relaxed in their shirtsleeves with knotted neckerchiefs at their necks. It was good, too, to see the village girls in their finery with their hair fashionably styled and their faces made up. The land girls from Shillingbury Farm looked the most altered – no headscarves, boots and working breeches for them tonight! Clarissa had just spotted Molly dancing with her husband, the vicar, when she heard a decidedly well-spoken voice at her side.

'Now tell me why a stunning girl like you isn't dancing?'

Clarissa turned and found herself staring up into the strikingly handsome face of a dark-haired airman.

'I haven't been asked,' she replied smoothly.

'Well, that can easily be rectified.'

Before she knew it, he had taken her glass, placed it on a nearby table and had her firmly in his arms.

'You might have asked me properly,' she said, feeling some kind of protest was required of her.

He grinned. 'I couldn't take the risk you'd say no.'

'Is there any reason why I should have said no?'

'Plenty!'

'Give me one.'

'I'm afraid they're all classified.'

She laughed and allowed him to lead her around the dance floor. When the music came to an end, he said, 'This will never do, I haven't even introduced myself; just where are my manners?'

'Where indeed?' she said with a raised eyebrow.

He gave her a salute. 'Flying Officer William Dallimore, at your service. And you would be?'

'Clarissa Allerton.'

'Well, Clarissa, I've just made quite possibly the single most important decision of my life.'

'And what would that be?'

He tapped his nose. 'Classified, I'm afraid. Will you dance with me again?'

Never once thinking of her two left feet, she danced with him all night, a night that seemed to pass in the blink of an eye as the music played by the band – 'Moonlight Serenade', 'I'll Be Seeing You', 'The Very Thought of You', 'You Made Me Love You' – seemed to keep her within his embrace like a magnetic force.

When the band had played its last song, 'When I Grow Too Old to Dream', and it was time to go, he insisted on walking her home. 'But don't you have to return to the airfield with the rest of the men?' she asked.

'In theory, yes. However, seeing you home safely is far more important.'

Thinking of Leon, Clarissa hesitated, but with no sign of him in the hall, she accepted William's offer only too readily.

The velvety dark sky was studded with stars and a bright full moon of magical silvery whiteness. 'It's a bomber's moon,' William remarked, taking her hand in his, 'when all is laid bare. There's no hiding on a night like this.'

Clarissa had the strongest feeling he was talking of more than just the moon and stars above their heads. She wasn't at all surprised when some minutes later, after an owl hooted and swooped out from the trees to their left, he slowed his step, turned to face her in the moonlight and kissed her on the mouth. Without a second thought, she kissed him back, filled with a sense of elation, her heart beating fast, her head spinning with the potent desire to make this moment last forever.

How had it happened, she thought later, lying in bed unable to sleep? How could this stranger appear from nowhere and eclipse every emotion she had felt before? How was it possible she could meet somebody and in an instant, with no more than a few words exchanged between them, feel as though they were in perfect harmony and destined to be together?

Chapter Thirty-Nine

'How soon was it before you married him?' asked Lizzie in an awed voice when the flow of Mrs Dallimore's words came to an abrupt stop.

'Less than two months later. Charles gave me away, Molly was my bridesmaid, Mrs Cook made the cake and Lily helped me turn one of my favourite *Belle Etoile* evening gowns into a wedding dress. Our honeymoon was a night spent in a cottage by the sea in Norfolk, which Polly arranged for us. We couldn't stay there for more than the one night because William couldn't get leave for any longer, not when the Battle of Britain had just begun to be fought in earnest.'

'That really was a case of being swept off your feet, wasn't it?' Lizzie said, yet more of her preconceived ideas about the old lady vanishing.

'It was a coup de foudre for us both,' Mrs Dallimore said quietly. 'It might sound absurdly improbable to someone of your age, particularly so in these less than romantic times, but that night when we met, when William said he'd just made the single most important decision of his life, it was that he knew I was the woman he would marry. I felt the same about him by the end of the evening; I was literally dazzled by the way he made me feel and wanted to experience that emotion for the rest of my life.'

She closed her eyes briefly and let out a long, heartfelt sigh. 'Lizzie, my dear, would you mind if we left it there for now? I suddenly feel extremely tired.' Her voice contained a note of melancholy.

'Of course,' Lizzie said, worried that she'd tired the old

lady out. 'Would you like to have a nap? I could take you back to your room if you want.'

Mrs Dallimore made a placatory gesture with her hand. 'No, that won't be necessary, thank you. I'm quite comfortable here. Off you go now. I've taken up far too much of your time.'

Lizzie was reluctant to leave the old lady alone, but seeing her retreat into a meditative silence, she knew she had been politely dismissed.

Funny, she thought as she went back up to the house, how time spent with Mrs Dallimore made everything else fade into the background. Not once had she thought of Curt while she'd been listening to Mrs Dallimore. Come to think of it, the queasiness in her stomach had all but gone. The woman was a miracle worker!

When there was nothing else to do and she'd changed out of her overall, Lizzie went to find her bike to cycle home. A part of her didn't want to go home. The atmosphere between her parents that morning had not been good. She had never known them to snipe at one another, but there had definitely been some tetchiness between them at breakfast with each rushing to see to Freddie before the other did, as though trying to make a point.

She had just cycled to the end of Woodside's driveway when she decided to ring her brother. With a bit of luck she'd catch him on his way home from work. Her bike propped against the gatepost, she made the call. He answered on the second ring. 'You free to talk?' she asked.

'Yes, I'm still in the office. What's wrong?'

'Nothing's wrong, why would you think that?'

'I don't know, it's just that lately it seems like it's one thing after another.'

His voice sounded abnormally morose as if weighed down with all the cares of the world. 'Come on, big bro,' she said, 'tell me what's going on. What's making you sound like Homer Simpson when he finds his last doughnut's been pinched?'

She heard a small laugh in her ear and was glad she'd managed to cheer him up. 'It's nothing,' he said, 'just a bad day at work, that's all. What's new with you?'

'Oh, you know, same old same old, on the verge of world domination, if only I could get my lucky break.'

'It'll come. How're you doing otherwise?'

'You mean, Curt-wise?'

'Yes.'

'Better. Definitely better.'

'That's good. You do know he isn't worth a single second of regret, don't you? Because I guarantee he hasn't lost any sleep over you. Sorry if that sounds harsh.'

'It is harsh, but I think you're right; he played me for a complete fool. But it still hurts.'

'But maybe now the hurt is knowing you fell for his lies.'

'Hurt pride, you mean?'

'It's always been your Achilles heel. Don't let it get the better of you this time. Promise?'

'I promise, Big Bruv.'

'So, how's it going at Woodside?'

'Actually it's okay. There's this old lady called Mrs Dallimore who's been telling me about when she was a young girl. It's riveting and addictive stuff; I could sit and listen to her all day, given half the chance. It's made me realise that under that one roof there are all these people with a great stash of stories to tell.'

'I can remember Mum saying much the same when she started working there.'

'Talking of Mum, she and Dad were weirdly ratty with each other last night, and this morning. I felt like Freddie and I were caught in the crossfire.'

'That's not like them,' Luke said after a pause.

'I know. And the ridiculous thing is, it's all because Freddie fell in the pond yesterday on Dad's watch and he's—'

Lizzie suddenly realised she wasn't supposed to let on about Freddie's dunking accident. Not when it might get back to Ingrid. Although, as she'd pointed out to her parents, Freddie was now getting to the stage when he could easily spill the beans himself.

'When you say he fell in,' Luke said, 'what do you mean exactly?'

Uh-oh, bad Lizzie! 'Well,' she said, mentally picturing the precarious minefield she had just created for herself, 'I wasn't there in person, so all I know is … well … I think Freddie just got a bit, you know, excited and probably fancied a paddle. Nothing to worry about. Freddie's absolutely fine. If he wasn't, you'd have been the first to know. Mum and Dad would never keep anything serious from you when it comes to Freddie. I bet he's had tons of little accidents which you've never heard about.' She finally located the *off* button and hit it hard.

'None of what you're saying is really helping to put my mind at rest, Lizzie. Quite the reverse, if I'm honest.'

'I'm sorry, Luke, I'm doing my best to back-pedal over something that really would be neither here nor there if we weren't all so scared of how Ingrid would react. She always goes over the top when it comes to Freddie. You know that. And you also know we all walk on eggshells around her.'

When Luke didn't say anything, Lizzie feared she'd blown it. 'Are you there, Luke?' she asked anxiously.

'Yes, I am,' he said slowly. 'I was just selecting a larger shovel for you to use to dig yourself an even bigger hole. You might want to rethink your interpretation of back-pedalling.'

'Oh Luke, you know what I'm like, sometimes I just open my mouth and rubbish pours out.'

'I disagree. You usually speak straight from the heart and say what others are too afraid to say.'

'Yeah, but not this time,' she lied, trying to make good the damage her big mouth had caused – even she could see that as salvage operations went, she had her work cut out. 'This time I was shooting my mouth off like the idiot I am. Just forget I ever said anything. Please?'

Hearing her brother mutter some sort of assent, and desperate to change the subject, she told him about Simon turning up out of the blue. 'Thank God I wasn't at home when he called in,' she said, 'I'd have died on the spot. Mind you, if I had been there, I might have been able to stop Mum blurting out that Curt had just dumped me. Instead, Simon's probably now punching the air that I've got my come-uppance.'

'I doubt that. Simon isn't that kind of guy. I ought to go; I still have a few things I need to finish before leaving.'

One of these days, thought Lizzie irritably when she'd said goodbye to Luke and climbed back on her bike to set off for home, she would learn to keep her big yapper shut. It was one thing for her brother to suspect his family might view his wife in a certain way, but to have it confirmed was quite another matter.

She had only been cycling for a short while when she heard somebody calling her name. She turned to see Jed powering towards her on his mountain bike. Drawing level, he gave her a megawatt, campaign-poster smile. 'Fancy risking another drink at the Riverside with me?' he asked.

They sat at the same table as they had two evenings ago. 'I have news for you,' he said, after he'd taken a long, apprecia-tive drink of his beer. 'My friend at Skylark Radio says he'd like to meet you. He's looking for a researcher who might want to do a bit of presenting work to cover some maternity leave. And I'm all too aware that Bury St Edmunds is not the sexy centre of broadcasting action you've always dreamt of, that it's very much the wilderness in your eyes, but it could suit you until something better comes along.'

'You're kidding me, aren't you?'

He passed a hand across his face. 'Sorry, did I have my joker's face on then?'

'I don't know,' she said, 'it's difficult to tell with you when you appear to take so little seriously.'

'Well, here's a newsflash: in this instance I am being serious, and so is Ricky. He said to ask you to give him a call to set up a time when you could go into the studio to meet him.' From his pocket, Jed pulled out a scrap of paper with a phone number written on it. 'Thank me anytime you feel like it.'

She took the piece of paper and put it safely in her bag. 'Thank you,' she said, 'and I'm sorry if I sounded ungrateful, it's just that I really didn't expect anything to come of our previous conversation.'

'Ah, you thought I was all talk and no do. Sorry to disappoint you.'

'You haven't. You absolutely haven't. Thank you again for what you've done, I appreciate it.'

He smiled. 'Don't go overdoing the gratitude, or I'll think I'm on a promise.'

She tutted and rolled her eyes. 'And there you go again, spoiling a special moment of magic between us.'

He laughed. 'Story of my life.'

'Now there's a story I wouldn't mind hearing: yours.' She gave him a long appraising stare. 'Did you grow up round here? Are you a local boy?'

'I'm a local boy through and through. Apart from time spent away at school and university. And yes, before you climb up onto your high horse, I am what you call a posh boy who went to boarding school. You can fight that particular battle with my parents if you want.'

Remembering how rude she'd been the other evening with him, Lizzie apologised again. 'I'm sorry I had a go at you about that. I was out of order.'

'Yes, you were. Especially as I only ended up at boarding school because my parents were going through a messy and acrimonious divorce and it was deemed better for me to be somewhere that would provide more stability than either of my parents could.'

'I stand fully corrected. How are things with them these days?'

'Dad sold his business and is enjoying retirement in the South of France with wife number three. Mum hasn't fared so well. She's got motor neurone disease, and that's the reason I've moved back here from London, to take care of her.' He glanced away briefly, then took a mouthful of his beer. 'She sees herself as a burden and hates it.'

'How awful for her. And for you to know that she's suffering this way. What were you doing in London before?'

He turned to look at her directly from behind his sunglasses. 'What would give you the most pleasure to hear me say?'

'I don't know what you mean,' she said with a frown.

'What's been the most hated profession in the last few years? Come on, you can work it out.'

'*No!* You were a banker?'

He tipped his sunglasses up and gave her a long stare. 'Yep, a fully fledged City banker. I was pretty good at it, too, in case you're wondering. And just as I predicted, I can see the look of triumphant disgust in your eyes. Now my fate is sealed; throw me that noose you keep in your back pocket and I'll slip it over my head now.'

She smiled. 'I'll hold onto it for a while longer, if you don't mind. I'm sure you've got worse to tell me yet.'

He laughed. 'It's good to know you regard me so highly.'

Lizzie took a sip of her beer and considered what Jed had told her. Dressed in shabby jeans and a faded T-shirt, and with his tanned face, muscular arms and thick, golden-brown hair that looked like it needed a good brush, there was nothing of the City banker about him. She tried to picture him in a smart suit doing whatever it was bankers did, and failed totally.

A thought occurred to her. 'Presumably, as a banker, you

were making a ton of money; couldn't you have paid for a carer for your mother?'

'Is that what you would do if it was your mother?'

Shamed by his question, Lizzie looked away, realising she had never stopped to think of what would happen if one of her parents wasn't around and the other was seriously ill. Perhaps subconsciously she'd always assumed Luke – always the more sensible and grown up of the two of them – would be the one to step in and sort things out. He was much more efficiently organised than she was.

'I see you're hesitating over your answer,' Jed remarked.

'Not for the reason you're thinking,' she said, turning to look at him again. 'It's just something I've never given any thought to before now.'

'We none of us do, not until we're face to face with the dilemma. And don't get me wrong, I didn't want to do it at first. I researched every other available avenue before giving in to the one unassailable truth – I'm all my mother has, barring a couple of close friends and some helpful neighbours. But then when redundancies at the bank were fluttering around like confetti, I took it as a sign to grab the financial package on offer and do the right thing.'

'Couldn't you have stayed in London and have your mother live with you?'

He shook his head. 'I didn't think it was fair to uproot her to suit my needs, which makes me sound more altruistic than I really am. It's more a case of being pragmatic – the medical opinion is of the view she'll be lucky to see her next birthday, so why not do the best I can meanwhile?' He leant forward in his seat. 'The one big scary fact I've come to understand in all this is that being responsible for another person is the ultimate act of growing up. Something I'd never been in any hurry to do previously.'

Thinking of the life he must have sacrificed in order to take care of his mother, Lizzie said, 'Do you ever regret what you've given up?'

'Sure, there are times when I miss London and the person I used to be, but for now my life's here. It might sound strange, but I've found it quite a liberating experience and have adopted a take-each-day-as-it-comes attitude. I'm lucky to have a fair-sized cushion of money in the bank, so I can pay for an excellent carer to keep an eye on Mum while I work part-time, with hours to suit our arrangement.'

Her curiosity piqued, she couldn't resist asking her next question. 'But why gardening work?'

He shrugged. 'Why not? I used to do it as a summer job when I was at university, so despite what you think, I do actually know what I'm doing. And more to the point, I enjoy it. I could be at home 24/7, but that would make Mum feel even more of a burden.' He drained his glass and looked at his watch. 'I ought to be going; Mum's carer will be leaving soon.'

After they'd parted, and after Jed had reminded her to get in touch with Ricky, Lizzie cycled home deep in thought. Jed had risen considerably in her estimation, but exponentially her view of herself had sunk without trace. She had done nothing but feel sorry for herself since losing her job. Enough was enough. It was time to shake off the pathetic whinger she had become and prove her mettle.

What was more, Luke was right when it came to Curt – it was mostly hurt pride that she was feeling. She had fooled herself into believing that Curt loved her, she could see that very clearly now. Oh, how she'd lapped up his every word about how awful his wife was, how since having their daughter he'd been frozen out and made to feel he was no longer needed. And Lizzie, idiot that she'd been, had kidded herself that she could undo all the harm his wife was causing.

Well, no more time would she waste dwelling on Curt and the consequences of her gullible stupidity. It was time to turn things around.

*

Luke made it home from work just in time to say goodnight to Freddie before he went to bed at Keeper's Nook.

Conversations with his son on FaceTime always made him smile as Freddie generally saw it as an opportunity to show him things, excitedly holding whatever it was up to the camera, either so close Luke couldn't see what it was, or so fleetingly it was no more than a blur. It was always Dad who was with Freddie when they chatted like this, but last night it had been Mum doing the pre-bedtime chat, and now Luke came to think about it, she had seemed slightly off-kilter, giving Freddie hardly any time to chatter on in his haphazard way. Had she been covering up for something? Or maybe it was just tiredness that was the problem: the work involved in taking care of a two-year-old was not to be underestimated.

After Freddie had kissed the screen by way of saying goodnight and run off to have his bath, Luke scrutinised his father's face and asked if everything was all right.

'All under control, as always,' Dad said cheerily. 'Nothing to worry about.'

'Dad, you would say if it's getting too much having Freddie Monday to Friday, wouldn't you?'

'Of course. But we love having Freddie here. He's no trouble at all. You'll never guess who we had a visit from the other evening – none other than Simon. Or did your mother tell you that last night when you called? Or maybe Lizzie's filled you in?'

Ingrid frequently told Luke that the problem with his parents was that it wasn't what they said that was important, but what they didn't say. 'That's the bit you have to listen to the hardest,' she claimed, 'those polite pauses, or those quick-to-change-the-subject moments.' Luke had always taken the view that it was human nature to mislead and dissemble and to do so quite unconsciously. But aware that his father had just neatly changed the subject, he said, 'I don't want you and Mum to feel we're taking advantage of you.'

'We don't feel that. And anyway, it won't be long before everything's back to normal, will it? What's the latest on the nursery front?'

They talked some more, all without Luke once referring to what Lizzie had told him about Freddie and the pond, and without his father bringing it up. Nor did Luke say anything of his disappointment in his family that they felt they had to tiptoe round the woman he loved, although it was dangerously on the tip of his tongue to ask his father if it were true.

'Hang on,' his father said now, 'I can hear Freddie calling for me to go up and kiss him goodnight. Better do as I'm told. The tyranny of a two-year-old – there's nothing like it!'

Luke smiled. 'Give him another hug and a kiss from me.'

'Will do. Roger and out.'

Dad always ended a FaceTime call that way.

For minutes afterwards, Luke stared absently at the screen. He was still sitting there some minutes later when he heard Ingrid's key in the lock.

While he cooked supper, Ingrid sat at the kitchen table and dealt with a list of emails she hadn't had time to answer during the day. Hearing her tapping away on her laptop, Luke thought how, instead of spending more time together of an evening while Freddie was at Mum and Dad's, he and Ingrid were actually spending less time together, both of them taking advantage of not having to rush off from work to collect Freddie from nursery. The thought had naively crossed Luke's mind that with a more leisurely start to the day they might linger awhile in bed like they used to – Ingrid had often said that she enjoyed sex first thing in the morning more than at any other time of the day. Not any more, he thought, trying to remember when they had last made love. Or even when they had enjoyed a fun evening out, just the two of them.

He was probably worrying unnecessarily, but thinking

how they had always promised themselves that work would never interfere with their relationship, here they were eating late and barely a word being exchanged between them.

'How about we take off for a couple of weeks' holiday,' he suddenly said.

Ingrid stopped typing.

'There's bound to be any number of last-minute bargains we could pick up,' he added.

'What's brought this on?' she asked, reaching for the glass of wine he'd poured for her.

He put down the knife he'd been using to slice mushrooms. 'I feel in need of a break, somewhere hot and sunny and with some five-star luxury thrown in. Wouldn't you like that?'

'Of course, who wouldn't? When were you thinking?'

'Next week. Or maybe the week after.'

Ingrid took a sip of her wine and drew her brows together. 'I couldn't possibly get away. I'm in the middle of a big case, I can't just hand over the reins to somebody else because I fancy a holiday.'

He went back to slicing the mushrooms. 'Forget it, it was stupid of me. I should have thought.'

'Don't be silly. It was a nice idea, just not feasible right now. How was Freddie when you spoke to him?'

'As happy as Larry, like he always is with Mum and Dad. What about the weekend?' he persisted. 'We could go away to a classy hotel.'

'I'm sorry, Luke, but I'll have to work for at least one of the days over the weekend. And besides, we can't expect your parents to have Freddie on Saturday and Sunday as well.'

'I assumed he'd come with us.'

'A toddler in a classy hotel? It's not ideal, is it?' Her fingers had resumed tapping again at the keyboard.

He carried on chopping. What was the point? he wondered.

Seconds passed. 'What is it, Luke?' asked Ingrid. 'What's wrong?'

'Nothing's wrong,' he said. 'Everything's fine. Fancy an episode of *House of Cards* while we eat?'

And there we have it, he thought, he was just as bad as his parents. It's what we don't say that matters the most.

Chapter Forty

With her breath held tight and her heart hammering in her chest, Lizzie snapped her eyes open with a start. She blinked and took a moment to work out where she was. And then relief kicked in. It was a dream. Just a dream. It wasn't real.

But the vividness of what she'd been dreaming still had the power to convince her she was mistaken, and as her body convulsed with a shudder of horror, she felt compelled to rush to her parents' bedroom to check they were all right, that they weren't both lying amidst the bloodied wreckage of a car crash. She didn't, though. Instead she shuddered again at the thought of the twisted remains of her father's car, which she had been driving in the dream. The accident had been her fault. She hadn't been concentrating; she'd been too busy looking for her mobile in her handbag on her lap, her hands off the steering wheel as she hunted through all the rubbish in her bag to find the phone.

'It'll be Curt,' she'd said happily, ignoring her father's instruction to keep her eyes on the road, 'he'll be ringing to say he's sorry and will I forgive him for what he said.'

She'd found the phone just as the car skidded off the road and went careering down the slippery, grassy slope of a steep hill and no matter how hard she banged her foot on the brake pedal, the car wouldn't stop. Faster and faster the car went, until finally it crashed headlong into what was the only object for miles around, a colossal oak tree. Then, as if she were suspended above the wreckage of the car, she was calling to her parents. 'I'm sorry,' she was crying, 'I'm sorry for what I did!'

Sitting up now, Lizzie took a deep breath. Two things, she told herself, trying to make sense of the dream. First, Curt is never going to ring and beg forgiveness, and second, never would she forgive him. *Never.* Not even if he turned up here in person with tears running down his cheeks and a choir of heavenly angels singing to her.

She thought again about the dream and what had caused her subconscious to create such a nightmare. Did its roots lie in the conversation she'd had with Jed about his mother? Certainly it had left her thinking whether she could be as selfless as he had been. 'Being responsible for another person was the ultimate act of growing up,' Jed had said. It sounded a bit preachy, but maybe he was right.

In the dream she had been driving without care or thought for anybody else; all that mattered was the ringing of her mobile – was that a sign that she lacked responsibility, that she didn't think enough of others before herself? Was that how she'd been lately? She had a dreadful feeling that maybe it was true, for hadn't her every waking thought revolved around herself since Curt had turned her world upside down? And hadn't she, in her haste to throw herself into an affair with Curt, isolated herself from her friends, not caring a jot about how they felt? Was it any wonder so many of them had taken Simon's side and deserted her?

Putting Curt from her mind, she asked herself again if she could ever be as selfless as Jed.

Or as selfless as Mrs Dallimore. Look what she had done when she was years younger than Lizzie. Without a back-ward glance she had thrown herself into not just helping her grandparents, but caring for two young refugee children. And not forgetting Leon, the Polish refugee. What had driven Mrs Dallimore to be so generous and to do so much good at so young an age? And why hadn't Lizzie felt the same, because when she thought back to when she was twenty and what she was getting up to, the comparison didn't bear thinking about.

Feckless and without purpose – that just about summed her up. By rights the admission should have depressed her, but it didn't. It made her think that the time had come to ditch her bad old ways and get a grip on what was important.

Jed had given her the chance of a job, albeit a job she wouldn't have previously considered, but beggars couldn't be choosers and she might just as well accept that and see what transpired. It was always possible this Ricky character wouldn't think she was suitable for the role at Skylark Radio, but the first step was to get in touch with him. She had entered the contact details into her mobile and planned to make the call this morning before she went to Woodside. Knowing how desperately her parents wanted her to find a job that would get her back on her feet, she hadn't mentioned Jed or the opportunity that he had passed her way in case it got their hopes up, only for them to be dashed.

To get the ball rolling on her new-found determination to be more positive, and since all was quiet in the house with everybody else still sleeping – it wasn't quite six thirty – she decided her first selfless act of the day would be to surprise her parents by making breakfast for them.

But when Lizzie got downstairs, she found her mother was already in the kitchen, the kettle coming to the boil.

'Hello, love,' Mum said. 'You're up early.'

'So are you.'

'The birds woke me. They've been at it since four.'

'You haven't been awake since then, have you?'

'Off and on. Tea or coffee?'

Remembering her first act of selflessness for the day, Lizzie said, 'Why don't you sit down and let me do it?'

'It's no trouble.'

'I know it isn't, but I'd like to do it for you.'

Her mother looked at her.

'What's that look for, Mum?'

'I'm not aware of giving you a look.'

'Well you did, now out of the way. What would you like, tea or coffee?'

'Tea, please, and no sugar.'

'I know you don't have sugar in your tea, Mum. And nor does Dad. Honestly, the way you're carrying on anyone would think I never make you a drink.'

Her mother neither confirmed nor denied her comment. Instead she said, 'Seeing as it's such a lovely morning, shall we have our drinks in the summer house?'

'Good idea. You go and plump up the cushions, I'll be right with you.'

Dad had built the summer house for Mum last year as a birthday present, and it was her favourite place in the garden to sit. He had also made her a sign that read *Tess's Retreat*, and he'd run an electricity cable from the house to the summer house so that it could be lit up with little lanterns in the evening. Mum and Dad often enjoyed a gin and tonic in there – but when was the last time they had done that? Certainly it hadn't happened since she'd moved back home.

The drinks made, she carried them outside and settled herself in the chair next to her mother. How beautiful the garden looked, she thought, bathed as it was in a golden wash of early morning sunlight. The only sound to be heard was the joyful chorus of birds singing their hearts out.

'Birds always sound so happy to be awake first thing in the morning, don't they?' Lizzie remarked. 'Do you suppose that's because they don't have anything to worry about?'

Her mother looked at her. 'That sounds like a question only somebody with too much to worry about might ask.'

'It wasn't meant to,' Lizzie said. She drank some of her tea, taking care not to scald her lips. 'You might find this hard to believe,' she said at length, 'but before I came downstairs I was trying to sort out some of the clutter going on inside my head.'

'Why would you think I'd find that hard to believe?'

Lizzie shrugged. 'I know how people see me, Mum, that

I'm a hopeless flibbertigibbet who can't get anything right.'

'That's not true. I've told you before, you mustn't be so hard on yourself.'

'Okay then, give me an example of something I've achieved.'

'Well, from what I hear, you're a big hit at Woodside, particularly with Mrs Dallimore.'

'That's hardly an achievement.'

'Isn't it? I'd say it is. All somebody like Mrs Dallimore wants is the company of someone who's genuinely interested in what she has to say. And you do that.'

'But I like spending time with her.'

'Not everyone would. And initially you weren't too keen on the idea of going to Woodside, were you? But instead of complaining about it, you rolled your sleeves up and in the short time you've been there, you've made a success of it.'

'All right, I'll concede that one maybe, but if you put that to one side, there isn't anything else I can be proud of, is there? Everything I touch turns into a gigantic mess. In one fell swoop I hurt Simon badly, I destroyed your friendship with Lorna and Keith, I lost my job into the bargain, and all because I was stupid enough to fall for the oldest trick in the book, a married man who had no intention of ever leaving his wife.'

Her mother tutted. 'As always you're blaming yourself too much. I doubt you're the first person Curt has lied to, and probably not the last, so try to take some solace in that. Do you mind if I ask you something?'

Lizzie smiled. 'Mum, since when have you asked permission to interrogate me?'

'I've never interrogated you!' her mother remonstrated.

'Well, maybe we'll have to agree to disagree on that point. What is it you want to know?'

'Do you think if Curt hadn't come along when he did you might have stayed with Simon?'

'Good question,' Lizzie said as she watched a pair of

sparrows hopping along the path. 'We'd hit a sort of fork in the road, I suppose, and you could say I chose the wrong road.'

'Have you thought of speaking to him?'

'Oh, Mum, you'd love nothing better than to see me back with Simon, wouldn't you?'

'He's such a lovely boy.'

Lizzie smiled at her mother's description.

'And it was good of him to come and see us the other evening.'

'It was. You're right, he was always very thoughtful. But maybe I don't deserve somebody so decent and good.'

Her comment produced a tut of gigantic proportions. 'That's utter rubbish, Lizzie, and I never want to hear you say anything like that again.'

Loving her mother for always rushing to defend her, Lizzie said, 'I'm going to turn the tables on you now and ask you something.'

'What's that then?'

'Why have you and Dad been acting so strangely these last few days? Have you rowed?'

Her mother immediately looked flustered and bent down to pick up a leaf from the floor of the summer house. 'It's my fault entirely,' she said. 'I blamed him quite unfairly for Freddie falling in the pond. I overreacted. And all because I'm so scared of what Ingrid might say. What if she declares us unfit grandparents?'

'I think she'd have a tough job getting that one past Luke. And Freddie, for that matter. He loves you and Dad to bits. Besides, an accident is just that, an accident.'

'I know, but in the heat of the moment I wasn't thinking rationally when I blamed your father. And he'd probably admit that his reaction wasn't altogether rational either.'

'Why, what did he say?'

'He shouted at me. Accused me of making a drama out of everything, of not supporting him. And then he stormed out. I'd never seen him like that before. He was so cross. I've tried apologising to him, but I don't think he's forgiven me.'

'He will. Dad's not one to harbour a grudge.' But then, nor was he the kind of man to shout or storm out, Lizzie thought. 'Would it help if I spoke to him?' she asked.

'I don't know. He might be upset that I've been tittle-tattling to you about him.'

Lizzie sipped her tea thoughtfully. Then from nowhere, a gem of an idea struck her. What her parents needed was time on their own, an evening without Freddie or her. She would book a table at their favourite restaurant for tonight and deliver it as a fait accompli. That's if she could book it in time. She'd call in at the post office to make a withdrawal from her bank account, and give them the money to dine out in style. It would make a serious dent in what little money she had, but it would be worth it. It would be her way of trying to make amends for the turmoil she was putting them through.

Lizzie cycled into the centre of the village, propped her bike against the bench in front of the duck pond – scene of Pond-Gate – and sat down to tackle the first of the phone calls she needed to make, both of which had to be done out of range of her parents overhearing.

When Ricky Chambers answered her call he sounded breathless. In the background she could hear birds singing and the distant noise of a car engine.

'Sorry,' he panted, when she said who she was and hoped she wasn't disturbing him, 'I don't always sound like this, but I'm in training for a half marathon I've agreed to take part in. Stupidest thing I ever said yes to. What's yours?'

'Err ... sorry?'

'What's the stupidest thing you've ever agreed to?'

Okay, he was testing her, putting her on the spot with a classic left-field interview question. *Think carefully, Lizzie,* she warned herself, *think very carefully.* But before her brain had time to filter out the raft of wrong answers, her runaway mouth had seized control and to her horror she heard herself say, 'Agreeing to have a drink with my last boss ranks prettily highly as the stupidest thing I ever agreed to.'

'Interesting. Jed's told me a little about you and since I know him of old, I know to trust him. How about you come into the studio tomorrow and we can have a chat?'

'What time shall I come?'

'I'll be on air from twelve o'clock until three, so why don't you arrive towards the end of the show?'

With the first task of the day crossed off her list, and hardly daring to believe anything would come of it, Lizzie then rang the restaurant in Lavenham to book a table for her parents that evening. With that done, she called in at the post office to drain her bank account. It's for a good cause, she reminded herself when she saw the paltry amount she had left.

Next stop Woodside, and back on her bike and pedalling fast, she realised she was looking forward to seeing Mrs Dallimore again, in the hope she would hear what happened next after she'd married her dashing pilot.

But there was no sign of Mrs Dallimore that morning, and when Lizzie asked after her she was told the old lady hadn't slept well and was in the medical wing. Alarmed that something might be seriously wrong, Lizzie spent the next few hours on the lookout for her.

By lunchtime there was still no sign of Mrs Dallimore, and as she helped Mr Sheridan take his seat at the table in the dining room, she asked him if he knew anything.

'She looked a touch peaky last night during supper,' he said. 'Told her as much, which she didn't like one little bit. Lovely woman,' he said wistfully. 'Wish I'd known her years ago, after my wife passed away. I think we would have had some fun together in our twilight years.' He sighed heavily.

That sigh stayed with Lizzie during lunch while she helped oversee things, giving help to those who needed it, but holding back respectfully from those who had not yet reached the stage when they were prepared to ask for assistance. It broke Lizzie's heart to see poor old Mr Jenkins, who suffered badly with Parkinson's disease, trying to feed himself, and she longed to take hold of his hand and steady it so that the food from his plate made it to his mouth and not down his front. Sitting on the same table as him was a new resident, a woman who had quickly gained herself the reputation amongst the staff as being 'difficult'. Her name was Mrs Lennox, and she had arrived two days ago and told anyone who would listen that she wouldn't be staying here long; it was just a stopgap until her son found her somewhere more suitable. Observing the disgust on her superior face as she watched Mr Jenkins doing his best to feed himself, Lizzie very much hoped the woman's son would find somewhere more suitable, and soon.

She was just helping to clear away the plates from those who'd finished eating when Jennifer approached. 'Could I have a quick word?'

'Of course,' Lizzie replied. 'What is it?'

'It's Mrs Dallimore, she's—'

Lizzie's heart sank. 'What?' she cut in. 'She hasn't died, has she?'

The woman frowned. 'Heavens no, whatever made you think that?'

'She's been in the medical wing all morning and Mr Sheridan said she wasn't looking so good last night, and—'

'She's fine; her blood pressure just went a bit haywire. She's in her room resting, and knowing how fond she's grown of you, I wondered if you'd like to take her some lunch and sit with her for a while. Would you?'

'Of course.'

Chapter Forty-One

'Such a lot of fuss about nothing,' said Mrs Dallimore with a dismissive wave of her hand. 'A rise in my blood pressure and everybody's getting ready to measure me up for my coffin.'

'Better to err on the side of caution,' Lizzie said, conscious that, despite the fighting talk, the old lady did indeed look more frail than yesterday. 'Are you sure you can't eat any more lunch?' she asked. 'You haven't eaten much.'

'I've never really been a fan of poached salmon if I'm honest; it has the habit of repeating on me. But I'll have that bowl of fruit salad now. So what news do you have for me? How's Mrs Lennox settling in? Is there anyone left she hasn't offended with her superior airs? She rather reminds me of dear old Virginia Charlbury.'

Lizzie removed the plate of half-eaten food from the tray resting on Mrs Dallimore's lap and replaced it with the dessert bowl and spoon.

'Now you know I couldn't possibly comment on one of your fellow residents,' she said good-humouredly.

Mrs Dallimore laughed. 'How very diplomatic of you, my dear. Well, if you won't give me any snippets of gossip of that nature, tell me what's going on in your own life. Stopped moping over that married man yet?'

Lizzie smiled. 'Getting there.'

'Good, I'm very pleased to hear that. Somebody once told me that the cure for infatuation is simply to get to know the person better. Which you now have. How's Jed? Taken you out for another drink yet?'

'As a matter of fact he has, he—' Lizzie did a double take.

'Hang on, how did you know that Jed had asked me out for a drink previously?'

'Because I suggested it to him.'

'*You didn't!*' Her exclamation coming out as a high-pitched squeak, Lizzie's mouth stayed open in a circle of disbelief.

'What an absurd thing to say, of course I did. What else am I supposed to do here but meddle in other people's lives? Did you have a pleasant time together?'

'Never you mind.'

Mrs Dallimore chuckled happily. 'He's a nice chap; I like him. And there's more to him than meets the eye, wouldn't you say?'

Lizzie smiled. 'What a wily old thing you are, Mrs Dallimore! If you eat some more fruit, I'll tell you some more.' The deal struck, Lizzie explained about Jed putting in a word for her at Skylark Radio and her going to the studio tomorrow to meet one of the station's presenters.

'Part of me wants you to get the job,' said Mrs Dallimore when Lizzie finished, 'but selfishly, I shall miss not having you around.'

'I probably won't be offered the job, given my run of bad luck, but if I do, I could still come and visit you,' Lizzie said, 'if you'd like me to.'

'Oh, I expect you'll be much too busy to do that.'

Lizzie took the now empty dish from Mrs Dallimore. 'I shall make time,' she said firmly, meaning it. 'After all, I might want to do some meddling of my own regarding you and Mr Sheridan.'

Wiping her mouth with a paper napkin, Mrs Dallimore's eyes twinkled. 'Playing me at my own game? Well, I deserve that, I suppose. But as pleasant a man as Mr Sheridan is, I'm prepared to let somebody else snap him up.'

'A case of him not being a patch on your husband, is that how it is?' asked Lizzie. 'Was Mr Dallimore the one true love of your life?'

The old lady paused a beat, and, as if giving the question careful deliberation, she turned her gaze reflectively towards the open French doors. 'We were very happy,' she said faintly, 'but for so short a time.'

'How short?'

'Two years, which was longer than a lot of marriages lasted, given the war. William died not in the air, as I dreaded, but during an air raid one night. The airfield was targeted, and since it was so close to the village, the village was also hit. My grandmother and I were at a WVS meeting in the village hall when suddenly it seemed as though the whole world had exploded. To all intents and purposes it had; Shillingbury had become my world and I lost not just my husband that night, but my grandmother and my friend Molly. It was a terrible, terrible night ...'

In a hushed voice, not wanting to appear crass, Lizzie said, 'I can't begin to imagine what it must have been like for you.'

Mrs Dallimore slowly turned away from the French doors, her gaze now back on Lizzie. 'No, you probably can't. Unless you lived through those times, you have no idea. And I don't mean to be patronising when I say that.'

'I know you don't. How did you carry on?'

'There was no alternative. Besides, it was what one had to do; one had to keep going. Would you like to hear what happened next?'

'Only if it won't tire you out. I don't want you ending up back in the medical wing again.'

'Don't concern yourself with that – it's my resolute intention to stay away from there for as long as possible.'

Chapter Forty-Two

Autumn and winter 1943, Shillingbury, Suffolk

They say that for everything you lose, you gain something new, but it was hard to believe this was true the night the bombs rained down on Shillingbury, the night when Clarissa lost so much.

The horror of the bombing raid made them all realise how lucky they had been, because until that night they had escaped what London and many other cities around the country had endured on a regular basis. Now the war had come directly to them. And claimed some of their own.

Lavinia died shortly after Clarissa and two others managed to drag her from the burning inferno of what had been the village hall and where they'd been attending a WVS meeting. The scene was one of utter chaos: of men and women screaming as they frantically searched for loved ones amidst the wreckage, while others did their best to put out the fires that had taken hold. Thatched cottages were ablaze in an instant, turning the sky into a flaming cauldron. At Jimmy's command, a human chain was formed from the water pump, but the buckets of water thrown at the flames made little impact. Then suddenly, as if it were an act of God, it began to rain, and when the first fat drops turned to a dramatic downpour, a loud cheer went up. By the time the ambulances and fire engines arrived, the worst was over. Half a dozen houses had been lost, including Mrs Cook's cottage, and the dead were laid out on the village green – Lavinia, Molly, Vera Hubbard, Joan Bidwell, the elderly Finch sisters and

Virginia Charlbury. It was a miracle anyone had survived from inside the hall, so people started to say.

Soaked to the skin, her teeth chattering with shock and cold, Clarissa was taken home where she had to break the awful news to Charles. The next morning, and still in a daze, she received the news that the airfield had been hit by several bombs at the same time as the village hall had, and William was one of five airmen who'd died. His end, so she was assured, had been mercifully quick. Inconsolable, Clarissa sobbed her heart out for what felt like an eternity. She was convinced the profound pain of her grief would be too much for her to bear. Poor William. One minute so full of life and the next no more.

His parents, who'd already lost one son when the Spitfire he'd been flying had been shot down over the English Channel, wanted William to be buried in Kent in their parish church. Numb with grief, Clarissa went along with their wishes. It was only later that she realised her mistake – having William's grave to tend to in Shillingbury would have given her somewhere to visit when she wanted to feel close to him.

But that regret was soon assuaged when Dr Rutherford diagnosed that the acute tiredness and sickness she was experiencing had little to do with mourning, but was morning sickness: she was pregnant. The news had the effect of lifting her spirits: she might not have William, but she had his child, a child who would give her the strength and courage to carry on.

It was a courage that was put to the test a month later when Clarissa went in search of Charles to tell him lunch was ready. Since his wife's death, Charles was a much altered man. Never loquacious before, now he was even more taciturn and withdrawn, and spent nearly all his time alone, either in the greenhouse or in the drawing room listening to the daily news broadcasts. Thomas and Walter took to listening to the news on the wireless also, wanting to understand fully what was going on. They had been so very fond of William, and of Lavinia, too, who had become something of a grandmother figure to them. The shock of what had happened understandably prompted them to speak about their parents more, asking Clarissa question after question about them, desperately needing reassurance that their mother and father were still alive, that they would see them again, and soon. All Clarissa could do was tell the boys that they had to live in hope; it was all any of them could do.

With no sign of Charles in the house, Clarissa went out to the garden. She found him in the greenhouse, slumped in his wheelchair, his left hand hanging limply at his side. At first she thought he'd fallen asleep, but when he didn't stir at the sound of her voice, or her hand on his shoulder, she feared the worst and felt for his pulse. Unable to find it, but knowing from the stillness of his body that it would serve no purpose other than to confirm what she already knew, she went to call Dr Rutherford. The cause of death, so the doctor wrote on the death certificate, was a massive stroke, but Clarissa felt the real truth was that with Lavinia gone the fight had gone out of Charles; he'd lost the will to live.

Immediately after the funeral service, and back at the house where those who'd been at the church had gathered for a drink, Henry Willet took Clarissa discreetly to one side and said there were certain things he needed to discuss with her.

'Will it take long?' she asked tiredly.

'No more than half an hour,' he said. 'I just thought it would be better to do it today, rather than drag you to my office. But if you feel—'

'No, no,' she said, 'let's do it when the other guests have left.'

They sat in the drawing room, or, more precisely, she sat while Henry paced the floor in front of the fire burning in the grate, his well-manicured hands clasped behind his back.

No longer did he resemble the awkward country lawyer she had first encountered in the Primrose Tea Rooms. Dressed today in an elegant dark suit with a black tie, his hair oiled and smoothed into place, he would not have looked out of place in a smart city law firm.

'As I'm sure you're aware,' he began, 'Charles and Lavinia had no real money to speak of; things did not go well for them after the Depression. I mean no disrespect when I say that Charles's judgement was less than sound when it came to investments, and so—'

'Yes, yes, I know all that,' Clarissa interrupted him, wishing he would get to the point. Henry had turned into a pompous and monumental bore. Pedantry might be considered an asset for a lawyer, but Clarissa had no time for it. Her grandfather had often made the same observation, especially so after Henry had been declared unfit for active service. But a pedant was a safe pair of hands, Charles had maintained, saying there was nobody he would trust more to handle his affairs.

Henry was, Clarissa strongly suspected, a deeply unfulfilled man – a man who, still unmarried, continued to live with his mother. William had met Henry once and had not taken to him. 'The man strikes me as having a cushy war and doing rather well out of it,' he'd said. In Clarissa's opinion William had been a shrewd judge of character.

It had been after she was married, and at her American lawyer's insistence, that Clarissa had made a will. Henry had drawn it up, but without ever knowing the exact extent of her wealth. Again at her lawyer's insistence, the bulk of the money inherited from Grandma Ethel, along with a wide variety of investments, was to remain in America until the war was over. For now a generous monthly allowance was transferred by wire.

Soon after her wedding to William, Effie had written to congratulate Clarissa, declaring herself to be the most jealous girl in all the world. '*Why can't a handsome pilot fall in love with me?*' she'd written. Her comment was a nod towards Ellis, who was then based in Newport Beach, California carrying out submarine patrol missions. A letter from Ellis arrived several weeks later, accusing Clarissa of wantonly breaking the hearts of the only two men who were remotely worthy of her affections – he and Artie. Artie had also sent her a brief letter of congratulation, and more recently a heartbreakingly compassionate note of condolence after she'd written to say that William had been killed. Artie was now in Italy reporting on the advancement of the Allied troops – with the US so heavily involved in the war since the bombing of Pearl Harbor, his skill as a reporter was in even greater demand. Rarely in his letters did he refer to what he was witnessing; instead he enquired after Clarissa and Thomas and Walter. The boys also wrote to Artie, or Uncle Artie as they now called him.

'I'm very sorry,' Henry said, coming to a stop in front of the fireplace, his hands still clasped behind his back. 'After everything you've endured, this must be dreadfully wearisome for you, but I wanted to set the scene, so to speak.'

Lord! How much had she missed while her mind had wandered? Clarissa rapidly corralled her wits. 'For which I thank you,' she said, 'but it's been a long day, most of which I've spent on my feet, and I'd really like to get this over with so I can rest.'

'Of course.' Henry's gaze flickered hesitantly from her face to her swelling abdomen. She had the feeling he found the sight of her in this condition vaguely unpalatable. 'Perhaps I could request Mrs Cook make you a cup of tea,' he said. 'I'm sure she's not too busy to do that for you.'

There was something horribly proprietorial about the way he was standing there on the hearthrug, and also in the manner he referred to Mrs Cook, whose devotion to Clarissa was matched only by Clarissa's devotion to her. With the poor woman's cottage rendered uninhabitable after the night of the bombing, she had been living here at The Grange ever since. There had been times when, distraught with grief, Mrs Cook had been the only person to whom she could turn.

'That's all right,' Clarissa replied. 'Mrs Cook's done quite enough for the day. If she has any sense she'll be sitting down having a well-earned cup of tea herself. So, to the point, Henry. Which is presumably the contents of my grandfather's will.'

'Yes, indeed.'

'And given that I have absolutely no expectations, please don't feel you have to sugar-coat anything for me.'

'Thank you, I appreciate your frankness. Which deserves equal frankness. To this end, I'm sorry to tell you things are far worse than Charles would have ever wanted you to know. He kept the worst of it from Lavinia, wanted to shield her from anything unpleasant. As you may recall, I spoke with him after Lavinia's funeral and he requested I draw up a new will and appointed me as sole executor. In that respect, he was at least thorough.'

And still he hasn't got to the point, thought Clarissa irritably as the ormolu clock on the mantelpiece struck the hour – it was now four o'clock.

'What with increased taxation due to the war and death duties to take into account,' Henry continued relentlessly, 'it's my very sad duty to inform you that while Charles has bequeathed you this house, there will be nothing left once the bank and the taxman have claimed what is owed to them. In fact, I fear you will have to sell the house to pay off in full what is owed. And therein lies a further problem, for the cost of the outstanding repairs required, repairs that Charles kept putting off, such as the leaking roof, the damp and the …' His words trailed off. He pressed his glasses firmly to the bridge of his nose. Then: 'Perhaps now is not the time to further distress you with regard to the poor state of the house. But there is a solution, and one I think you might find agreeable. Since I know how much you love this house and regard it as your home, you could request funds from America to resolve the situation.'

Wondering where he'd got the idea that she loved the house, Clarissa said, 'It's more or less how I assumed my grandfather had left matters.'

He nodded. 'I so wish it could be otherwise.'

'But it isn't,' Clarissa said firmly, 'and if there's one thing I've learned, it is that we must face these things head-on and with all the grit we can muster.'

He came and sat on the sofa next to her. 'How brave you are, my dear, but Clarissa, I want you to know that you don't have to face this alone. If there's anything I can do, you only have to ask.' He took her hand and held it between his, the palms of his hands clammy against hers. 'You know how very much I've always admired you,' he said. 'And perhaps ... well, perhaps if things had been different, if we had met long before the war broke out, before you became saddled with so much responsibility, I might have had the courage to ask you to—'

'Please, Henry,' she interrupted him, appalled and dismayed at what he was on the verge of saying. She removed her hand from his. 'Now is not the time.'

'You're right,' he said. 'Forgive me. It's just that I can't stand to see you suffer.'

'I'm not suffering,' she said. 'Compared to what some people are going through, I'm fortunate.' She had told herself this so many times she almost believed it.

'That's an admirable thing to say. But what do you intend to do?'

'About the house?'

He nodded. 'It's become your home. Surely you can't bear to part with it?'

'Funnily enough, I can. And what is more, it's already arranged for me to leave.' She rose to her feet. 'You see, a few days ago I was informed that the house is to be requisitioned and used by the airfield.'

Henry rose to his feet also, his face a picture of alarm. 'Have you agreed?'

'Agreement doesn't come into it. It was an order. And a quite understandable order at that. The air raid destroyed much of the sleeping quarters and the officers' mess,' she continued, as though he hadn't spoken. 'The house is needed.'

'But where will you go?'

'I have plans in place. Tomorrow I'm going to sign the lease for a cottage on Colonel Brook's estate. It's been empty for some time and is a little run-down, but fixing it will be part of the fun of moving there.'

His brows drawn, Henry had now resumed his pacing in front of the fireplace. 'This is all so sudden, Clarissa,' he said. 'Are you sure you know what you're doing?'

Annoyed by his patronising tone, and sensing he was put out that his role of caring lawyer gently leading her by the hand had been snatched from him, Clarissa forced herself to smile. 'Never more so, Henry. Mrs Cook will be coming with me, as will Thomas and Walter, and Leon too. Sadly we'll be losing Jimmy, but he'll be nearby working for the Colonel and will be available to help with a few jobs for me should the need arise. Of course, the cottage will be a lot more cramped than we're used to, but in the circumstances that really does seem neither here nor there, don't you think?'

'It still leaves you with the problem of paying off the bank,' Henry rallied, ever the lawyer.

Clarissa was ahead of him. Well ahead. 'I've spoken to a very helpful and understanding man at the bank,' she said, 'and whatever is owed I shall personally deal with. The taxman will have to wait until after the war.'

With nothing more to be said on the matter, Henry saw himself out and Clarissa went to find Mrs Cook.

'Glory be, you look tired!' the woman exclaimed when she saw Clarissa. She pulled out a chair and made her sit down at the table. 'What you need, my girl, is a nice cup of tea.'

'That would be lovely, thank you.'

'How did it go with Mr Willet?'

'He didn't tell me anything I didn't know already, but I had the satisfaction of surprising him fairly and squarely.'

'Good for you. Ah, here's Leon. I swear that lad knows the precise moment when I put the betsy on the stove.'

Leon had had his Enemy Alien status downgraded to Friendly Alien and was now working as a civilian at the airfield, putting his engineering training to good use as a mechanic. He still managed to fit in time to help with what was now a scaled-back kitchen garden. The evening of the dance, when Clarissa had met William, and when she'd seen Leon post something, it had been a letter in which he'd offered his services to the war effort as an engineer. He had not expected to be put to work at the Shillingbury airfield, but was pleased he was. The same day he started work there, Lily responded to a new call for women to do their bit and went to work in an ammunition factory in the Midlands. Now and then she would send a card telling them about the friends she had made, and how hard and tiring the work was. The romance between Leon and Lily that Clarissa had hoped for had got no further than Leon walking Lily home after the dance the night William had walked Clarissa home, but secretly Clarissa still had hopes for them.

In the middle of November, the day before Shillingbury Grange was to be requisitioned, Skylark Cottage became Clarissa's new home, along with those for whom she now felt wholly responsible – Thomas and Walter, Leon and Mrs Cook. The cottage was as cramped as she had anticipated, but with no regrets about the decision she had made, and though heavily pregnant, she set about the task of turning it into a home. Leaving Leon and the boys to clip back the unruly hedges and tame the wild garden that had been left to its own devices, she and Mrs Cook scrubbed the bare and dusty wooden floorboards and cleaned the walls. Grimy and unloved as it was, it did have running water and electricity, unlike some of the surrounding cottages on Colonel Brook's estate.

To Mrs Cook's delight, the blackleaded range Clarissa had installed in the kitchen was a vast improvement on the one they had left behind. In no time, their combined efforts removed all last traces of the dismal sense of neglect Clarissa had encountered when she'd first seen the half-timbered thatched cottage. Colonel Brook hadn't wanted her to see it, claiming it was much too shabby for her to live in, but Clarissa had fallen in love with its name, and insisted it would be perfect for her needs. In her mind's eye she had pictured her unborn child – William's child – growing up there, playing amongst the apple trees in the long grass with Thomas and Walter.

It was just before Christmas when Clarissa, bringing in the filled log basket, experienced the first sign that her baby had decided it was time to make its appearance. The sudden sharp pain in her lower back was considerable and made her cry out. When it passed, she took a deep breath and smiled to herself, pleased to have her suspicions confirmed – she had woken early that morning with the strongest feeling that today would be the day, and so had spent every hour she could getting as many jobs done while she was still able.

Knowing that labour could be a long-drawn-out affair, Clarissa placed the log basket to one side of the hearth and calmly got down on her hands and knees to make a fire. She crumpled old newspaper into balls, placed them on top of a few logs and added a generous amount of dried kindling. She put a match to it and watched the flames take hold. Just as they did, a bolt of pain shot through her and another cry escaped her lips unbidden. She waited for it to pass before going through to the kitchen to wash her hands. Drying them, she wondered what she should do. She was alone in the house – Leon was at work, the boys were at the vicarage rehearsing for the Christmas Eve carol concert and Mrs Cook was at a WI meeting.

No need to worry yet, she decided; plenty of time before she had to involve anybody else. Both Dr Rutherford and the midwife had explained at length that first babies were never in a hurry to arrive; they always took their time. She made herself a mug of hot blackcurrant juice and braced herself as another all-consuming bolt of pain made it feel as though her spine was being wrenched from her body.

When the pain had passed, she took the mug through to the sitting room to sit by the fire. She switched on the wireless and once she had lowered herself into her favourite armchair and was comfortable, she picked up the knitting she was part way through. Knitting kept her busy, kept her mind from straying to the fear that the world was hell-bent on destroying itself. In this instance, it kept her mind from dwelling on the inevitability of the next painful contraction.

Many an evening she and Mrs Cook had sat here either side of the fire knitting and planning for when the baby arrived. Mrs Cook was convinced it would be a girl, but Clarissa was sure it was a boy – a boy who would look just like William; a boy who would always remind her of the man who'd swept her off her feet.

The decision to marry William had been one of the easiest of her life. There had been no hesitation in her response when, during a picnic one sunny afternoon during a weekend of leave, he had got down on one knee and proposed to her, producing a ring to put on her finger. Every ounce of her being knew it was meant to be.

Full of fun, William hadn't taken anything too seriously, other than his love for her and his determination to play his part in fighting the Germans. Thomas and Walter had warmed to him immediately and had loved to hear about the missions he flew. Not once did they fear he would take Clarissa away from them, as they had with Henry. Perhaps that was because William remained stationed at the airfield and only stayed at Shillingbury Grange on his rare time off. Clarissa would never forget the first time they made love in her bedroom while doing their best not to make any noises that would alert the rest of the household as to what they were doing. At one stage they had both got a fit of the giggles and had to bury their faces in the pillow.

Naively she had believed the strength of their love for each other would put an impenetrable shield around the two of them and keep them safe from the war. How utterly absurd that now seemed. Her eyes suddenly brimming with tears, she longed for William to be here with her, to know he was about to become a father. But her sadness was held in check by a wave of pain so tremendously powerful she let out a loud and agonising cry.

She forced herself to breathe through the pain the way the midwife had explained to her, and just as the worst was over and she began to relax, she heard a knock at the front door.

Hauling herself out of the armchair, she went to see who it was.

Chapter Forty-Three

December 1943, Skylark Cottage, Shillingbury

The sight of a bearded, but vaguely familiar man standing on the doorstep in the half-light of a cold and damp winter's afternoon briefly threw Clarissa off balance, and it took her a moment to register fully who it was. '*Artie!*' she cried. 'What a surprise!'

'A good one, I hope,' he said with a smile.

She ushered him inside. 'Oh, it's the best, the absolute best!' And such was her joy at seeing him after all this time, she threw her arms around him. He hugged her back and kissed her on the cheek, his lips icy-cold against her warm skin.

'But how did you know where to find me?' she asked. 'I haven't had a chance to write and tell you my new address.'

'I was told by a guard in the gatehouse at Shillingbury Grange where to find you. Things have obviously changed round here.' Artie's gaze took in the large bump that filled the space between them. 'Especially you.'

She smiled shyly. 'Come on through to the sitting room, I have a fire going nicely in there.'

They'd made it as far as the doorway when she suddenly grimaced and almost fell to her knees with the pain. She struggled to breathe. 'I don't want to alarm you,' she gasped, 'but your arrival may well coincide with the arrival of my baby.'

'Oh, jeez! Really?'

Her uncontainable groan told him the answer to his

question. He held her firmly and guided her towards the sofa. 'What's best for you,' he asked, 'lying down or sitting?'

She shook her head and trying not to let the excruciating pain of the contractions panic her – they were definitely getting stronger and more painful – she ignored the sofa and occupied her mind and body with the task of putting one foot in front of the other and walking over towards the window, counting as she did so. She then turned around and did the same back towards Artie, who had now removed his hat, coat and scarf.

'What can I do?' he asked. 'Have you called the doctor?'

'I was waiting,' she murmured, the worst of the pain ebbing away.

'What for?'

She let out a long breath, relishing the heady relief of the contraction tailing off. 'For things to progress,' she murmured.

He looked at her incredulously. 'I'm no expert, but I'd say they've progressed far enough. Give me the number and I'll ring the doctor. Or shall I get you to the nearest hospital?'

'Calm down,' she said. 'There's no hurry. Truly there isn't.'

His expression doubtful, he gently lowered her to the sofa. Kneeling on the floor beside her, he stroked her cheek. 'How about some hot water? That's always needed; I've seen it in the movies.'

Smiling, she closed her eyes at his touch, abruptly tired. 'It's exhausting being in labour,' she said quietly. 'They don't tell you that.' She opened her eyes. 'It's wonderful to see you. It's been too long since you last visited.'

He carried on stroking her cheek until the next contraction seized hold of her. 'Take my hand,' he told her, 'squeeze it as hard as you can. That's it, harder still. Go on, you can do it.'

When again the pain had passed, he said, 'I'm not taking no for an answer now. You have to give me the telephone number for the doctor, or the midwife.'

She was just telling him where it was written down when a voice called out to her. It was Mrs Cook.

'Saints alive!' the woman declared after no more than a cursory look at Clarissa. 'The baby's on its way, isn't it? Had I known, I would have hurried back sooner. Now then, who might you be, young man?'

'This is Artie,' Clarissa said.

Mrs Cook gave him an appraising stare. 'Is it indeed? Well now, Artie, it's very nice to make your acquaintance, but if you'd like to make yourself useful, there's a number for the doctor by the telephone on the hallstand. You do that while I get our mother-to-be upstairs to where she should be. And when you've made the phone call, you can find your way to the kitchen and heat up some water. Got that?'

'He's not a child, Mrs Cook,' said Clarissa, smiling at Artie.

'I'm just making sure, that's all. Can you stand?'

'Of course I can. I keep saying that there really isn't any hurry, these things take forever and—'

She was silenced by another contraction. By the time it had passed, Artie had phoned the doctor and was on his way to the kitchen as instructed.

'Seems like a decent enough young man,' Mrs Cook said when they'd made it to the top of the stairs, 'even if he is an American.'

'He's a very decent man,' Clarissa said, 'so you be nice to him.'

By the time Mrs Cook had her in bed, another contraction held Clarissa in its grasp. She didn't hold back from letting out an almighty scream.

'You shout and scream as much as you want,' Mrs Cook encouraged her. 'It'll do you a power of good. That's it; you're doing splendidly. Just keep thinking that before the evening's out you'll be saying hello to your baby.'

*

It was less than an hour later when Clarissa said her first hello to her son. The midwife arrived just in time to perform the delivery, and declared mother and baby to be in rude health before hurrying off to deal with another arrival. 'It's this war,' she said, gathering up her things, 'it's brought on a rush of marriages and babies. I've never been busier!'

Mrs Cook gave Artie permission to sit with Clarissa while she went downstairs to make some tea.

On their own, the swaddled baby sleeping peacefully in Clarissa's arms, Artie looked intently at him and then at her. 'Does he look very much like his father?' he asked.

'I can't tell. He's too scrunched up to know. But ... but I hope he does,' she added quietly, thinking how much William would have enjoyed this moment, how he would have held his newborn son with such loving pride.

Artie smiled. 'How does it feel to be a mother?'

'Scary,' she said, willing back tears of sadness. 'But magical. I don't ever want to forget this moment.'

'You won't. And nor will I. Have you decided what you're going to call him?'

'I know exactly what I'll call him – Nicholas William Dallimore. How does that sound?'

'It sounds a fine name,' said Artie. 'He's going to be a lucky boy having such an amazing mother. I hope I'll get the chance to remind him of that in years to come.' He leant forward and kissed Clarissa tenderly on the forehead. 'You know that if there's anything I can ever do to help you and Nicholas, you have only to ask. Never forget that.'

'I won't,' she said softly, again holding back the tears that William wasn't here. Then more briskly she said: 'You look very distinguished with your beard. But you've lost too much weight. There's nothing of you. Has it been very awful in Italy?'

He ran his hand over his beard and looked at her gravely. 'The worst part was when I was in Naples in October, after Italy declared war on Germany; the German soldiers did unspeakable things to those who they viewed as betrayers. You hear about barbarism, but when you actually see it with your own eyes, it makes you lose hope for mankind, it makes ...' He paused and blinked hard. Then swallowed. 'Let's not talk about that now.'

As if in agreement, the bundle in Clarissa's arms gave a small start and a snuffle, but didn't wake. Beyond the room came the sound of hurried feet clattering on the wooden staircase. A light knock at the open door followed, and then two faces peered in. 'Can we see him, please?' whispered Walter. 'Mrs Cook said we could if we were very quiet.'

'Of course,' Clarissa said. 'Come on in. And look who else is here.'

The boys' faces lit up. 'Uncle Artie!' they both cried out excitedly, forgetting all about keeping quiet.

They went to him and hugged him hard. Then, remembering the baby, they clustered round the bed. 'He's very small,' observed Thomas seriously. 'Is he meant to be like that, all wrinkly like a raisin?'

'Of course he is,' answered Mrs Cook as she came in with Leon behind her carrying a tray of tea things. 'I dare say you looked just as small and wrinkly when you were born.'

Both boys laughed, and, dismissing the idea as nonsense, they eyed the tray hungrily.

Leon put the tray down on the dressing table. 'It's better I leave now, I think,' he said solemnly, politely averting his gaze from looking at Clarissa in bed.

'Please don't go, Leon,' Clarissa said. 'Stay and have a cup of tea with us. It wouldn't be the same without you.'

'You can give me a hand passing these cups of tea round,' said Mrs Cook, 'as well as keep any thieving little hands clear of them biscuits I made this morning.'

With everyone gathered around her, and all looking so pleased and happy for her, Clarissa suddenly found she couldn't hold back the tears any longer and they streamed freely down her cheeks.

Walter looked at her, concerned. 'Are you sad because William isn't here?' he asked with surprising insight.

'Yes and no,' she managed to say, stroking the top of his head. 'I do wish William was here, but at the same time I know I'm lucky to have you all in my life.'

Chapter Forty-Four

Christmas was going to be different in every way this year.

Last year Clarissa had been looking forward to William spending the day with her, along with Charles and Lavinia and Leon and the boys. This time there would be no William and no Charles and Lavinia. But her sadness was assuaged by the delight of having Nicholas, who was proving to be such an easy baby and never failed to make her smile, even when he woke in the night. There were times when she wondered what sort of world he'd been born into, and whether he would only ever know a world at war, but then he would nuzzle up to her and nothing else mattered.

With extended leave, Artie was staying with them at Skylark Cottage until the New Year. Leon had kindly offered to share his room with him, but Artie had insisted he sleep on the sofa, not wanting to put anybody out. He was the perfect house guest and gained Mrs Cook's adoration by helping with anything that needed doing, like peeling the potatoes, or ensuring the blackout curtains were in place at night.

At a time when rationing was challenging even Mrs Cook's ability to conjure edible and nutritious meals from next to nothing, the delivery of two large Christmas parcels all the way from America, one from Betty and one from Effie, had them crowded around the kitchen table as they excitedly unwrapped the thoughtful treats: tins of peaches, cake, and ham, stem ginger, packets of chocolate and prettily wrapped bars of rose-scented soap. 'Luxury soap,' enthused Mrs Cook dreamily, holding a bar to her nose. 'When was the last time we had anything so extravagant?'

On Christmas Eve afternoon, after enjoying the carol concert in the village church, Clarissa pushed a sleeping Nicholas home in his pram with Mrs Cook at her side, leaving Artie and the boys to fetch the Christmas tree from the grocer's.

Letting themselves in at the back door of Skylark Cottage, Clarissa's mouth watered at the delicious smell of a rabbit casserole slowly cooking in the oven. The rabbit had been given to them by Jimmy, who might or might not have come across it legitimately. Nobody had asked him for details. Leaving Nicholas in the warmth of the kitchen while Mrs Cook pulled on her apron and started work on making a suet pudding for supper that evening, Clarissa went through to the sitting room to get a fire going. By the time she had it done, Nicholas had stirred and with his eyes open and his little fists waving in the air as if reaching out for her, she settled in the chair to the side of the range to feed him.

'I've got just enough treacle left over to make a hot sauce for the pudding,' Mrs Cook said. 'Lord knows when we'll see any more.'

'I'll help,' Clarissa said, staring at the contented child at her breast.

'You'll do no such thing,' Mrs Cook replied. 'You'll sit tight and take it easy.'

'But I don't feel like taking it easy,' Clarissa said. 'I'm not ill.'

'And that's the way I'd prefer it to stay, thank you very much. Now do as you're told. I'm not having you overdoing things. Especially not at Christmas.'

'I had no idea you could be such a tyrant,' Clarissa said with an affectionate smile.

'If you'd known my Norman, God bless his soul, he'd have put you right soon enough.' She cocked her ear. 'Now who's that ringing at the front doorbell? If it's them boys back with the Christmas tree and up to no good when there's a perfectly good back door to use, I'll tan their behinds, so I will!'

But it wasn't Thomas and Walter; it was Henry Willet. 'I told 'im you was busy and to wait in the sitting room until you was free,' Mrs Cook informed Clarissa when she bustled back into the kitchen, looking thoroughly put out.

'Why the high dudgeon?' asked Clarissa.

'You know my thoughts on Mr Willet. For such a small man he has a lot to say for 'imself. Much too much. And none of it worth hearing.'

'Did he say what he wanted?'

'No. I enquired, but he as good as told me to mind my own flippin' business, as though I were nothing but a common busybody poking and prying. As if I had time for such goings-on. He's got some nerve, let me tell you. If I wasn't so good-natured, I'd give him what for.'

'Perhaps you'd tan the behind off him?' suggested Clarissa, greatly amused at the woman's outrage, and glad the door had swung shut so there was no danger of them being overheard.

Mrs Cook stopped what she was doing – weighing suet – and roared with laughter. 'Now there's an idea!'

It was another ten minutes before Nicholas was finished, and after Clarissa rubbed and patted his back as the midwife had shown her, she laid him in his bassinet and made a pot of tea to take through to Henry. What had brought him here on Christmas Eve? she wondered.

She found him bending down to the fire where he was dropping a large log into the grate, then pushing it into place with the poker. If she had found Leon or Artie doing the same thing she would have thanked them, but seeing Henry making himself so at home irked her.

'Hello, Henry,' she said. 'I'm sorry for keeping you.'

He put the poker back in its place and came over to take

the tray from her. 'That's all right,' he said. 'Here, let me do that for you. You should have asked Mrs Cook to bring it in.'

'No need, I'm quite capable of carrying a tray.' And to prove it she sidestepped him and put the tray down on the table in front of the window, which overlooked the front garden. 'I took the liberty of making you tea, but if you'd prefer something stronger, I can find you some ginger wine, or some sherry or whisky.'

'Tea would be most welcome, thank you,' he said. 'You've really done wonders with this cottage, Clarissa; you've quite transformed it. I must confess I doubted the wisdom of you taking it on when it was in such a poor state of repair, but once again you've shown me just how very capable you are. Nothing stops you in your tracks, does it? I'm always telling Mother how confident and talented you are.'

'I find a positive attitude goes a long way,' she said lightly, pondering why on earth Henry should be discussing her with his mother. There was, she reflected as she poured their tea, something different about him today. She couldn't put her finger on it, but he seemed more animated than usual, as if he had something he couldn't wait to impart.

She passed him his cup and saucer and indicated the sofa for him, while she sat in the armchair nearest the fire, not for its warmth, but for making it impossible for Henry to place himself next to her. 'So what brings you here, Henry?' she enquired.

He smiled. 'There you go again, straight to the point. You have many fine attributes which I admire, one of which is your marvellous ability always to be so refreshingly candid.' He stirred his tea, placed the spoon in the saucer and looked around him, as if inspecting the worth of the furniture she had brought with her from The Grange, although she had been forced to leave behind the bulk of the furniture as it was mostly too large. 'As comfortable as you might feel here,' he said, 'it is only until the war is over, isn't it? Once life returns to normal, you'll want to live somewhere – somewhere more in keeping with a woman of your standing.'

'Goodness,' she said, 'I had no idea I had any kind of standing worth keeping.'

He crossed his legs and flicked at a speck of something on his suit trouser leg. 'Come now, Clarissa, your family connections are impeccable, so let's have no false modesty.'

'I assure you my modesty is far from false, and as for where I choose to live, this cottage may be a snug fit, but it's relatively draught-free and economical to run and suits my needs perfectly, as well as those of everyone else who sees it as their home and for whom I feel responsible.'

'That's truly admirable of you, but—'

'And when I consider all those poor people in London and around the country who have lost their homes and all their possessions,' she continued, determined to make her point clear, and not caring that she was sounding as pompous as Henry, 'I'm only too glad to be able to count my blessings that I have a roof over my head.'

'And I, too, count my blessings,' he said, nodding his head, 'and chiefly amongst those blessings is what I want to discuss with you. You see, my situation has changed since I last saw you. Much to my surprise I've been left a substantial bequest from a great-aunt who died recently.' He swallowed. 'And, well, the thing is, with the unexpected change in my fortunes I feel able to say what has been on my mind for some months. I say it in the hope that you might now regard me more favourably in this new light.'

Rigid with dismay, Clarissa said, 'Henry, really, please don't say any more, there's no—'

His cheeks glowing pink, he held his hand up to stop her. 'Clarissa, you have a child now, which means that more than ever you need a man you can trust to be by your side. Wouldn't William want you to be well cared for by a man who would want nothing but the best for you? Wouldn't William want a man for you in whom you have complete faith and can rely upon, a man who is now not without his own means? Clarissa, I believe with all my being that William would approve of me, and I would deem it a very great honour, the greatest honour of my life, if you would allow me to be the one to walk by your side for the rest of your life.'

With every word he uttered, Clarissa had grown more distressed, willing him to stop. Now that he had, she opened her mouth to speak but was distracted by the sound of voices heading their way. The door then swung wide on its hinges and Thomas and Walter burst in with Artie following behind, carrying a Christmas tree almost as tall as he was.

'Look, Clarissa!' cried Thomas happily. 'Look at the tree we've got!'

'It was the most expensive, but Artie said it didn't matter, that we had to have the best for you because you deserved the best Christmas ever, and we bought you a present, and—' Walter's voice halted abruptly when he realised she wasn't alone.

'Henry came to wish us a happy Christmas,' Clarissa said brightly, filling in the crashing silence. 'Wasn't that nice of him?'

The excitement the boys had bounded in with evaporated in an instant and, nodding politely at Henry, they slipped quietly out of the room, leaving Clarissa to introduce Artie.

'Henry, this is Artie, a very dear friend who's staying with us.'

Putting his cup and saucer down on a side table, Henry rose slowly to his feet and gave Artie a long cool look of scrutiny. 'I didn't realise you had company, Clarissa,' he said stiffly. 'Had I known, I wouldn't have called unannounced and disturbed you.'

'Don't be silly, it's not a disturbance seeing you,' she said gaily – a little too gaily, such was her relief that Henry couldn't now expect her to respond to his proposal.

With his free hand, and appearing to tower over Henry,

Artie formalised the introduction. 'Looks like I'm the one who should be apologising for barging in,' he said. 'I'll put the tree in the hall and leave you to carry on talking. We need some more logs chopping, Clarissa, so I'll go and do that before the light goes entirely.'

'No, that won't be necessary,' Henry said. 'I've stayed too long as it is. Mother will be expecting me. Clarissa, I'm sorry if once again I've misjudged things and spoken out of turn.' His gaze slid back towards Artie. 'I have clearly misjudged the situation.'

In no hurry to disabuse him of the conclusion he'd reached, Clarissa walked him to the front door, where he hurriedly put on his hat and coat, making it clear he couldn't wait to be gone. 'I wish you had not allowed me to make such a fool of myself,' he said tersely. 'You might at least have paid me that courtesy.'

'Henry, I tried to say something, but you wouldn't let me speak.' Again she made no attempt to correct him on the assumption he had made. If it meant he would no longer pester her with his affections, then so be it.

'From now on I propose we keep our dealings on a strictly business footing,' he said.

'Perhaps you're right,' she replied meekly, prepared to make whatever concessions he required so he could walk away with his head held high.

'Would I be right in thinking I didn't exactly ingratiate myself with your visitor?' asked Artie, when later he was alone with Clarissa. They were in the kitchen clearing up after supper. Nicholas was sleeping soundly upstairs and Leon and Mrs Cook were tempering Thomas and Walter's zeal to decorate the Christmas tree in the sitting room.

'I think that would be a fair assessment,' Clarissa said.

'And presumably that's because he saw me as a threat in some way?'

'He did. I'm embarrassed to say, in his endlessly

roundabout fashion, Henry had just proposed to me when you and the boys walked in.'

'Embarrassed?'

'Mortified would be a fairer description. I thought I'd managed to convince him some months ago that I wasn't interested, but he had other ideas.'

'Is he a serious problem?' asked Artie, putting away the plates he'd dried.

'Not now. I think he'll leave me alone from here on, having branded me a woman of questionable reputation who has wilfully deceived him, even though I gave him no encouragement. As if I would, when William's been dead hardly any time at all!' She banged down the pan she was scrubbing on the wooden draining board. 'How could he even think I would welcome a proposal from him? How could he even think he compared to William, or that I was now over him?' Her heart thudded against her ribcage with the familiar ache of grief. Tears filled her eyes. She blinked them away, but fresh ones coursed down her cheeks and suddenly she was overwhelmed with a deep sorrow for the man who had so briefly come into her life, but who had left her with a son who would forever be a joyful and poignant reminder of him. The sadness fuelled yet more tears, and no matter how hard she tried, she could not hold back the flood.

From behind her she heard Artie saying something, and then she felt his arms around her. She sank against his chest and sobbed. He held her close, but didn't speak, for which she was grateful. There were simply no words for what she felt.

Chapter Forty-Five

December 1943, Skylark Cottage, Shillingbury

On Christmas Day they all went to church in the morning, but Mrs Cook didn't return to Skylark Cottage with them. Clarissa was adamant that she should spend the day with her family in the village, especially as Lily was home for a short break.

Still feeling raw following her breakdown in the kitchen with Artie, Clarissa was determined not to give in to any mawkish feelings today. Today her priority was to give everyone the best Christmas she could. Watching Artie at the other end of the table carve the brace of pheasants Colonel Brook had personally delivered, and which Clarissa had cooked, she listened to Leon promising to help Thomas and Walter make the model airplanes she had surprised them with that morning. Not for the first time she thought how like a family they were. Except they weren't a normal family; they were a family of refugees brought together through an act of prodigious wickedness on the part of Nazi Germany. But out of that evil had come a great blessing, because without these dear loved ones sitting around the table with her, Clarissa knew her life would be immeasurably poorer.

With everyone's plate now filled, Leon cleared his throat and slowly stood up. He raised his glass of gooseberry wine. 'I would like to say something,' he said. 'I would like to thank you, Clarissa, not just for giving me a home, but for making me feel an important part of it. I owe you so very much. Maybe there will come a time when I will be able to repay you for your kindness.' His cheeks pink, he sat down quickly and took a gulp of his wine.

Touched by the formality of his speech, Clarissa smiled lovingly at him. 'Leon, you owe me nothing, please don't ever think you do.' She raised her glass. 'Happy Christmas to you all. And I don't want anyone saying my cooking isn't as good as Mrs Cook's!'

The boys laughed and grabbed their knives and forks.

The pheasants, roast potatoes and parsnips swiftly despatched, Clarissa brought in the plum pudding, which was met with a rousing cheer. 'This is the happiest day of my life,' declared Walter after he'd taken a mouthful. 'I wish we could have plum pudding every day!'

'But then it wouldn't be so special,' Artie said.

'It would,' sighed Walter, scooping up another spoonful. 'When the war is over I shall eat plum pudding every day for the rest of my life.'

Thomas looked at him scornfully. 'Then you will be the fattest person in the world.'

'But the happiest,' retaliated Walter.

'Well, I for one can't remember a better Christmas lunch,' said Artie.

Clarissa smiled. 'Just don't say that in front of Mrs Cook, or she'll abandon us.'

'I don't want anyone to leave,' said Walter. 'I wish we could all live together like this forever and ever. And I wish Mutti und Vati were here too,' he added quietly, his gaze lowered.

Nobody spoke for the longest moment.

It was Leon who broke the silence around the table. 'You are making a lot of wishes today,' he said to Walter.

'I do every day,' Walter replied seriously, casting a glance at his brother. 'I just don't usually say them aloud.'

'Perhaps we should all make a wish,' Artie said. 'What about you, Thomas, what would you wish for?'

'To be a famous artist,' he said without hesitation.

'And I have no doubt you will,' said Clarissa with an encouraging smile. 'What about you, Leon?'

Unlike Thomas, he did hesitate. After a short pause, he said, 'I think I would like very much to have a second helping of plum pudding.'

Clarissa smiled at him, grateful that he had lightened the mood. 'I think that could easily be arranged,' she said.

'For me too?' asked Walter.

'Of course.'

'Uncle Artie, what would you wish for?' This was from Thomas.

'Right now I wish I could stay here with you for another few weeks, but sadly I have to return to Italy.'

'Why do you have to go back?' asked Walter.

'To report what's going on there. That's my job.'

'But you might be killed.'

Artie exchanged a look with Clarissa. 'Walter,' he said, 'I'll be fine; you're not to worry, nobody's going to kill me, I'm really not worth the trouble.'

Walter looked glum. 'I've changed my mind now about my wish; I wish you didn't have to go. I like you being here.'

Artie reached over to him and patted his arm. 'I promise I'll be back before you've even had time to miss me.'

'You promise?'

'Yes. And I never break my promises.'

Being the consummately good baby that he was, Nicholas woke from his nap with perfect timing just a few minutes after they'd finished eating and had made a start on clearing up. Artie and Leon immediately shooed Clarissa out of the kitchen, banishing her to the sitting room beside the fire to feed her son. It still amazed her that she had a son, that she was a mother. But at the same time it was as if she had known no other existence, that Nicholas had always been a part of her.

In the corner of the room stood the Christmas tree, its

brightly coloured glass baubles catching in the lamplight. It reminded Clarissa poignantly of her own childhood Christmases with her parents, when she had never given it a second thought that life would be any different. How she wished her parents were still alive to know their grandson. 'And just what would Grandma Ethel make of all this?' she asked Nicholas.

His answer was to flutter his eyes open and stare at her while wrapping his little hand around her thumb. It was such a small gesture, but it melted her heart. 'My hand will always be there for you to hold,' she whispered to him. 'I'll never let you down, and that's a promise.'

Her words made her think of the promise Artie had made to Walter. Just as Walter didn't want Artie to leave, nor did Clarissa. Nobody had asked her what her wish was; had they done so, she would have said she wished Artie could stay here with them at Skylark Cottage out of harm's way. Perhaps it was hearing Walter say aloud what was in her heart that made her now fear for Artie's life more than she ever had before.

They were in the middle of playing a game of snakes and ladders when there was a knock at the front door. Thomas went to see who it was and came back with a beaming Mrs Cook and a very smart-looking young woman dressed in a red dress with lipstick to match. It wasn't until the woman spoke that Clarissa recognised her – it was Lily!

'I couldn't come to Shillingbury and not see you all, miss,' she said. 'Here, you two,' she said, delving into a basket hooked over her arm, 'I've got some chocolate for you.' Thomas and Walter all but fell on her. She held out a small package to Clarissa. 'And something for you, miss.'

'Lily, you really shouldn't have.'

'Why ever not? You gave Auntie Dot something to give me.'

'But that was just a box of dates. This,' Clarissa said, the wrapping now removed from the package, 'is so much more extravagant.' She held up the packet of stockings. 'What a luxury! Thank you so much.'

Lily then turned to Leon and smiled brightly at him, which in turn had his face turning almost as red as her dress. 'I got you something as well.'

Leon took the gift from her, but seemed to have lost the power of speech. Rooted to the spot, he stared at Lily.

'Go on,' she said, 'don't just stand there, open it then.'

His fingers, usually so adept at fixing things, suddenly seemed incapable of undoing the simple bow of the ribbon. When he had it done, Leon opened the slim box and showed everyone what was inside: a pen.

'It's so that you can write to me,' she said with a wink.

If it were possible, poor Leon's face turned an even deeper shade of red.

'Don't I get a kiss, then?' she asked. 'I call that a very poor show. I've been gone for what feels like forever and was expecting a bit more of a welcome back.'

Mrs Cook laughed. 'Get on with you, you saucy baggage. Stop teasing the poor man. Now who's for a nice cup of tea?'

'Never mind tea, where's the baby? He's the one I've really come to see. I've got him a present.'

Right on cue, Artie appeared behind Lily carrying Nicholas. 'Oooh, look at him,' she exclaimed, 'he's the living spit of his dad!' Her expression dropped and she looked at Clarissa. 'Sorry, miss, perhaps I shouldn't have said that, but gawd, I'm as giddy as a kipper to see you all again!'

'Don't be silly,' Clarissa said with a smile. 'And do please stop calling me miss. Call me Clarissa. Would you like to hold Nicholas?'

'Just you try and stop me!'

Over tea and cake – the one in the tin Effie had sent from America – Lily regaled them with her tales of life in the Midlands and the munitions factory she worked in. Clarissa marvelled at the change in her – how confident she now seemed, and infinitely more mature and knowing. She had changed the way she spoke as well, her pronounced East Anglian accent barely discernible.

'The girls I work with are always talking about how life will never be the same again,' she was saying now, 'that there'll be a New Order when we will all do more for each other. We'll have a fairer society and us poor folk won't be put upon like we always have been.'

'You better not go round talking like that too much,' said Mrs Cook, 'or you'll be accused of being a communist.'

'And what if I was?' replied Lily. 'Isn't it right that we all get our proper share? And I'll tell you this for nothing, I'm not going to be told by no hoity-toity Lord and Lady what I can and cannot do when this war's over. No, you take it from me, we're all going to be better off when we've done Hitler in. Especially us women. We're all soldiers in this war for the liberation of humanity.'

'Good for you, Lily,' said Artie, clapping his hands. 'That's an admirable sentiment.'

Clarissa smiled, proud of Lily. How good it was to see her so full of confidence. It made her feel she should be doing more herself. 'If I'm not mistaken, I see a future member of the British Parliament before me,' she said.

Lily laughed and held Nicholas up to her face so he was just inches from the end of her nose. 'What do you think, little fella?' she asked him. 'Do you see a great future for me?'

His answer was to hiccup loudly.

Later that night, when the house was quiet and Clarissa was soothing Nicholas after changing his nappy and feeding him, she thought how perfectly Lily had summed things up. She was right, things would never be the same, and that perhaps would not suit everybody. Some would want life to go back to how it was. But how could it? Women were doing the jobs of men, and for the most part doing them just as well. They were independent as a result and for many that was a freedom never before experienced. How many of them would want to slip back into the old ways? She for one could not conceive of her old life when all Grandma Ethel had wanted for her was a good marriage.

When she eventually got Nicholas off to sleep again in the bassinet by the side of her bed, she tightened the belt of her dressing gown and crept quietly downstairs to make herself a cup of tea. She made it as strong as she dared, hearing in her head Mrs Cook's often spoken words that it wouldn't be long before they'd be reduced to drinking tea made with a single reused tea leaf.

She sat in the chair by the side of the range and no sooner had she taken a sip of tea than she heard footsteps and the door creaked open. It was Artie, also in his nightclothes.

'I thought I heard you,' he said. 'Were you up with Nicholas?'

'Yes. He took a little longer to get back to sleep than usual. I think he's decided it's time to start being more alert. Would you like me to make you a drink?'

He motioned her to stay where she was. 'I'll do it.'

While he waited for the kettle to boil, he said, 'I meant it earlier today when I said I wish I could stay here longer with you.'

'I know you did,' she said softly. 'And if anybody had been interested in my wish it would have been for you to do exactly that. The boys love having you here, and I can see that Leon really appreciates having another man about the place.'

'What about you, do you appreciate having another man around? After all, you are heavily outnumbered.'

She smiled. 'I don't mind that one little bit. But as Effie might say, it's been a real hoot having you around.'

He smiled too. 'Good, I'm glad about that.' He turned away to make his drink then came and sat opposite her. His expression had changed now; gone was the smile and in its place was a look of grave solemnity, his eyes dark behind the lenses of his glasses. 'When I'm back in Italy, will you do something for me?' he asked.

'Of course.'

'Would you wish for me to return, please?'

She frowned. 'Are you asking for me to pray for you?'

'I suppose I am. Just so that all my bases are covered, so to speak.'

'I'm not sure that God will listen to me; I'm hardly one of the faithful, am I?'

'Neither am I. And if we're going to be pedantic, God doesn't seem to be listening to anyone in the world right now.'

She leant forward. 'What's brought this on, Artie? Why do you suddenly feel that you're in danger?'

'We're all in danger, every minute of the day. Look what happened right here in Shillingbury the night William—' He broke off. 'Sorry, I shouldn't have—'

'It's all right,' she said, 'you can talk about William without me falling apart again like I did yesterday.'

He shook his head. 'You didn't fall apart; you simply expressed your feelings for the husband you loved. You probably haven't done enough of that. My guess is that you've been too busy holding the fort for everybody else. Am I right?'

'I wouldn't go so far as to say that.'

'I would. I've seen how you mother everyone here and how they adore you in return. Just as I love you. But you've always known that, haven't you? The very first night we met on board the *Belle Etoile*, I knew that we would have a special relationship. And don't worry, I'm not about to embarrass you like Henry Willet did, I'm not that stupid. So will you be my guardian angel when I'm in Italy?'

Touched by his words, and the depth of his feelings for her, she reached out and took his hand in hers. 'You know I will. I shall do all I can to ensure you keep your promise to

Walter. But I don't understand why you're now so concerned about your safety.'

'It's quite simple, really: having had the courage to admit to myself how much I love you, I feel I have more to lose if I were to die.'

Chapter Forty-Six

April 1944, Skylark Cottage, Shillingbury

It was now April, and in the months that had passed since Artie had left for Italy, Clarissa had worried about him constantly.

When he had first gone, she had tried to ignore how empty the house felt without him, or how often she accidentally laid a place setting for him at the table, or looked forward to telling him something. Always trailing in the wake of her thoughts for Artie was a pervading sense of guilt that she was betraying William. But her aching heart whispered that Artie was alive, and no amount of guilt was ever going to bring William back.

It wasn't that she was trying to replace William with Artie, she really wasn't; William was William and Artie was Artie, the two men couldn't be more different. William had quite literally swept her off her feet and instilled in her a reckless abandon and the belief that they had a duty to live for the moment, to snatch whatever happiness they could. Despite their time together being cruelly cut short, Clarissa frequently consoled herself with the knowledge that they had made each other exceedingly happy for that time.

More than once she was reminded of the passionate love her parents must have felt for one another, a love that had made her mother defy her family and run away to France. Without a doubt Clarissa would have done the same with William. She would have done whatever he'd asked of her.

In contrast, the emotions she felt for Artie were grounded in the mutual trust and understanding they had for each other. He was more thoughtful and measured than William had been, less of a risk taker too. He was not the sort to rush headlong into something, and would be the first to say that he was an observer of life, hence the work he was doing. What she had always found so admirable about Artie was his integrity and absolute loyalty. He never exaggerated or said anything he didn't mean, which was why she had been so alarmed by his asking her to be his guardian angel. It made her wonder if he'd experienced some sort of premonition that something bad lay ahead for him. Or had he simply seen so many awful things as a war correspondent that he couldn't put his faith in surviving such a brutal war?

The day he left she had clung to him with a fierce, protective love. 'Please be careful,' she had implored him. 'You know how dear you are to me; I couldn't bear for anything to happen to you. You have to stay out of danger.'

'I'll do my best,' he'd said, 'because there's nothing I want more than to see you again. I love you, Clarissa.'

She couldn't bring herself to say the words in return, despite knowing that it was how she felt – her conscience forbade it – so instead she had kissed him, not on the cheek, but on the lips. 'I'll be waiting here for you,' she'd said. 'We all will. Goodbye, my darling.'

Every day since she had avidly followed the news of what was going on in Italy. In January she had read of the Allied advance on Rome, how thousands of British and American troops had stormed ashore at Anzio taking the Germans by surprise. Then in February she had read of the bombing of Monte Cassino, of the massed formation of Flying Fortresses that had unleashed their deadly load of bombs. It seemed as if the Allies had the upper hand and were winning the battle there, but any optimism Clarissa felt was outweighed by her concern for Artie.

She wrote to him as often as she could, giving him any amount of inconsequential news from the village, her letters posted to the address he had given her. She eagerly awaited the postman, desperate to receive word from him. He wrote intermittently, but always said how much he valued her letters to him.

She wasn't the only one waiting for the postman to call. With the fountain pen Lily had given him, Leon now wrote to her and always had a smile on his face after he'd read one of Lily's letters.

With the arrival of spring came not just the pleasing sight of leaf buds on the trees and daffodils with their trumpets of yellow in the sun, and the sound of the skylarks singing in the meadows, but an influx of American air personnel in the area.

The peace and quiet of Shillingbury had long since been disrupted by the presence of military vehicles and aircraft, but now the noise and number of servicemen and women had swelled enormously with the arrival of the US Eighth Air Force. New airplanes, which Thomas and Walter expertly informed Clarissa were B-24 Liberators, became a regular sight in the sky as the pilots practised close-formation flying and bombing skills. It was common knowledge that they were carrying out intensive training in readiness for invading occupied Europe. Nobody knew when, but it had to be soon. The heavy bombers made a thrilling sight, and the thunderous noise they made stirred the senses.

This new Fighter Group with its airbase a short distance away to the south-west of Shillingbury gave rise to a surge of high spirits in the village, especially when word went round that the Americans had brought with them more food than they knew what to do with. It was, of course, an exaggeration, but in no time delighted women in the village were showing off legs clad in nylon stockings and children were licking the chocolate from their lips given to them by the generous American servicemen. Hearing so many American voices at the same time made Clarissa realise how very English she had become.

Then one sunny afternoon, when she was on her way home with Nicholas in his pram, after queuing at the butcher's for more than thirty minutes only to find all that was left were a few scraps of liver being fought over by three determined women, Clarissa came to a sudden stop. There by the wooden gate to Skylark Cottage was a military motorcycle propped on its stand. What would somebody from the military want here? Unless … unless it was to deliver bad news?

Oh, please not Artie. Not Artie as well as William.

Chapter Forty-Seven

April 1944, Skylark Cottage, Shillingbury

Clarissa could have wept with joy when she saw who was sitting at the kitchen table chatting to Mrs Cook. It was Ellis, dressed in a uniform which gave him an added vitality and achieved what she wouldn't have believed possible: it made him even more handsome.

'Here you are at last, Clarissa,' he said, casually stubbing out the cigarette he'd been smoking and getting to his feet. 'Mrs C and I thought you were never coming home.' He spoke as though they had seen one another only yesterday.

The relief that it was Ellis here, and not somebody to deliver bad news about Artie, suddenly welled up inside Clarissa and she threw her arms around Ellis in a rush of elation.

Clearly he wasn't expecting such a warm reception. 'Now that,' he said, 'is a definite improvement on the welcome I received the last time I saw you.'

Pushing her away from him, but keeping hold of her hands, he held her at arm's length. 'You're looking well,' he declared approvingly. 'Motherhood suits you. Where is the little guy? I've brought him a present.'

'Captain Randall's brought us all presents,' remarked Mrs Cook with a broad smile – the kind of smile that told Clarissa she'd been totally charmed by Ellis. 'Take a look in the box over there on the dresser – there are tins of apricots, evaporated milk, corned beef, salmon and packets of sugar, chocolate and coffee. And chewing gum for the boys.'

Clarissa went over to take a look. 'And stockings,' she murmured. 'Ellis, you shouldn't have.'

'Don't talk so daft, of course he should!' said Mrs Cook. 'We'll take all the help we can, thank you very much. He's just been telling me he's stationed practically on our doorstep.'

'Really?' asked Clarissa.

Ellis smiled. 'Station 174, Sudbury. I arrived last week. Didn't I say I'd be over one day to save you from those pesky Germans?'

'You did,' she said, flicking his shoulder playfully, 'but you took your time about it.'

'Believe me, I'd have been here sooner, but the might of the US military moves at its own pace. Come on, show me your son. Where've you hidden him?'

She took Ellis outside to where she'd left Nicholas sleeping in the pram. He was awake now and staring contentedly up at the washing on the clothes line flapping in the breeze. Ellis bent over to take a closer look. 'Yep, just as I suspected, he's a looker – just like his mother.'

To Clarissa's surprise, Ellis reached into the pram and lifted Nicholas out. Half expecting Nicholas to object, she made to take the child from Ellis, but he didn't so much as wriggle or draw breath in readiness to cry. Instead, he rewarded this handsome stranger with one of his heart-melting smiles and poked a curious finger at his face.

'He likes you,' Clarissa said.

'Sure he does, everybody likes me.'

'How wonderful it is to see you haven't changed in the slightest,' she teased. 'You're as modest as ever.'

'Don't be fooled, I've changed. We all have. War does that to you. Look at you, a widowed mother now.'

For a moment neither of them said anything and in the silence, as if without a care in the world, a robin sang out from the branches of the cherry tree that was in full blossom.

'Why didn't you write and tell me where you were going to be stationed?' Clarissa asked at length.

'I didn't know exactly where I'd end up. Plans change in the blink of an eye in this game. I thought I was on my way to somewhere on the south coast. Not that I would have been allowed to tell you, had I known. I didn't even know what ship I was going to board to cross the Atlantic until I set eyes on it; it was our old friend the *Belle Etoile*.'

Clarissa felt a pang of poignant nostalgia for those four days spent on board the luxurious liner – four days that had led to her life being changed beyond belief. It was inconceivable that any of them would experience that same level of luxury ever again. 'I'd read that the liner had been put into service,' she said. 'It must have been a very different crossing for you.'

He smiled ruefully. 'There were no cocktails and no one to dance with, certainly.' He shifted Nicholas into a more comfortable position and set off down the garden towards the apple tree where Leon had fixed a swing to one of the branches for Thomas and Walter.

Clarissa fell in step beside him. 'I can't believe you've been posted here,' she said. 'What are the chances?'

'It's fate,' he said, turning his head to look at her.

She said nothing in response; she knew him too well to fall for such a comment, and waited for him to laugh sardonically and say 'Fate be damned!' But he didn't.

'Do you know what your first mission is?' she asked.

'I have a fair idea. But I'm not going to tell you. So don't fish.'

With Nicholas beginning to wriggle now, Clarissa offered to take him. Relinquishing her son, Ellis put his hand in his shirt pocket and pulled out a silver chain with a St Christopher pendant attached. 'It's not much of a present for a baby,' he said, 'but I like the idea of him having it. It was given to me by my grandmother when I was born.'

'Don't you want to wear it?'

327

'Why, to protect me when I'm flying?'

'Why not?'

'Because fate will decide whether my number's up, not a necklace.' He pushed the sleeve back on his jacket and looked at his watch. 'I'd better scoot.'

'So soon? But we've had hardly any time to chat. I haven't heard from Effie in a while. Have you?'

'She's fine,' he said, ducking his head and kissing her cheek. 'I promise to return when I can.'

He returned a week later on an afternoon when Clarissa was alone – Mrs Cook had taken Nicholas to the shops in the pram and then to visit a friend. Leon was at the airfield on his shift and Thomas and Walter were at school. The sun was shining brilliantly from the clearest of skies and Clarissa was digging in the garden, preparing the vegetable plot for planting potatoes. Wearing a pair of rubber boots, a pair of Leon's cast-off overalls and with her hair tied up with a cotton scarf, she smiled at the expression on Ellis's face when he saw her.

'So this is what the Brits mean by digging for victory?'

'If I didn't think you'd be so hopeless with your soft pilot's hands, I'd ask you to help,' she said.

He raised an eyebrow. 'You think I can't dig?'

'A privileged boy like you, I'll bet you've never picked up a spade in your entire life.'

The challenge was irresistible, just as she knew it would be, and with a glint in his eye he threw off his cap and leather flying jacket and rolled up his sleeves. 'Right,' he said, grabbing the fork that was balanced against the wheelbarrow, 'show me what needs digging.'

'Help yourself to that end of the plot, and we'll see who reaches the middle first. And mind you dig thoroughly – I don't want the crop of potatoes ruined because you didn't get your back into breaking up the clods of earth.'

'Yes, ma'am,' he said, giving her a salute.

'Let's see if you're still saluting me in an hour's time.'

Within minutes Clarissa realised she had misjudged Ellis; he was ploughing through the earth with a powerful efficiency that had her surreptitiously watching him with new respect.

'Stop watching me and get back to your digging, Dallimore!' he ordered. 'Or I'll change my mind about taking you to the dance at the airbase a week on Saturday.'

'Who says I want to go to a dance?'

'Sure you do. Every girl for miles around will want to go.'

'But in my case I don't think it's really appropriate, do you?'

He stopped what he was doing and narrowed his eyes. 'When would be appropriate?'

'I don't know. It just seems ...'

'Wrong for you to enjoy yourself as a widow?' he finished for her. 'Is that it?'

'Something like that, yes.'

'How about I make a pact with you to guarantee you don't enjoy yourself?'

She smiled. 'You mean you'd promise to be your usual horrible, sneering self?'

'Yeah, I could easily arrange that. Or you could see it as voluntary work to raise the spirits of a bunch of pilots a long way from home missing their loved ones, not to say terrified they might not return from their first mission the following week.'

She gave him a long, searching look and knew he was being serious. 'I'll see if Mrs Cook will look after Nicholas for me.'

They finished the digging and went inside to wash their hands. There was some home-made ginger beer in the pantry, and after pouring two glasses, they went back out to the garden and sat on an old blanket on the grass where the blossom had begun to fall from the cherry tree.

'I hear Artie spent Christmas with you here,' Ellis said. 'What's more, he very nearly ended up delivering your baby.'

'Did he tell you that?' asked Clarissa.

Ellis drained his glass and lay down on the blanket. 'Of course not, it was Effie. I haven't heard from Artie in a while. I miss him. I miss him badly.' His tone was abruptly pensive, as if mourning a time when the world was a very different place. 'But then I guess he's got more important things to do than write to me,' he went on. 'The action in Monte Cassino is hotting up now. The reports I've read make for grim reading.'

'Is there anything in the news that isn't?'

'True. As for Effie, she's on her way over here.'

'No!'

He smiled up at her. 'Yeah, I thought that would surprise you. She's coming to do her bit, to sing to the troops. Heaven help them, I say.'

'I hope I get to see her. She will come here, won't she? Oh, she must!'

'Try stopping her,' Ellis said dryly.

'Why didn't she write and tell me?'

'She wanted it to be a surprise for you, except I've gone and spoilt it. But then, I'm known for spoiling things.'

Delighted at the news, Clarissa lay back on the blanket next to Ellis and stared up at the pale sky through the blossom. She smiled. 'Effie coming here,' she said happily, 'I can't believe it.' In her mind she was picturing Effie the first time she saw her, standing at the top of the stairs of the dining restaurant on the *Belle Etoile* knowing that every eye was on her, and loving it.

Ellis turned to look at her. 'Clarissa,' he said, 'can I ask you something?'

She twisted her head. 'Of course.'

'Why am I not irresistible to you?'

Caught up in a mood of jollity at the prospect of seeing Effie again, she laughed. 'Now why on earth would you ask me that?'

'Because I'm curious. You once kissed me in a way that suggested we might become more than friends.'

'I think you'll find it was you who kissed me.'

'I clearly remember the way you responded.'

'I did so out of politeness.'

He raised himself up onto his elbow and smiled down at her, his finger tapping her on the nose. 'You're such a liar.'

She batted his hand away. 'Oh, all right then, I admit it, I was nothing but a gauche young girl taken in by the dazzle of your arrogant charm.'

'Couldn't you find it in your heart to be that gauche young girl again? I had such fun teasing you.'

She rolled her eyes. 'You're quite the most dreadful man I've ever had the misfortune to know.'

He tipped his head back and laughed.

Then from behind them came the sound of somebody very ostentatiously clearing their throat. 'I'm not disturbing you, am I?'

Clarissa slipped out from beneath Ellis, and saw to her horror Henry Willet, briefcase in hand, staring back at them.

'I don't believe we've met,' Henry said pompously, when both Clarissa and Ellis were on their feet and she'd introduced him. The look of disgust he gave Ellis was matched only by the expression of contempt he gave Clarissa.

'I guess not,' Ellis said quite calmly, but making no attempt to shake Henry's hand, which was extended before him. Instead he smoothed back his hair and went over to where he'd earlier left his cap and flying jacket on a garden chair. 'If you have business to conduct, I'd better leave you to it,' he said, taking out a packet of cigarettes and lighter from one of the jacket pockets.

'No, don't rush off,' Clarissa said, willing him to stay. She didn't feel comfortable at the thought of being left alone with Henry. Why was he here when he'd made it clear on Christmas Eve that any future dealings they had would be conducted in his office?

His cigarette lit, and blowing a ribbon of smoke into the

air, Ellis looked at Clarissa with narrowed eyes. 'It's getting late,' he said, 'but perhaps I'll stick around a while longer so I can see Thomas and Walter when they come home from school.'

'And Mrs Cook would love to see you again,' Clarissa added, giving him a grateful smile. 'How about I make us some tea?'

'That would be splendid,' said Henry, looking and sounding as if it would be anything but.

Inside the house, while Clarissa occupied herself with boiling the kettle and setting out cups and saucers, Henry opened his briefcase and produced some papers. 'It's nothing much, Clarissa,' he said, 'but if you could just sign these I'll be on my way.'

'What are they?'

'Just the usual thing, declarations of income for the Inland Revenue.'

'I don't recall signing anything like that before,' Clarissa said, going over to take a look.

'It's slightly different this year in that ...' He paused and adjusted his spectacles. 'There's now your war widow's pension to take into account.' He held the pen out towards Clarissa. 'I just wanted to make things as trouble-free as possible for you.'

'Perhaps you should give Clarissa time to read through them,' Ellis said from across the table, casting his gaze in the direction of the papers.

Henry's reaction was to slide them away from him and nearer to Clarissa.

'Ellis is right, Henry,' she said. 'I should read them, shouldn't I? It's only sensible. Especially as it's something so official.'

'Of course. I merely wanted to make things as painless as I could, knowing how difficult this time of mourning must be for you.' His eyes slid meaningfully from Clarissa to Ellis, then back to her.

'And I appreciate that, I really do,' said Clarissa. She held out her hand for the papers. 'I'll look over them this evening when Nicholas is in bed and post them back to you tomorrow. Unless you're in a hurry and need my signature right now?'

'It's nothing to do with me,' said Ellis, his fingers drumming the table, 'but in my experience, in business, anybody who requires a signature in a hurry is to be regarded with the utmost suspicion.'

Henry gave him a look of hatred. 'You're right,' he said, his nostrils flaring, 'this really is nothing to do with you.' He shoved the papers back into his briefcase and fastened it. 'Clarissa, I've acted on your behalf, and on your grandparents' behalf, and never with a word of complaint from anyone.' He puffed his chest out. 'I really don't take kindly to being treated in this manner, as though I were trying to do something underhand. If you'd rather I didn't handle your affairs any more, please just say so, and you can find yourself a new solicitor. I shall see myself out.'

'Far be it from me to offer you any advice, but there goes a man I wouldn't trust as far as I could throw him,' remarked Ellis as they listened to the sound of Henry driving off at speed.

'I'm inclined to agree with you,' Clarissa said thoughtfully. 'I wonder what it was he was so anxious for me to sign?'

'And which he patently didn't want you to read.'

Chapter Forty-Eight

May 1944, Skylark Cottage, Shillingbury

'How long do you think this awful war will go on for?'

'For some of us it might end sooner than we'd like.'

Clarissa turned sharply to look at Ellis, knowing what he was referring to – next week was when he and many others would finally get to do what they'd been sent here to do. 'You're worried about next week, aren't you?' she said.

Ignoring her question, Ellis pointed to where he was looking. 'Those birds that are singing like they have nothing better to do, and swooping in and out of the grass, what are they called?'

'They're skylarks, and they're looking for somewhere to nest in amongst the meadow grass. They've become my favourite bird; I love their song.'

'I could get to like them, too,' he said thoughtfully.

Clarissa smiled. 'They're the reason I chose to live in this cottage; I couldn't resist the name: Skylark Cottage.'

They were standing at the end of the garden and leaning against the fence. It was late afternoon, and a gentle breeze was rippling the surface of the meadow. Off in the distance the low rumble of a tractor was just discernible, as well as the bleating of lambs in the lower fields of Colonel Brook's estate. This was what Britain and the Allies were fighting for, Clarissa thought; for freedom. Whereas Germany was fighting to destroy freedom.

It was moments like this that she clung to, when war felt a very long way away, when it was almost conceivable to

334

believe that what she read in the newspapers and heard on the wireless wasn't real. When she could almost believe that Artie wasn't in danger, or that Ellis wasn't about to embark on a dangerous mission that could end his life.

She closed her eyes and raised her face to the sun and, as she so often did, sent up a prayer to keep safe those she loved – her beautiful and precious son, Nicholas, Thomas and Walter, Leon and Mrs Cook, and, of course, Artie and Ellis.

She would never have thought it possible to love two such very different men in the way she did, but somehow it had happened. Probably she always had loved them, even when she married William, for without a doubt, Artie and Ellis had each stolen a part of her heart that she now accepted she had willingly surrendered for the rest of her life.

'You've gone quiet on me,' Ellis said. 'What are you thinking?'

She turned again to look at him. 'I was thinking of you and Artie, how different you are from each other, but how much I care for you both.'

He reached into his jacket pocket for his cigarettes. 'What do you mean by that word, *care*?' he asked, when he had the cigarette lit.

'For heaven's sake, can't you ever just accept a statement without tearing it apart?'

He frowned. 'And can't *you* ever really say what's in your heart?'

'What, like you?'

He inhaled deeply on his cigarette, then looked at her through the ribbon of smoke he blew into the air. 'What would you say if I told you I loved you?'

'I'd say you were playing a game with me. It's what you do best.'

'And prevaricating is what you do best. Supposing I genuinely thought you and I could have an interesting life together?'

'*Interesting*,' she repeated. 'What a peculiar way to describe a marriage between two people who supposedly love each other.'

'How would you rather I put it?'

'I'd rather you didn't, frankly. Not when we both know that it's Effie who you're going to marry.'

'Says who?'

'Ellis,' she said gently, 'your life is back in America, with your family and the business you'll be expected to run one day. My life is here in England with my son. I feel rooted here, this is where I'm meant to be.'

'Things change, Clarissa.'

'I know that, better than anyone. But I know this is home for me. It always will be.'

'No negotiation on that, then? You wouldn't consider leaving here to be with a man who thinks you'd be an ideal partner for him?'

She shook her head.

He drew long and hard on his cigarette once more, then exhaled deeply. 'And your decision wouldn't have anything to do with Artie, would it?'

She smiled at him sadly. 'You had to ask, didn't you?'

'Sure I did. Well?'

'Please don't make me answer that. It's not fair.'

'Which is answer enough,' he responded with a shrug. 'But you could at least soften the blow, for the sake of my battered ego, and say you love me just a little bit more than Artie. Have you no heart?'

She knew he was teasing her now. 'Oh my darling Ellis,' she said, 'I do so hope you never change.'

'I shan't,' he said. 'And I shan't even feel jealous of Artie. I mean, what's he got that I haven't? Apart from being the most decent man I know, and the best friend a man could ever have. Will you still come to the dance with me tomorrow evening?'

'If you're sure you'd still like that.' It never failed to amaze

Clarissa how Ellis conducted a conversation, how he could seamlessly switch from one line of questioning to another.

'Yeah, I could probably stand it,' he said. 'But no disgraceful flashing of those beautiful eyes of yours at anyone else.'

'I've never flashed my eyes at anyone in my life,' she said indignantly.

He laughed. 'You're doing it at me now.'

She laughed too. 'Those are my angry eyes.'

'A look I've frequently been on the receiving end of since the day we met.'

'And will continue to be so for a long time yet.'

He put his arm around her. 'Well, I'm glad we have that sorted out. Now tell me what you've done about Henry Willet. Have you fired him and found yourself a new lawyer?'

'I haven't had a chance yet; it's been a busy week.'

'I shouldn't hang about if I were you; it gives him more time to hide any irregularities he might have been cooking up. Would you like me to instigate a few checks of my own to see what he's been up to?'

She shook her head. 'You have quite enough to do with winning this war. I can fight my own battles, thank you.'

'Don't we all know it?'

She dug him in the ribs with her elbow. 'What's the latest news on Effie?'

He groaned. 'Dear God, if it's not Artie, it's Effie you want to talk about. Don't you understand I'd much rather talk about me?'

'Oh, do get on with it,' she said, amused.

'She's in London, arrived a few days ago. She wanted to come straight here, but whoever is in charge of things her end denied her leave. Which won't have gone down well with her. Effie only knows one way to behave, and that's to get her own way.'

Not unlike you, Ellis, she thought. 'I can't wait to see her,' Clarissa said. 'Will she even recognise me, I wonder?'

'Sure she will. And if she doesn't, she'll pretend she does. She's a real pro, that girl!'

'That's why she would make you the perfect wife. Why don't you just propose to her and have done with it?'

'What, when I'm on the rebound from you?'

Clarissa laughed. 'Don't be absurd, how can you be on the rebound from me when we've only ever been friends?'

'But in my mind we've been so much more. I've lost count how many times we've made love. I might say that, with a little more practice with me, you'd really make the model lover.'

Her cheeks flushed. 'Ellis, you're a disgraceful show-off! I'll bet you've had more affairs of the heart than all the men in your squadron put together.'

He put a hand to his heart. 'I'm all talk. I've been as chaste as a pope all these years, just waiting for you to give me the green light. Couldn't you take pity on me just once? It could be your gift to me in case I don't return from a mission.'

'That's low, Ellis, even by your standards. Shame on you.'

He winked. 'Worth a try, though.'

The next day, and after Clarissa had taken Nicholas for a routine health check at the doctor's surgery, and had queued at the greengrocer's and the butcher's, then posted a letter to Artie, she returned home and telephoned Polly in London to ask her if she could recommend a solicitor to take over from Henry.

Polly came up trumps and put her in touch with her own solicitor, the senior partner of a firm in Bishopsgate who, she claimed, she would trust to guard her very last bar of rationed chocolate.

Another telephone call made, and Clarissa put the matter of Henry Willet to one side; she had done all she could.

More important now was getting ready for the dance that evening. Despite the sadness it provoked – the last dance she had attended had been the night she met William – she was looking forward to it. Mrs Cook was more than happy to look after Nicholas, as well as Thomas and Walter who, at ages thirteen and eleven, declared they didn't need looking after. There was a strong element of truth in this, particularly so with Thomas, who often spoke of when the time came for him to take his part in the war. It depressed Clarissa that a child of his age and sensitivity could think of there being no foreseeable end to the war, that, in his young eyes, it stretched dauntingly on forever, as though it were simply a way of life.

As before, Leon escorted her to the dance, Ellis having extended the invitation to include him. One way or another, most of the girls in the village, along with the land girls, had also been invited, all eager to meet the Yanks, who were, to all intents and purposes, a different breed.

This time, however, Leon and Clarissa didn't walk; he took her on the back of his Norton, the US airbase being six miles away. Ellis had offered to fetch her, but she said it was a waste of petrol for him to make the journey. It wasn't the first time Leon had given Clarissa a lift on his motorbike, which was his pride and joy and on which he lavished much time and attention. To her great delight, he'd taught her how to kick-start his precious Norton and had been impressed with her ability to handle the heavy motorbike for a short distance. This evening, with dusk settling in, it felt especially exciting as they raced along the country lanes, the wind snatching at the silk scarf which she had tied around her head in a vain attempt to protect her hair.

They weren't late when they arrived, but judging by the blaring music they were met with, along with the unmistakable smell of alcohol, the dance was clearly well under way.

'How do I look?' she asked Leon when they dismounted and she'd released her hair from the scarf.

'You look great,' he said a little shyly.

'As do you,' she said. She slipped her arm through his. 'Shall we make our entrance?'

The band was playing at such a volume Clarissa soon realised that conversation would be almost impossible. Leon mimed that he would go in search of something to drink for them both.

Watching people jitterbugging with wild abandon to the raucous music was incredibly exhilarating and before she knew it, Clarissa was swaying to the beat as she looked around the hall for Ellis and anyone she might recognise. She spotted a couple of girls who worked in the Primrose Tea Rooms – they looked very different in their best dresses and with their hair elegantly pinned in place, and their scarlet mouths smiling as their uniformed partners whirled them around the dance floor.

She felt a hand on her shoulder and started: it was Ellis. Without asking her, he pulled her onto the dance floor just as the band started playing Glenn Miller's 'In the Mood'. He then proceeded to alternate between twirling, pushing or pulling her to him. Dizzy and breathless, and not knowing the steps, she had no choice but to follow Ellis's lead.

'When did you learn to dance like that?' she asked, when at last the band brought the song to an end and she caught her breath.

'Just another of my many talents,' he said, not at all out of breath.

From behind them the bandleader called for quiet. 'Ladies and gentlemen, we have a special guest here tonight – would you please put your hands together for the one and only Effie Chase!'

Clarissa's jaw dropped as, from behind a flimsy curtain on the stage, Effie appeared, resplendent in a khaki uniform, complete with tie and cap. 'Why didn't you tell me?' Clarissa gasped as the place erupted with wild applause and the stamping of feet.

'Effie wanted to surprise you,' Ellis said above the crescendo. 'And the expression on your face tells me she succeeded.' He put his fingers in his mouth and gave a piercing whistle. Effie turned to look, spotted him and then saw Clarissa. Clarissa waved madly at her and just as enthusiastically, Effie waved back. But then she turned to the bandleader and nodded, who in turn nodded at the band members and they struck up with 'Boogie Woogie Bugle Boy'. Clarissa wanted to stand and stare, to enjoy Effie's performance, but Ellis was having none of it. He grabbed her and they were off again, dancing with everybody else.

Chapter Forty-Nine

May 1944, Skylark Cottage, Shillingbury

It was almost two in the morning when Clarissa and Leon finally made a move to set off for home. They'd had a wonderful carefree night – a high spot for Leon being on stage with Effie and singing with her. The dance had officially finished at midnight with Effie closing the show with 'The Very Thought of You'. 'What a hoot this war is!' she had declared happily when they were alone and a round of drinks had materialised from somewhere. 'Who'd have thought I'd end up here in England, singing in a Nissen hut!'

Rolling his eyes, Ellis had said, 'Only Effie could describe this war as a hoot.'

She smacked his hand as she would a naughty child. 'You know exactly what I mean.'

'Indeed I do. Now if you and Clarissa could make your arrangements when you're next going to see one another, we can all get some sleep.'

'Sleep!' Effie had cried. 'I can't possibly sleep now. Clarissa and I have far too much catching up to do to waste time sleeping.'

But in the end, the sensible option had been to finish their drinks and agree for Effie to visit Skylark Cottage in the morning. Sadly she was leaving to perform at another US airbase.

Now, clinging onto Leon as they rode carefully along the lanes towards Shillingbury, the only light in the blackout darkness to guide them provided by a half-moon that was intermittently hidden behind banks of clouds in the sky, Clarissa hummed another song Effie had sung at the dance, 'Midnight, the Stars and You'.

She was conscious that the alcohol had flowed with a generous hand all evening and very likely she was just a little tipsy. But what the heck! See, Herr Hitler, she thought, you can throw as many bombs at us as you see fit, but you'll never stop us from enjoying ourselves. One way or another, we'll always find a way to do that! A bubble of mirth rose up within her and she started to laugh.

'What's so funny?' shouted Leon over his shoulder to her.

'Everything!' she shouted back, unpinning her hair and letting it stream out behind her.

'Well, don't do anything silly, will you?' he yelled at her. 'Remember to hang on tight.'

'Ah, don't be a spoilsport, Leon!' Nonetheless, she did as she was told and put her arms around his waist.

They were a mile from home, approaching the deceptively sharp curve in the road, when from nowhere there was a loud bang and a jolt that went right through her. What happened next seemed to go on for an eternity, but really it was in no more than a blink of an eye.

To Clarissa's horror, Leon seemed to lose control of the motorbike and they began to zigzag wildly across the road. A puncture was her first thought as she tightened her grip on Leon, expecting him somehow to get the motorbike under control again. But slumped forward, taking her with him, he showed no sign of being able to stop the motorbike from hurtling down the sloping road. Fear made her scream out to him when she realised they were heading straight towards the ditch at the side of the road, but he paid her no heed. With a terrible inevitability that had her screaming and frantically shaking Leon to do something, they careered off the road straight into the ditch and at the looming outline of what could only be a large tree.

Clarissa braced herself for the crash, but when it happened

it wasn't as bad as she'd feared. For a moment she lay very still, assessing what part of her was hurt. Miraculously she didn't think anything was broken, but perhaps that was because she was lying on top of Leon; he must have cushioned her from the worst. 'Leon,' she said, crawling off him, 'are you all right?'

He didn't answer. 'Leon,' she said more loudly, 'can you hear me?'

Again he didn't reply. On her knees, just as she was gently turning him over, she heard footsteps. Hurried footsteps. Thank God! Somebody must have heard the accident and was coming to help. She peered into the blackness. 'Over here,' she called out, instinctively raising a hand to alert whoever it was to where she was, even though it was unlikely they would see her at any distance. 'Over here,' she repeated more urgently. It was then that she became aware that her hands were wet. Not only her hands, but her arms and her chest. A heart-stopping thought occurred to her; straining her eyes in the darkness, she looked at Leon more closely and saw what was causing the wetness: it was blood, Leon was badly injured – he was bleeding profusely. Lowering her head to his face, she tried to detect if he was still breathing. She felt for his pulse, but couldn't find one. A tremor ran through her and in the darkness she put her hand to his bloodied chest feeling for his heart. But unlike her heart, which was pounding painfully against her ribcage, there was nothing from Leon's. 'No!' she cried desperately, panic filling her. 'No, no, *no!*'

'On your feet and put your hands above your head! Do as I say and I will not hurt you.'

Clarissa froze at the distinctive sound of English being spoken with exaggerated care. She slowly turned her head. Looking down at her was a man wearing the flying suit of the Luftwaffe. Even in the darkness, she could make out the pistol in his hand, pointed directly at her. How many times had they laughed in the village about the chances of coming upon a German airman on the run, or a German spy hiding in a barn or coal shed? Only the other day, when they'd been alerted that a German plane had come down near Ipswich and the pilot was unaccounted for, they hadn't taken it seriously. Old Mrs Bladon had said she'd arm herself with a frying pan and a rolling pin if she found a German sneaking about in her outside privy. Then it had all seemed amusing, but there was nothing remotely funny about the situation in which Clarissa now found herself.

'I said stand up!' the German ordered her.

She looked at the gun, then back at Leon, recalling the loud bang she had imagined was a tyre blowing. 'You shot my friend!' she said incredulously. 'He's dead!'

'And I will shoot you if you do not do as I say.'

His words brought Clarissa up short as she realised this man would have no hesitation in shooting her. Fear seized hold of her at the thought of never seeing Nicholas again, and she began to shake uncontrollably.

'I want only your motorcycle,' the German said. 'Do as I say and you will not come to harm.'

She didn't believe him. He had killed Leon – poor Leon, who had escaped the ruthless purge of Jews by the Nazis in Poland only to lose his life on a quiet country lane after a carefree night out; this ruthless man wouldn't think twice about killing her as well.

He waved the gun at her. 'I need to escape, but I need your help.'

Never! she wanted to shout at him. Never would she help him so he could return to Germany and climb into another airplane and drop more bombs on innocent people! 'What do you need me to do?' she said, rising slowly to her feet.

'I need you to help me lift up the motorcycle.'

It was then that Clarissa noticed the left sleeve of his flying suit was ripped and badly stained with blood. 'You're injured,' she said.

'It's nothing. Now will you help me?'

She looked over to where the Norton lay on the other side

of Leon's inert body. 'I doubt it will work now,' she said. 'You shouldn't have stopped us the way you did.'

The airman moved around her, all the time keeping the gun trained on her. She watched him stoop to inspect the motorbike in the ditch and wondered if she dared consider trying to prevent him from escaping. He was injured, after all. But what could she do?

'Come here,' he ordered her. 'Come and lift the motorcycle for me.'

She did as he said, but with her senses on full alert. There had to be a way to stop him. It took all her strength to heave the motorcycle from the bottom of the ditch; twice she had it almost out, before it slipped back down. She was scrabbling around in the ditch when her hand knocked against something rough and hard in the long grass: it was a brick, or more precisely, two-thirds of a brick that somebody must have dumped here. Here was her weapon! If she could somehow find a way to use it when the airman's back was turned, she might stand a chance of grabbing the gun. She then had an idea.

'Hurry up!' he ordered.

Opting for a different approach, she let out a long sigh. 'I'm sorry,' she said weakly, 'I'm doing my best, but the motorbike's so heavy.'

'It cannot be that heavy,' he barked back at her. He remained where he was staring down at her, the gun still raised.

When at last she had the bike out of the ditch, she said breathlessly, 'Take it, then, before it falls back into the ditch.'

He stepped forward to grab hold of one of the handlebars, first putting the gun into his left hand. 'Where is the key?' he demanded. 'It is not there. What have you done with it?'

'I haven't done anything,' she lied. 'It probably fell out when we crashed.'

'I do not believe you. You have taken it. Give me the key. Now!'

'But I don't have it.' She began to cry. 'Please don't shoot me,' she pleaded, dropping to her knees, her head bowed in supplication. 'I've done all I can to help you. Just go. I won't tell anyone I saw you. I promise. I just want to go home to my baby.'

'Be quiet!' he snapped. 'I cannot think if you make that noise.'

Once more she did as he said.

'You must help me look for the key,' he said.

'But it could be anywhere.'

'No. It will be here somewhere in this ditch. I will search also. But remember, I have the gun and if you disobey me I will use it.'

'I won't disobey you,' she said. 'I promise.'

He let go of the Norton, resting it on its side on the verge, and switched the gun back to his right hand. He then carefully climbed down into the ditch and began hunting through the grass in the dark. Clarissa did the same, surreptitiously watching him, biding her time until he made his mistake. Which he did when he bent down with his back turned to her. In a flash, summoning every violent need in her to avenge not just Leon's death, but William's, she raised the brick in her hands and brought it down with a sickening smash against the back of the German's head. At first she didn't think she had hurt him at all; he just stood there. But then he dropped to his knees and fell with a heavy thud. Had she killed him? No time to tell!

She took the gun, then removed her stockings; together with her scarf, they were all she had with which to tie him up. She'd just got him securely tied – his hands fastened behind his back and his legs bound together at the ankles – when he grunted and opened his eyes and gave her a look of savage fury. Summoning all her energy, she heaved the motorcycle upright and inserted the key she had earlier removed into the ignition. She tried to remember what Leon had taught her when kick-starting it, but the engine failed to respond.

Frantically she tried again to get the engine to catch and was just about to give up and run for help when it spluttered into life with a throaty roar.

She took off hesitantly and headed for the nearest house, which was Colonel Brook's. She banged on his front door with all her might, ringing the bell as well. After what seemed like an eternity, the door opened and Colonel Brook stared back at her, looking far from happy in his dressing gown with an expression as rumpled as his pyjamas.

'German airman!' she blurted out before he could utter a word of remonstration. 'I left him tied up on the Shillingbury road. Call for help!'

She was hailed as the 'Amazing Mrs Dallimore' in the local newspaper, the woman who had captured a German airman with nothing but her stockings and a headscarf. The national newspapers picked up the story and all but made out that she had single-handedly taken on the might of the entire German Luftwaffe.

She wanted none of the accolades paid her. How could she when Leon was dead? Thomas and Walter were devastated; they had lost somebody who had been father, brother, friend and uncle rolled into one. There wasn't an empty pew to be had in the church for the funeral. Once more the village was mourning one of its own. For they had, despite some initial resistance when Leon first arrived in Shillingbury, come to regard him as exactly that.

But then, just when Clarissa thought things couldn't get any worse, they did.

Chapter Fifty

A knock at the door made Lizzie start. In her spellbound state it was all she could do to stop herself from telling whoever had interrupted them to go away.

Mrs Dallimore stared at the door blankly. She then looked around her, before tilting her head and intensifying her gaze on Lizzie for the longest time, and in an oddly puzzled manner.

'What is it, Mrs Dallimore?' asked Lizzie, concerned. 'What's wrong?' It was as if the old lady was looking at her while trying to figure out who she was. It was very alarming.

'Shall I see who that is?' asked Lizzie, when Mrs Dallimore still hadn't spoken and a lengthy awkward moment had passed, followed by another knock at the door. An anxious, uncertain nod was all the response she got, and rising from her chair, she went to the door.

It was Mr Sheridan. 'I don't want to be a nuisance,' he said in a hushed voice, 'but I was just wondering how Clarissa is.'

'I think she might be a little tired,' Lizzie said, thinking that maybe she had exhausted Mrs Dallimore and she ought to fetch Matron to check on her.

'Is that Mr Sheridan?' came a voice from behind Lizzie. She turned to see Mrs Dallimore looking much more her usual self. There was barely a trace of puzzlement in her face now.

'Permission to be granted entry?' asked Mr Sheridan, leaning in to peer round the door.

'Of course,' replied Mrs Dallimore.

Once Mr Sheridan was seated in the chair Lizzie had just

vacated, she picked up the lunch tray she'd brought in earlier and offered to rustle up two cups of tea.

'That would be perfect,' said Mrs Dallimore, 'and I do apologise if I went on for too long.'

Lizzie shook her head. 'You didn't at all. Far from it. I'll be back in a jiffy with your tea.'

After having a word with Jennifer about the confused state Mrs Dallimore had briefly displayed, Lizzie went to sort out the library. She had made the suggestion that it needed an overhaul and had been given the job. Jettisoning tatty old paperbacks that had seen better days, she set about reorganising the shelves. A number of residents wandered in while she was working, browsing the books she had piled up on the floor and lingering to chat with her. One woman came in to return a book she'd finished reading and after asking if Lizzie had read it, which she had, they had a great discussion about the ending, both agreeing that it was highly unsatisfying.

It struck Lizzie, as before, just as her mother had said, that for many of the people here a simple chat with somebody who showed an interest made all the difference to their day. But wasn't that true of everyone? She thought of her life back in London, of always being in a hurry, of sitting cheek by jowl with strangers on the tube and on the bus and never once communicating, other than to make it plain there was an invisible barrier in place that was never to be breached.

When she had the shelves neatly ordered, and after saying goodbye to a group of residents in the sitting room watching *Escape to the Country*, she called in on Mrs Dallimore, but found her fast asleep in her armchair, her head resting against the wing of the chair. On her lap was a photograph album. It was so tempting to take a sneaky look, but Lizzie resisted and instead, very carefully so as not to disturb Mrs Dallimore, slid the album off her lap and put it on the bed.

She cycled home, thinking of all that Mrs Dallimore had told her, in particular her extraordinary bravery in tackling the German airman. What was the bravest act Lizzie had ever done? She racked her brains but could think of nothing. Not a thing. How pathetically dull and uneventful her life was compared to Mrs Dallimore's! What would she have to tell anyone when she was the same age? A week or so ago the thought might have depressed her, but now as she cycled home, the fields of wheat either side of her golden in the August sunshine, she had a sense of being on the cusp of some great change in her life.

But cusp or not, she had to tell her parents about the surprise she had in store for them. She should perhaps have texted them in the day to warn them not to plan anything else for the evening, but that would have spoilt the pleasure of giving them their surprise face to face.

She arrived home to find Freddie stripped down to nothing but a sunhat and chasing her mother round the garden with the hose. His squeals of unfettered glee made Lizzie smile. Her father appeared at the back door carrying a towel. 'I'm not sure who's going to need it more, your mother or Freddie.'

'I'd lay odds on Mum's need being the greater,' said Lizzie.

Suddenly spotting her, Freddie gave a whoop of delight and began running across the lawn. The part of the hose lying on the lawn had other ideas and tripped him up, sending him sprawling. Fortunately he didn't seem to mind too much and Lizzie scooped up her nephew and demanded a kiss. He obliged fulsomely, and after she'd pressed her mouth against his tummy and blown the requisite number of fruity raspberries, she swung him round and carried him to the summer house where her parents were now seated, Mum rubbing her face with the towel.

'I have a surprise for you,' she said to them. 'At seven thirty you're booked in for dinner at the Great House in Lavenham.'

'But—'

'No buts, Mum, it's my thank you to you both for putting

up with me and the fallout of some disastrous decisions I've made lately.'

'But you can't possibly afford—'

'Hello? Is my message not getting through? There are no buts involved, Dad. Oh, and by the way, I wasn't going to tell you this, but I have a job interview tomorrow, so think positive thoughts for me while you're enjoying your dinner.' Lizzie looked at her watch. 'You have an hour to get ready. So how about you both scram and leave me to give Freddie his tea and put him to bed?'

'Not bed,' Freddie said, shaking his head. 'Not bed yet.'

Lizzie hugged him. 'No, not bed yet – we have plenty of fun to get through before then.'

'It really does feel all wrong accepting Lizzie's offer,' Tom said, after they'd handed the menus back to the waiter, the job of selecting and ordering their food now complete. They were seated at a table in the window overlooking the pretty cobbled Market Place in Lavenham.

'But it would have hurt her feelings to have said no,' said Tess, casting her gaze round the small restaurant and the smartly dressed diners. 'It was such a lovely thing for her to have planned.'

'You're right, I know; but she can't afford to pay for a meal here.'

'Well, let's hope her job interview goes her way tomorrow. She's due some good luck.'

Watching through the window a car reversing into a parking space, Tom said, 'Have you thought what she'll do if she gets the job? She'll carry on living at home with us, won't she?'

'Don't you want her to?'

He frowned. 'It's not really a matter of what I want; it's what's best for Lizzie. Living at home with her parents at her age isn't exactly ideal, is it?'

Tess knew what Tom was saying, but she didn't want to

think that far ahead. Nor did she want to be the kind of parent whose help was conditional, or had its limits. 'It's a stopgap until something better comes along,' she said.

Tom didn't look convinced. 'I suppose I'm worried it'll all become too comfortable for her, that she'll settle for the easy option instead of seeking out something more stimulating and challenging. Remember how she always used to say that London was where she wanted to be, that she couldn't imagine living anywhere else?'

'Lots of young people say that, but for many of them the dream doesn't live up to expectations. And who knows, maybe Skylark Radio will give her something she didn't know she was looking for.'

Tom suddenly smiled. 'I remember a certain young girl saying something very similar to me a long time ago.'

Tess smiled back at him, remembering the day they met and how suddenly she'd felt as though she'd found something she hadn't realised she'd been looking for. Quite unconsciously she'd fallen in love with Tom in a heartbeat. They'd been inseparable from that day on, and everyone said they were made for each other. Having experienced such a happy marriage herself, she had badly wanted Luke and Lizzie to be equally blessed.

She looked at her husband, seeing him not as the middle-aged man she'd snapped at so heatedly the other day, but as the kind-hearted and affectionate man she had always loved. 'I'm sorry I was so horrible to you when Freddie fell in the pond,' she said. 'I didn't mean anything I said, not really, anxiety just got the better of me.'

'I was just as horrible to you,' Tom said, 'and I'm sorrier than I can say. It's absurd, isn't it? We brought up two children perfectly successfully, but for some reason we fret more over Freddie than we ever did with Luke and Lizzie.'

'It's a different kind of responsibility,' Tess said. 'Especially with Ingrid being such a stickler for ... well, for being such a stickler. Do you suppose our parents fretted the way we do when they became grandparents?'

'Who knows? But one thing I do know with certainty is that the first of this evening's culinary delights is heading our way, so I suggest we forget all about our children and grandchild and thoroughly enjoy ourselves on this rare night when it's just the two of us. Agreed?'

Tess nodded happily. 'Agreed.'

When the waiter had left them alone with their 'comical bush', as Tom liked to refer to the *amuse bouche*, he raised his glass of wine to Tess. 'Here's to worrying less and laughing more.'

'And to Lizzie's interview tomorrow.'

With Freddie happily tucked up in bed, Lizzie surveyed the wreckage of the kitchen and wondered where on earth it had all come from. There were pots and pans, bowls, plates, a sieve, spoons, forks, knives, a cheese grater, an empty milk carton and the remains of an uncovered hunk of Cheddar. All this for one dish of macaroni cheese for a two-year-old, she thought.

With nothing else for it, she poured herself a glass of wine from the open bottle in the fridge and began clearing things away, stacking the dishwasher, wiping down surfaces, sweeping up uncooked macaroni that had dropped on the floor, and all the while listening out for Freddie. When she had the kitchen looking more or less how Mum liked it, she tiptoed upstairs and looked in on Freddie who was fast asleep clutching Nellie, the knitted elephant Mum had made him.

Back downstairs, she went outside with her glass of wine, which was actually a glass of Dutch courage.

She had decided to make an important phone call. It was a call she needed to get exactly right, so she had to make absolutely sure she sounded one hundred per cent genuine. She would hate to be accused of insincerity. Very probably her apology would be viewed as too little too late, but it was suddenly important to her to make the attempt to put things right, as right as she could at any rate.

When she'd rehearsed what she wanted to say, she picked up her mobile. She scrolled through Contacts, found the name she wanted, swallowed the lump of apprehension in her throat and pressed her forefinger against the screen. She heard the dialling tone and willed it not to direct her to voicemail. No way did she want to leave a message.

When he answered, Simon's voice was freighted with equal amounts of surprise and caution. 'Lizzie?' he said, the question mark clearly audible in the saying of her name.

'Yes, it's me, Simon. Have I caught you at an okay moment to have a quick chat?'

'I'm just back from the gym, so doing nothing more important than contemplating what to eat for supper.'

'That sounds energetic,' she said.

'The gym or the contemplating?'

'I'll leave you to decide,' she said, forcing out a small laugh, but resisting the urge to comment on him having been at a gym, something he'd never previously been keen to do. He'd probably joined one now on a mission to shake things up and explore a world of new interests and hobbies. And to meet people. To meet a new girlfriend.

'So how are you?' he asked. 'I heard things didn't work out with you and Curt.'

Ouch! Straight to the jugular, then. 'You heard right,' she said, mustering what scraps of dignity she was still in possession of. 'I was an idiot to believe anything Curt said, he had no intention of leaving his wife, I see that now. But that's not why I'm ringing,' she added hurriedly. She didn't want Simon to think the two were connected. 'I just wanted to say …'

'Yes?' he prompted when she hesitated.

'That I'm genuinely sorry for the way I treated you. I don't expect you to forgive me, I really don't, but I do want you to know that I've come to realise that I behaved appallingly. I was so wrapped up in myself that I lost the plot on what constituted decent behaviour.'

'I know you did, and that's why it's no problem to forgive you.'

'Really?'

'What you felt for Curt was clearly so much more than you ever felt for me, so I guess I have to be thankful you discovered that before we took things any further. Like get married.'

Lizzie should have welcomed Simon's matter-of-fact acceptance, as well as his generous forgiveness, but his reason for it saddened her. It sounded horribly final, too, as though there was nothing else to be said. Which wasn't how she felt. 'I don't think I'd ever compare what we had to what I experienced with Curt,' she said.

'That's exactly my point.'

'No, no! I meant that with Curt it was all smoke and mirrors; none of it was real. Whereas with you, it was always real.'

'Just not what you wanted in the end,' he said flatly.

'Do we ever know what it is we really want?'

'I think we do when we find it, yes. Can I ask you something?'

'Of course.'

'Do you regret what you did?'

'I regret hurting you.'

'But not falling for Curt?'

'Oh, that too. I regret every stupid, reckless second I spent in his company. I lost so much because of what I did, but, and this doubtless sounds toe-curlingly unoriginal, it's given me pause to think about what's really important in life.'

'Well, that's good.'

'What about you, what's new with you?'

'Not a lot.'

'The gym's new.'

'True.'

'Anything else?'

'Are you asking if I've met somebody?'

'No, of course not, I wouldn't be so crass.' *Yes, yes, of course she was!*

'I've been out a couple of times with a girl from work,' he said.

Lizzie had a mental picture of a work colleague doubling up as Simon's gym buddy; she would be fresh-faced, long-legged and with a stomach like that girl from the annoying *Are You Beach Body Ready?* advert. 'That's good,' she lied brightly.

When he didn't respond, she could see no point in furthering the conversation; plainly they'd run out of things to say. 'I'd better let you get back to contemplating your supper, then,' she said.

'Thanks for ringing,' he said. 'Say hi to your parents from me.'

'Will do.'

For some minutes after she'd ended the call she sat motionless, staring at nothing in particular. Her purpose in ringing Simon had been to say sorry and, in the manner of making a confession, she had hoped it would make her feel better about herself. So why, given that he had been so understanding, did she feel a whole lot worse?

Chapter Fifty-One

Skylark Radio was situated in Abbey Crescent, a stately semicircle of Georgian terraced buildings a short walk from the abbey gardens. Having allowed herself plenty of time to find the studio, Lizzie decided to go for a calming stroll in the gardens.

No sooner had she passed through the gate than she thought of a young Mrs Dallimore coming here with Henry Willet, and then afterwards having a drink in the Angel Hotel on the other side of the road. She pictured Mrs Dallimore dressed in a pretty dress with a hat and gloves, and Henry in a suit, both of them carrying gas mask cases.

Did Henry Willet figure in Mrs Dallimore's story any further? Lizzie wondered. Although story wasn't the right word to use: story implied something made up, and Lizzie didn't think for a moment that the old lady was spinning her along with a monumental yarn; it was all much too real and detailed to be made up. But what a life story it was and what a shame it would be lost when Mrs Dallimore died. Not for the first time Lizzie felt a wave of sadness at the thought of the old lady not being around any more. She thought also of Mrs Dallimore's apparent confusion yesterday, when she seemed not to know her surroundings, or Lizzie. It was as if she had been so caught up in reliving the past, she had been momentarily unable to relocate the present.

Passing a flowerbed bright with summer bedding plants, Lizzie rehearsed her carefully worded interview spiel: she was looking for a change of direction, a smaller provincial radio station might be less constrained than the one she'd been used to, and more personal; it might also give her more of a chance to engage fully with the listening audience. All of which sounded reasonable enough, if a little pat, but from nowhere she heard Curt and his drawling sardonic voice – a voice that she had previously always found so sexy: 'Yeah, yeah, heard it all before, love, give me something original.'

At the thought of Curt her confidence, which had been steadily growing, suddenly collapsed and she thought how he would view her stressing over a small-time job for a small-time radio station in a small-time town as utterly pathetic. It would be his idea of hell. He'd said once that he'd sooner rip out his own tongue and stamp on it than fall so low.

But because of him she *had* fallen that low! She had lost *everything*! She had fallen so low she was in danger of suffering the bends if she ever surfaced again, and it was all thanks to Curt and her stupid, stupid—

She stopped herself short. What had got into her? Why was she thinking of Curt and what he might think? The only thing that counted was what *she* thought. And come to think of it, what exactly had she lost? Hadn't she had to remind herself of this before? But so be it if she had to do it again and again to get the message through.

One: she'd lost a lying, cheating boyfriend who wasn't even a boyfriend.

Two: she'd lost a job that she'd loved, which was a shame, but there were other jobs she would perhaps love, maybe a job that would be more fun and give her more of a challenge.

And three: she'd lost her flat and – no two ways about it – that was a real downer. Would she be able to afford to rent something if she got this job? Because one thing she knew, it wasn't fair to outstay her welcome with Mum and Dad. Coming home was only ever meant to be a brief stopgap until she was back on her feet. Not that her parents would ever say anything, but she knew their lives had been hugely disrupted this summer. So there was nothing else for it but to find a place of her own. What kind of place did she fancy? Here in Bury St Edmunds? Or perhaps something more rural?

While living in London she had never once thought she would swap city life for rural life, but she had really enjoyed cycling along the lanes to Woodside, being out and about in genuine fresh air, not that stuff in London that was loaded with toxic fumes and lord knows what else. What was more, she'd noticed this morning when getting dressed that she'd lost weight – the favourite black trousers she'd put on for her interview were definitely looser than when she'd last worn them.

She sat on a bench and continued to redress the harm caused by thinking of Curt. Something Mrs Dallimore had once said came into her head – *For everything you lose, you gain something new.*

Lizzie hoped it was true. There again, maybe she had evidence of that being the case already, for while she had lost all her old friends in London, she had gained a new one in Jed. It just went to show that it was true: when the chips are down, that's when you know who your true friends are.

The ringing of her mobile had her reaching into her bag. She hoped it wasn't somebody from Skylark Radio calling to say the interview was cancelled, that the post had been filled.

It wasn't; it was Jed.

'You must be telepathic,' she said. 'I was just thinking about you.'

'You were? In a good way, I hope. Anyway, I'm here with Mrs D and she was adamant that we had to get in touch to wish you good luck. Not that you need it, I told her, but she said everybody needs a bit of luck from time to time.'

'Tell her I really appreciate that.'

'You can tell her yourself. Hang on and I'll put her on for you.'

'Is that you, Lizzie?' asked Mrs Dallimore a few seconds later.

'Yes, it is, and I'm really touched you should be thinking of me.'

'How could I not when you're so very much on my mind? Now off you go and knock them for six at the radio station with your sparkling personality. I'm sure I won't need to, but I shall keep my fingers crossed for you. I'll say goodbye now, as the last thing you need is to be held up. Oh, wait a moment, Mr Sheridan wants to speak to you.'

Another fumble accompanied by a rattle of throat-clearing and Mr Sheridan's voice boomed in Lizzie's ear. 'Ditto with the sparkling personality, my dear, and if you're in need of a good reference, I'm your man.'

'Thank you, Mr Sheridan,' she said with an unexpected lump in her throat, 'I'll bear that in mind.'

After some more fumbling, Jed came back on the line. 'You did remember to polish up your sparkling personality, didn't you?' he said.

'I might be a little lacking in that department.'

'You'll be fine. And if you feel like a chat afterwards, give me a call. I'm sure Mrs D would like to know how you get on. In fact, the whole of Woodside will probably want to know.'

'Please tell me you're joking.'

''Fraid not. As I speak they're clubbing together to buy you a leaving present. You're going to be greatly missed.'

'You mean they can't wait to be rid of me, more like.'

'If I could give you a word of advice before going in for your interview, try not to speak so glowingly of yourself, nobody likes a show-off.'

'Okay, point taken.'

'Good. Now go! Go and impress Ricky.'

'Jed?'

'Yes?'

'Thank you. Thank you for setting this up for me.'

'Don't start being nice; you'll have me welling up. I prefer it when you're a regular pain in the chuff.'

She laughed. 'That works both ways.'

With the amount of luck she was carrying on board, as dispensed by her parents and brother, and now Jed and Mrs Dallimore and Mr Sheridan, she felt a surge in her spirits. Moreover, she felt compelled to do her absolute best. This might not have been the job she wanted a short while ago, but now it was, and not just for herself, but for all those who were cheering her on. At the back of her mind was the vaguely stirring thought that, somehow or other, this was meant to be, as if it was sort of all tied up with her being at Woodside, where she'd met not just Jed who had a friend at Skylark Radio, but Mrs Dallimore who'd lived in a house called Skylark Cottage. Connections. Coincidences. She'd take whatever portents were on offer.

So with that in mind, and ignoring the possibility that she was clutching desperately at the thinnest of straws, she retraced her steps out of the gardens and walked purposefully in the sunshine towards Abbey Crescent and Skylark Radio. At the entrance, she pressed the buzzer to be admitted and after signing her in, the girl on reception invited her to take a seat.

Afternoon With Ricky was piped through to the foyer, the walls of which were decorated with framed photographs of the station's presenters. She located Ricky's – he looked about thirty-five, thirty-seven, give or take, and instantly likeable. She then gave her concentration to listening to him in case he tested her on anything he'd said. She hadn't actually had a chance to listen to his show previously as it coincided with her hours at Woodside, but she'd done her research; in particular she'd checked out the listening figures. The station was still in its infancy, but the numbers were definitely moving in the right direction, with the average daily reach having gone up from 13 per cent to 18 per cent in the last year.

At the moment Ricky was doing a down-the-line interview

with a second-generation local thatcher – a Master Thatcher, no less. Whoever had done the research had done it well; Ricky was asking all the right questions, referring to the difference between water reed and straw, also slipping in a question about hazelwood brotches. Such was Ricky's seemingly easy-going technique, he allowed the expert to speak with passion about something he patently loved. By the end of the interview Lizzie felt she knew almost enough about thatching to have it as her specialist subject on *Mastermind*!

At three o'clock *Afternoon With Ricky* came to an end for the news, and no sooner had the news finished than the door at the other end of the foyer opened and Ricky appeared. He was taller than she'd expected from looking at his publicity photograph, but seemed friendly enough.

'Hi, Lizzie,' he greeted her, extending his hand. 'You found us all right, then?'

'No problem at all,' she said. 'You have a great location here.'

'We're thoroughly spoilt. Come on through to my office, or what I laughingly refer to as my office. We'll do the grim stuff first, the part when I grill you by asking some excruciatingly impertinent questions, and then I'll give you a tour round the studio.'

Swiping his ID card in the security lock to the right of the door he'd just appeared through, he led the way down a narrow corridor passing a glass window beyond which was a studio where a presenter called Sian Stewart was under way with her show. She waved at Ricky as they passed.

He hadn't exaggerated when he said his office was small; there was just enough room for a desk and two chairs, a bookcase and a hatstand that, rather curiously, was decorated with a number of hats. Perhaps they were part of the interview process and she'd be asked to choose one to wear and explain why.

'Well then,' Ricky said once they were both seated. 'According to your CV you've done a variety of jobs over the years, and latterly you were working in London for Starlight Radio. May I ask why you left?'

Lizzie had prepared herself meticulously for this question and opened her mouth to rattle off the spiel she'd come up with, when she had a complete change of heart. She didn't want to sit here and lie her way into a job. She wanted to hold her head high, to prove to herself that she could shake off the last vestiges of her shame. Besides, there was something about Ricky that fostered a sense of openness and honesty. There was also that comment she had blurted out on the phone to him about regretting having a drink with her boss. He would be bound to raise that. She could also hear Mrs Dallimore urging her on to be brave and to fear nothing.

'It would be the easiest thing in the world to give you the highly edited version of events as to why I left,' she said, 'but since you could easily find out the truth, I don't want to do that.'

'Fair enough,' he said.

So she told him.

Clarissa was in the garden watching Jed; once more he was deadheading the roses. He was a competent gardener, but then she suspected he was competent at most things he put his mind to. Such a shame about his mother, but what an admirable thing he was doing, putting his life on hold to take care of her. The woman was fortunate to have a son who was prepared to make that sacrifice.

A shadowy movement over in the trees caught Clarissa's eye. Was it Ellis? She put a hand to her brow to shield her eyes from the sun to see better. It was him, all right. Leaning against a tree, he waved and beckoned her over. Silly man, she thought, how do you expect me to walk all the way down there? As if reading her mind, he pointed towards Jed. Of course! Jed could push her wheelchair down to the trees.

She called over to him. 'Jed, I know you're busy with those roses, but could you help me for a moment, please?'

'It'll be my pleasure, Mrs D,' he said, pushing his secateurs into the tool holder around his waist. 'What's it to be?'

'I'd like to go and sit in the shade of the trees, please.'

'Consider it done.'

As he wheeled her down the sloping lawn, Clarissa asked if he had heard anything from Lizzie.

'Not yet.'

'I do hope she takes the job if she's offered it, and isn't hankering to go back to London. Do you ever hanker to go back to London, Jed?'

'Now and then I miss my old life there, but for now I have no complaints.'

'How is your mother?'

'So, so. Where would you like to sit?' he asked, when they were on the flat.

'Over there would be perfect.' She pointed to the tree where Ellis had stood. There was no sign of him now, but there wouldn't be, not with somebody else around.

When he had her positioned, Jed said, 'Give me a wave when you're ready for me to fetch you back up to the terrace, okay?'

'Thank you, you're very kind.'

When she was sure he was far enough away not to hear her, Clarissa looked around her, further into the shadowy darkness of the trees. 'Ellis,' she called, 'I'm here, just as you commanded.'

She waited for him to show himself.

'Oh, how typical of you,' she said crossly. 'I go to the trouble of doing as you say, only for you to disappear. You don't change, do you?'

In the absence of a reply, she sighed and closed her eyes. She felt unaccountably weary today; the slightest thing seemed to sap her of energy. At her age it shouldn't surprise her, yet it did. What she hated most was the sense of losing control, of not being herself. And there was no getting away from the fact that the instances of feeling muddled were definitely gaining momentum. More and more she found herself doing something and not knowing why she was doing it, or staring into the face of somebody and not having a clue who they were. But then, as if somebody had put a shilling in the meter, she would suddenly spring to life and see things perfectly lucidly.

She caught the sound of a lighter being flicked, followed by the smell of tobacco. She opened her eyes. Sure enough, there was Ellis, just where she'd seen him earlier.

'It's nearly time, Clarissa,' he said, blowing smoke into the air.

'Time for what?'

'You know.'

'But I'm not ready.'

'Who is? Do you think I was?'

'I still have things to do.'

'Then do them.'

Chapter Fifty-Two

Lizzie didn't know who to speak to first. She knew Mum and Dad were waiting anxiously to hear how she had got on, but she felt she owed it to Jed to tell him first; after all, he was the one who'd made this opportunity possible.

However, it was Luke who made the decision for her by ringing to hear how the interview had gone – she had texted him first thing to let him know about it.

'So how did it go?' her brother asked when she was unlocking Mum's car, which she'd borrowed for the day.

'Better than I thought it would,' she said.

'How much better?'

'I got the job! I couldn't believe it when Ricky just came right out with it, saying he thought I'd fit in perfectly. I still can't believe it. All I can think is that they must be absolutely desperate with no interns to turn to.'

'Are you going to take the job?'

'I'd be a fool not to.'

'That's not exactly answering my question, is it? Do you *want* to work for Skylark Radio?'

'Are you asking that because you think I shouldn't, that I should wait for something better?'

'I'm not asking anything of the kind. I just want you to be sure this is what you want, that you're not settling for the first convenient thing that comes along.'

'Actually, I really do fancy working at Skylark Radio. I liked the whole set-up. Everyone I met couldn't have been nicer and there was a refreshing absence of ego about the place. There's even a chance I could do some presenting.'

'Then it sounds like it's a done deal, congratulations.'

Lizzie couldn't think why, but there was nothing congratulatory in her brother's voice. 'What's up?' she asked.

'Nothing's up, I'm fine.'

Now seated in the car, Lizzie caught the unmistakable lie in her brother's reply. It was the defensiveness in his voice that was the giveaway. 'You're so not,' she said. 'This is twice now you've sounded far from your usual merry self. What's going on?'

'Nothing's going on.'

'Give me a clue: trouble at work, or at home?'

'Neither. I told you, I'm fine.'

'Is it anything I can help you with?'

'Lizzie, are you listening to anything I'm saying?'

'It's what you're not saying that I'm listening to. And don't forget, we're twins, so I always know what you're thinking.'

'If that's true, why don't you tell me what's supposed to be bothering me?'

Twin or not, Lizzie couldn't say with any great certainty what she thought was the matter, but knowing that her brother had always taken work in his stride and had never once to her knowledge got anxious about it, she took a wild stab in the dark, or perhaps not so wild as she knew what the two things were that really mattered to Luke. And since she knew that Freddie was perfectly all right at home with Mum and Dad, she opted for the only choice left. 'It's Ingrid, isn't it?'

'Actually, no,' he said after a long pause, 'it's not Ingrid. It's everybody else.'

Once more she heard the unfamiliar ring of defensiveness in his voice. 'When you say *everybody else*, could you narrow it down a touch?'

Her request was met with another silence from Luke, during which she could hear the sound of traffic, then to make matters worse, the connection started to break up. While she waited for him to move into an area where the signal was better, she had a sudden and appalling thought that all was not well between her brother and Ingrid; that maybe their marriage was in trouble. From there it was but a short hop to the awful scenario in her mind of poor Freddie being shunted between warring parents, of Luke only seeing his precious son for alternate weekends and her, Mum and Dad being pushed out of Freddie's life. Lizzie felt the pain of her imaginings so keenly she wished she hadn't pushed things, that she'd just kept her stupid big mouth shut.

But if there was a problem, wasn't it better that Luke shared it with her? Yet what would her advice be? She could hardly say that she had always found Ingrid to be a bit too prickly and aloof for her liking, and that she invariably felt she had nothing to say to her sister-in-law who, with her ferocious intelligence, probably viewed Lizzie as an idiot who couldn't be trusted to blow her own nose, never mind be a responsible and loving aunt to Freddie.

'Are you still there, Luke?' she asked anxiously.

A moment passed and then she heard Luke's voice as clear as a bell. 'That corner in the road is always a signal black spot,' he said.

'Would you rather we had this conversation another time?' she asked.

'There's not much to say,' he said. 'Forget I said anything.'

'I can't, Luke, I've got myself all worried that you and Ingrid aren't happy, that—'

'Ingrid and I are okay,' he said, 'but since you've raised the subject, can I ask you something?'

'Yes,' she said.

'Do you actually like Ingrid?'

'Honest answer?'

'Why else would I have asked?'

'I'm scared of her, if you really want to know. And I don't think she likes me very much.'

'So you tolerate her because she's my wife?'

'No, it's not like that; you mustn't think that. I think the problem is that we don't feel as if we know her any better than when you first brought her home.'

'Are you speaking on behalf of Mum and Dad?'

'I suppose I am. But would you say that's a fair comment I've made?'

'Yes, I guess so,' he said simply.

She steeled herself. 'Are you having problems, Luke?'

'No more than the average couple with a child and busy work commitments. I just wish that Ingrid felt more comfortable around you and Mum and Dad. You know she's always thought that as a family we never say what we're really feeling, that we shove anything unpleasant or awkward under the carpet.'

'That pretty much describes most families, doesn't it?' A thought occurred to Lizzie. 'Exactly what unpleasant or awkward things does Ingrid think we shove under the carpet? And come to think of it, aren't I usually told I blurt things out a bit too readily?'

'I think it's Mum and Dad she's referring to, in the main.'

'But they're as open as the day is long!'

'Are they? Are they really?'

'As open as they need to be, I reckon,' Lizzie said. Loyalty to their parents forbade any kind of admission about their little glitch this week to her brother. She couldn't bring herself to give Ingrid's observation of them as a family an ounce of credence. 'What exactly does Ingrid want from us all?' she went on.

'Transparency, I think.'

'That's a dangerous commodity, Luke; isn't that what causes most families to self-combust? Isn't a degree of well-meant deception essential for the sake of family accord?'

'That depends on what the deception revolves around and what lengths those involved are prepared to go to.'

Lizzie frowned. 'This is beginning to sound like a whole can of worms best not approached, never mind opened.'

'You're right,' Luke said with a sigh. 'Forget everything

I've said. Go home and celebrate landing your new job. I shouldn't have got all serious and spoilt the mood for you.'

Lizzie drove out of Bury St Edmunds unable to do as her brother said. How could she forget what he'd said? Especially as she strongly suspected he'd been holding out on her. Which was ironic when he'd just been saying that Ingrid wanted more honesty from them.

Home wasn't her destination, not yet at any rate. She was on her way to Woodside. She hoped Jed would still be there; she wanted to thank him for putting in a good word for her with Ricky. For how else could she have been so lucky as to be offered the job on the spot?

Luck, she thought, as she slowed to let a taxi pull out from a side street, was she finally, at long last, in for a small share of it? She hardly dared to hope it was true, but certainly Ricky had been very enthusiastic about her joining the radio station. Before he'd given her a tour of the studio, he'd asked a classic interview question – what did she think her personal contribution to the station would be? Thinking fast, she had surprised herself by pitching him an idea about introducing an item into his show about hidden lives, about seemingly ordinary people doing extraordinary things. 'Tell me more,' he'd said, leaning back in his chair and nodding his head.

Before she knew what she was doing, Lizzie had told him about Woodside and Mrs Dallimore, and the German airman she'd captured single-handedly during the war. 'She just looks like any normal, sweet old lady you've ever come across,' Lizzie had explained, 'yet the reality is, she's this amazing woman who's done all these amazing things. Stories like hers need to be told, before they're lost forever.'

Smiling, Ricky had readily agreed with her. She couldn't help but think that maybe it was a combination of Jed putting in a good word for her and her story about Mrs Dallimore that had led to her being offered the job. If so, she owed Mrs Dallimore a massive thank you.

As to Lizzie's confession about her regrettable affair with Curt and subsequent dismissal – her face could not have been redder as she briefly gave her explanation – Ricky had all but passed over it. 'We've all made errors of judgement,' he'd said, 'but thank you for being so honest, I admire your courage.'

During the tour round the studio, he had introduced her to a number of people, and it was when they were in the small staff room that her eye caught a note on the notice-board – *Lodger wanted to share two-bedroomed terraced house a short walk from Abbey Crescent*. At the time it had seemed presumptuous to ask for any more details, but Lizzie had discreetly made a note of the phone number.

At Woodside she left Mum's car in the staff car park and, after changing into her tabard, hurried out of the staff room and promptly collided with Jennifer, who was on her way to the medical wing.

'How did the interview go at Skylark Radio?'

'They've offered me the job,' Lizzie said, 'but it seems only sensible to wait until I've received the official offer before I get too excited.'

'I'll keep my congratulations until then, in that case. But I shall be sorry to lose you; you've fitted in here very well, the residents will miss you. It's not everyone who has the gift you have, you know.'

'What gift is that?' asked Lizzie, bemused.

'The ability to listen to people, to listen properly and show that you care.'

Lizzie smiled. 'Maybe I'm just nosy and like listening to other people's stories.'

'To which I'd say you were being disingenuous. When do you think you'll be leaving us?'

'I'm not sure. I know this might seem odd, but when I do leave, will it be all right for me to come back and visit Mrs Dallimore?'

'Of course. And don't forget Mr Sheridan, and Mr

Jenkins, I know they'll be only too delighted to see you, as would many of the others. By the way, you did a great job in the library; I don't think I've ever seen it looking so good.'

Unable to remember the last time so much praise had been heaped on her, Lizzie went outside to the garden to round up people for dinner.

'Here she is!' shouted Mr Sheridan, when Lizzie approached the terrace where half a dozen residents were sitting at the larger tables. Mrs Dallimore was there too.

'Well,' enquired Mr Sheridan, 'can we uncross our fingers now?'

Everyone around the table, including Mrs Dallimore, held up their hands to show their crossed fingers.

At the sight of poor Mr Jenkins' trembling hands, Lizzie's throat tightened with a knot of profound sadness. She was going to miss this remarkable group of people and the warmth of their friendship.

Chapter Fifty-Three

Tom rarely had the chance to spend any time alone with Luke, but on Friday evening when his son came to take Freddie home for the weekend, he suggested he didn't rush off straight away but that they walked down to the Bell for a quick beer. Tom had rather stage-managed things, in that he'd put the idea into his grandson's head that he had to have a bath before leaving, so that ensured Tess was busy. Lizzie was also conveniently out of the way.

It was Lizzie who had tipped him off that maybe some dad-and-son time together might be good. As had often happened down the years, Tom and Tess had been so pre-occupied with Lizzie they were guilty of overlooking their son. That was the trouble with Luke: such was his steady and easy-going temperament, he had never given them cause for concern. But after Lizzie had told him of a worrying conversation she'd had the other day with Luke, Tom was determined now to pay more attention to his son.

Their beers bought and the two of them seated at a table in the beer garden of the pub, Tom adopted what he thought was his most casual tone and asked his son how work was going.

Luke lowered his beer glass and looked at him hard. 'What's Lizzie been saying?'

'Why on earth would you ask that?' asked Tom, disappointed that he had given himself away so easily.

'Because we're having a drink here,' Luke said, 'and not at home. Because it's just the two of us, and you're asking about my work.'

Tom tried to shrug his shoulders in a gesture of innocence. 'I thought it might be nice, you and me having a chinwag on our own. When was the last time we did that?'

'Good question. And mine remains: what's Lizzie been saying?'

Tom capitulated. He'd never been good at subterfuge. 'Don't be cross,' he said, 'but Lizzie mentioned you didn't seem your usual self. I'd say she's right, you do seem a bit on edge.'

Luke frowned. 'I wish she hadn't said anything, you and Mum have enough on your plate as it is.'

'Not at all, and anyway, we would never be so busy we couldn't help you, you must never think that. Is there something wrong?'

'How much did Lizzie tell you?'

'Very little, just that she thought you and Ingrid were a bit snowed under right now with one thing and another.'

Luke's frown deepened. 'She said just that, or more? Knowing Lizzie, I find it hard to believe she didn't give you the full story. And a lot more besides.'

Tom knew what Luke meant, but in this instance, and despite Tom having tried to get Lizzie to expand, she had refused point-blank to do so. 'Let's forget about Lizzie for the moment,' he said. 'All I know from your sister is that she's worried about you and Ingrid. Which means now I'm concerned. What can I do to help?'

'I'm not sure you can. And I'm not convinced I want to talk about Ingrid behind her back – it doesn't feel right.'

'I'd feel the same way talking about your mother,' Tom said. 'But Luke, whatever you say will stay between us, if that's what you want.'

Luke didn't look convinced. 'I'm worried that if I say what I really think, it'll be like letting the genie out of the bottle: impossible to get back in.'

'But would bottling up something make it worse for you? Is that what you've been doing?'

'Sort of, I suppose.' Luke took a long swallow of beer, as did Tom as he waited patiently for his son to continue. His patience was rewarded.

'Ingrid and I don't seem to have the same closeness that we used to have. And – and I think part of the problem is that she resents the fact that I have you and Mum and Lizzie.'

'You mean she's jealous?'

'Yes. It's probably all to do with the way she was brought up, she didn't have the same kind of family life we did.'

'But in that case, surely she'd welcome being part of our family, wouldn't she?'

Luke shook his head. 'It doesn't seem to work like that, Dad. I reckon that you helping us out this summer by looking after Freddie highlights all that she never had when she was a child. It's like she doesn't know how to be a member of a real family.'

Tom thought about this. He and Tess knew very little of their daughter-in-law's parents; just enough to know the ties had all but been cut between Ingrid and them. Out of respect to Ingrid it was not a subject they had liked to delve into too much. Had that been a mistake on their part? Had their discretion been misinterpreted in some way? Did Ingrid see them as horribly smug, constantly reminding her of their happy marriage and happy family life? 'Have we ever given Ingrid cause to think we've been less than welcoming to her?' he asked anxiously.

'No,' said Luke vehemently. 'It's almost as if the more welcoming and helpful you are, the more she resents it. She's so independent; she hates to think she can't be on top of everything and that you and Mum have to pitch in. I think she sees it as weakness. To my knowledge, she's never once asked for help from her own parents.'

'Poor Ingrid,' Tom said. It was a sentiment he was ashamed to acknowledge he had never before imagined saying about his cool and unapproachable daughter-in-law. 'What can we do to help her feel more at ease around us as a family?' he asked.

'I wish I knew. I really do. I—' Luke broke off, his gaze suddenly caught by something over Tom's right shoulder.

'What is it?' asked Tom.

'It's Keith. And Simon.'

Tom turned in the direction Luke was looking. Keith spotted him at the same time and Tom automatically waved his hand in recognition. He was tired of the stand-off caused by Lizzie splitting from Simon. Moreover, he missed Keith; he missed their convivial chats at the pub when, and with complete impunity, they could have a grumble about whatever was bothering them, or better still, enjoy an inappropriate laugh over something neither of their wives would find funny.

To Tom's relief, Keith raised his hand in return. Simon did the same.

'Why don't we invite them to join us?' suggested Luke.

'Why not?' said Tom. 'Let's see if four reasonably intelligent men can't mend a few bridges over a drink.'

'Shouldn't that be fences?'

Tom smiled. 'Those too.'

Lizzie had offered to help that Friday evening at Woodside and was assisting with serving supper.

While she helped Mr Jenkins with his soup – it was the first time he had asked for her assistance – Lizzie listened to Mr Sheridan holding court at the table. He was regaling them with an amusing tale of when he worked for the Foreign Office and how his limited Mandarin had had him very nearly arrested and thrown into prison in Hong Kong. Everybody seemed in a good mood, apart from Mrs Lennox who still continued to look down her nose at everybody else, as well as reminding them she would soon be moving somewhere more to her liking.

It was two days since Lizzie had gone for her interview with Skylark Radio, and in the post that morning she had received the official job offer, though a start date had yet to be decided. In those two days she had scarcely had time to speak properly with Mrs Dallimore, but today the old lady had proposed that when supper was over and Lizzie had helped clear the tables she might like to come to her room for a chat and a cup of tea. Eager to hear another instalment of Mrs Dallimore's wartime experiences, Lizzie had agreed only too readily.

With everything cleared away and most of the residents now in the sitting room or the library, Lizzie checked there wasn't anything else that needed doing before making a pot of tea and knocking on Mrs Dallimore's door.

The old lady was sitting in her armchair with a photograph album on her lap and a faraway look in her eye. She looked at Lizzie as if seeing straight through her, and once again Lizzie was troubled that the old lady didn't know who she was, even though they had spoken not half an hour ago. 'I've brought you some tea,' she said brightly, 'tea to go with our chat, just as you requested.' When still the old lady seemed not to know her, just stared at her with hauntingly blank eyes, she felt compelled to add: 'Mrs Dallimore, it's me, Lizzie. Are you okay?'

Slowly the blank expression faded from Mrs Dallimore's face and was replaced with a smile. 'Lily,' she said, 'is that really you? Has Ellis sent you? Is William coming, too? And Artie?'

Lizzie's heart sank. 'No, it's not Lily, it's *Lizzie*,' she said with added emphasis.

'Lizzie? Oh, of course, how silly of me. I – I ...' Her words trailed off, and for a terrible moment the old lady looked so confused and upset, almost like a lost child, Lizzie was worried she was going to cry. Never had the poor woman looked more frail or vulnerable. Hurriedly putting down the tray she was carrying, Lizzie went and sat in the chair next to her.

'It's happening more often,' the old lady said, her head nodding fretfully.

'What is?' asked Lizzie.

'The moments of not knowing ... of not knowing where I am, or what I'm doing, or who people are.'

Lizzie didn't know what to say, so she took hold of one of Mrs Dallimore's thin, veiny hands resting on top of the photo album and squeezed it gently. The old lady turned her face up to Lizzie's, her faded blue eyes brimming with tears.

'I'm getting worse; I know I am. What frightens me is when I no longer can tell the difference. It's been happening for a while now. Can I tell you a secret?'

'Of course,' Lizzie said solemnly.

'Ellis and Artie regularly visit me. Sometimes Effie comes as well. But the trouble is, they seem so real, and yet they can't really be here, can they? But they talk to me. And I talk to them. It feels as real with them as it does sitting here with you.'

Lizzie didn't know what to say. All she could think was how cruel it was that nature should make the mind deteriorate in this horrible way. It wasn't fair!

'I know what you're thinking,' said Mrs Dallimore, 'that I'm losing my mind, or as you young people say, losing the plot.'

'I would never think that of you, Mrs Dallimore. But maybe it's just your imagination getting the better of you. Maybe it's your brain's way of allowing you to be with the people who meant the most to you.'

'But then why hasn't Nicholas visited me? Or William?'

Lizzie tried to come up with a logical reason that would satisfy the old lady in her anxious state. 'Perhaps they're waiting to surprise you. You know, like a surprise party is being arranged for you and Nicholas and William are hiding behind the curtain waiting for just the right moment to jump out and say, *ta dah!* A bit like when Effie appeared on the stage at that dance you went to at the American airbase.'

Mrs Dallimore smiled and for an instant a brightness shone in her eyes. But then the brightness was gone and she pursed her lips. 'I shouldn't ask you this,' she murmured, her eyes filling with tears, 'but please don't tell anyone that we've had this conversation, or that I mistook you for Lily. If you do, I shall have to leave and go somewhere else, and I don't want to do that. You see, I know I'm going to die soon, and I want to die here. I came to Woodside because it seemed such a pleasant place to end my days. Is that too much to ask, to die in modestly comfortable surroundings with people who care?'

Lizzie's throat tightened with compassion for this poor woman who was haunted by the spectre of dementia. Did everyone at Woodside live with the same fear, of losing their footing on the slippery slope of infirmity with its inevitable consequences of being cast out? Lizzie knew what the policy was at Woodside, knew too that it existed for a good reason, to ensure the elderly were given the care required for their specific needs, but she hated to think of Mrs Dallimore being uprooted and forced to go somewhere else, to a place where she might not be treated with as much respect and dignity as she was here. 'I won't tell anyone,' she said. 'I promise.'

It was a promise Lizzie fully intended to keep, but in truth it meant little, because the physical and mental well-being of every resident was very closely monitored, just as it should be, and besides, Jennifer was already aware that Mrs Dallimore was experiencing episodes of mild confusion.

Close to crying, Lizzie let go of Mrs Dallimore's hand and stood up. 'How about I pour our tea before it goes cold?'

Mrs Dallimore wiped away the tears that had trickled down her pale, crumpled cheeks. 'Thank you, that's a very good idea. And then if you have time, I'll show you some photographs.' With what seemed an effort, she tapped the album on her lap.

'I'd love to see them,' Lizzie said.

She now had her back to the old lady and was blinking

hard as she busied herself with the tea. 'And if you feel like chatting,' she went on, her voice tight, and desperately wanting to talk about something more cheerful, 'I'd love to hear what happened after you'd captured that German airman. I still can't get over how brave you were that night.'

'I wasn't brave at all,' Mrs Dallimore said. 'I just acted instinctively. As I have all my life.'

Chapter Fifty-Four

May 1944, Skylark Cottage, Shillingbury

The Ritz,
Mayfair,
London.

Darling Clarissa,

What a hoot it is here in London! And how different to the last few weeks of touring round the airbases. I only arrived two days ago and already feel I never want to leave. I've met the most charming people, including any number of fancy Lords and Ladies. Wouldn't it be a hoot if I bagged myself a Marquess like Kathleen Kennedy?!

Yesterday I was invited to the Berkeley and then a crowd of us went on to The Four Hundred Club just off Leicester Square – it was full of the most handsome American and British pilots. I kept expecting to bump into Ellis!

The day after tomorrow I fly home in an army transport plane. I wish I didn't have to leave London, but my father insists, apparently he's negotiating a new contract for me with MGM in the absence of any stage roles coming my way. Between you and me, I don't care if I never make another movie. Do you suppose I shall ever be free to make my own decisions? I know you've suffered the appalling loss of your husband, and now your dear Polish refugee, but how I sometimes envy you

*your life, Clarissa. I don't mean that to sound flippant or
insensitive but what I wouldn't give to live in that sweet
little cottage of yours, surrounded by adorable children,
and with nobody telling me what I should and should
not be doing.*

> *Fondest love as always,*
> *Effie*

> *PS Remember me to darling Ellis, tell him to stay safe
> and to write without delay.*

It was towards the end of May, three weeks after Leon's
funeral, that Ellis came to see Clarissa. She hadn't seen him
since the night of the dance, the night that Leon had so needlessly lost his life. They all knew in the village that the US
airbase was now fully operational and carrying out heavy
bombing missions over Belgium and Germany. Every time
Clarissa heard or saw a formation of B-24s climbing high
into the sky in the direction of the North Sea, she sent up a
silent prayer for Ellis to come home safely.

It was late, nearly ten o'clock, Mrs Cook had already
gone to bed and Clarissa was locking up, when she heard
the throaty roar of a motorcycle, followed by a knock at the
back door.

'Where do you keep the whisky?' Ellis demanded after
she'd let him in. 'Even if you don't want any, I do.'

Straight away she knew he had the worst of news to share
with her. Her heart racing, she found two glasses and opened
the cupboard where she kept a bottle of sweet sherry and
another of whisky.

'Here, let me do it,' he said impatiently, when she couldn't
get the top off.

She watched in silent foreboding while he poured out two
measures. *Not Artie*, she thought, *please not Artie*. But she
knew it was. Nothing else would bring Ellis here at this late
hour, looking so stricken.

383

'There's no easy way to tell you this,' he said, passing her one of the glasses. 'I heard about an hour ago that Artie's dead. He was with the 3rd Infantry Division at Anzio and—' Ellis's voice broke. He swallowed and tried again. 'It was last week ... the bloody fool was trying to rescue some goddamned injured soldier when he got himself shot.' Ellis raised his visibly shaking hand and downed the whisky in one. He banged the empty glass down on the table. 'All anyone can talk about is that the Allies successfully launched a breakout offensive. But the cost, Clarissa, the bloody awful cost! Four months of slaughter, of brutal carnage. It's beyond comprehension. And why the hell did Artie have to be there? He wasn't a soldier. He should never have been there!'

'He knew he wasn't coming back,' Clarissa murmured, without answering Ellis. 'I think I knew it too, but I didn't want to believe it.' She closed her eyes and tried to quell the terrifying tremor building within her. Artie. Dead. Her dearest Artie. Never to see him again. Never to read one of his beautifully written letters again.

When she opened her eyes, she gave Ellis her untouched glass of whisky. 'You have it,' she said. 'You loved him as much as I did. As I *do*.'

He took the glass from her, his eyes bloodshot and wet with tears. After he'd drunk the whisky, she put her arms around him, and together they cried out their grief. When the worst was over for them both, Clarissa said, 'Poor Ellis, you've lost the one person in the world you truly loved, haven't you?'

He froze in her arms. 'It's all right,' she said softly, 'I know what Artie meant to you; he was so much more than a friend to you, wasn't he?'

Ellis tilted his head back from her. His face was ravaged with raw pain. 'You knew?'

'Perhaps only subconsciously – until now. Now it makes sense.'

'I expect you're shocked. Disgusted, even.'

His expression saddened her, for he looked so disgusted with himself. 'Oh, Ellis, how could you think that of me? You're the same to me now as you were before. My love for you hasn't changed.'

'Then you pity me, don't you? Which I don't want. I don't want to be pitied. Not ever!'

'I promise you I don't.'

He regarded her sceptically. 'Most others would regard me as abhorrent, something vile and utterly loathsome.'

'I'm not most other people,' she said firmly. 'I'm Clarissa, your friend.'

Ignoring her and shaking himself free of her, he sank into the chair by the side of the range. 'I don't think Artie ever knew,' he said. 'I was always so careful around him. I didn't want to do anything that might make him hate me. I just wanted to be near him. You have no idea how much pleasure that gave me, just to be in the same room as him.'

'He wouldn't have hated you,' Clarissa said. 'Not Artie. Do you think Effie knows?'

Ellis looked at her, the downward curve of his mouth lifting at the corners. 'She's always known. She's come across enough men like me in her business to spot the signs a mile off.'

She knelt on the floor in front of him. 'I'm sorry I kept trying to encourage you to marry her. That must have hurt you.'

'Not really. I'm used to it. My family are permanently trying to marry me off. And who knows, Effie and I may yet walk down the aisle together. In so many ways, as you once said, we're perfect together. She knows all there is to know about me and often says that a conventional husband would be the least agreeable thing for her.'

'Why did you ask me to marry you?'

He dragged a hand over his face. 'All part of the disguise. Why do you want to know, are you reconsidering my offer?'

'I think I'd make a better friend to you than a wife,' she said with a smile.

He shook his head. 'Sometimes I wish I were different, but I'm not. I am what I am. I can't change it.'

She took his hands in hers. 'You're *who* you are, not *what*.'

He stared back at her, his eyes still wet with tears. 'Artie's dead, and here I am talking about myself.' He brought his fist down hard on the arm of the chair. 'What kind of man am I?'

'You're a man in shock. A man mourning someone he loved.'

'But I should be comforting you.'

'You can do that another time.'

He sighed deeply. 'There were times when I was mad with jealousy knowing that Artie loved you. God, how I wanted him to feel that way about me. It hurt knowing that he never would.'

'But he cared deeply about you, I know he did. Perhaps like a brother.'

With the gentlest of touches, Ellis stroked Clarissa's cheek. 'Would you have married Artie if he'd asked? If William hadn't come along? Or if he'd returned from this godawful war?'

Clarissa nodded. 'Yes, but only if he'd agreed to live here with me. I couldn't go back to America. Not now.'

'Trust me, Artie would have agreed to stay with you wherever you wanted to be. Can I stay here tonight? I can't face going back to the base.'

'Of course you can.'

They slept together in Clarissa's bed, she cradling Ellis in her arms.

Early in the morning, just as the first rays of dawn filtered through the curtains at the window, and the birds began their noisy chattering, she woke to find that Ellis was gone.

Something about the sight of the side of the bed where he had slept, the dented pillows and the scent of his cologne left behind on the sheets, tore at her heart and opened the floodgates of her grief. Burying her face into the pillow, she sobbed. Not just for Artie, but for William. And Leon. How many more people she loved would she have to lose before this dreadful war was over? Or maybe it would go on and on until nobody was left to grieve ...

By the time the children woke and were clamouring for their breakfast, Clarissa had pulled herself together. Mrs Cook knew something was wrong, but discreetly kept her counsel until Walter and Thomas had left for school. Taking Nicholas from Clarissa to soothe him – he'd been fractious since waking, as though picking up on her sadness – Mrs Cook asked what was the matter.

'Oh Lord,' she said when Clarissa had told her, 'how will you tell Thomas and Walter? They were so fond of him.'

'I know, and poor Walter made Artie promise he would come back. How will he ever believe anything anyone tells him, or trust anyone sufficiently to love them?'

'It's a tough lesson, but he will. In my experience children often bounce back better than adults. For now, I'm going to put Nicholas in his pram and go for a walk. Why don't you see if you can get some sleep? You look exhausted.'

After Mrs Cook had bounced the pram off down the lane, Clarissa dismissed the idea of resting and set to work on clearing up the breakfast things. She then scrubbed the floor on her hands and knees, before cleaning the small-paned window that looked out onto the garden. It was while she was polishing the panes of glass with a piece of newspaper that she heard the sound of the letter box being pushed open.

The second she saw the airmail envelope, she knew who it was from. She would recognise Artie's handwriting anywhere. With trembling hands, she opened the letter.

My dearest Clarissa,

I am writing this in the hope that, should I die, my instructions will be carried out and you will receive my last letter to you.

You knew when I left you in January that I had the strongest sense that my luck was due to run out. I shan't waste time explaining why I felt that way, and why I still do, not when I have so much more I want to say.

Whenever I think of our meeting on board the Belle Etoile, I marvel at the chance of our paths crossing and how it has led to the moment of me writing this letter, which is essentially a love letter in its purest form.

I wish it wasn't so, but a singular truth in our existence is that we will lose people we love. Another truth, and one close to my heart, is that we will come to understand that no matter how much time we spend with someone we love, it will never be enough. This is how I feel about you, Clarissa. I felt it that night on board the Belle Etoile when we danced together; I just knew that I had to get to know you better. Thank God I have been granted the joy of doing that, even if for so little time. I daresay a lifetime spent knowing you would not be sufficient, so I have to count myself lucky I've had what I've had.

Thank God also that you have given Thomas and Walter such a wonderful home. My instinct is that they will never be reunited with their parents, and I pray you will be with them to soften the pain of their loss. I would trust nobody better than you to undertake this task.

Now I must speak about Ellis. Poor Ellis. He's really not as tough as he portrays himself, and I fear my death will affect him badly. Please do all you can to be the friend he so badly needs. I know he has Effie, but you are far stronger than she is.

You must know by now that had William not come

*along when he did, I would have summoned the courage
to ask you to be my wife. I will never know if you would
have said yes, but then perhaps it's better for me to die
never knowing your answer. I don't think I could have
borne a rejection from you.*

*Now my love, I have said all there is to say. In
the years to come, I hope you will look back on our
friendship and remember it fondly. I also sincerely hope
you find the happiness you so richly deserve.*

*With all my love,
Artie*

Ellis was reported dead less than a week later. His aircraft
came down in the North Sea while returning from an operation over Merseburg. His crew all managed to escape and
were rescued not far from Lowestoft on the Suffolk coast.
Ellis's body, and his alone, was not recovered. It was hard
for Clarissa not to believe that this was how he wanted it to
end.

Chapter Fifty-Five

February 1947, Skylark Cottage, Shillingbury

> *Skylark Cottage,*
> *Shillingbury,*
> *Suffolk.*
> *15th February 1947*

Dear Betty,

Thank you, thank you, THANK YOU! I can't tell you what joy your food hamper brought us when we opened it – you are an angel to think of us! I'm ashamed to say we have already gorged ourselves thoroughly on the tins of ham and salmon, and the cake and chocolate. It was like Christmas all over again!

More seriously, I'm sad to say the stirrings of unrest are gaining momentum here. The general feeling is that we have lived with rationing quite long enough, that we should not be expected to continue making sacrifices during peacetime. It was easier somehow to bear the lack of food and hardship during the war years because we had a just cause to get behind. Now we just want to feel that the war was worth it, that we can get back to living normal lives again and can go to the shops and come home with a basket full of delicious things to eat. Hunger and deprivation is a terrible thing and I wonder if this will be what breaks our spirit – something even Hitler was unable to do.

We're now enduring a transport strike, which is

preventing food reaching the shops and to make matters worse, with sub-zero temperatures and snow blizzards sweeping across the country, there are fuel shortages which means thousands of factory workers can't get to work, which in turn means for long periods of time we're without heat or light – we've run out of logs for the fire and are down to our last sack of coal and I have no idea when we will see the coalman next. At night we go to bed wearing as many clothes as during the day, if not more, and are scarcely able to move beneath the weight of blankets and eiderdowns. With ice on the inside of the windows, I've had Nicholas sleep with me, cuddling him close to ensure he stays warm. Thomas and Walter have also shared a bed to keep warm.

I confess that there are times when I come close to losing my adopted stiff upper lip and succumb to the desire to weep at the unrelenting gloom. But what good would that do? I have the boys to fight for.

Talking of the boys, specifically Thomas and Walter, my worst fears may well come true, that I shall soon have to part with them. For now I'll say no more, in case putting it down on paper makes it a reality.

And now that I've thoroughly depressed you with such a tale of woe and misery, I must end before I depress myself further!

Thank you again for the hamper, you brightened our day wonderfully.

With all my love and endless thanks,
  Clarissa

PS I can't remember if I mentioned in my last letter that Henry Willet wanted to buy Shillingbury Grange from me. In case I didn't, I'd better start the story at the beginning. When the war came to an end, The Grange was no longer required by the RAF and was officially given back to me. It was in a terrible state of repair, and since I had no desire to live in the house, even though I could well afford to return it to its former glory, I decided to sell it. Of course, with so little money around these days, few people were interested in taking on such a costly proposition, but then along came Henry who said he'd always admired the house and offered what he said was his best price. I accepted his low offer, despite objections from my solicitor in London, but frankly I just wanted to be rid of the problem, so really I have only myself to blame. However, I heard a few days ago that Henry has now sold The Grange to a builder for nearly double what he paid me. This man plans to build about a dozen houses on the land after bulldozing The Grange to the ground. Jimmy swears blind that Henry must have been in cahoots with somebody in the planning department to pull off a stunt like this, but to be honest, I don't care. If this was Henry's way of getting back at me, then so be it.

PPS Apologies for the ridiculously long PS!

Harbour View,
Falmouth,
Cornwall.
26th April 1947

Dear Clarissa,

I write with the sad news that William's father passed away in February. As you know, he had been ill for some time and in many ways his death was a blessing.

I'm afraid that one way or another I have not been the best of mother-in-laws to you, or a good grandmother to Nicholas. I blame myself entirely, especially when you have been so good as to keep me up to date with my grandson's progress. I should have made more of an effort to visit you, but the war made everything so much harder, and then my husband was ill and confined to bed and all my time revolved around him.

Last month I moved down here to Falmouth, having made the decision to be near a dear friend who also recently lost her husband. I would be happy to have you and Nicholas to stay when I have got myself straightened out, although I do appreciate it would be a very long journey for you to undertake with a young child.

Please continue to write as often as you can.

Yours affectionately,
Audrey Dallimore

Skylark Cottage,
Shillingbury,
Suffolk.
30th August 1947

Dear Eva and Rudy,

Thank you for your letter and assurances that you will take the very best care of Thomas and Walter. As you must have come to realise from my previous correspondence with you, Thomas and Walter are as precious to me as my own son is, and parting with them is going to be an enormous wrench. I'm still not convinced that it's the right thing for them to leave here, but I know I have no choice in the matter, that it would be wrong to stand in their way.

There will always be a home for them here, should they have a change of heart.

Kind regards,
Clarissa

Four months after Clarissa wrote that brief but difficult letter to Eva and Rudy Neumann, the day had come for Thomas and Walter to leave Skylark Cottage.

They were now sixteen and fourteen years of age and since the end of the war, when the world discovered just what evil atrocities the Nazis had carried out in the concentration camps, Thomas and Walter had grown up fast. Knowing that their mother died within six months of being taken to the camp in Dachau, and that their father was later moved from Dachau and taken to Auschwitz, where he perished in the gas chambers, had brought about a swift end to their childhood. When they read of the Nazi war criminals who had been tried and found guilty at Nuremberg and subsequently executed, Thomas had spoken with a wisdom that had chilled Clarissa. 'Those men died believing they had done nothing wrong,' he said. 'There will be others who believe the same. It won't stop. Not ever.'

Then shortly before Christmas last year a letter had arrived from Palestine. It was from a woman called Eva Neumann who claimed to be Thomas and Walter's distant cousin. She had survived Auschwitz and was now living on a kibbutz on the outskirts of Jerusalem with her husband Rudy. After contacting the International Red Cross and those who had organised the Kindertransport, she had eventually tracked down Thomas and Walter, and as their only surviving relative she believed it her duty to offer them a home with what she referred to as their *real* family.

Clarissa's first response had been to throw the letter into the fire and pretend she had never received it. How dare this woman say where Thomas and Walter should live! Shillingbury was their home. This was where they were loved and cared for. How could this stranger even contemplate two young boys going to live in a country that was rife with conflict, where people were regularly being killed?

But Thomas had seen the letter with its Palestine stamp and postmark, and besides, Clarissa knew she had no right to keep something so important from him and his brother. Their reaction to the letter had been mixed. Walter had been adamant that he wasn't ever leaving Skylark Cottage, but Thomas had not been so ready to dismiss the contents of the letter; he was curious to know more. It was a stab to Clarissa's heart when he asked if he could write to Eva Neumann himself.

In the weeks and months that followed, during which time Thomas corresponded regularly with Eva and Rudy Neumann, Clarissa felt powerless to curb the zeal of what was plainly a growing conviction within him that England was no longer his home: Palestine was.

Reports in the newspapers of Arabs and Jews killing each other appeared to hold no fear for Thomas, and in July, when the refugee ship *Exodus 1947*, carrying 4,500 Jewish refugees, was thwarted from entering Palestine, Clarissa had hoped Thomas might review the situation, that he might see how dangerous it could be for him and his brother to make the journey, but perversely it made him all the more determined to go. 'We're going so that our parents did not lose their lives for nothing,' he declared.

He had suddenly become very much more politically and socially aware, eager too to embrace what he now saw as his true identity – he was Jewish and proud of it. He wanted to explore that identity and discover what it meant in its true context, and in his eyes there was only one way to do that.

Even when Clarissa reminded him of his dream to go to art school in London, he parried with Eva and Rudy Neumann's promises of him being able to study in Jerusalem. He then decided that art no longer interested him; he wanted to study politics and Hebrew.

Though it pained her to do so, Clarissa had to accept that Thomas was set on a course of action from which he would not be budged. Furthermore, he was a boy on the verge of manhood with a cause firmly fixed in his mind; it was a cause that terrified her.

Now here they were, on a bitterly cold December morning, preparing for the separation that Clarissa had dreaded. At her side stood Mrs Cook with a handkerchief thrust to her eyes.

'I can't bear it,' the poor woman said. 'Skylark Cottage just won't be the same without those boys. It's not right them going. Not right at all. Why do they want to go? I don't understand how they could do this, and after everything you've done.'

Overhearing this as he came down the stairs, a rucksack slung over his shoulder and a case in his hand, Thomas put his luggage down and gave Mrs Cook a hug. 'But think how much less work you'll have to do without us around.'

She dabbed furiously at her eyes. 'I've never complained about how much I do round here. Never.'

'Yes you have,' said Thomas gently. 'You've always complained at us for eating you out of house and home, and how we use all the hot water and make more mess in the bathroom than a pair of water hogs.'

'I might well have said something along those lines,' she replied with a sniff, 'but it doesn't mean I won't miss you.'

'And we'll miss you, Mrs Cook,' he said kindly. 'But it's time we found our own way now.'

Walter was next to come downstairs. There was less resolve in his manner, but he was devoted to his brother and would follow him anywhere. Trailing behind him, as if he were going too, was Nicholas carrying a small bag of toys with the head of his teddy bear poking out. It was enough to set Mrs Cook off again with a fresh burst of tears.

With a confused Nicholas looking on, Clarissa suggested it was time they set off. She was now the owner of a smart little Austin Seven and with the luggage stowed in the boot, Clarissa sat behind the steering wheel with a heavy heart. She was driving them to London, where Thomas and Walter would then take the train down to Southampton before boarding a ship bound for Haifa.

The final goodbye on the platform was too much for Clarissa. She clung to Walter as though through the sheer force of her love for him she might be able to persuade him not to go. She knew she was being unreasonable, but the agony of letting them go was just too awful.

Such a loving and gentle boy, Walter had tears in his eyes when she reluctantly released him. Thomas stepped forward and placed his hands on Clarissa's shoulders – he was so much taller than her now. 'We will never forget all the love and kindness you've shown us,' he said. 'Nobody could have done more. I hope that one day you will be proud of Walter and me, that you will realise this is something we had to do.'

His words, so formal and final, drilled straight through to her heart. 'I'll always be proud of you,' she said. 'Always.'

The three of them stood facing each other on the crowded platform in excruciating awkwardness. It was almost a relief when the guard's whistle blew and suddenly they were caught up in the commotion of people rushing to get on the train. Standing back, Clarissa watched the boys follow suit. The whistle was blown again, and in a great cloud of steam, the train surged forward and began to pull away. Leaning out of the carriage window, Walter called to her. 'I'll write to you,' he shouted, 'every week. I won't forget you, Clarissa! I promise!' His words breached the last of her reserves and she started to run after the train, her hand raised, her eyes blurry with tears.

When the train was moving too fast for her to keep up, she reluctantly watched it disappear into the distance. For the longest time she stood perfectly still, rooted to the spot, unable to move, unable to think.

'Clarissa, is that you? Why, yes it is!'

She turned to see none other than Polly Sinclair staring back at her. It was ages since they'd last seen each other, or had even been in touch, but the sight of Polly now was so welcome that Clarissa practically threw herself into her arms.

'Oh, my poor darling, whatever is the matter?'

Clarissa tried to explain, but hysterical sobs prevented her from uttering anything remotely coherent. Polly's solution was to take command and drive Clarissa home with her.

'What you need, my dear girl, is a large gin and it,' she said, bundling her into the front of her car as Clarissa continued to sob, 'and only once you've drunk it will I allow you to explain why you're so upset. Not a word until then!'

Cosseted in a sagging but immensely comfortable armchair, and soaking up the warmth of the fire burning brightly in the grate, Clarissa drank what she was given, and when her glass was empty she told Polly about Thomas and Walter.

'I warned you this might happen,' Polly said. 'It's an all-too-familiar story, but these children have to live their lives the way they want to. As much as they sometimes come to love the host families who have given them a home, they know it's not their true home and will perhaps spend the rest of their lives searching for what, for many, may well be elusive.'

'But I thought I'd done that,' said Clarissa, 'I thought I'd given them a sense of permanence, a place where they knew they were loved and were secure.'

'And so you did,' said Polly. 'Nobody could have given those boys more love and stability than you gave Thomas and Walter, other than their own mother and father, but you were only ever meant to be a temporary mother to them. You knew that right at the start.'

Her hackles up, Clarissa wanted to accuse Polly of not understanding. *You've never had children in your life*, she wanted to say, *you don't know the emotional pull they have on you*. But she didn't. 'I know all that in my head,' she said calmly, 'but my heart says otherwise. And the worst of it is, I know what Thomas plans to do. He wants a cause to fight for and he'll do whatever it takes to do that in Palestine, or the State of Israel as it will soon be called. He'll get himself killed; I just know it. And poor Walter will follow him only too willingly. It breaks my heart.'

'You don't know any of that for sure,' Polly said firmly. 'For now it sounds like Thomas wants to prove himself; all boys do at that age.'

'But I feel as if I've failed not just him and Walter, but their parents. They effectively entrusted their sons into my care and look what's happened.'

Polly rose from her chair, took Clarissa's empty glass and refilled it with yet more gin and vermouth. 'Clarissa, my darling,' she said, handing the glass back to her, 'you have two choices: you can either keep on berating yourself like this and go mad into the bargain, or you can square your shoulders and hope with all your being that Thomas and Walter will be all right. Those are your options, and I would advocate the latter – if not for your own sake, then for the sake of your son, Nicholas.'

At the mention of Nicholas, Clarissa sat up straight. 'Oh good lord, what was I thinking? I need to get home! I shouldn't be sitting here, drinking gin with you! Poor Nicholas and Mrs Cook will be wondering what's happened to me. I must get back to the station where I left my car.' She was up on her feet, all her anxiety now focused on her son.

'For heaven's sake, calm down,' Polly ordered. 'You're not going anywhere with the amount of gin I've poured into you. You must ring Mrs Cook and tell her you're staying the night here with me. And later, over supper, we must decide what you're going to do with the rest of your life.'

'What do you mean?'

'You need a job, my girl.'

'But I have one, I'm Nicholas's mother and—'

'I'm well aware of that,' Polly interrupted her, 'but you need more than motherhood to one small boy to keep you sane. An occupation will provide you with a fresh perspective.'

Once again Clarissa felt her hackles rise. 'What precisely do you propose?' she asked with a hint of sarcasm.

'Later,' Polly said. 'For now, ring Mrs Cook, then you can come into the kitchen and peel some potatoes for supper.'

Chapter Fifty-Six

Lizzie's first thought when she woke the next morning was of Mrs Dallimore, in particular the contrast between the frail old lady she had come to know, and the one she wished she had known – the young and extraordinarily selfless woman who had devoted herself to others, but who had suffered heartache after heartache. It made Lizzie want to vow she would never again whinge about anything bad that happened to her. Yet human nature being what it was, she would very likely break the promise before the day was over.

But whatever else she failed to do, she fully intended to keep the promise she'd made to Mrs Dallimore, that she wouldn't tell anyone about her so-called visits from her old friends. If it was all right for a child to have an imaginary friend, she reasoned, why couldn't a sweet old lady who was as harmless as a daisy be left to enjoy the same flight of fancy? As rational as the argument was, Lizzie knew that for most people it was missing the point. Even so, her lips would remain sealed.

She knew all about how old people's recollections steadily became far clearer than those of the more immediate past, and even the present, but observing it close up with Mrs Dallimore really brought home to Lizzie just how true it was. Had anyone, she wondered, actually figured out yet why the brain could enable a person like Mrs Dallimore to recall events that took place seventy years ago, and with an extraordinary depth of detail, but at the same time play tricks on her, such as steal her ability to recognise Lizzie?

The buzzing of her mobile interrupted her thoughts. These

days, with her circle of contacts shrunk to no more than a handful of people, the mere fact that the device had sprung into life with a text was a surprise to Lizzie.

An even bigger surprise was that it was Simon who had texted. *Am home for the Bank Holiday weekend, fancy lunch today?*

After a small hesitation, she replied: *When and where?*

His reply came back in an instant: *The Bell, 12.30. If that's ok.*

I need to be somewhere for 2.30, so it'll have to be a quick lunch.

Let's make it 12.00 in that case.

See you then!

The invitation had to be as a result of Dad and Luke running into Simon and his father last night. Luke had come back to the house on his own, leaving Dad chatting to Keith and Simon. It wasn't exactly how Lizzie had hoped the evening would pan out. Dad was supposed to be having a one-to-one with Luke, but judging from his jovial manner when he'd returned home during the ten o'clock news, it was obvious he'd thoroughly enjoyed himself. Lizzie had watched her mother doing her best to be pleased for him, but she could see it rankled, as if Dad had broken ranks by fraternising with the enemy.

Time to get up, she thought after glancing at her watch, but no sooner had she pushed aside the duvet than she heard her father whistling his way up the stairs, followed by a knock on her door.

'Come in,' she said, 'I'm wide awake.'

'Cup of tea,' said her father, putting the mug on the bedside table. Going over to the curtains, he drew them back. 'It's another day in—'

'Paradise,' Lizzie finished for him.

He smiled. 'As reliably predictable as a Swiss cuckoo clock, that's your old dad.'

'We wouldn't want you any other way,' she said with a

402

smile of her own. 'You didn't tell me how you got on yesterday with Luke. Did you manage to get anything out of him?'

Her father sat on the end of her bed. 'Yes, and rather more than I expected to.'

'Is it bad?'

'It certainly isn't good. Some of which I said I wouldn't repeat, so no trying to extract it from me. Okay?'

'Of course. Tell me what you think you can.'

While her father spoke, Lizzie drank her tea. 'The question is,' he said eventually, 'how we as a family can help resolve the problem.'

'Can we?' asked Lizzie. 'Isn't it for Ingrid to accept that Luke has a family that cares for him? And for her, too?'

'True, but the question is how can we help her do that?'

Lizzie puffed out her cheeks. 'I don't know. How worried does Luke seem?'

'More worried than I'd like him to be.'

'You know, I never thought I'd say this, but I can sympathise with Ingrid, in that I hated having to ask you and Mum for help when I lost my job. I felt such a failure having to admit I'd messed up. It was like being a child again. Not that Ingrid has messed up; it's just that, from what you say, she hates to ask for help. It probably makes her feel less capable, which may well stem from some sort of insecurity.'

Her father took a moment to consider this. 'I hadn't thought of it quite like that,' he said, 'but I think you could be right.' He rubbed his chin, thinking. Then: 'Do you think you could be the one who Ingrid might open up to if you talked to her?'

'Me?' blurted out Lizzie, shocked. 'Oh, I don't think that's a very good idea, especially as I'm sure she doesn't really approve of me.'

'I'm equally sure that isn't true. More likely the two of you just haven't found the right common ground yet. I've suggested to your mother that we have a family barbecue on Monday afternoon when they come to drop off Freddie.

Why don't you see if you can get Ingrid on her own for a chat?'

The suggestion appalled Lizzie. 'You really think she'll talk to me? Why not you, or Mum? You two are so much more careful about what you say.'

'And therein lies the problem, in all likelihood. What's needed is some good old-fashioned openness, and you, Lizzie, are so much better at that than the rest of us.'

'But what if my mouth runs away with itself and I make things worse?'

'You won't, I have every confidence in you.'

Which is more than I have in myself, thought Lizzie when she surprised herself by agreeing to talk to Ingrid.

Well, this is a day of surprises, she found herself thinking when later she was sitting in the garden of the Bell with Simon. With the arrival of identical plates of chargrilled burgers and two small bowls of fat chips, they each reached for the salt at the same time.

'You first,' Simon said. He seemed a lot more at ease than Lizzie was. But then he had nothing to feel guilty about; she was the one who was riddled with self-recrimination and regret.

'Dad really enjoyed himself last night,' she said, sliding the salt mill across the table after she'd used it. 'I do hope things go back to how they were between them before I threw a spanner in the works.'

'So do I. I know my father misses Tom, they were such good friends.'

'What about Lorna?' Lizzie asked cautiously. 'Any change there?'

Simon pulled a face. 'Still a work in progress, I'm afraid. I'm working on her.'

'I don't want to sound critical, but what's her problem? Does she blame Mum for what I did?'

Simon chewed on a mouthful of burger. When he'd

finished, he said, 'I think she's got herself into a tight corner and doesn't know how to come out of it with her pride in place.'

'That's probably where Mum is right now. And if I'm honest, I was in a similar place myself when I had to leave London with my tail firmly between my legs. Talk about the long walk home of shame, my pride was so low it was practically digging its own grave.'

'And now?'

'Now I'm fast developing a new perspective, and can see that some of the things that used to seem important to me just aren't.'

'Such as?'

'The whole London-centric thing.' She smiled. 'Mind you, that could just be my battered pride flexing its muscles, making out that the job I've just been offered with a small provincial radio station is the last word in career moves.'

Unfolding his paper napkin, Simon wiped his mouth. 'Who knows, it might well be.'

'How about you?' she asked.

'You'll be pleased to hear I've abandoned my five-year plan, and not just because we're no longer together; I suddenly realised how ridiculous it was.'

She frowned and put down her knife and fork and reached for her glass of water – despite an initial need to quell her nerves with a large glass of wine, she'd deemed it better not to turn up at Woodside with alcohol on her breath. 'It wasn't ridiculous, Simon,' she said. 'There's nothing wrong in having a plan.'

'It was the wrong plan at the wrong time. And ...' he paused to take a sip of his beer, 'I lost you because of it.'

'Don't say that. It really wasn't anything you did: it was *me*. I lost my head for somebody who turned out to be nothing but a lying cheat.'

He put down his glass and gave her one of his close-scrutiny looks. The one she had always found so attractive in

405

the past. And as if seeing him through fresh eyes, she thought how well he looked. Was it her imagination, or did he seem freer than before, as though he were more himself? He'd had a change of haircut, had left his hair to grow slightly longer on the top so its natural curve was visible. It suited him. The pale blue T-shirt he was wearing was new and picked up the blue of his eyes. Was he getting style tips from the work colleague he'd mentioned on the phone? *No*, she warned herself, *don't go there, it's none of your business.*

'Perhaps I shouldn't say this,' he said, 'but – and please don't think I'm saying it with any kind of sick pleasure – I heard on the grapevine that Curt is up to no good with your replacement.'

Surprised that she felt no hurt at Simon's words, just a sickening disgust with herself that she had fallen for a low-life serial adulterer, Lizzie shook her head and shrugged. 'How does he get away with it?' she said.

'Some just do,' said Simon. 'And again, I don't want to speak out of turn, or appear as though I'm revelling in this, but aren't you glad you discovered what Curt was like when you did, rather than get any more involved with him?'

'You can say anything you want to me,' she said, and meaning it, 'you've earned that right. And yes, I'm now at the point when I can see that I had a lucky escape.'

Their burgers finished and their plates taken away, Simon looked at her. 'I've enjoyed this,' he said. 'I was worried it might be difficult, but it hasn't been. Well, not from my side of the table. How's it from your side?'

She smiled at his tact. 'It's okay,' she said. 'But there's a bit of me that keeps waiting for the sting in the tail, for you suddenly to give it to me with both barrels.'

'If it puts your mind at rest, I can assure you I've passed that stage.'

'So there was a moment when you might have given it to me with both barrels?' she said.

'Oh yes, I'm human, not a saint, Lizzie.'

'I'm sorry. Truly I am.'

'Apology accepted.' He glanced at his watch – the retro digital watch she had bought him for his birthday two years ago. 'I don't want to hurry you,' he said, 'but didn't you say you had to leave here at two o'clock? It's five to.'

'That time already?' she said, disappointed. She could happily stay here for the rest of the afternoon. 'I see you kept it,' she said, pointing at the watch.

He frowned. 'Of course I did. Why would you think ...? Oh, I see, you think I should have thrown it away in a fit of anger? Or taken a hammer to it to exorcise my feelings for you?'

'Something like that. Which is probably what I would have done, had Curt actually bothered to give me anything other than a ton of regret.'

'A cheapskate as well as a twenty-four-carat-gold shit?' remarked Simon with a raised eyebrow. 'Is there a worse combination?'

She laughed. 'None that I know of.'

He smiled back at her. 'Would it be inappropriate to say how good it is to see you again?'

'Not at all. I've been thinking the same. But I really should be going.' She dug around in her bag for some money.

'Put it away, it's my treat. After all, it was my idea.'

'That's not fair. You know I always like to pay my way.'

'How about you do the next one?'

She looked at him. 'You're sure you want a next one?'

'I wouldn't have suggested it if I didn't mean it.'

She cycled away from the pub in the very best of moods. Life was good, she thought with a carefree happiness as she pedalled out of the village. It was good to know that from the wreckage of one of the worst decisions she'd ever made in her life she and Simon could be friends.

Her mood was further improved when she arrived at

Woodside just in time to join in with singing happy birthday to Mrs Coleman, and to help pass slices of birthday cake round. It was the woman's ninety-second birthday and with her wispy white hair specially washed and set for the occasion, she looked as pleased as punch with the fuss being made of her. Her family were gathered around her wheel-chair, the handles of which had balloons tied to them, and a couple of great-grandchildren were running around and causing a mixture of mayhem and delight amongst the residents. An unnaturally smartly dressed boy of about thirteen was enthusiastically showing Mr Sheridan something on an iPad. There should be more days like this, Lizzie thought, not just birthday parties, but times when children came in to entertain the residents. The only person who seemed not to be enjoying herself was Mrs Lennox, who repeatedly tutted and complained of the noise.

When the party was over and Lizzie had helped clear away and stack the dishwasher in the kitchen, she went in search of Mrs Dallimore. As she so often did, she had the rose arbour to herself. Her head was tilted forward, her chin tucked in and her lips were moving, as if she were reciting something, praying even, or maybe she was talking to herself. Or was this a visit from her old friends? Lizzie felt awkward coming upon her in this way and hung back for a moment, uncertain whether to proceed or just leave well alone. She had noticed during Mrs Coleman's party that Mrs Dallimore had had a vague and distracted air about her, gazing off into the distance at times as though lost in her own world. Chances were Lizzie wouldn't have been the only one to notice.

'Is that you, Lizzie?'

'I thought you were asleep,' lied Lizzie, hurrying forward, 'that the party had been too much for you.'

'I must confess I do feel a little tired,' the old lady said weakly. 'Do you have time to sit awhile with me?'

Lizzie smiled. 'All the time in the world for you.' She

settled herself next to Mrs Dallimore. 'I had lunch with my ex-boyfriend today,' she said.

Mrs Dallimore turned to look at her, her brows drawn. 'Who?'

'Simon,' she explained, 'the boyfriend I treated so badly when I fell for Curt, the married man.'

'Oh, him,' the old lady said vaguely, as if still not entirely sure who Lizzie was talking about.

'It was good seeing him again,' Lizzie continued, 'although I did feel incredibly nervous initially. He suggested we should meet again some time.'

'Will the two of you get back together, do you think?' asked Mrs Dallimore. Like the flip of a coin, the vagueness of before was replaced with a razor-sharp frankness.

Lizzie shook her head. 'No. I wouldn't trust myself not to hurt him again, and he doesn't deserve that. Oh, and get this, Simon told me he'd heard that Curt is already at it again with the girl who took over my job at the radio station.'

Mrs Dallimore sighed. 'A dirty dog of the highest order! What a lucky escape you had, my dear.'

'I said much the same thing to Simon. I've decided to stay away from men for the time being, until I feel I can be trusted to make the right choice.'

'What about Jed?'

'What about him?'

'You're not going to stop being friends with him, are you? That would be a great shame, in my opinion.'

Lizzie smiled. 'Are you matchmaking, Mrs Dallimore?'

'He's a fine young man; you could do a lot worse.'

'And I'm sure he could do a lot better. Did you never want to marry again, Mrs Dallimore?' she asked, changing the subject.

'No. Nicholas was my priority, and I always considered myself lucky to have known what I had. Rightly or wrongly, I didn't believe anyone would have lived up to William, or Artie.'

'What about Effie, did she marry in the end?'

'Ah, dear Effie. The poor girl had three marriages, all of them doomed because she could never find a man to replace Ellis. He was the light of her life.'

'If Ellis hadn't died, do you think they would have married,' asked Lizzie, 'even though he was gay?'

'Almost certainly, and probably *because* he was gay. She told me some years after the war that she would have done anything to protect him.'

'That would have been quite some sacrifice.'

Mrs Dallimore shook her head. 'Back then, people were more inclined to make sacrifices than they are today. And anyway, sex wasn't that important to Effie. She had, she confided in me, a low sex drive, practically non-existent, she said. I expect that was a contributing factor to her unhappy marriages. Very likely her relationship with her father somehow played its part, too, although it was never anything we discussed. I thought it very cruel when her second husband, a film producer, accused Effie of being "glacial" in bed. It was an unnecessarily unkind comment from a man who was a notorious womaniser and would bed anything that moved.'

'Sounds like somebody I know! Have you stayed friends all these years?' asked Lizzie, as ever fascinated by the old lady's reminiscences. 'Is Effie still alive?'

'We stayed in regular contact right up until she died in a car crash back in the sixties. She and her husband had been at a party and after she'd seen him flirting outrageously with a girl half his age, she drove home despite having drunk too much. The newspapers said some vile things about Effie being a faded star who'd taken to the bottle to compensate for a lack of fulfilment. Oh, it was quite dreadful.' The old lady looked at Lizzie. 'You know, I'm surprised you haven't applied your great researcher's mind to finding out more about my friends for yourself. Their lives are fairly well documented, particularly Effie's.'

Lizzie smiled. 'It did cross my mind to do that, but it

would have totally spoilt my enjoyment of hearing you tell me all about them.'

Mrs Dallimore patted her hand. 'You've been a good listener, and I'm very grateful to you for giving me the opportunity to relive a special time in my life. It means a lot to me.'

They sat in silence for a few moments listening to the swell of birdsong, and while watching a trio of cabbage white butterflies chasing each other before flying off, Lizzie thought of Mrs Coleman being surrounded by her family for her birthday, and of her great-grandchildren running about the place. It made her wonder about Mrs Dallimore's son. Last night the old lady had shown her a number of old black-and-white photographs, including Nicholas when he was about ten years of age, along with older ones of Mrs Dallimore with William, and Artie, Effie and Ellis. It had been intriguing seeing pictures of these people after hearing so much about them, and Lizzie would have loved to investigate the album further, but Mrs Dallimore had suddenly shown signs of exhaustion and of having had enough company.

Lizzie hardly dared to ask the question, given how many loved ones Mrs Dallimore had lost, but she did so anyway. 'What about your son, Nicholas?' she asked. 'And Thomas and Walter, what happened to them after they left you?'

Mrs Dallimore swallowed and blinked hard. 'I'm afraid my worst fears came true with Thomas and Walter.'

Chapter Fifty-Seven

November 1948, Skylark Cottage, Shillingbury

Not quite a year after parting with Thomas and Walter, Clarissa received a letter from Eva Neumann, a letter informing her that along with Rudy, both boys had been killed in a bomb explosion in the centre of Jerusalem. Never had Clarissa hated anyone as much as she did when she held that letter in her hands – if Eva and Rudy Neumann had not interfered, Thomas and Walter would still be in England alive and perfectly safe, their whole lives stretching out before them.

The next day she sat down to reply to Eva's letter and gave vent to her feelings, letting the flow of anger pour out of her. It was vitriolic and unashamedly condemnatory; four pages of grief in which she explicitly blamed the woman for selfishly exposing two young boys to a needless danger which they ultimately paid for with their lives. She wrote of Thomas's wish of becoming an artist one day, and of Walter's kind and sensitive nature. '*I hope you can live with yourself, and that you never know a day when your conscience isn't pricked by your actions,*' she wrote. She signed the letter, sealed it and put it ready to post the next morning.

But the next morning as she listened to Nicholas humming happily to himself at the breakfast table while he methodically dipped fingers of toast into the egg she had boiled for him, her heart softened and fresh tears of sadness for the two boys he had adored as brothers threatened to spill over. She hadn't had the heart yet to explain to Nicholas that he would never see Thomas and Walter again; she needed to wait until she was feeling stronger.

True to their word, Thomas and Walter had stayed in touch and occasionally sent Nicholas small presents, the last a wooden camel carved from olive wood. He kept it on his bedside table next to a photograph of him with Thomas and Walter. The juxtaposition of her precious son's innocence and the shameful cruelty contained within the pages Clarissa had written yesterday wounded her painfully, and going over to the dresser she ripped the letter up and threw it into the bin. She would write again tomorrow, she told herself, and would endeavour to be gracious; Eva Neumann had lost her husband, after all.

Meanwhile, and with Mrs Cook due back this afternoon from Broadstairs in Kent, where she'd been on holiday for a week staying with an old friend who ran a guest house, Clarissa did what she always did when she was upset: she threw herself into a frenzy of activity. Rolling her sleeves up, and with Nicholas's help, she set about making an iced lemon cake, a dozen strawberry jam tarts, a round of short-bread and then some fish paste sandwiches with thinly sliced cucumber – Mrs Cook's favourite.

At a quarter to three, with Nicholas bouncing excitedly in the front seat beside her, Clarissa drove the short distance to Shillingbury station. It was a miserable November day, wet and cold with a powerful gusting wind that was ripping the last of the leaves from the trees. The rain was falling in earnest and already the light was fading. She switched on the car's headlamps and concentrated on the road ahead. The windscreen wipers thumped to and fro and had almost no effect in helping her to see more clearly.

They made it to the station, where Billy Moss the station-master waved to them from the open door of the ticket office. A couple of minutes later the branch line train of just three carriages – two third-class and one first-class – came to a halt and Mrs Cook stepped onto the platform. 'Lawd love us!' she exclaimed after Clarissa had stowed her luggage in the boot and Nicholas had jumped into the back of the car to make room for Mrs Cook in the front. 'What shocking weather.'

'I'm afraid it's not much of a welcome for you,' Clarissa said, turning out of the station and joining the road for home. 'How was your holiday?'

'Terrible! I couldn't wait to come back.'

'Oh dear, what a shame. What was the problem?'

'Edie's turned into such a bitter old woman, not got a good word for anyone. I know she's had some bad luck in her time, but I tell you, she's a caution to the rest of us that, no matter what life throws at us, we have to keep positive and not let the beggars get us down. In the end I told her she'd better pull herself together or she'll end up with no friends whatsoever.' Mrs Cook twisted round in her seat to look at Nicholas. 'Now then, you little rascal, have you been a good boy while I was away? Did you miss me?'

'Yes, yes, *yes*!' he chorused. 'Have you brought me a present?'

'Why, you cheeky little monkey!'

'We've made a surprise for you,' he said, grinning and leaning forward so his body was jammed between the two seats.

'Have you indeed? And what would that be?'

His eyes wide, he put a finger to his lips. '*Ssh!* I can't tell you, it's a surprise.'

Clarissa smiled. Thank heavens for Nicholas, she thought, he was such a joyful ray of sunshine. Even on a day like today.

The real surprise of Mrs Cook's welcome home party was that there were two guests joining them – Lily and her husband. Lily's married name was Porter, and she and her husband lived in Bury St Edmunds where Derek worked as a clerk in a solicitor's office. Having learned typing and shorthand at

414

night school when the war was over, Lily was now employed as a secretary to the editor of the local newspaper, *The Bury Messenger*. Clarissa had no doubt that her ambitions didn't stop there.

As for her own ambitions, and frequent nagging from Polly that it was high time Clarissa did something more with her life, other than motherhood, she was now working as a teaching assistant at the village school. Shortly after Nicholas had started attending the school Mrs Russell, the headmistress, had approached Clarissa to ask if she would be willing to spend three afternoons a week listening to the children read. Then when Miss Todd, who taught the infants, left unexpectedly due to ill health, Clarissa was asked if she would step into the breach until a more permanent replacement was found. At Mrs Russell's encouragement she was seriously contemplating training to be a teacher.

Mrs Cook was delighted to see Lily, and while they caught up on family news, Derek helped Nicholas with the jigsaw puzzle Mrs Cook had bought for him. Then it was time for tea, which they had in the cosy warmth of the kitchen – where Clarissa always gravitated. The table was laid with a white linen cloth embroidered with flowers, and the best china, so rarely used, had been dug out from the sideboard in the dining room in Mrs Cook's honour. With the greatest of care, Nicholas offered Mrs Cook a sandwich. 'I helped Mummy makes these,' he said proudly, the plate wobbling precariously in his small hands.

'In that case I'll enjoy them even more,' said Mrs Cook with a wink.

Helping to pass cups of tea round, and after exchanging a look with her husband, Lily said, 'Clarissa, you'll read about it in the *Messenger* tomorrow, so there's no harm in telling you this now, but we heard yesterday that Henry Willet has been arrested for fraud.'

Clarissa put the teapot down. 'Go on,' she said steadily.

'You tell her,' Lily urged her husband, 'you know more about it than I do.'

Placing his cup back in its saucer on the table, Derek took up the story. 'It turns out Willet had been fiddling some poor old woman's accounts for years,' he said, 'siphoning off small amounts here and there so that no one would ever notice, but then he got greedy and when the old girl died, he produced a will in which everything was left to him, lock, stock and barrel.'

'What made anyone think there was anything wrong?' asked Clarissa.

'It was the housekeeper and her husband, the gardener; they smelt a rat when their employer died and left them not a penny piece. They also knew that their employer had written a previous will in which they were both named as beneficiaries. They had worked for the woman for years, and the amount promised them would have set them up nicely in their own little cottage when they retired.'

'I always knew he was a bad 'un,' declared Mrs Cook. 'So did you, Clarissa, that's why you gave him his marching orders. Thank the lord you did!'

'What's more,' went on Derek, 'all his previous clients' financial affairs are being looked into. I would imagine that will include you as well, Clarissa.'

'So now we all know how he could afford to buy The Grange,' Clarissa said grimly, remembering how horribly smug Henry had been at the time of the sale. 'He once told me he'd inherited some money from an aunt – perhaps that was a lie, too.'

'The man probably didn't have an honest thought in his head,' said Mrs Cook. 'What's more, you being such a wealthy woman, you were a target like no other for him. Another woman in your situation, recently widowed with a baby on the way, might have welcomed his attention, but thank God you had more sense or he'd have been stealing from you.'

Later that evening, after Lily and Derek had left to go and see Jimmy and Nicholas was tucked up in bed, Clarissa gave Mrs Cook Eva Neumann's letter to read.

When she'd read it, she removed her spectacles and blew her nose, then dabbed her eyes. 'Those poor, poor boys,' she murmured. 'As if they hadn't suffered enough in their young lives.'

Clarissa told her about the letter she'd written and which she'd thrown away that morning. 'I'm ashamed of myself when I think of what I wrote,' she said, 'and I know this is selfish, but I can't help but worry how much more will be taken from me. It seems that anybody I love, I'm destined to lose. I was kissing Nicholas goodnight and I suddenly—'

'No!' interrupted Mrs Cook fiercely. 'You're not to think that. Not ever. Nicholas is going to grow up to be a fine young man, and he'll be there by your side when you're a very old lady.'

'I hope you're right. I really do.'

Chapter Fifty-Eight

When Mrs Dallimore fell silent, Lizzie turned to look at her. Very gently, she said, 'Please tell me Mrs Cook was right.'

'She was almost right. Nicholas grew up to be the best son any mother could have. I had a tendency to be overly protective of him, but given all those I'd lost, I'd defy any mother to behave differently.'

'If my mother had been in your shoes, she'd have watched over my brother and me every second of the day,' said Lizzie.

'That was my natural inclination, but I had to stand back and let him go free. He excelled at school, took up a place at Cambridge and eventually became the surgeon he'd always wanted to be.' She smiled ruefully. 'He was teased at school as a teenager for having such small, neat hands. He never minded, just laughed off the comments saying nobody wanted a clumsy, big-handed surgeon.'

'Did he marry and have a family?'

Mrs Dallimore nodded. 'He married in his thirties, but sadly the marriage didn't work out.' She waved a hand airily. 'There was no real fault involved, their lives were just going in different directions and so they did the sensible thing and divorced. Pam remarried some years later, but Nicholas never really felt settled again. His feet had become itchy and he developed a need to spread his wings; London was no longer enough for him. Then, in what one might call a completing of the circle, he took up a post offered to him by a prestigious teaching hospital in Boston and went to live in America.'

'Did you visit him there?' asked Lizzie. 'It must have felt strange going back after all the years you'd been away.'

'I never went. I wasn't the least bit curious to return to a place I'd been so keen to leave. I felt I had closed that chapter in my life and didn't want to reread it. Besides, Nicholas flew home so regularly to see me, he was often in London for medical conferences and so forth, so I never felt the need to make the journey myself. I was also quite busy running my own school.'

Lizzie did a double take. 'You had your own school?'

The old lady let out a low chuckle. 'Oh yes,' she said, 'I became quite the schoolmarm. When Colonel Brook died and his estate was to be sold, I bought the house and land and turned it into a prep school. It was called Shillingbury House School. I set up a trust to provide a wide selection of scholarships for children whose families couldn't afford the fees – that was very important to me.' After a lengthy pause, she went on. 'It was with great reluctance that I sold the school when it was time for me to retire. It was a hard decision for me to make, but I had to accept it had become too much for me. So I left Shillingbury and wanting a change of scene, I went to live in Long Melford. And that's where I stayed until I came here.'

'Does the school still exist?' asked Lizzie, curious. She had never heard of it.

'Sadly no. Shillingbury House is now an upmarket hotel.'

'I bet you were a wonderful teacher,' said Lizzie, 'really inspirational.'

'I don't know about that, but I think my achievements, if that is what I can call them, came down to one very simple thing: the desire to nurture and take under my wing those in need of encouragement and support. I suppose that sounds rather hackneyed and self-righteous to you.'

'Not at all. It's a shame more of us can't say the same thing. Including me!' Then, realising they'd moved away from the subject of Mrs Dallimore's son, Lizzie said, 'And Nicholas, what about him? Does he still live in America?'

The old lady shook her head slowly. 'My darling Nicholas died of a heart attack shortly before his fiftieth birthday, not long after he'd returned to London to live.' Her voice, already faint, faded almost to a whisper. 'He'd had no previous problems, no warning signs. I'll always be grateful the end was quick for him, that he didn't suffer a long-drawn-out illness. He would have hated to have lived what he called a half-life; he had to be constantly doing something, physically as well as mentally. His friends said the only time he ever stood still was in the operating theatre.'

'I'm so sorry,' Lizzie said. 'You've lost so many people, haven't you?'

'I've outlived them all,' the old lady murmured, looking off into the distance. 'Every last one of them. But soon – very soon – I'll be gone too.'

'Don't say that.'

Mrs Dallimore returned her gaze to Lizzie. 'Dear girl, one must never shirk the truth. The clock is ticking, and now I have a sense of being ready to go. I wasn't before. But now I am.'

Lizzie struggled to speak. 'I think you're the most extraordinary person I know. I'm not sure I would have half your resilience if faced with what you've gone through.'

'Nonsense. Look how you've coped this summer with everything that's gone on for you. A lesser person might have gone under, but not you. You didn't want to come and be a befriender here at Woodside, and yet you did, and what's more, you've made a great success of it.'

Lizzie smiled. 'Remember how I nearly knocked you out of your wheelchair on my first day?'

Mrs Dallimore smiled, too. 'How could I forget? That gave me something to chortle about, I can tell you.'

Thinking of all the people that had come and gone from Mrs Dallimore's life and how she'd obviously cared deeply for them, Lizzie said, 'Have I been somebody you wanted to take under your wing and nurture?'

The old lady stared unblinkingly at her. 'What do you think?'

Chapter Fifty-Nine

Ingrid picked up on the atmosphere at Keeper's Nook straight away.

Everybody was being unnaturally upbeat, and Lizzie in particular was behaving very out of character. Since when did her sister-in-law comment on what Ingrid was wearing, or ask where she'd bought her shoes? The real giveaway came when Lizzie ordered Tess to go and sit in the garden with a glass of wine, and then asked Ingrid to help her with making the salads. Lizzie, doing something useful in the kitchen? What was *that* all about? Meanwhile, a beer apiece, Tom and Luke were dancing attendance on the demands of the gas-fired barbecue, which, much as it rankled with Ingrid, was probably a fair representation of most families this Bank Holiday Monday.

Standing at the kitchen sink washing her hands before handling the food, Ingrid watched Freddie in the paddling pool where he was playing with a plastic tea set, busily pouring out miniature cups of tea. Every now and then he stood up to pass one to Tess, who took it and gave a credible performance of drinking it with huge enjoyment. In one of the very few photographs Ingrid had from her own childhood, she was wearing a hideous frilly pink swimsuit, playing much the same game. Except the adults in the picture – her mother and stepfather – were not playing along; they were ignoring her, deeply engrossed in each other. She might just as well have not been there. Ingrid had no idea who had taken the photograph, but it pretty much captured her childhood. That sense of isolation eventually became the norm, to the point where it was what she thrived on; it strengthened her, gave her the kind of independence she vowed never to give up. She'd always counted herself lucky that Luke understood not to crowd her, or try to change her.

Until now.

As much as she wanted to pretend she was imagining it, there was no getting away from the fact that just lately there had been friction between them. She was conscious of frequently saying the wrong thing, or more precisely, not saying what he wanted to hear.

'Here we go then,' Lizzie said, staring at a mound of ingredients that had been piled on the work surface. 'What shall we do with it all?' she asked. She sounded like one of those irritatingly jolly girls at Freddie's nursery who were relentlessly bright and cheery. Ironically, that jolliness would be a welcome balm in eight days' time when the nursery reopened. Yesterday morning they had received an email letting them know that the damage caused by the flood was in the final stages of being put right. Ingrid longed to resume their old routine; she missed seeing Freddie of an evening, of enjoying a bath with him and then reading to him.

Surveying the pile of food, she said, 'I'll make a watermelon and mint salad. Pass me that packet of feta, will you?'

'How clever you are,' said Lizzie. 'I'd never have thought of that. I'll chop some cucumber and tomatoes and then just throw it in a bowl with that bag of lettuce, shall I?'

'Why not?' said Ingrid, evenly.

On Saturday, when Luke had come off the phone after telling his parents about the nursery reopening, he'd told Ingrid a family barbecue had been proposed by way of celebrating Lizzie's new job. Ingrid's initial reaction had been to flag up the work she had to do, and suggest he went and enjoyed himself while dropping Freddie off for the week ahead – his last week with his grandparents. But Luke had vetoed her suggestion before she'd had a chance to get the words out. 'I told Dad we'd go,' he'd said.

She'd balked at what she saw as his high-handedness. 'You might have checked with me first,' she'd replied.

'And had I done that, what would you have said?'

She had known from the look on his face that it would have been reckless to give him an honest answer, so she'd fudged it by saying it would have been nice for her to be included in the conversation. She'd then made her point by getting up extra early that morning to do the work she'd planned to do at a more civilised time. Annoyingly, instead of facing the day fuelled with a sense of virtuous energy, she'd felt deflated as well as mean and petty, especially when Freddie insisted on her playing with him as well – he was not to be fobbed off with just Daddy, or Peppa Pig, the usual saviour in such situations. 'Mummy play,' he'd said, trying to drag her away from her laptop by her arm. 'Mummy *and* Daddy.' He'd beamed when the three of them were kneeling on the floor putting his Duplo train set together. With the memory of her mother's singular lack of maternal instinct never far away, Ingrid had thrown herself into amusing Freddie – her son would not grow up thinking his mother hadn't cared. Whatever else he might think of her, it would not be that she didn't care.

'*Damn!*' she suddenly exclaimed. She'd been so deep in thought she'd managed to slice her finger while cutting the watermelon into cubes.

'You okay?' asked Lizzie, coming over to look.

'It's nothing,' she said crossly. 'Just me being clumsy.'

Lizzie pulled a face. 'That's more than nothing.' She grabbed some kitchen roll and wrapped it around Ingrid's finger. 'Stay there and I'll get the box of plasters.'

Wishing Lizzie would stop making such a fuss, Ingrid winced when she saw that the paper towel around her finger was fast turning red.

'Here we go,' Lizzie said, brandishing a box of Mr Bump plasters. 'Mr Bump was always my favourite of the Mr Men, probably because I was always falling over or bumping into something.' She tipped the plasters out of the box onto the work surface. 'Funny that it should be you who cuts yourself – that's normally my job.'

'My mind was elsewhere. That one should do,' said Ingrid, not trusting Lizzie to pick the right size plaster.

'Which was yours?'

'Sorry?'

'Which was your favourite character from the Mr Men?'

'I didn't have one.'

Having ignored Ingrid's advice, Lizzie was now applying an enormous plaster to her finger. 'Is that because you didn't like the books?' she asked.

'I didn't have them.'

'Were you more of a Beatrix Potter girl? Or maybe Winnie-the-Pooh was more your thing?'

'Neither. Pippi Longstocking books were what I read. It was the Swedish influence.'

'Oh, of course. I had a bit of a thing about Pippi when I was seven – I used to get Mum to plait my hair just like her.'

A memory Ingrid hadn't thought of in a very long time flashed into her head. 'I used to plait my own hair, and then put pipe cleaners inside my plaits so they would stick out,' she said.

'Genius! Now why didn't I think of that!'

Ingrid suddenly smiled at the recollection of standing in front of her small dressing table mirror in her bedroom and turning herself into a blonde version of Pippi Longstocking, imagining, of course, that she too had extraordinary super-powers.

'There, that's you done.'

Her cut finger almost forgotten, Ingrid looked at the plaster, which, much to her surprise, had been far more neatly applied than she'd expected. 'Thank you,' she said, picking up the knife she'd been using earlier. She washed it and was about to get back to the task of chopping the melon when Lizzie passed her a glass of white wine. 'I'd better go easy,'

Ingrid said, 'I expect I'll be the designated driver later.'

'Would you prefer a soft drink?'

'No, this is fine, I'll just make it last. Thanks.'

And there was another example of the *niceness* she was being treated to, thought Ingrid. And for that matter, when had she and Lizzie ever been in the same room together without anybody else around? Chopping the mint for the salad now, she supposed the situation in which she found herself was alien to her because she and Lizzie had probably taken great pains to avoid it. In the lengthy silence that followed, and for something to say, she felt she ought to enquire about Lizzie's new job.

'How do you plan to get to and from Bury?' she asked after Lizzie had elaborated and said she would be starting at Skylark Radio in two weeks' time.

'Mum's said I could borrow her car, which would be dead handy. Otherwise I'll have to make do with the bus. Another option is house-sharing. Somebody at the radio station is looking for a housemate for a place in the centre of town, so I plan to look into that.'

'Sounds like you've got it all organised.'

'It's the new me.'

Had the inconceivable finally happened? Lizzie had grown up?

Another silence followed.

'Ingrid?'

Assuming it was going to be a question about the salads they were making, Ingrid replied absently, 'Yes?'

'It's been a funny old summer, hasn't it?'

Ingrid turned to look at her sister-in-law. 'In what way?'

'Well, we've all been thrown into a situation none of us saw coming. Me coming back home after losing my job, and Freddie staying here with Mum and Dad, it's made everything all sort of topsy-turvy, hasn't it?'

Thinking that anybody with an ounce of sense would have seen Lizzie's affair with her married boss ending the way it did a mile off, she said, 'Everything will soon be back to normal.'

'Maybe that's not a good thing.'

Ingrid frowned. 'Why do you say that?'

'I just think that perhaps some things might need to change. Or rather, *should* change. Like – like the way we've never really got on.'

Ingrid returned her attention to the mint, adding it to the watermelon. 'I don't know what you mean,' she said warily. 'Of course we get on. You're my sister-in-law.'

'I get it, I really do,' Lizzie continued in a blithe tone of voice. 'I can quite see that I must be the most irritating person on the planet to you. I'm all over the place, always messing things up, always getting it wrong. Whereas you, you get everything right. You've always known what you're doing and what you plan to do. I'm in awe of you; you're so efficient and competent, you make Superwoman look like a total slacker.'

Ingrid stopped what she was doing and looked at Lizzie. 'Is that how you see me?'

'More or less, give or take. But I'm right, I do wind you up with my incompetence, don't I?'

The directness of Lizzie's question was unnerving, yet at the same time Ingrid had to respect the girl for being so candid. 'Incompetence in general winds me up,' she said carefully. 'I've always been that way.'

'So it's not just me personally, then? Or do I get your hackles up more than most?'

'Lizzie,' she said, mystified why the girl was pursuing the subject so doggedly, 'where are you going with this?'

Lizzie stared back at her with a surprisingly steady gaze. It made Ingrid realise that eye contact between them was actually quite rare. 'I just want us to be friends,' Lizzie said. 'If that doesn't sound too embarrassingly needy. Do you think that would ever be possible, if only for Luke and Freddie's sake?'

'What's brought all this on?' asked Ingrid, deliberately avoiding the question. If she'd been suspicious before that Luke's family were behaving oddly, this conversation confirmed it. This had to have been a set-up from start to finish. But why? Unless Luke had been tittle-tattling to his sister and parents? And saying what, exactly? Oh, she should never have agreed to come. She should have ignored Luke's insistence and stayed at home to work.

'Luke hasn't seemed his usual self,' Lizzie answered her. 'I suppose that's why I'm having this chat with you. And before you leap to any rash conclusions, he had no idea I planned to corner you this way. If you want to blame anyone, blame me.'

Ingrid picked up her glass of wine and took a long sip. 'You're very protective of your brother, aren't you?'

'We're protective of each other. That's just how we are.'

'You don't think that stops you from learning to stand on your own two feet and fighting your own battles?'

'No. And isn't it nicer knowing that someone has got your back? Isn't that what you do with Freddie? I bet there isn't anything you wouldn't do for him.'

Ingrid turned to look out of the window. In the garden Freddie was carefully crossing the lawn towards Luke, a plastic cup of water in one hand and a teapot in the other. She watched Luke bend down and take the cup from him. The happy smile on her son's face sent an arrow straight to her heart. She watched him run back into the waiting arms of his grandmother, bouncing on his toes in the comical way he often did. Seeing the loving expression on Tess's face and the obvious affection Freddie had for her, Ingrid battled a painful emotion building inside her.

It was a familiar pain, and one that she constantly fought to keep at bay: it was the pain of rejection, the thought of all that she had missed out on as a child. For so many years now she had trained herself to regard the emotion as the enemy – an enemy that she had to be constantly on her guard against. It meant that she had never truly allowed herself to cross the line of being accepted, for fear of it leading to rejection. By casting herself in the role of outsider and hiding behind an invisible barricade, she was able to keep herself from being hurt. Now here was this wretched girl blundering in and dismantling that wall of defence.

Or rather it was Freddie who was doing that: Freddie, her precious son for whom she would do absolutely anything. So on that score, Lizzie was right. To her fury, tears pricked the backs of her eyes, and then suddenly the pain of the struggle to keep her composure had her within its grip. She put down the glass in her hand and fought all the harder. She would not cry. She would not let Lizzie see this other side of her, this unbearable weakness that was not to be tolerated. Anger, she thought desperately, mentally thrashing around for a life support. Anger was her last resort; it gave her the strength to overcome anything.

But with that thought came the unbidden memory of the girls grouped around her in her first week at boarding school. She was twelve years old and they had formed a mob, a mob to put her in her place and to brand her forever more as the Ice Maiden. Every day they found a way to corner her, to make it clear that she would never be welcome to be a member of their clique. But no matter what they did, she refused to show weakness. Not once did she cry, in front of them, or in private.

Then one day, after she'd found a dead rat in her bed, she'd had enough and she fought back and unleashed a volcanic eruption of ferocious anger. She grabbed the ringleader and, in an act of wholly satisfying and instinctive aggression, she headbutted the girl and broke her nose. Instantly suspended from school for two weeks, much to her mother's horror – and annoyance that she was put to the inconvenience of having Ingrid at home – she was made to write a letter of apology to the girl she'd injured. On her return to school she was forced to read the letter out in assembly. It was the single most demeaning experience of her life, and she swore never to lose control again, or to be treated so unjustly. She also promised she would never tell another living soul what she'd done, or what she was capable of doing if pushed too far.

Staying in control was paramount, leading her life in such a way that that there would be no danger of any cracks appearing. Distancing herself from her mother and stepfather was another way to preserve the person she had now become. She wanted no reminders of what had gone before. And then along had come Luke, so loving and kind and easy-going. Falling in love with him made it even more important to her to maintain the facade of who she was.

All the while she was remembering that shameful episode from her childhood, she was balling her hands into tight fists to strengthen her resolve not to cry, yet the tears were spilling over. Even worse, she could hear Lizzie offering sympathy and, to compound her misery, the wretched girl was now handing her a box of tissues. The gesture invoked what Ingrid could only describe as a howling sob from her.

With his arms around Ingrid, Luke sat on his sister's bed in a state of shock.

When Lizzie had come out to the garden and quietly said that Ingrid needed him, he was ashamed to admit he'd been suspicious that she was faking a headache, or some other problem in order for them to go home. Inside the house Lizzie had apologised and said it was all her fault, that she must have said something to upset Ingrid and that she was upstairs crying. Baffled, he'd taken the stairs two at a time and entered his sister's room. He had never before seen Ingrid cry, and the sight of her doing so had been like a body blow. She was crying so hard it had taken a while for her to speak, but when she had, he had listened in silence, letting her pour out every last word of what she seemed to need to say.

When finally her words came to a stop, he tilted his head

back to look into her eyes to reassure her – so what, she'd broken a girl's nose, it sounded like the bitch had deserved it – but before he could say anything, Ingrid said, 'So you see, I'm not the person you think I am. I've conned you.'

'You haven't done anything of the kind,' Luke said. 'We're all capable of thumping someone when pushed. Do you think for one moment I love you any the less because of something that happened to you when you were a child? Do you really?'

'I wouldn't blame you if you did. It's what I've always feared, that you'd discover the real me. My mother once accused me of being unlovable, that I was too detached.'

'You're mother's a fool,' Luke said firmly, 'and has a lot to answer for, in my opinion.'

Ingrid blew her nose, then threw the tissue into the waste-paper basket at the side of the bed. 'How did you ever fall in love with me?' she asked.

He smiled, and stroked her hair away from her face. 'It was the easiest thing in the world. And if you want to know the truth, I love you even more after what you've told me.'

'Why? That doesn't make sense.'

'Love doesn't. Nor is it conditional. Not real love. And I know you might find it hard to believe, but my family love and care for you, too. All they've ever wanted is for you to feel a part of the family.'

'I think I know that deep down, but I never allowed myself to trust it. Just as I've worried at times that maybe I'd been wrong to trust your love for me.'

'So the more Mum and Dad tried to show their love for you, the more you resisted it, is that it?'

She nodded. 'Better to reject them than to face their inevitable rejection of me.'

He kissed her. 'That's never going to happen. Just as Freddie and I will never reject you. You're stuck with us. Now what do you want to do? Stay here, or go home? Mum and Dad will quite understand if you don't want to hang about.'

'No, let's stay.'

'You're sure?'

She nodded again. It was then that Luke noticed the Mr Bump plaster wrapped around her finger. 'What did you do?'

'It's nothing. Just a cut. I was careless. I'm sorry for causing such a scene.'

He hugged her. 'You've done nothing to be sorry for. How about I be the one to drive us home later this evening, and you be the one to enjoy a few glasses of wine?'

'You know, it would be a lot easier for me if you could be just a bit more horrible.'

'I'll do my best,' he said with a smile.

Chapter Sixty

The next day dawned clear-skied and spectacularly tranquil, the stillness broken only by the uplifting chorus of birdsong. It didn't seem possible that the glorious weather could continue, but it really did appear to be set to do so for a while yet.

Downstairs in the kitchen and still in her nightclothes, Tess took her first cup of tea of the day outside to enjoy in the summer house. Opening the doors, she was met with the airless, woody smell she always associated with childhood, of keeping her father company in his shed at the end of the garden. Funny how some things never leave you. Like memories of the summer school holidays, the endless carefree days of sunshine with the sound of doves cooing, the call of a cuckoo, afternoons spent strawberry-picking, the taste of ice lollies brought from the ice-cream van with its tinny chiming rendition of 'Edelweiss' that lured the children to the street like the Pied Piper. She smiled. How easily the tedious days when it rained had been erased from her memory.

What a powerful instrument the memory was, she thought, thinking of poor Ingrid. What a dreadfully lonely childhood the girl must have endured. Her need to stay in control explained so much about her, and Tess's sincere hope was that maybe now, now that Ingrid had revealed this vulnerability to them as a family, she would feel more able to accept their love and care in the way they had always wanted her to.

Thank God Luke was like his father, blessed with a patient nature, and would, now he knew the full story, be able to encourage Ingrid to believe that she was loved just as she

433

was. Wasn't that the basis of every healthy relationship, an acceptance of who and what we are? Goodness, if Tess had to hide all her bad habits and insecurities from Tom, she'd never have time in the day to get anything done!

When Tom had told her that he'd asked Lizzie to try and speak to Ingrid on her own, Tess had been against it; it had seemed like a recipe for disaster, and it almost had been, provoking poor Ingrid to a state of near collapse. Lizzie had been devastated at what had happened as a result of her getting Ingrid on her own, but Tess had told her that it only went to show just how precariously balanced Ingrid had been, and that if that moment of breakdown was going to happen, better it was done amongst those who cared about her.

Tess had urged Luke and Ingrid to stay over last night, but Luke had wanted to drive them home and, much later, when Ingrid was sleeping, he'd phoned to reassure them all was well. He'd sounded relieved more than worried. From what Tom had shared with Tess, it sounded as though Luke had been anxious that there was a far greater problem lurking within their marriage.

What an afternoon it had been, and what a way to start the new week – Freddie's last week with them. How odd it would be not having him here with them. But at least with Freddie back at nursery it meant that she would be able to return to helping regularly at Woodside; she was looking forward to that.

She sipped her tea and wondered how long it would be before Lizzie found a place of her own. When that happened, Keeper's Nook was going to feel very quiet without Lizzie and dear little Freddie around.

Until the next drama in their daughter's life, perhaps, Tess thought with a wry smile. Or Luke's, for that matter. She and Tom must never make the same mistake they had recently, of overlooking Luke because he so rarely caused them any trouble.

Hearing Freddie's voice calling to her – 'Hello, Nana!' – Tess looked up to see Lizzie standing at the back door with Freddie in her arms.

'Hello, Freddie!' she answered him, rising happily to her feet. It was time to get on with another day.

Chapter Sixty-One

Increasingly Clarissa had little idea what day of the week it was, they each blurred into one after another, but today she knew it was Friday and that it was Lizzie's last day at Woodside. It seemed like only yesterday when the girl first started working here.

Just as Lizzie was leaving Woodside, so too would Clarissa. Her dear old friends and family, the people she loved most in the world, were constantly on her mind and she longed to be with them; she had been parted from them for long enough. She had told Ellis she was now ready to go to them. 'So you've finally come to your senses, have you?' he had said to her in the early hours of this morning.

She had been woken by a brilliant flash of light in the room, and seconds later a terrific clap of thunder had made her heart nearly leap out of her chest. That was when Ellis had appeared at the window. 'You always did like a dramatic entrance,' she'd said to him. 'You could outdo the Grim Reaper himself!'

He'd laughed. 'I should hope so.' Then, coming over to the side of the bed, he'd peered down at her. 'I've come for you, you know that, don't you?'

'One more day,' she'd bargained with him.

Shoving his hands into his trouser pockets, he'd paced the floor and demanded to know if she was ever going to put a stop to her procrastinating. 'Aren't you tired of living this way?' he'd asked. 'When the smallest of things takes so much effort? Wouldn't you rather be with us and be young again?'

436

'I want to say goodbye to Lizzie,' she'd told him firmly, 'it's her last day. Then I'll be ready. I promise.'

'I shall hold you to that.'

Through the window now, Clarissa watched Jed surveying the storm-damaged garden before setting off with his wheelbarrow to start work.

Earlier, and using what little strength she still possessed, she had managed to open the French doors – for one more time she had wanted to breathe in the cool, damp afternoon air that smelt of wet earth and leaves. It was a smell that reminded her of being a child, of being with her parents in France, of a time when she had seen them at their happiest, when life had revolved around the simplest of pleasures – of her father lifting her up onto his shoulders so she could pluck a lemon from the tree; of helping her mother to fill a large china bowl with the first cherries of the season. Of piling into their ancient jalopy with a picnic and driving down the hillside through the olive groves to the coast. How different life might have been if her father had been able to support his little family with his writing and they could have remained in France. There would have been no returning to Boston, no having to work at the bank, no ending of his life and leaving behind a heartbroken wife and daughter.

But then, if none of that had happened Clarissa might never have left America and found a new home in England and led the life she had. There would have been no *Belle Etoile*, no Artie, Ellis or Effie, no Betty, or even the ghastly Marjorie. She would never have got to know her English grandparents, there would have been no William and her precious Nicholas, and no Thomas, Walter, Lily and Mrs Cook – oh, and so many others who had played their part in making her life so complete.

Over the course of her long life, she had often been asked if there was anything she would have done differently if given the chance to live her life again. It was a good question, and she had never found an answer that truly satisfied her. For as much as she wished she hadn't lost the ones she loved, she knew that a meddle here would inevitably lead to a meddle there, and before she knew it, the colourful and intricately woven tapestry that was her life would unravel and be unrecognisable. Moreover, she was pragmatic rather than sentimental – age did that – and she could see nothing to be gained in hypothetical speculation.

Much to Clarissa's amusement, Lizzie had come up with the idea of taking her for a drive so Clarissa could show her the landmarks of her life in Shillingbury. It was sweet of the girl to think of it, but Clarissa was much too weary to be bundled into a car and hauled off to see what she had left behind.

Out in the garden, Jed had moved on to tidying the flowerbed directly in front of Clarissa's room. He was putting plant supports in place, and tying string around the flattened clumps of stonecrop and achillea. Cutting off a length of string, he looked up and saw Clarissa observing him. He waved and she raised her hand in return. How odd it was that her hand felt so heavy, that it took so much effort just to lift it.

Jed had admitted to Clarissa that he was going to miss having Lizzie around. He wouldn't be alone in that; there would be quite a few at Woodside who were going to miss her, the girl had won many a heart here. Clarissa hoped that before too long Lizzie would view Jed as more than just a friend – anyone with half a brain could see they would make a well-suited couple.

Tugging on the woollen blanket that had slipped off her legs, Clarissa closed her eyes. She was sleeping a lot these days. At first she had fought to resist the lethargy, but she soon gave in, powerless to prevent her eyelids from closing and her head drooping. Sometimes she woke with a start to find a hand adjusting the cushion behind her back, or somebody asking if she wanted a cup of tea. Sometimes she woke so disorientated that she looked around wondering where on earth she was, or wondering who all these people were crowded into her home. But then, like the slow clearing of a mist on an autumnal day, the confusion passed and she remembered.

Autumn would soon be here, but knowing that she wouldn't experience this one, that she would miss the glorious spectacle of leaves turning colour before being shaken from the trees in the chilling winds, did not upset her. Instead her heart was filled with peaceful acceptance. She had promised Ellis she was ready to call it a day, and she meant it. Everything was as it should be now. And as she gave herself up to a deep, enveloping sleep that took her gently in its inviting embrace, she heard the sweetest sound – it was a skylark singing for her; it was calling her home, calling her back to Skylark Cottage.

For Lizzie it was the end of term all over again, that feeling of happy excitement underpinned with a hint of sadness that there were friends and classmates she wouldn't see again. Funny to think that that was how she now viewed all those she'd got to know at Woodside. Her mother, who was enjoying being back at the care home, had said the experience would do Lizzie good, and she'd been right.

Something else Mum had been right about was that her friendship with Lorna was broken beyond repair. Last week Simon had texted Lizzie to say his parents were moving to Southwold. If that was Lorna's solution to avoid bumping into Mum in the village, it seemed an extreme step, but the day after the sale board went up at Orchard House, Dad met Keith for a drink at the Bell and came home saying that the move had been on the cards for some time. Nobody at Keeper's Nook was convinced.

On Monday Lizzie would be starting work at Skylark Radio and over the weekend, with Mum and Dad's help, and Jed's, too, she was moving to Bury St Edmunds into a flat a short walk from the radio station. She'd lost out on the lodging opportunity, but then Ingrid had come up trumps with a friend of hers who wanted somebody to rent her flat during an overseas posting.

Lizzie was under no illusion that a month ago Ingrid would have considered her sensible enough to make use of a friend's flat, but things had changed, and for the better. Ingrid was much easier to be around these days; she was less prickly, and had even allowed Mum to give her a proper hug one day. All this meant that Luke was looking much more his old relaxed self, which meant Mum and Dad were happy again. The weekend of the Harvest Supper in the village, they had offered to have Freddie for the weekend so that Luke and Ingrid could treat themselves to some time away together, just the two of them. It also, rather conveniently, got Mum off the hook from having to help at the supper.

That particular weekend, Jed had invited Lizzie to visit a friend of his who had a boat over in Wroxham on the Norfolk Broads. She was looking forward to it. However, determined to keep her promise not to get involved with anyone too soon after her disastrous relationship with Curt, she was keeping it light with Jed. He seemed perfectly happy with the arrangement, so that was good.

Meanwhile, she had her last day at Woodside to get through. Mr Sheridan had put in a request after lunch that she play backgammon with him, a game he had taught her to play.

She found him in the library where he was waiting for her with the board all set up. They'd been playing for a while when he asked if she had seen Mrs Dallimore today.

'Not yet, I'm seeing her after you've once again thoroughly annihilated me at this wretched game,' said Lizzie. 'I'm going to feel quite sad saying goodbye to her, even though I'll pop in next week to annoy you all.'

'She's had enough,' Mr Sheridan said gruffly, moving one of his pieces on the board. 'I've seen it before.'

'What do you mean, she's had enough?' asked Lizzie.

'Exactly what I say. She's hung on for long enough and now she's preparing to make her exit. She told me as much yesterday. Mark my words: you won't see her again. I saw it with my wife. She'd been ill for some months when, out of the blue, she said it was time to say goodbye. I didn't believe her, but she asked me to round up the family so she could talk to them for the last time. I did as she said, and the next day, just a few hours after our youngest son managed to get a flight from Paris where he was working, she died. It was as if she had it all planned. I'd heard before that people can hang on until they've decided they're ready to die, but I didn't believe it. Not till I saw it with my own eyes.'

Lizzie was shocked. 'But surely you don't think Mrs Dallimore is about to die, do you?'

Mr Sheridan stared at her from beneath his bushy eyebrows. 'Haven't you noticed a change in her? It's like the stuffing's suddenly gone out of her.'

The truth was, Lizzie *had* noticed the change, but she hadn't wanted to dwell on it. She knew, though, that a much closer eye was being kept on the old lady, and that in the fortnight since the Bank Holiday weekend she was spending a lot more time asleep. Their conversations had been less frequent and were often curtailed by Mrs Dallimore nodding off, or her forgetting where she was.

Half an hour later, and with Mr Sheridan's unblemished record of backgammon champion still intact, Lizzie hurried away to Mrs Dallimore's room.

After she'd knocked twice and still didn't get a response, she turned the handle and pushed the door open.

The old lady was sitting by the French doors, which were ajar and letting in the chilly damp air. Motionless, her head resting against the back of the armchair, she looked to be sleeping peacefully. Lizzie was about to retreat when she thought better of it. What if the old lady wasn't asleep? What if …?

Filled with unease, she stepped further into the room.

Close up, the unnaturally pale colour of Mrs Dallimore's face added to her concern. Hardly daring to, Lizzie touched one of the old lady's hands. She almost let out a gasp at the coldness of it. She turned to cross the room and press the call bell to summon help, when a muscle twitched in Mrs Dallimore's face and her eyelids fluttered open.

'Is that you, Lizzie?' she asked faintly.

'Yes, it's me,' said Lizzie, relief flooding through her. 'I'm just going to shut the window, it feels a bit cold in here for you.' When she had the window shut, Lizzie knelt in front of the old lady and tucked the blanket around her. 'How about a nice cup of tea to warm you up? Maybe even a hot-water bottle?'

Mrs Dallimore blinked. 'There's no need.' She leaned forward. 'You've been a dear friend to me these last weeks, Lizzie,' she murmured. Her voice was unbearably weak and her pale lips trembled. 'But now it's time to say goodbye.'

Lizzie took hold of Mrs Dallimore's cold and insubstantial hands. 'But it's only goodbye until I see you next week. Remember I said I'd come back and tell you how my new job is going?'

For the longest moment, the old lady stared directly into Lizzie's eyes. Then, as if exhausted by the effort, she sank back into the chair, her shoulders sagging. 'No, Lizzie,' she said so weakly Lizzie instinctively moved in closer, 'I shan't be here next week. This is – this is a forever goodbye.'

Tears sprang into Lizzie's eyes. 'Don't say that, Mrs Dallimore. Please don't.'

The old lady's mouth quivered and her chest visibly rose as though she were struggling to breathe. With her heart hammering against her ribcage, Lizzie's own breath got caught in her throat. 'Shall I ring for Matron?' she managed to ask. 'Are you feeling unwell?'

Very slowly Mrs Dallimore moved her head from side to side, her eyelids drooping. 'I waited for you,' she murmured, 'to say goodbye. Now it's time for us to part company.'

Tears trickled freely down Lizzie's cheeks. 'I wish we didn't have to,' she said. 'I'm going to miss you so much. I've learnt so much from you this summer. You really did take me under your wing, you know.'

'All you needed was a fresh perspective.' The old lady's voice, little more than a rasp, faded away and her breathing became more laboured. Then, letting out a long exhalation of breath, her head tipped to the side and her eyes closed.

Lizzie felt the colour drain from her face. 'Mrs Dallimore,' she said softly, 'can you hear me?'

But even as she asked the question, she knew she wouldn't get an answer. With a calmness she didn't know she could feel, she rose to her feet, pressed the call button and then returned to kneel in front of the old lady. In the still silence, she held Mrs Dallimore's hands and quietly cried for this extraordinary woman.

Chapter Sixty-Two

Dear Lizzie,

You must excuse the formality of this letter, but I dictated it to my solicitor, who then had it typed for my signature.

If my instructions are followed correctly, you will, in due course, receive a letter from this same solicitor. I won't go into the details now, but suffice it to say I have arranged to leave you some money in my will. It is a modest gift to thank you for your refreshing company this summer. The gift comes with just the one proviso: you must do something 'worthwhile' with it, something of which I would approve. I have every confidence you will think of something!

Forgive an old lady preaching to you, but I want you to believe what I do, that you have so much more to offer the world than you give yourself credit for. Yes, you have encountered a run of bad luck and made mistakes in the past, but so have we all, so please do not make the bigger mistake and allow yourself to be defined by these things. 'Pick yourself up and fight another day' is as good a motto as any in my experience.

Since there is no one else I know who would be remotely interested in my photograph albums, or the bundles of letters I've kept all these years, I'm leaving them to you too. If they become a burden to you, then you have my permission to destroy them.

Thank you again for your friendship and kindness. I wish you a long and fulfilled life.

With fondest best wishes,
   Clarissa Dallimore